HEAVEN'S KEEP

HEAVEN'S KEEP

A NOVEL

WILLIAM KENT KRUEGER

ATRIA BOOKS
New York London Toronto Sydney

ATRIA BOOKS

A Division of Simon & Schuster, Inc.
1230 Avenue of the Americas
New York, NY 10020

First Atria Books hardcover edition September 2009

ATRIA BOOKS and colophon are trademarks of Simon & Schuster, Inc.

For information about special discounts for bulk purchases, please contact Simon & Schuster Special Sales at 1-866-506-1949 or business@simonandschuster.com.

The Simon & Schuster Speakers Bureau can bring authors to your live event. For more information or to book an event contact the Simon & Schuster Speakers Bureau at 1-866-248-3049 or visit our website at www.simonspeakers.com.

Designed by Davina Mock-Maniscalco

Manufactured in the United States of America

10 9 8 7 6 5 4 3 2 1

Library of Congress Cataloging-in-Publication Data

Krueger, William Kent.
  Heaven's keep : a novel / by William Kent Krueger.—
1st Atria Books hardcover ed.
    p. cm.
1. O'Connor, Cork (Fictitious character)—Fiction.   2. Private investigators—
Minnesota—Fiction.   3. Minnesota—Fiction.   I. Title.
  PS3561.R766H43 2009
  813'.54—dc22

                                                          2009003081

ISBN 978-1-4165-5676-3
ISBN 978-1-4391-6571-3 (ebook)

For Danielle Egan-Miller,
who saw the spark in this writer's heart
and inspired it to flame

ACKNOWLEDGMENTS

I often begin a novel nearly blind and it's only through the guidance of others that I find my way. In the writing of this book, I was guided much and well.

Thank you, first of all, to my editor at Atria Books, Sarah Branham, whose eye is true and whose suggestions are always dead-on. Thanks also to the early readers at Browne & Miller—Danielle, Joanna, and Alec—who flagged the problems with structure, language, and logic and helped me, as much as I was able, to banish those troublemakers. And as always, a big thanks to all the members of Créme de la Crime.

I owe a tremendous debt to the experts: Philip Donlay, professional pilot and fine thriller writer; Lt. Col. Keith Flanagan of the Minnesota Wing of the Civil Air Patrol; and Jeff Cohen, developer extraordinaire. Thanks, guys, for your expertise and your generosity.

Finally, I'd like to thank the people of Rice Lake, Wisconsin, for letting me take suspenseful liberties with their wonderful community, and also the people of the state of Wyoming, particularly the residents of Cody, Thermopolis, and Dubois, for their hospitality and for the stories, true or not, that they shared with me about the remarkable landscape they call home.

PART I
LOST

PROLOGUE

In the weeks after the tragedy, as he accumulates pieces of information, he continues to replay that morning in his mind. More times than he can count, more ways than he can remember, he juggles the elements. He imagines details. Changes details. Struggles desperately to alter the outcome. It never works. The end is always the same, so abysmally far beyond his control. Usually it goes something like this:

She waits alone outside the hotel in the early gray of a cloudy dawn. Her suitcase is beside her. In her hand is a disposable cup half-filled with bad coffee. A tumbleweed rolls across the parking lot, pushed by a cold November wind coming off the High Plains.

This is one of the details that changes. Sometimes he imagines an empty plastic bag or a loose page of newspaper drifting across the asphalt. They're all clichés, but that's how he sees it.

She stares down the hill toward Casper, Wyoming, a dismal little city spread across the base of a dark mountain like debris swept up by the wind and dumped there. As she watches, a tongue of dirty-looking cloud descends from the overcast to lick the stone face of the mountain.

She thinks, I should have called him. *She thinks,* I should have told him I'm sorry.

She sips from her hotel coffee, wishing, as she sometimes does when she's stressed or troubled, that she still smoked.

George LeDuc pushes out through the hotel door. He's wearing a jean jacket with sheepskin lining that he bought in a store in downtown Casper the day before. "Makes me look like a cowboy," he'd said with an ironic grin. LeDuc is full-blood Ojibwe. He's seventy, with long white hair. He rolls his suitcase to where she stands and parks it beside hers.

"You look like you didn't sleep too good," he says. "Did you call him?"

She stares at the bleak city, the black mountain, the gray sky. "No."

"Call him, Jo. It'll save you both a whole lot of heartache."

"He's gone by now."

"Leave him a message. You'll feel better."

"He could have called me," she points out.

"Could have. Didn't. Mexican standoff. Is it making you happy?" He rests those warm brown Anishinaabe eyes on her. "Call Cork," he says.

Behind them the others stumble out the hotel doorway, four men looking sleepy, appraising the low gray sky with concern. One of them is being led by another, as if blind.

"Still no glasses?" LeDuc asks.

"Can't find the bastards anywhere," Edgar Little Bear replies. "Ellyn says she'll send me a pair in Seattle." The gray-haired man lifts his head and sniffs the air. "Smells like snow."

"Weather Channel claims a storm's moving in," Oliver Washington, who's guiding Little Bear, offers.

LeDuc nods. "I heard that, too. I talked to the pilot. He says no problem."

"Hope you trust this guy," Little Bear says.

"He told me yesterday he could fly through the crack in the Statue of Liberty's ass."

Little Bear's eyes swim, unfocused as he looks toward LeDuc. "Lady Liberty's wearing a dress, George."

"You ever hear of hyperbole, Edgar?" LeDuc turns back to Jo and says in a low voice, "Call him."

"The airport van will be here any minute."

"We'll wait."

She puts enough distance between herself and the others for privacy, draws her cell phone from her purse, and turns it on. When it's powered up, she punches in the number of her home telephone. No one answers. Voice mail kicks in, and she leaves this: "Cork, it's me."

There's a long pause as she considers what to say next. Finally: "I'll call you later."

In his imagining, this is a detail that never changes. It's one of the few elements of the whole tragic incident that's set in stone. Her recorded voice, the empty silence of her long hesitation.

"Any luck?" LeDuc asks when she rejoins the others.

She shakes her head. "He didn't answer. I'll try again in Seattle."

The van pulls into the lot and stops in front of the hotel. The small gathering of passengers lift their luggage and clamber aboard. They all help Little Bear, for whom everything is a blur.

"Heard snow's moving in," Oliver Washington tells the driver.

"Yep. Real ass kicker they're saying. You folks're getting out just in time." The driver swings the van door closed and pulls away.

It's no more than ten minutes to the airport where the charter plane is waiting. The pilot helps them aboard and gets them seated.

"Bad weather coming in, we heard," Scott No Day tells him.

The pilot's wearing a white shirt with gold and black epaulets, a black cap with gold braid across the crown. "A storm front's moving into the Rockies. There's a break west of Cody. We ought to be able to fly through before she closes."

Except for Jo, all those aboard have a tribal affiliation. No Day is Eastern Shoshone. Little Bear is Northern Arapaho. Oliver Washington and Bob Tall Grass are both Cheyenne. The pilot, like LeDuc, is Ojibwe, a member of the Lac Courte Oreilles band out of Wisconsin.

The pilot gives them the same preflight speech he delivered to Jo and LeDuc the day before at the regional airport outside Aurora. It's rote, but he throws in a few funny lines that get his passengers smiling and comfortable. Then he turns and takes his seat at the controls up front.

They taxi, lift off, and almost immediately plow into clouds thick as mud. The windows streak with moisture. The plane shivers, and the metal seems to twist in the grip of the powerful air currents. They rattle upward at a steep angle for a few minutes, then suddenly they've broken into blue sky with the morning sun at their backs and below them a mattress of white cloud. Like magic, the ride smoothes out.

Her thinking goes back to Aurora, to her husband. They've always had a rule: Never go to bed mad. There should be a corollary, she thinks: Never separate for a long trip with anger still between you.

In the seat opposite, Edgar Little Bear, not a young man, closes his purblind eyes and lays his head back to rest. Next to him, No Day, slender and with a fondness for turquoise and silver, opens a dog-eared paperback and begins to read. In the seats directly ahead of Jo and LeDuc, Washington and Tall Grass continue a discussion begun the night before, comparing the merits of the casinos on the Vegas strip to those on Fremont Street. Jo pulls a folder from the briefcase at her feet and opens it on her lap.

LeDuc says, "Hell, if we're not prepared now, we never will be."

"It helps me relax," she tells him.

He smiles. "Whatever." And like his old contemporary Edgar Little Bear, he lays his head back and closes his eyes.

They're all part of a committee tasked with drafting recommendations for oversight of Indian gaming casinos, recommendations they're scheduled to present at the annual conference of the National Congress of American Indians. Her mind isn't at all on the documents in her hands. She keeps returning to the argument the day before, to her final exchange with Cork just before she boarded the flight.

"Look, I promise I won't make any decisions until you're home and we can talk," he'd said.

"Not true," she'd replied. "Your mind's already made up."

"Oh? You can read my mind now?"

She'd used the blue needles of her eyes to respond.

"For Christ sake, Jo, I haven't even talked to Marsha yet."

"That doesn't mean you don't know what you want."

"Well, I sure as hell know what you want."

"And it doesn't matter to you in the least, does it?"

"It's my life, Jo."

"Our life, Cork."

She'd turned, grabbed the handle of her suitcase, and rolled it away without even a good-bye.

She's always said good-bye, always with a kiss. But not this time. And the moment of that heated separation haunts her. It would have been so easy, she thinks now, to turn back. To say "I'm sorry. I love you. Good-bye." To leave without the barbed wire of their anger between them.

They've been in the air forty-five minutes when the first sign of trouble comes. The plane jolts as if struck by a huge fist. LeDuc, who's been sleeping, comes instantly awake. Washington and Tall Grass, who've been talking constantly, stop in midsentence. They all wait.

From up front, the pilot calls back to them in an easy voice, "Air pocket. Nothing to worry about."

They relax. The men return to their conversation. LeDuc closes his eyes. Jo focuses on the presentation she's put together for Seattle.

With the next jolt a few minutes later, the sound of the engines changes and the plane begins to descend, losing altitude rapidly. Very quickly they plunge into the dense cloud cover below.

"Hey!" No Day shouts toward the pilot. "What the hell's going on?"

"Fasten your seat belts!" the pilot calls over his shoulder. He grips the radio mic with his right hand. "Salt Lake, this is King Air N7723X. We have a problem. I'm descending out of eighteen thousand feet."

The folder that was on Jo's lap has been thrown to the floor, the pages of her careful presentation scattered. She grips the arms of her seat and stares out at the gray clouds screaming past. The plane rattles and thumps, and she's afraid the seams of rivets will pop.

"Goddamn!" No Day cries out. "Shit!"

LeDuc's hand covers her own. She looks into his brown eyes. The left wing dips precariously, and the plane begins to roll. As they start an irrevocable slide toward earth, they both know the outcome. With this knowledge, a sense of peaceful acceptance descends, and they hold hands, these old friends.

Her greatest regret as she accepts the inevitable—Cork imagines this, because it is his greatest regret as well—is that they didn't say to each other, "I'm sorry." Didn't say, "I love you." Didn't say good-bye.

ONE

Day One

After Stevie took off for school that morning, Cork O'Connor left the house. He headed to the sheriff's department on Oak Street, parked in the visitors' area, and went inside. Jim Pendergast was on the contact desk, and he buzzed Cork through the security door.

"Sheriff's expecting you," Pendergast said. "Good luck."

Cork crossed the common area and approached the office that not many years before had been his. The door was open. Sheriff Marsha Dross sat at her desk. The sky outside her windows was oddly blue for November, and sunlight poured through the panes with a cheery energy. He knocked on the doorframe. Dross looked up from the documents in front of her and smiled.

"Morning, Cork. Come on in. Shut the door behind you."

"Mind if I hang it?" Cork asked, shedding his leather jacket.

"No, go right ahead."

Dross had an antique coat tree beside the door, one of the many nice touches she'd brought to the place. A few plants, well tended. Photos on the walls, gorgeous North Country shots she'd taken herself and had framed. She'd had the office painted a soft desert tan, a color Cork would never have chosen, but it worked.

"Sit down," she said.

He took the old maple armchair that Dross had picked up at an estate sale and refinished herself. "Thanks for seeing me so early."

"No problem. Jo get off okay?"

"Yeah, yesterday. She and LeDuc flew out together. They stayed in Casper last night. Due in Seattle today."

"You and Stevie are bachelors for a few days, then?"

"We'll manage."

Dross folded her hands on her desk. "I don't have an application from you yet, so I can't really consider this a formal interview."

"You know those exploratory committees they form for presidential candidates? This is more like that."

Cork had hired her years ago when he was sheriff, and she'd become the first woman ever to wear the uniform of the Tamarack County Sheriff's Department. She'd proven to be a good law officer, and when the opportunity had come her way, she'd put her hat in the ring, run for sheriff, and won easily. In Cork's estimation, she'd filled that office well. She was in her late thirties, with red-brown hair, which she wore short, no makeup.

"Okay," she said. "So explore."

"Would you consider me seriously for the position?"

"If you apply, you'll be the most experienced applicant."

"And the oldest."

"We don't discriminate on the basis of age."

"I'll be fifty-one this year."

"And the man you'd replace is sixty-three. Cy Borkman's been a fine deputy right up to the end. So I'm guessing you might have a few good years left in you, too." She smiled, paused. "How would you feel taking orders from an officer you trained?"

"I trained that officer pretty well. So no problem there. How would you feel giving orders to the guy who trained you?"

"Let me worry about that one." She lost her smile and leveled at him a straight look that lasted an uncomfortably long time. "You told me a year and a half ago, after the shootings at the high school, that you would never carry a firearm again."

"No. I told you I would never fire one at another human being."

"Does that mean you'd be willing to carry?"

"If required."

"The job definitely requires it."

"In England the cops don't carry."

"This isn't England. And you carry with the understanding that someday you might have to use your firearm. That's why all our deputies certify on the range once a year. Your rule, remember?"

"How many times since you put on that badge have you cleared your holster and fired?"

"Yesterday is no predictor of tomorrow. And, Cork, the officers you work with need to believe you're willing to cover their backs, whatever it takes. Christ, you know that." She sat back, looking frankly puzzled. "Why do you want this job? Is it the litigation?"

"The lawsuit's draining me," he admitted.

"You've built a good reputation here as a PI."

"Can't spend a reputation. I need a job that brings in a regular income."

"What'll you do about Sam's Place?"

"Unless I win the litigation, there won't be a Sam's Place. And unless I can pay for it, there won't be a litigation."

"And if you win the lawsuit, are you out of here again? I've got to tell you, Cork, you've been in and out of uniform more times than a kid playing dress-up."

"I was never playing."

She looked away, out her window at the gorgeous November sky and the liquid sun that made everything drip yellow. "I've got a dozen qualified applicants wanting Cy's job, young guys itching for experience. I hire one of them, he'll be with me for years. I can start him out at a salary that'll be healthy for my budget. I can assign him the worst shifts and he won't complain."

"Did I ever complain?"

"Let me finish. The feeling around here is that I ought to hire you. You're clearly the popular choice. Hell, you brought most of our officers into the department yourself. These guys love you. But I have to look beyond the question of how well you'd fit in here. I have to think about the future of this force. And I also have to think about the welfare of the officer I hire." She gave him another long, direct look. "What's Jo think about this?"

"That it's not the best idea I've ever had."

"An understatement on her part, I'm sure."

"This is between you and me, Marsha."

"Until I run into Jo in the produce aisle at the IGA. I can't imagine that would be pretty."

"You're saying you wouldn't be inclined to hire me?"

"I'm saying we both probably have better options."

It was Cork's turn to eye the promising blue sky. "I don't know anything but law enforcement."

"I heard the new casino management firm might be looking for someone to head up security."

"All paperwork," Cork said.

"Sixty percent of what we do here is paperwork."

"I guess I have my answer." Cork stood up. "Thanks for seeing me, Marsha."

They shook hands without another word. Cork headed out, passed the contact desk, where Pendergast gave him a thumbs-up.

TWO

Day One

Cy Borkman's enormous butt ate the stool he sat on. "Coffee, Janice," he said to the young woman who was serving the counter at Johnny's Pinewood Broiler. He looked at Cork, who, until Cy arrived, had been sitting alone. "So, what did Marsha say?"

"That although she might be tempted, she wouldn't actually burn my application."

"Come on. What did she say?"

Cork sipped his coffee. "She encouraged me to pursue other career options."

"She say why?"

"To make way for youth."

Janice brought Borkman's coffee and asked him, "Anything else?"

"Yeah. Two eggs over easy, patty sausage, hash browns, and wheat toast."

"Tabasco?"

"*Naturellement.*"

Janice walked away, without writing on her pad.

"You ever think about security at the casino?" Borkman asked. "They're always looking for guys."

Cork shook his head. "Checking IDs, throwing out drunks, not for me."

"What do you think you'd be doing as a deputy? Hell, a lot of it's checking IDs and dealing with drunks."

"Maybe so, but I'd prefer doing it with a deputy's badge."

Borkman clapped a beefy hand on his shoulder. "Pride cometh before a fall, Cork." He took one of the little containers of half-and-half from the bowl on the counter, creamed his coffee, stirred in a packet of Splenda. "What about your PI business? You've got a good rep."

"And not enough work to afford to pay a lawyer."

"Why won't Jo take your case?"

"She says it's best to have a disinterested third party handle it."

"Even if it breaks the bank?"

"She's encouraged me to settle."

"What would that mean?"

"Letting the bastards surround Sam's Place with a lot of fucking condos."

"You'd make a lot of money."

"And ruin everything that Sam Winter Moon loved. And, hell, that I love, too. I'm going to win, Cy. I'm going to fight these bastards and I'm going to win."

"What did Jo think about you applying for my job?"

"About what you'd expect." Cork pushed his cup away. "Got things I have to do. When's your last day?"

"Two weeks from tomorrow. They're throwing me a shindig at the Four Seasons. You better be there."

"Wouldn't miss it."

Cork dropped plenty for the coffee and a good tip on the counter and headed outside.

In Aurora, Minnesota, things got quiet in November. The fall color disappeared. The stands of maple and oak and birch and poplar became bone bare. The tourists lost interest in the North Country. Deer-hunting season was nearly finished, and the orange vests, like the colorful foliage, were all but gone. There were still fishermen on Iron Lake, but they were the hardy and the few and came only on weekends. In town, the sidewalks became again the province of the locals, and Cork recognized most of the faces he saw there. November was usually a bleak month, days capped with an overcast and brooding sky, but the last week had been different, with the sun spreading a cheerful warmth over Tamarack County. Cork wished some of that cheer would lighten his own spirits.

He drove his Bronco from the Pinewood Broiler to the gravel access road that led to Sam's Place. He stopped at the chain that had been strung across the road and that had been hung with a No Trespassing sign. He wanted to drive right through, break the chain into a dozen pieces. Instead, he simply drove around the barrier. He followed the road over the Burlington Northern tracks and pulled into the parking lot of Sam's Place, where he got out and stood looking at what was, in a way, the vault of his heart.

Sam's Place was an old Quonset hut built on the shore of Iron Lake. More than forty years before, it had been bought and refurbished by an Ojibwe named Sam Winter Moon. Sam had divided the structure in half. In the front he'd installed a freezer, a grill, a deep fryer, a shake machine, and a soft drink dispenser, and had begun serving burgers, fries, and drinks during the tourist season, May through October. It had become one of Aurora's icons, a destination, a place for many that, until they patronized it, their vacation wasn't complete. Sam, when he died, had passed the place to Cork, who'd been like a son to him. Years before, when Cork had lost his job as sheriff, he'd poured himself into keeping the spirit of the wonderful old burger joint alive. He'd brought his own children in to work the windows and flip the burgers and learn, in the way he'd learned, when he was their age, both the necessity and, ultimately, the pleasure of a job well done.

He heard the water lapping gently against the shoreline, and he walked down to the lake. There was an old dock where folks could tie up their boats, disembark, and order a meal. Ever since the chain had gone up across the access from town, that dock was the only legal way to come at Sam's Place.

To the north stood a Cyclone fence that separated Cork's property from the BearPaw Brewery. Cork's land, two acres of mostly open field full of native wild grass and wildflowers, ran south along the shore of Iron Lake and stopped just short of a copse of poplars that surrounded the ruins of an ancient ironworks. Beyond the poplars, the open land continued until it hit Grant Park. Except for the lake, Cork's property was bounded on all sides by land now owned by the Parmer Corporation, a development company headquartered

in Odessa, Texas. Parmer intended to turn the entire lakefront, from
the BearPaw Brewery, which they now owned, to Grant Park, into a
large condominium resort community. All they needed to complete
their ownership of a quarter mile of prime lakefront was to acquire
Cork's property. They'd offered him a lot of money, three-quarters
of a million dollars. He'd turned them down. They'd offered him
more, a full million this time. He'd declined the proposition. They'd
made one more offer, one and a quarter million. He told them to
take a hike.

Cork had an easement agreement with those who, before Parmer,
had owned the property that stood between Sam's Place and Aurora.
This gave his customers access to the old Quonset hut along the road
over the Burlington Northern tracks. But Parmer's lawyers had
wormed their way around the language of the agreement and, near
the end of August, had chained off that access. Cork had gone to court,
seeking a temporary injunction until the easement dispute could be
resolved. The court had turned him down. He'd had so little business—only from boats on the lake—that he'd been forced to close
Sam's Place six weeks earlier than usual, cutting significantly into the
cash that might otherwise have been available for legal fees.

From the beginning, Jo had overseen her husband's interests. As
the depth of Parmer's pockets and the corporation's resolve to string
the proceedings out over years, if necessary, became more apparent, Jo
had explained to Cork that it might be best to retain someone who
was an expert in this kind of dispute and who could, perhaps, bring
about a more expeditious resolution. She recommended a firm in
Minneapolis. It was, she cautioned him, going to cost enormously.

Then Parmer had offered a compromise. Cork could keep Sam's
Place. They would build around it; in fact, they would incorporate the
old landmark into their design. Cork simply had to sell them the re-
mainder of his property at the last price they'd offered. He'd drafted
his own response, told them to go fuck themselves, that he'd sell at no
price, that only over his dead body would they ruin the shoreline of
Iron Lake.

Jo had carefully pointed out that Parmer held all the cards, that if
the lawsuit did, in fact, go on for years, and access to Sam's Place con-

tinued to be effectively blocked, Cork would be forced out of business and they would have to find a way to shoulder a significant legal debt. She cautiously suggested that compromise might be possible.

Christ, of all people, she should have been behind him. Of course she was a lawyer, but she was his wife first. Compromise? Settle? Hell, fold up like a card castle, that's what she wanted him to do.

Now he stood at the edge of the lake, looking south, where the shoreline met the sapphire reflection of the sky, thinking how he'd be tempted to kill to protect that unspoiled view.

"Howdy."

Cork turned and watched a man emerge from the shadow of Sam's Place and approach him over the gravel of the parking lot, smiling cordially as he came. He was tall and lean, sixtyish, a face like a desert landscape full of deep cuts and hard flats, with a couple of blue-green oases that were his eyes. He wore jeans, a tan canvas jacket open over a blue work shirt, and a Stetson that matched the color of his jacket.

"Morning," Cork said.

The man stopped beside Cork and spent a moment admiring the view. Under the bright sun, the water sparkled. Along the far eastern shore, a ragged line of dark pines cut into the blue plank of sky like the teeth of a saw. The man breathed deeply and seemed to appreciate the smell of clean water and evergreen.

"Beautiful spot," he said.

"I've always liked it."

"Yours?"

"For the time being."

"Lucky man. Business good?"

"In season," Cork said. "Visitor?"

"Yep."

"Fisherman?"

"Nope."

"Fall color's gone and hunting season's basically over."

"Depends on what you're hunting." He stuck out his hand. "Name's Hugh Parmer." The man's fingers were long and steel-cable strong.

"Cork O'Connor," Cork said.

"Figured."

"Hugh Parmer." Cork drew his hand back. "As in the Parmer Corporation."

"That'd be me, son."

"You're trespassing."

Parmer looked back toward the chained access and smiled. "Appears to me we've both stepped a little outside the law."

"What do you want?"

"In general? Or right at this moment?" He kept smiling. "Just wanted to see for myself the parcel of land that's holding things up."

"It's not the parcel that's in the way. Look, Parmer, why don't you just forget about this place and go back to your other developments? I understand you've got a number of them in the works."

"Here and there."

"Not here, not if I can help it."

Parmer used the tip of his forefinger to nudge his Stetson an inch higher on his forehead. "My people have told me about you. Burr under the saddle, they say."

"I don't need people to tell me about you."

"You sum up a man easy."

"Some men."

Parmer shrugged. "Me, I think everybody's complicated, and I confess that sometimes I never do get the exact measure of a man."

"In town long?"

"I haven't decided."

"I'd prefer not to see you here again."

"I understand. Much obliged, Mr. O'Connor." He eyed the shoreline once more. "Nice," he said. "Very nice."

Cork watched him cross the parking lot and hike the gravel access toward town. He watched until Hugh Parmer was a small figure well beyond the Burlington Northern tracks. Then he turned and promised the lake, "Over my dead body." He picked up a rock and threw it far out and watched the ripples spread. "Over my dead and rotting body."

THREE

Day One

He spent much of the day at Sam's Place working on the only paying investigation he had at the moment. He made calls to several police departments in Tamarack County and in the three adjoining counties. He'd been hired by Covenant Trucking to look into break-ins at a couple of their depots, and he was trying to find out if there might be a more widespread pattern to the crimes, something he'd seen a few years before, when he was sheriff.

At three thirty he turned onto Gooseberry Lane and pulled into the driveway of his home, a two-story white clapboard nearly a century old. The house had been in his family since its original construction and was known in Aurora as "the O'Connor place," a designation that would probably continue long after the last O'Connor was gone from it. A huge elm stood on the front lawn, with a rope scar visible on one of the low, thick branches where for years a tire swing had hung. A tall hedge of lilacs edged the driveway. In spring the fragrance from the blossoms was the next best thing to heaven, but now the bushes were a thick, unpleasant mesh of bare branches. Cork parked in front of the garage and went in the side door to the kitchen. He let Trixie, the family mutt, in from the backyard, where she'd been drowsing in the sun.

He was home five minutes ahead of Stephen. At thirteen, Cork's son was just beginning to get some height and bulk to him. He'd always been a small kid, but in the last few months, the growth hormones had kicked in and Stephen was mushrooming. His coordination hadn't caught up with his muscle development, and he was heart-wrenchingly awkward these days and knew it. His voice was changing, too. He was self-conscious about everything. Including his name. Until the last few weeks, he'd been known to everyone as Stevie. Now it was Stephen, a name he felt had more substance to it, more sophistication.

Stephen stumbled in carrying his school pack, which he slung onto the kitchen table. Trixie jumped up and pawed Stephen's thighs and licked his hand. Stephen petted her fiercely in return. "Hey, girl. Miss me?"

"How'd it go today?" Cork asked.

"Okay." Stephen turned from the dog and made a beeline for the refrigerator. He hauled out a carton of milk, grabbed a glass from the cupboard, and filled it to the brim. He gulped down half the milk, then refilled his glass.

"Cookie with that?" Cork asked.

"Mmmm," Stephen grunted.

Of all Cork's children, his son most visibly showed his Anishinaabe heritage. His eyes were dark walnuts, his cheekbones high and proud, his hair a fine black with, in the proper light, hints of red. Despite all Stephen's awkwardness, both of Cork's daughters had declared that he was growing into a bona fide hunk.

While Cork pulled out the cookie jar—Ernie from *Sesame Street*, a ceramic relic that had survived mishap for a dozen years—Stephen picked up the phone and listened to the messages.

"Nothing for me," he said, disappointed. He'd been begging for a cell phone of his own, but Cork hadn't knuckled yet. "There's a message from Mom."

"Let me listen." Cork put the phone to his ear and replayed the message.

"Cork, it's me." Long pause. Was that the wind he heard in the absence of her voice? "I'll call you later."

It was a simple message, nothing of import, but for some reason, Cork saved it on voice mail.

He looked at his watch. He thought she was supposed to be in Seattle around 1:00 P.M. PST. He adjusted for the time zones and figured she should be there by now. He said to Stephen, "I'm going into your mom's office and give her a call."

Around a mouthful of cookie, Stephen asked, "What's for dinner?"

"Mac and cheese."

"How about we go to the Broiler for fried chicken?"

"We're on a tight budget, buddy. But tell you what, I'll slice up a few hot dogs and throw 'em in."

"I like fried chicken better."

"Maybe after dinner we could hit the Broiler for a little pecan pie à la mode."

Stephen shook his head. "I'm going over to Gordy Hudacek's house."

"Video games?"

"Yeah."

"What about homework?"

"I'll have it done before dinner."

"See that you do."

Cork headed through the living room and down the hallway to Jo's home office. She ran her law practice from a suite in the Aurora Professional Building, but she kept an office at home as well, and she often used it in the evening or on weekends to keep up with her cases. It was done in oak panel, with bookshelves across three of the walls. Plants hung in every window, and a big, healthy ficus stood in a pot in one corner. The office was neat and clean, and the smell of it—thick books and heavy paper—reminded Cork of Jo.

He used the phone on her desk to call her cell. She didn't answer. He left a message: "Sorry about yesterday. Call me when you get a chance. I love you, you know."

Dinner was a quick affair, both of them wolfing, not saying much. When Jo was there, they took more time, and in her motherly-lawyerly way, she questioned Stephen about his day. He tended to give brief answers, along with the sense that he was uncomfortable being quizzed, but Jo managed to squeeze enough information out of him that both of his parents had a pretty good window on his life. Cork appreciated that about his wife.

Stephen cleared the table and loaded the dishwasher—his part of the bargain—then headed out to Gordy Hudacek's house. Cork grabbed the *Duluth News Tribune* and settled onto the sofa to catch up on news from the outside world.

He hadn't been reading long when Trixie, who'd nestled on the floor near his feet, lifted her head and barked. A moment later, the front doorbell rang. Cork was surprised to find Sheriff Dross standing on his porch. He thought for a moment—hoped, actually—that she was coming to say she'd changed her mind about him applying for the position that Cy Borkman was vacating, but when he saw her face, he knew it was something gravely serious.

"Could we sit down, Cork?"

"Sure." He motioned toward the living room.

Dross wore jeans and a brown turtleneck, and Cork wasn't sure if this was a personal or a professional call. When they were seated, she said, "Have you heard from Jo?"

"No. Why?"

He saw her prepare herself, a moment of resolution, and he knew something terrible had happened.

"We received a call from the sheriff's department in Owl Creek County, Wyoming. This morning around nine A.M., a charter flight out of Casper disappeared from radar over the Wyoming Rockies. Radio contact was lost and hasn't been reestablished. Jo was listed on the flight's passenger manifest."

Cork sat a moment, stunned. "It crashed?"

"They don't know the status for sure, Cork."

"What happened?"

"According to the control tower in Salt Lake City, which was tracking the flight, the plane ran into bad weather. It began a rapid descent southwest of Cody—they're not sure why—and pretty quickly dropped off the radar over an area called the Washakie Wilderness. They've tried contacting the pilot. Nothing."

"It went down in the mountains?"

"Not necessarily. The Wyoming authorities are calling all the local airports and every private airstrip in the northern Rockies to see if the plane might have been able to land somewhere."

"And if it didn't land?"

"You know the routine. They'll mount a search and rescue effort."

For a moment he didn't say anything. Couldn't say anything. He struggled just to breathe. Then he looked at Dross and realized there was more. "What else?"

She took a deep breath. "They're in the middle of a bad snowstorm out there. Blizzard conditions. If they can't locate the plane at an airfield, they won't be able to begin the search until the storm passes. According to the current weather forecast, that might be a while."

"Oh, Jesus," Cork said. He looked down at his hands, which he'd clenched into hard white balls. "If that plane's gone down and Jo and the others are exposed, Christ, Marsha, you know the odds."

"Cork, we don't really know anything yet. Probably we'll hear that they made it to an airfield. In the meantime, the Owl Creek County authorities are doing everything possible. We're in constant contact with the sheriff's people. Anything we know, you'll know, I promise." She put her hand on his arm. "Cork, we have every reason to hope for the best."

He looked at her long and hard. "Same line I used to deliver to the loved ones when we were beating the bushes for somebody they'd lost."

"And more often than not you found the lost ones. Trust the people out there, Cork. They know what they're doing." She stood up. "I'm on my way to the reservation to deliver the news to George LeDuc's wife." She looked into his face, and her own was full of concern and compassion. "Cork, I'm so sorry."

"Yeah. Thanks."

He watched until her truck pulled away. He turned out the porch light and closed the door. Then his legs gave out. He sank to the floor and sat with his back against the wall. He tried to think straight, but his brain was caught in a whirlpool, spinning round and round, and every rational thought got sucked into some dark nowhere, until he was left with only a desperate, mindless repetition to cling to: *Oh God, no . . . Oh God, no . . .*

Eventually he pulled himself up. He walked to the telephone and dialed the number of the Hudaceks' home. Gordy's father answered.

"Dennis, it's Cork O'Connor."

Hudacek said something amiable in reply, but the words didn't register. Cork simply told him, "I need to have Stephen come home. I need to have him come home now."

FOUR

Day One, Missing 12 Hours

He sat at the kitchen table, a cup of cool coffee at his elbow. He held the phone in his right hand and, with his left, punched in the number of Jo's sister.

"Rose, it's Cork. Sorry to call so late."

Because of either the lateness of the hour or the somber tone of his voice, she didn't waste time. "What's wrong, Cork?"

"I've got bad news. Jo was on a charter flight to Seattle. This morning while it was flying over Wyoming, it disappeared from radar and radio contact was lost."

There was a long moment of silence as Rose absorbed this information. "What does that mean exactly? Did the plane crash?"

"Not necessarily. The authorities are checking all the airports in the area to see if it might have landed somewhere. They're in the middle of a big snowstorm, and it sounds like everything's kind of confused."

"So it could have landed in some out-of-the-way place and because of the weather they can't get word out. Is that it?"

That was the positive read. He said, "Yes."

He waited, staring out the window at the night beyond that was as black as the cold coffee in his cup.

"Just a moment, Cork," Rose said. "Mal's here." She covered the phone, and he couldn't hear anything except the emptiness of the line. He thought of the silence in the middle of the message Jo had left him, and again he felt the knife of regret.

Mal was Cork's brother-in-law. He'd once been a Catholic priest serving the parishioners of St. Agnes in Aurora. Then he'd fallen in love with Rose. Now they were married—five years—and living in Evanston, Illinois.

Rose came on the line again. "Do the kids know?"

"I called Jenny and Anne. They both wanted to come home right away, but I convinced them to stay put until I know more."

"How's Stephen doing?"

"Taking it hard. He's up in his room right now."

"And you?"

"Not good either. I would have waited to call until I knew more, but with this kind of situation it won't be long before the media picks up on it. I wanted to make sure you both heard it from me."

"We're coming up there, Cork." Rose, always a strong woman, had already put away her despair and girded herself for action.

"Rose, there's no reason—"

"You'll have your hands full. We'll leave first thing in the morning. End of story."

For many years before she married Mal, Rose had lived with the O'Connors. She was part of the family. Cork could have resisted more, but the truth was that he liked the idea of her being there. He also understood that worry was multiplied by distance and silence, and coming to Aurora would put her closer to the situation, to any news that came.

"Thanks, Rose."

"If you hear anything, you'll let us know."

"Of course."

"We'll see you tomorrow, Cork. In the meantime, we all have a lot of praying to do."

Cork had the television on, tuned to The Weather Channel. The storm in the upper Rockies was one of the stories they were tracking. On radar, the area of snow was a huge white blob gobbling up most of western Wyoming, as well as large parts of Montana, Idaho, and northwestern Colorado. He went to the bookcase in the corner of the living room, pulled out an atlas, opened to the map of Wyoming, and located Owl Creek County and the Washakie Wilderness. He'd been through Wyoming a couple of times, but always far to the south, on I-80. He'd never been to Yellowstone, never been anywhere near the Washakie Wilderness. He tried to imagine it, and what he visualized were the mountains in the cowboy movies of his youth—distant, blue, beautiful, formidable.

The phone rang. Caller ID told him it was the Tamarack County Sheriff's Department. It was Dross. "I'm back in the office," she told him. "I just wanted you to know I'm here all night and in constant contact with the sheriff's department in Owl Creek County."

"Mind giving me the number of the people out there you're talking with?"

"I'm sure they're busy and doing everything they can."

"I'm sure," Cork said. "I'd still like the number."

She gave it to him, though he could tell it was with reservation.

"I'm watching The Weather Channel," he said. "Doesn't look good."

"Local conditions vary a lot, you know that."

"Right. Thanks, Marsha."

He called the number she'd given him.

"Sheriff's office." A tired male voice.

"My name's Cork O'Connor. My wife, Jo O'Connor, was one of the passengers on the flight that's missing there in the Rockies. I'd like to talk to someone about what you folks are doing."

"Just a moment."

The moment turned into two minutes. Cork assumed a couple of possibilities. First, that the department was overwhelmed. Second, that they were taking time to verify his identity via caller ID and whatever information the Tamarack County Sheriff's Department had given them.

"Mr. O'Connor, this is Deputy Quinn." Sounded like he had a cold, something rattling in his chest.

"I'm wondering, Deputy, if you could give me a rundown on where things stand."

"All right. The FAA is still trying to contact all the possible landing fields. That's not easy because there are a lot of private airstrips, some pretty remote, and the storm's brought down a lot of power and telephone lines. It's snowing like blazes and it's dark as pitch." The deputy coughed away from the phone, then came back. "If a search becomes necessary, we've already got a number of Civil Air Patrol volunteers standing by. And our own search and rescue people are geared up and ready. They're good. They've done this kind of thing before. As soon as we get a break in the weather, if necessary we'll be out there looking. Believe me, Mr. O'Connor, we're doing everything we can."

"Are you familiar with the area where the plane disappeared from radar?"

"We know where it dropped off the radar, but we don't know that it actually went down in that particular area. The folks at the FAA are doing their best to advise us."

"I was told it's called the Washakie Wilderness. Could you tell me about it?"

"As I said, we have no reason at the moment to believe that the plane went down there."

"Tell me anyway."

A too long pause. "It's remote, rugged. Mostly big mountains and no roads."

"What's the local weather forecast?"

"Just a moment." The deputy covered the phone, but not well enough that Cork couldn't hear him hacking something up. He came back on. "They're saying the snow could last another twelve to eighteen hours. We're looking at total accumulations in the high country of four, maybe five feet. Mr. O'Connor, Sheriff Dross has told us about your law enforcement background, so I'm guessing you know to a certain extent our situation. Believe me, we're doing everything we can, and we'll keep you well informed."

Which translated into "please don't call us."

"I appreciate your time, Deputy Quinn."

"No problem, Mr. O'Connor."

He was no place different from where he'd been ten minutes before. Absolutely lost.

Stephen wandered down the stairs and slumped onto the other end of the sofa. He looked at the television screen, which was delivering the "Local on the 8s." In northern Minnesota tomorrow, the prediction was for another beautiful day. A minute later, the coverage returned to the storm in the Wyoming Rockies.

"Is she dead?" Stephen said.

"Why would you think that, Stephen? There's every reason to hope that she and the others are safe."

"I don't care about the others. I just want Mom to be okay." He stared at The Weather Channel, the shifting of white against green that was the digital image of the snowstorm, a simple representation of a crushing fear. "I wish I could be looking for her."

"She'll probably turn up by morning and she'll have a hell of a story to tell, buddy. And remember, there are good people out there who know what they're doing."

"They don't care like I do."

"Sometimes, Stevie, in really tight situations it's best to have someone who's not emotionally involved. They think clearer."

"My name's Stephen and that's bullshit. If I was out there, I'd be looking for her right now."

"Sorry about the name. And I'm sure you would," he said gently.

Stephen fell asleep on the sofa. Cork covered him with an afghan Rose had knitted for Christmas one year. He settled into the easy chair with the phone at hand and closed his eyes. He couldn't sleep. He kept going over the possibilities, searching for some reasonable alternative, something to hold on to, but his thinking kept coming back to the darkest prospect—a plane in pieces in the mountains, slowly being buried by snow.

He picked up the phone and listened again to the message Jo had left.

"Cork, it's me." During the long silence that followed, he heard the wind in the background like the whisper of a ghost. He saw her outside somewhere. He didn't know Casper, Wyoming, didn't know the geography, and he imagined her in a vast nowhere standing against a sky that was gunmetal gray, her blue eyes searching the empty horizon, the wind pulling at her hair. "I'll call you later," she finished.

But she hadn't. And despite all the hope he was trying to give his family, in his own mind he fought not to hear the bleak, bitter voice of his terrible fear telling him she never would.

FIVE

Day Two, Missing 20 Hours

The phone woke him. He'd been dozing all night in the easy chair in the living room.

"Yeah, hello."

"Cork, it's Marsha."

He sat up and squeezed his eyes to force the sleep out. "What's up? Any word?"

"They contacted every airstrip they know of, public and private, and they've come up empty. There are still a few that haven't responded, but they're beginning to focus on the probability of search and rescue. It's still snowing heavily out there, but the sheriff's people expect it to begin tapering off before noon. They've also had a report from a couple of snowmobilers who say they heard a low-flying plane sputtering overhead around the time the charter dropped off the radar yesterday, which puts it, apparently, in the east-central section of the Washakie Wilderness."

"It was still flying?"

"If it was the charter, yes. They couldn't see anything. The snow and cloud cover was heavy, but they're pretty sure the plane was heading southeast."

Still flying, Cork thought and grabbed hold of hope.

"How're you doing?" Dross asked.

"Hanging in there."

"When I hear anything more—"

"I know. I'll be here."

The phone hadn't woken Stephen, and Cork let him sleep. He pushed himself out of the chair and went to the kitchen to make coffee. Outside, the sky was clear and the approach of dawn had softened the hard black of night. His muscles were tense, sore as if he'd taken a beating. He watched the coffee slowly fill the pot, then he poured a cup, sat down at the kitchen table, stared at the wall clock, and thought about the fact that she'd been missing nearly twenty-four hours. He'd been involved in enough winter search and rescue operations in the Minnesota wilderness to know that unless the plane was intact or its passengers had at least some protection from the cold and wind, their odds, by the hour, would plummet. He realized his hand was shaking uncontrollably and he put his coffee cup down.

The phone rang.

"Mr. O'Connor, this is Julie Newell. I'm a reporter for the St. Paul *Pioneer Press*. I know this is a difficult time for you, but we've been notified that your wife's name is on the passenger manifest of the plane that's gone down in the Wyoming Rockies."

"There's no confirmation that it's actually gone down," Cork said.

"Of course. I'm wondering if I could talk to you a few minutes in order to let our readers know who your wife is and how you're responding to this situation."

"I'm responding badly," Cork said.

"I understand. I'm also wondering what your reaction is to the allegation that the pilot was drinking the night before."

"What?"

"You didn't know? I'm sorry."

"Tell me."

"There's strong evidence indicating that the pilot, Clinton Bodine"—she pronounced the name "Bo-dyne"—"was in a bar the night before, drinking heavily."

"Evidence?"

"As soon as news of the plane's disappearance became public, a bartender in Casper came forward. So did a cabdriver. I'm surprised no one's told you this."

"Jesus," Cork said. "I don't know anything about it."

"Does this upset you?"

"What do you think?"

"The pilot was an Indian, Mr. O'Connor. You're part Indian, too, as I understand."

"The word is Ojibwe."

"Of course. How do you feel knowing that an Indian—Ojibwe—pilot, who allegedly had been drinking, might be responsible for your wife's disappearance?"

"Mostly I feel like ending this conversation." And he did.

He called Dross.

"I hadn't heard, Cork," she told him. "You know how it goes. Sometimes the media is ahead of us. I'll see what I can find out."

Cork didn't know much about the pilot. He'd had only a glimpse when Jo got on the plane at the Tamarack County Regional Airport. He knew he was Anishinaabe—Ojibwe—from a Wisconsin band, he thought. A drunken Indian? Christ, that was going to feed the stereotype.

Stephen stumbled into the kitchen looking beat. He poured himself some orange juice and sat silently at the table, while Cork flipped pancakes and fried a couple of eggs for each of them. He wasn't hungry, but he knew they had to eat, and Stephen, when the food was set before him, ate voraciously. These days he always did.

"I heard the phone ring," Stephen said.

"There's been some hopeful news." Cork told him about the two snowmobilers. "I don't know what it means exactly, but it looks like the plane was headed southeast, maybe back toward Casper, where it had come from."

Stephen had stopped eating. His eyes were big and hopeful. "Maybe they've made it back."

"If they had I think we'd have heard by now. But it gives the sheriff's people a better idea of where the plane might be."

"They turned around because of the weather?"

"That. Or maybe mechanical trouble. But definitely going back."

Stephen squinted, putting it together. "So what you're saying is that they didn't just drop off the radar and disappear?"

"Yeah."

"But they still could've crashed."

"Gone down," Cork said. "I'm thinking this means if they did go down that the pilot may still have been in control. I think that's important."

"I Googled the Washakie Wilderness last night. It's in the Absaroka Mountains. They're like thirteen thousand feet high."

"Mountains have meadows, places to put a plane down, Stephen."

His son thought about that, and although he didn't do cartwheels, he also didn't raise any further objections to the hope Cork was trying to offer. He finished his breakfast and went upstairs.

The phone rang again. Cork didn't recognize the name on caller ID, but the area code was 612. Minneapolis. Maybe another reporter from the Twin Cities. He let it ring.

He called George LeDuc's wife, Sarah. Her sister answered.

"Gloria, it's Cork O'Connor."

"*Boozhoo*, Cork."

"How's Sarah doing?"

"It's been a hard night. She's worried sick. We all are."

"Who's there?"

"Flora Baptiste, Lucy Auginash, Isaiah Broom, Wayne and Dorothy Hole-in-the-Day. A few others. Maybe a dozen."

Word had traveled fast on the Iron Lake Reservation, and relatives and friends had risen to the need of the moment. Cork told Gloria about the report from the Wyoming snowmobilers. Gloria told him that Sheriff Dross had already called. They discussed the implications.

Then Sarah came on the line. She was in her mid-thirties, more than three decades younger than her husband, with a pretty smile and deep brown eyes that were normally full of good humor. Cork imagined that this morning they were different.

"*Boozhoo*, Sarah. How're you doing?"

"It's hard, this waiting."

"I know. How's Akik?"

Sarah and George had a daughter, whose real name was Olivia, but whom they'd nicknamed Akik, which meant "kettle" in the language of the Ojibwe. She was a plump little girl of five, with a fiery temperament and given to letting off steam.

"I haven't explained the real concern to her. She's having a good time with all the relatives and friends here. How's Stevie?"

"Taking it hard."

"There's hope, isn't there, Cork? I mean, they haven't even started searching yet."

"Yeah, Sarah." He looked out the window at the street in front of his house, all golden in the morning sunlight. "There's lots of reason to hope," he said, trying to sound as if he believed every word of it. He hesitated before going on. "I got a call a while ago. A reporter from St. Paul. There's been an allegation that the pilot had been drinking the night before."

"No. Oh Jesus, no."

"Yeah. Marsha Dross is checking it out. You might be getting a call from that same reporter or others. Just thought you ought to know."

"Thanks, Cork."

He kept Stephen home from school. Father Ted Green, the priest at St. Agnes, dropped by to offer his help and his prayers. Cork thanked him for the prayers and told him he'd let him know about the help part.

The phone continued to ring. At first, he answered the calls from friends. After a while, he just let everything go to voice mail.

Around noon, Marsha Dross called again.

"Have you been watching CNN?" she asked.

"No, why?"

"That snowstorm coming across the Rockies, it's creating all kinds of problems from Canada down to New Mexico. CNN's giving it heavy coverage. They picked up on the story of the missing charter flight. And they've got the bartender on camera telling how the pilot was drinking like a fish the night before, bragging about owning his own company and that he was so good he could fly a plane through the crack in the Statue of Liberty's ass. I don't know how these people do this, but they've already got video from the security cameras in the bar, showing this guy slamming 'em back. They've also got a statement from the cabdriver who drove him to his hotel. The guy was so drunk the taxi driver had to pull over and let him out so he could puke."

Cork felt the scorch of fire behind his eyes. "The son of a bitch. If that guy wasn't probably already dead, I'd—" Cork stopped, realizing that he was caught in the web of a dreadful thought: *Already dead.* "Thanks, Marsha."

"I wish I had some good news, Cork."

"Yeah. Keep me posted whatever you hear."

"You know I will."

He put down the phone and stared at the wall.

Already dead? Was that really what he thought?

SIX

Day Two, Missing 26 Hours

Cork spent the early afternoon on the phone, frustrated and angry, talking to a number of airlines. He was hanging up a final time when the boxy green Honda Element pulled into the drive. Through the window above the kitchen sink, he watched Mal and Rose get out and begin to unload luggage. They worked together easily, touching often. Before she fell in love with Mal, Rose had been a stout woman. As far as Cork knew, she'd also been a virgin, deeply devoted to her Catholic faith. He'd never thought of her as pretty, but she'd always been beautiful in an ethereal, spiritual sort of way. Her marriage had changed that in ways that were both obvious and subtle. She'd lost weight and dressed to show it. There was a beauty in her face now that had an appealing earthy quality to it. It seemed to Cork that in marrying a man who'd worn a collar, she'd lost none of her faith but gained a very different and human kind of wisdom.

Cork went to the side door and greeted them. Rose's face wore a worried look, and she gave him a prolonged hug. "It's in God's hands," she whispered to him. "It's always in God's hands."

Mal hugged him, too. "What's the news from out there?"

"The snow's stopped, but blizzard conditions continue across a lot of the area. Airports are closed. Planes are still grounded. They think the wind'll let up later this afternoon. Even then it'll take them a while to clear the runways."

"Where's Stevie?" Rose asked.

"In his room."

"I'm going up to see him."

Rose headed directly toward the stairs. Mal set the two suitcases in the living room and came back to the kitchen.

As a priest, Mal Thorne had been a tortured man. The competing pull between his duty to the Church and his attachment to the world had nearly torn him apart. He was a decade older than Rose, and when he'd fallen in love with her, he'd seemed wrung out by life, thick in the middle, and often rheumy-eyed from booze. His marriage had changed that. He now looked trim and happy. He was fond of saying that in opening his arms to the earthly love of a woman, he'd found his way back to God, and the happiness had healed him. He was still a man of great spiritual depth—*once a priest*, Cork thought, *always a priest*—but, like Rose's, his wisdom was broader and his embrace of life much gentler. In Chicago, he ran a shelter for the homeless. Every day he helped people face bleak odds and tried to point them toward hope.

"If I made coffee, would you have some?" Mal asked.

"Yeah, thanks. But I can make it."

"Sit down," Mal said. "I know where everything is."

The room was full of afternoon sunlight. Silver darts shot off the stainless steel sink faucet and handles. A gold rhombus lay across the floor, stamped with Mal's shadow as he stood at the counter grinding beans and measuring into the filter. All day the room had felt close and stuffy, but Mal and Rose had brought in with them the perfume of the late autumn air.

"Mal, I'm going out there."

His brother-in-law hit the Brew button and turned back to Cork. "Seems reasonable to me. When?"

"I'm not sure. I've been on the phone talking to airlines all afternoon. The storm's wreaked havoc the whole length of the Rockies. A lot of flight cancellations, and none of them can get me a seat until tomorrow night. At the moment, it looks like I'll fly to Salt Lake and catch a connection to Cody first thing the following morning. It's the best they could do."

"Going alone?"

"That's my plan. I can't sit here doing nothing."

"Of course you can't. And don't worry about things here. We'll hold down the fort."

"Thanks."

Rose came downstairs from Stephen's room, followed by Trixie. The dog padded directly to Mal, who bent and gave her a good long petting.

"How's he doing?" Cork asked.

"For one thing, he's not Stevie," she said. "He's Stephen."

"Yeah, I should have warned you. He's kind of sensitive about it."

"He's also scared and angry," Rose said. "But he doesn't want to talk about it."

"You were up there awhile."

"I was doing most of the talking. I asked him if he wanted to pray with me. He told me he doesn't believe in prayer. If there is a God, the bastard never listens anyway. Direct quote. Since when has he been like this, Cork?"

"New development. Like the name thing. We haven't been pressing him on the issue."

She sat down at the table. It had been a long drive to come to a place full of despair. "That coffee smells heavenly," she said, and Mal reached into the cupboard for a mug.

"Cork's going to Wyoming," Mal said.

He handed Rose a mug of coffee, then gave one to Cork.

"Will that do any good?" Rose asked.

"I don't know," Cork said, "but I'll go crazy if I have to sit it out here."

"When do you leave?"

"At the moment it looks like late tomorrow afternoon."

"Are you going alone?"

"Yeah."

"Do the kids know?"

"Not yet. It'll be tricky, especially with Stephen. He'll want to go."

"Why not take him?" Mal said.

"Too many problems with that."

Mal shrugged, but it was clear he didn't necessarily agree.

"Maybe they'll find Jo before then," Rose said.

"Either way I want to be there."

Rose nodded. "We'll stay and cover here for as long as you need us."

Cork leaned to his sister-in-law and put his arms around her and laid his cheek against her hair, and for a long time they held each other.

"We argued before Jo left," Cork said, battling tears. "We were so angry that we didn't even say good-bye. Christ, what was I thinking?"

"That the next day would be like that day and the day before and you would have forever to make things right," Rose said. "You didn't know any of this was going to happen, Cork."

"I could've told her I love her, Rose."

She looked with great compassion into his eyes. "Oh, Cork, you think she doesn't know?"

The phone rang. Mal looked at caller ID. "Owl Creek County Sheriff's Office."

"I'll take it." Cork wiped at his eyes. "O'Connor," he said, and then he listened. "Thank you." He returned the phone to its cradle. "The wind's quit. Once the runways are clear, they'll have planes in the air."

His daughters arrived near dinnertime, pulling up to the curb in Jenny's old Subaru Outback. They hurried up the walk in the blue of twilight, and Cork greeted them at the door with his arms wide open. It felt good to hold them.

They were different from each other in many ways. Jenny was a scholar and a scribbler, in her senior year at the University of Iowa, where she hoped, on graduation, to be accepted into the Writers' Workshop. She had her mother's beauty, the same ice-blond hair and ice-blue eyes. For Annie, studies had always taken a backseat to athletics. While she was growing up, her big dream had been to be the first female quarterback for Notre Dame. That hadn't happened, but she'd been offered a scholarship to play softball for the University of Wisconsin. Tragedy in her senior year of high school had altered her life course dramatically, and she'd declined the scholarship in favor of enrolling in a small Catholic college in northwest Illinois, where she was preparing herself in all the ways she could for a life that would be devoted to serving God and the Church. Annie wanted to be a nun, which was the other dream she'd had since childhood. Physically, she looked more like Rose, with hair the color of a dusty sunset and freckles. And, like Rose, she had something calm in her eyes that made people trust her immediately.

They stood on the porch in the dying light. "Has there been any word?" Jenny asked.

"The weather's finally broken and they've started the search," he said. "So that's good."

"But they haven't found anything?"

"As far as we know, not yet." The evening air was cool, and Cork said, "Let's get inside and we can talk more. Rose and Mal are here."

"Where's Stevie?" Annie asked, looking past him into the house.

"It's Stephen these days," Cork said. "He took Trixie for a walk. He needed to get out for a while."

"Stephen?"

"He's been reinventing himself lately," Cork said.

"How's he doing?" Jenny asked.

"Not good. But then who of us is?"

Inside, Rose and Mal hugged them both, and they all said the things meant to bind them in their mutual concern and to offer comfort.

"It smells wonderful in here." Annie looked at her aunt. "Chicken pot pie?"

"Bingo. Get your things settled. Dinner will be ready soon."

Jenny paused at the bottom of the stairs. "Dad, we heard on the radio that the pilot had been drinking."

"At the moment, it's only an allegation. We'll know the truth soon enough."

It was dark by the time Stephen came home from walking Trixie.

Cork had begun to worry and was watching the street from the living room window. He saw his son shuffling along the sidewalk, head down, face in shadow as he passed under the streetlight. Stephen paused at Jenny's Outback, but the prospect of seeing his sisters didn't seem to raise his spirits at all. Even Trixie, often a little too exuberant to suit Cork, seemed to have been infected by Stephen's mood, and she walked subdued at his side. They mounted the front steps, and Cork opened the door.

"I was beginning to get a little concerned," he said.

"What for? I was just walking," Stephen said.

"Dinner's been ready for a while."

"You could've eaten. I wouldn't care."

"Stevie!" Annie shouted, coming down the stairs. She threw her arms around her brother.

"It's Stephen," he said in sullen reply.

Jenny came from the kitchen, where she'd been helping Rose. "Stephen," she said and hugged him with a purposeful courteousness.

Cork's son suffered their attentions grudgingly and was clearly relieved when they both stepped back from him. Trixie was much more enthusiastic in her welcome, and she danced around the girls in a joyous frenzy of barking and tail wagging that got her tangled in her leash.

Stephen freed her. "I thought it was time to eat," he said. He turned away and went to the closet to hang his jacket.

Dinner was an odd affair, surreal. So much family gathered, and still the dining room table felt empty. Cork left the television on in the living room, tuned to CNN in case there were any new developments. They tried to carry on conversation in a normal way. Then Cork made a mistake, though he didn't think of it that way at the time. He asked Annie a simple question about her faith.

"What I see when I look at the world, Dad, is challenge and opportunity. Everywhere I turn I'm confronted with challenges to my faith. And at those same places I'm given the opportunity to be an instrument of God's truth."

Without looking up, Stephen, who sat slumped over his plate, said, "That's such bullshit."

"Stephen," Cork said.

"So what's the big holy truth in what's going on with Mom?" he said. "Why did God do this to her?"

"You think God struck her plane out of the air?" Annie asked.

"Well, he sure as hell didn't keep it from falling."

"We don't know what's happened with her plane," Cork said.

"I do," Stephen shot back. "I checked out plane wrecks on the Internet today. I know exactly what happens when a plane slams into a mountain."

"Why are you so certain that's what's happened?" Jenny asked.

Stephen aimed at her the dark fire of his eyes. "Am I the only one who sees things the way they are? If the plane didn't crash, we'd have heard from Mom by now. If it did crash, it crashed in those big fucking mountains and ended up in little fucking pieces, and if anybody survived they're fucking Popsicles by now."

"Watch your language, Stephen," Cork said.

"My language? Mom's dead and you're worried about my language. Jesus Christ." He yanked his napkin from his lap, threw it on the table, got up, and left. Trixie, who'd been lying nearby, rose as if to follow, then seemed to change her mind. She simply watched him stomp up the stairs toward his room.

"He's scared," Annie said.

"And he's thirteen," Jenny added.

Cork slid his chair away from the table. "I'm going up to talk to him."

Upstairs, he knocked on Stephen's bedroom door.

"What do you want?" his son called from inside.

"To talk."

"I don't want to talk."

"We need to. Open up, Stephen."

The wait was long and Cork was beginning to think he'd have to assert his parental authority to barge in, but Stephen opened the door at last. He turned away immediately and went back to his desk. The only light in the room came from the computer monitor, which was full of pictures from a website, images of a plane wreck.

Cork sat on Stephen's unmade bed. "I can't imagine that's pleasant," he said.

"It's not supposed to be pleasant." Stephen looked at the monitor. "Did you know that they've changed the instructions for crash position? They don't want you to stick your head between your legs anymore. Know why? It's not because you have a better chance of surviving but because there's a better chance of keeping your teeth intact so they can use dental records to identify the remains."

"You found that on the Internet?"

"Yeah. And worse."

"And you believe it. And you think there's no hope."

Stephen pointed to the monitor. "You think there's any hope in that?"

"When my father died, I was thirteen," Cork said. "I was sitting at his bedside. Your grandmother was there, too. We watched him go. The doctors who attended him never gave us any hope. Because they were so sure, I didn't even pray that he wouldn't die. I just let him go. And you know what? I've always regretted that I didn't pray my heart out trying to keep him with us. I wonder to this day if it might have made a difference."

"What? Like a miracle or something?"

"Yeah. A miracle or something. Look, Stephen, nobody really knows what's happened out there."

Stephen said quietly, "I do."

"Oh? How do you know?"

"Because I dreamed it," he said.

"I don't understand."

The light from the monitor lit Stephen's face, giving his skin a harsh, unnatural sheen. For several seconds he didn't speak, and his lips were pressed into a thin, glowing line. "There was this dream I used to have when I was a kid, I mean really little. I was in a big yellow room and Mom was there but way on the other side. I was scared. I think maybe there was something or somebody else in there with us. I don't remember that part so well. What I remember is that

I tried to run to Mom but she disappeared through a door and the door slammed shut when I tried to follow her. The door was white like ice. I pounded on it but it wouldn't open. I screamed for her to come back."

"Did she?"

"I always woke up then. You or Mom heard me crying and came in and the dream was over."

"You used to have a lot of nightmares," Cork said.

"I had this one a bunch of times. It stopped and I pretty much forgot about it. Until today. Dad, it had to be about this, right? I mean, it *is* this. Only why did I have it so long ago when I couldn't do anything about it?"

"I don't know."

"Was there something I could've done to . . . I don't know . . . stop it? Is there something I should do now? I don't understand."

Tears gathered along the rims of Stephen's eyes. Anything still unbroken in Cork's heart shattered, and he reached out to his son, but Stephen shrank away.

"I want to understand," he pleaded.

"Why don't we talk to Henry Meloux?" Cork said. "He's the only man I know who understands dreams."

"Henry," Stephen said, and the dim light of hope came into his eyes.

"Not tonight though. It's late. First thing tomorrow."

"Tomorrow," Stephen said with a nod.

They sat for a while, silence and the distance of their great fear between them.

"Feel like joining the rest of us?" Cork finally said.

"Yeah, I guess." Stephen turned off the computer and followed his father out of the room.

Downstairs, the faces of the others were turned to the television screen.

"Dad," Jenny said, "check this out."

Cork stood behind the sofa and watched the CNN report. A small, energetic woman with black hair and dark, angry eyes stood talking with another woman, a reporter. She wore a leather vest over a western shirt. When she gestured, which was often, silver bracelets flashed on her wrists. She stood in front of a tan brick building that was bright in the sun and surrounded by an apron of snow. She squinted in the sunlight and spoke into the microphone the reporter held toward her.

"Do you think," she said, "that if this had been a plane full of white politicians these people would have waited so long to begin searching for them? But it was full of Indians, so who cares?"

"Who is she?" Cork asked.

"The wife of one of the men who was on the plane with Jo," Rose said.

"Our own people have taken up the search. And we will find them," the woman said emphatically.

A caption appeared under the picture on the screen: "Ellyn Grant, wife of Edgar Little Bear, a passenger on the plane missing in the Wyoming Rockies."

The reporter, a blonde in a long, expensive-looking shearling coat, asked, "I understand one of the Arapaho has had a vision that may indicate where the plane came down."

"Will Pope," Ellyn Grant replied. "Our pilot is looking in the area Will's vision guided us to, a place called Baby's Cradle. We've asked for help, but so far the authorities out here have given us nothing."

"Would you comment on the allegation that the pilot of the plane had been drinking the night before the flight?"

"I don't know anything about that. Right now, all I care about is finding the plane and my husband."

The segment that followed dealt with the charter pilot, Clinton Bodine, who'd allegedly been drinking the night before. A reporter in Rice Lake, Wisconsin, where Bodine lived and operated his charter service, told viewers that he'd obtained information indicating the pilot was a recovering alcoholic. Accompanying the report were pictures of the hangar at the regional airport that he used for his small enterprise. There was a brief statement by one of the officials at the airport who said he'd known Bodine a long time and he was surprised to hear about the drinking allegation. There were shots of the pilot's home and of his wife, a young woman holding the hand of a small boy, hurrying from her car to the front door to avoid reporters.

Mal said, "Why do I think that if they could they'd follow her into the bathroom?"

"Brace yourselves," Cork said. "Our turn may come."

SEVEN

Day Three, Missing 43 Hours

Another tragedy developed overnight, but this one didn't involve the O'Connors.

Cork slept on the sofa again, keeping company with the television and CNN in a drowsy, sometimes disoriented, way. Partly this was because it allowed him to monitor the news, but it was also because he couldn't sleep in the bed he shared with Jo. It felt too empty and he felt too alone. At 5:00 A.M. he roused himself, made some coffee, and stepped onto the front porch to breathe in fresh air and check the weather. The storm that hit the Rockies had slid south and east through Colorado and Nebraska and Iowa and had missed Minnesota entirely. The sky was black and clear and frosted with stars.

He was about to enter the third day since Jo's plane had gone missing. Cork wasn't praying anymore that they'd made it to some godforsaken airstrip. He was praying that wherever the plane came down it had remained in once piece. And he was praying that, when the search began again that morning, the plane would be quickly found.

He returned to the kitchen, poured himself a cup of coffee, stared at the wall clock, where the rapid sweep of the second hand was torture to him, and then headed back to the sofa.

CNN had come alive with coverage of a story breaking in Kansas. Outside a town called Prestman, population 1,571, a standoff had developed between law enforcement and a religious sect led by a man named Gunther Hargrove. Hargrove and his followers, a group estimated at around sixty people that included a number of children, had leased an abandoned farm several miles outside the isolated prairie town. Hargrove hadn't kept up with the rent, and a sheriff's deputy had gone with the property owner to execute a lawful eviction order. During the confrontation that followed, Hargrove's people had shot the property owner and taken the deputy hostage. Now the farm, which the sect had turned into a compound, was surrounded by law enforcement personnel. Hargrove claimed that enough explosives had been planted about the compound to blow western Kansas off the map. The situation was extremely tense, and a resolution wasn't anywhere in sight. From a cable news perspective, it was a perfect story, and in a way, it was helpful to Cork. It sent the missing plane full of Indians to the bottom of the network interest list. Cork hoped that as a result the media vultures who might have descended on Aurora to hound him and his family would be drawn to Kansas instead.

Mal was up long before the others. It was still dark when he came downstairs in his robe and slippers.

"Up early," Cork said.

"I'm always up early. And I smelled coffee." Mal went to the kitchen and came back with a cup. "Anything new?"

"Nothing from Wyoming. There's a situation in Kansas that's getting the coverage." Cork explained the standoff.

"So much harm in the name of God. Makes atheism look mighty appealing sometimes." Mal shook his head and sipped his coffee.

Cork went upstairs, showered, and put on clean clothes. When he came back down, Stephen was on the sofa with Mal. Rose and the girls were up, too. They filled the kitchen with breakfast preparations while the men and Stephen monitored CNN. Finally Rose called, "Breakfast's ready."

Another day of waiting had begun.

An hour after sunup, about the time Cork anticipated day would be breaking in western Wyoming, he phoned the Owl Creek County Sheriff's Department and spoke with Deputy Dewey Quinn.

"The weather there is clear," he reported to the others. "The planes are just taking to the air. They'll keep us informed."

"Did you ask him about that Arapaho's vision?" Mal said.

"He dismissed it. The man's a notorious drunk, and the area his vision indicates is nowhere near any of the corridors the plane may have traveled." Then to Stephen he said, "Let's go see Henry Meloux."

Cork drove his old red Bronco. He stopped at the Gas-N-Go for a pack of American Spirit cigarettes. He also bought himself a cup of coffee and some hot chocolate for Stephen. The defroster was giving him trouble, and he kept having to wipe the windshield as he drove. They headed north out of Aurora along the shoreline of Iron Lake. After twenty minutes they left the paved highway and began bouncing over the gravel washboard of a county road. Another fifteen minutes and Cork pulled to a stop near a double-trunk birch that marked the beginning of the trail that led to Henry Meloux's cabin. They got out and began to walk.

For almost a mile the trail cut across national forest land, then it entered the Iron Lake Reservation. It led in a fairly straight line through tall second-growth pines. The ground was a soft bed of shed needles, and the air was sharp with the scent of pine sap. The air was still, and the only sound was the occasional snap of twigs under their feet. In some places the sunlight came through the trees in solid pillars and in others it lay shattered on the ground, so that the forest had the feel of a temple partly destroyed.

They broke from the trees onto a long point of land covered with meadow grass that was still green so late in the season. Near the end of the point stood an ancient, one-room cabin. Smoke poured from the stovepipe that jutted from the roof, which Cork had expected. What he didn't expect was that dark smoke would be pouring from the windows and door as well.

"Come on!" he called to his son, and they began to run.

They reached the cabin together, and Cork called through the door, "Henry! Henry, are you in there!"

"Here," Meloux hollered back and emerged from the smoke with an old yellow dog at his heels.

Cork was greeted with another unexpected sight: Henry Meloux was laughing.

"Are you all right, Henry?"

Meloux was an old man, the oldest Cork knew, somewhere in his nineties. His hair was long and white. His face was as lined as the bark of a cottonwood. His eyes were like dark, sparkling water. And at the moment, his hands held what looked like a smoking black brick.

"Corn bread," the old man said.

Stephen had knelt down to pet the dog, to whom he was a well-known friend. "You okay, Walleye?" he asked.

The dog's tail wagged in eager greeting, and he licked Stephen's hands.

"What happened, Henry?" Cork said.

"We went for a walk. I forgot about the corn bread I was baking." He looked at the hard, burned brick cradled between pot holders. "The corn bread is a disappointment." He smiled at Cork and Stephen. "But the walk was not. It is a day full of beauty, Corcoran O'Connor."

Cork said, "We'd like to talk, Henry."

Meloux's face turned thoughtful. "I have heard about your trouble." He looked back at the cabin, where the smoke was beginning to thin. "I think it is a good morning to sit by the lake." He put the burned corn bread on the ground, where Walleye sniffed at it, then stepped warily back. The old man said, "Only a very stupid or a very hungry animal will eat that. In this forest, there are both." He went back into his cabin, and when he returned he carried a box of kitchen matches, which he slipped into the pocket of the red plaid mackinaw he'd put on.

A path led from the cabin across the meadow and through a breach in an outcropping of gray rock. At the edge of the lake on the far side of the outcropping lay a black circle of ash ringed by stones. Split wood stood stacked against the rock, and nearby was a wooden box the size of an orange crate. Meloux lifted the lid and pulled out a handful of wood shavings and some kindling. These he handed to Stephen. "We will need a fire," he said. He pulled the box of matches from his coat pocket and held them out to the young man.

Without a word, Stephen set to work.

Cork handed the pack of American Spirits to Meloux. The old man took the gift, opened it, and eased out a cigarette. He split the paper and dumped the tobacco into the palm of his hand. He sprinkled a pinch in each of the four cardinal directions and dropped the last bit into the fire Stephen had going at the center of the ring. They sat on sawed sections of tree trunk, and the old man passed a cigarette to each of them, then a stick that he'd lit from the flames. They spent a few minutes while the smoke from their cigarettes mingled with the smoke from the crackling fire and drifted skyward. Stephen had smoked with his father and Meloux before in this way because this was not for pleasure. In the belief of the Anishinaabeg, tobacco smoke carried prayers and wishes to the spirit world.

Meloux was an Ojibwe Mide, a member of the Grand Medicine Society. As far back as Cork could remember, the old man's guidance had been an important part of his life. When Meloux was a young man, his renown as a guide and hunter was legendary. He had the heart of a warrior and twice had saved Cork's life. His knowledge and understanding had also helped Stephen back to wholeness after the trauma of a kidnapping. This old man who'd turned corn bread into hard charcoal was remarkable in more ways than Cork could say.

"Tell me what I can do," Meloux said.

Stephen explained his dream. "I don't know what it means or why it came to me," he confessed. "Was I supposed to do something, or is there something I'm supposed to do now?"

The old man considered. "Sometimes a dream is just a dream, Stephen. It is a way for the spirit to examine pieces of this world."

"I think it's more than a dream, Henry. I think it was a vision."

"Tell me what you think this vision means."

"The white door has got to be the snow, right?"

The old man did not reply.

"Right?"

Instead of answering, the old man said, "You thought there was someone in the room with you. Who?"

Stephen frowned, trying to remember. "I don't know, but whoever it was, I was afraid of them."

"Afraid for yourself or for your mother?"

"For her, I think."

"This room, you said it was big. What else do you remember?"

"It was yellow. And full of white rocks," Stephen said suddenly.

"There were rocks in the room?"

"Yes. They looked like ice. Like the door looked."

The old man nodded. "Do you remember anything else?"

Stephen closed his eyes. "A light under the door."

"The door that hid your mother and closed itself to you?"

"Yeah, that one."

"Anything else?"

Stephen shook his head hopelessly. "It was a long time ago."

"Yet you remember much. I think you are right, Stephen. I think this is more than a dream."

"What does it mean?"

"I do not know. But I will tell you this. If there is a door, it can be opened."

"How?"

The old Mide shrugged. "Your vision. You will have to find the answer yourself."

"I don't even know where to start."

"You already have," Meloux replied. "A vision is never seen with your eyes, Stephen. Your heart is the only witness, and only your heart understands."

"So . . . what? I have to, like, talk to my heart?"

"I think listening will do."

"Henry, I need an answer now. My mom's in real trouble."

"All the more reason for everything inside you to be still, Stephen, the better to hear your heart."

"That's all you can tell me?" Stephen said.

"I am afraid so," the old man replied.

"Jesus." Stephen threw the last of his cigarette into the fire, stood up, and left the ring. He disappeared through the rocks heading along the path back to Meloux's cabin.

"He's scared, Henry," Cork said.

"He has reason to be. He holds a key, but does not know the lock that it fits."

They walked together to the cabin with Walleye following closely. Stephen wasn't there. Cork saw him far across the meadow, stomping along the path that would lead him through the forest to where the Bronco was parked. Meloux bent, picked up the black corn bread brick, and broke it open. The center was yellow and unburned.

"At the heart of most things that look bad is something that can be good and useful." He crumbled the edible section of the corn bread and spread it on the ground for the animals. "I am sorry for your situation, Corcoran O'Connor, and I hope that you discover some good in it somewhere."

Cork walked back the way he'd come. He found Stephen sitting in the Bronco, staring through the windshield. He got in, kicked the engine over, turned the Bronco around, and headed back toward town.

"Lot of good that did," Stephen said. "Listen to your heart. What kind of bullshit is that?"

"I'd never accuse Henry of offering bullshit."

"Okay, you tell me what it means. What door am I supposed to open?"

"I don't know."

"See? No help at all." Stephen folded his arms across his chest and slumped in his seat.

Cork had intended to use the trip to Meloux's to break the news to Stephen that he was flying to Wyoming, alone. But he found himself backing off, hoping a better opportunity might present itself, though he didn't have a clue how that might happen.

Halfway to Aurora, his cell phone rang. He pulled to the side of the road and answered. He listened and said, "Thanks, Mal." He put the phone away. "We need to get home," he told his son. "They've found something in the mountains."

Stephen's face brightened. "Mom?"

"No. They've spotted the door to a plane."

EIGHT

Day Three, Missing 49 Hours

Deputy Quinn was calling him Cork now.

"That's right, Cork," he said. His cold wasn't so much in evidence anymore. "One of our planes spotted debris in a high mountain canyon in the Washakie Wilderness. It's in an area that's part of a formation known as Heaven's Keep."

"Debris?" Cork said.

"What they could clearly see appeared to be the door of a plane. It's resting on a broad ledge that's free of snow because of the high winds. Which also means that it's going to be difficult to get to."

"Any sign of the passengers?"

"Not at the moment."

"How are you proceeding?"

"We have a chopper already in the air on its way to the location. If the pilot can find a reasonable place to land, he'll attempt it. We have EMTs onboard. We also have a ground team prepared to head in, but that will take much longer, of course."

"When will you know if the chopper's able to land?"

"Probably within the hour. I'll keep you posted. That's a solid-gold promise. And will you pass the information along to Ms. LeDuc?"

"I'll call her right now."

When he hung up, Cork told the others what he'd learned, which was no more than they already knew. He called Sarah LeDuc and explained.

"Only a door?" she said.

"It's a start, Sarah. At least we have a location. As soon as I hear anything more, I'll let you know. Stay near your phone."

When he hung up, Rose said, "I can't just sit and wait. I'm going to make some lunch. Anyone want to give a hand?"

Annie took her up on it, and the two of them headed to the kitchen. The others stayed in the living room. The television was tuned to CNN, but the sound was off. Cork stared at the screen, where the standoff in Kansas was center stage. Footage shot across the plains showed desolate hills, yellow-brown beneath a blue sky that, despite its swimming pool color, looked as empty and desolate as the land. There was nothing rising across the whole of the horizon except the dark, distant buildings of the compound where Hargrove and his followers were encamped. They'd chosen the place in order to be lost to the world, Cork figured, but they'd screwed themselves royally. Best laid plans.

Looking at all the emptiness made Cork realize how closed-in the house felt, how constraining. What he really wanted was to be in Wyoming, looking for Jo. He wanted to be on the helicopter that was at that moment speeding to . . . what? Her rescue? Only a door. That's all they saw. Only a door. And what did that mean?

"A door," Stephen said, as if he'd read his father's thoughts.

By now, everyone knew about Stephen's dream, which Meloux, like Stephen, believed was a vision.

"Maybe it's *the* door," he said.

Jenny said, "Don't get your hopes up."

Stephen gave his sister a challenging look. "Why not?"

"I'm just saying we don't really know anything yet." She was less than gentle in her reply.

What she meant, Cork thought, was that the door was wreckage. And wreckage wasn't good. Maybe she was trying to help Stephen see things more realistically, but her own nerves were frayed, and it came out as an accusation. They all were feeling the strain. He could see it in the pinch of their faces, hear it in the taut cadence when they spoke, feel it in the despair that hung in the house like fouled air.

He said, "Stephen, let's do some surfing on the Internet."

"Looking for what?"

"For hope," Cork said. "Come on."

They went upstairs to Stephen's room and for half an hour looked on the Net for stories of miraculous survival in frigid conditions. What they came up with was a half dozen tales of men and women whose luck and courage had brought them out of impossible situations: a party that had survived the ill-fated Scott polar expedition; the crash of a Canadian military transport in the Arctic; a man who'd survived a plane wreck in the High Sierra and hiked through wilderness for two weeks to reach safety despite a dozen broken bones.

Stephen's spirits seemed to rise with each miraculous tale, and he began pulling them off the computer and printing them to share with the others.

Downstairs, the doorbell rang. A moment later Mal called up, "Someone to see you, Cork."

To his profound surprise, Cork found Hugh Parmer standing in the shade of his porch.

"This isn't a good time," Cork said curtly.

"I'm sorry to intrude, O'Connor, but I have something to say to you that I thought you'd want to hear. It's important or I wouldn't bother you at a time like this."

Cork stepped outside. The morning was sunny and the temperature had climbed to forty degrees. Even in the shade of the porch, Parmer squinted, and Cork realized it was the natural state of the man's face. The face of a cowboy masking the mind of a real estate tyrant.

"Look, O'Connor, I know about your trouble, and I'm here to tell you that I'm putting the Iron Lake development on hold indefinitely. I'm not going to kick a man while he's down."

"You're dropping your plans for the lakeshore?"

"Let's take it one step at a time. Right now, I'm pulling back. I don't want you to have to worry about anything except your family. Later on, you and me can sit down, and I'm willing to bet we can hammer out something that works for both of us. But don't you even think about that right now. This is no bullshit."

He put out his hand, and after a moment's consideration, Cork accepted it. Parmer's palm was callused. Cork realized this wasn't a man who spent his time sitting in a plush office.

"There's nothing more important than family, O'Connor. You see to yours."

"The name's Cork."

"Call me Hugh. And listen, you need anything in all this, just let me know. Here." He pulled a card from an inside pocket of the jacket he wore and handed it to Cork. "That's my cell phone number. My Lear's parked down at the Duluth airport and I'm flying back to Texas tomorrow morning, but I can be reached anytime."

Cork said, "I misjudged you, Hugh."

"Not the first time that's happened. I'm a good businessman, Cork, but I'm a whole hell of a lot more."

"Look, we're about to have some lunch inside. You're welcome to join us."

"Thanks, but I didn't come here to intrude."

"You came with a good heart, Hugh. That's never an intrusion."

"I appreciate the offer, but all the same I'll be leaving now." He nodded toward the card. "I mean it. Call me anytime."

He walked down the steps and went to his car, a rented Navigator that was parked at the curb. He gave a wave as he drove off.

Cork's situation was so confusing that he understood he couldn't necessarily trust his judgment of Parmer. The man could have been setting him up in order to call in the note later, when they dealt with Sam's Place. That didn't matter. At the moment, Cork would have sold his soul to have Jo home safely. He eyed the card in his hand. A small white rectangle. He rotated it so that the long sides were vertical. It looked like a door.

"Dad," Annie called from inside. "Lunch is ready."

The phone call came a few minutes past noon, while Stephen was sharing with the others what he'd found on the Internet. Cork leaped up to answer.

"O'Connor," he said.

"It's Deputy Quinn."

"What's the word, Dewey?"

"Still uncertain. We got a report from Jon Rude." Quinn pronounced the name in a way that rhymed with *today*. "He's piloting the helicopter. A very good guy. The wind's a problem up there. It's kicking his chopper all over the place. But he thinks he's found a site where he might be able to attempt a landing. It's about a quarter mile from the ledge where the plane door was spotted, and after he lands there'll be some climbing involved. Even if he can set down, it will be a while before we know anything. Sorry I don't have something more solid for you."

"You're a big help, Dewey. Thanks."

Cork passed the news along to the others, then called Sarah LeDuc and did the same.

The next call came at one thirty.

"Cork, it's Dewey. Look, I have some bad news. Or maybe it's not bad, I don't know. They've reached the wreckage. It's not the plane your wife was on. It's a small Cessna that went missing five years ago, flown by a real estate broker from Rawlins. We spent a good long time looking for it then, but the search was centered much farther south. The team's found human remains, which they'll be bringing down. We've notified the pilots who've been helping with the current search, and they're going back into the air just as soon as they can. I'm sorry, Cork."

"Thanks, Dewey. I appreciate the call."

They all watched him expectantly. Cork braced himself and forced a smile. "Good news," he said. "It wasn't Jo's plane." He explained, trying to give the news the best possible spin. But after they'd heard, they seemed to sit a little lower, more heavily weighted than before. Hope was like that, Cork knew. It could be crueler than despair.

"I'm going to get a little fresh air," he said.

He went out onto the porch. The branches of the elm in the front yard had long ago been stripped bare, and the shadow they cast on the lawn made the ground look fractured. The air was cool and full of the scent of woodsmoke from the blaze in someone's fireplace. It would have been a beautiful day if not for the worry that dragged on all Cork's thinking.

Mal came out. "I haven't wanted a cigarette in years," he said.

"Right now I'd kill for one." He leaned against the porch railing. "You're leaving for the airport in a couple of hours and you still haven't said a thing to the kids about going to Wyoming."

"You think I don't know that?" When Cork heard the venom in his own voice, he apologized to Mal. Then he confessed, "I can't bring myself to tell Stephen."

"Take him with you."

"That's not a good idea, Mal."

"Why? Look, Cork, you can leave Rose and the girls. They have each other. For Stephen, you're it. And he's dying to be out there helping. You go and leave him behind, well, that'd be one big mistake, in my opinion."

The sun had dropped low enough to shoot fire at their feet, and they stood in a puddle that burned bright yellow on the porch boards.

Cork said, "It would be easier to operate if I were on my own."

"Maybe. But listen. One of the things you've told me about your father's death is that you've always felt there was something more you could have done. If Jo is lost to us for good, if ultimately that's what we all have to face, wouldn't you rather that Stephen faces it believing he did everything he could? Wouldn't you want to believe it of yourself?"

For a few long moments, Cork stared at the fire around his feet, then he decided. "Thanks, Mal. Let's go in and give them the word."

They didn't respond immediately when Cork told them he was going. He didn't know exactly what that meant.

"I think it's important to be there," he said.

"Are you going alone?" Jenny asked.

"No. I'd like to take Stephen with me. Is that okay with you, buddy?"

Stephen looked surprised, then he looked brighter than he had in days. "Heck, yes."

Cork said to his daughters, "Are you two okay with that?"

The girls looked at each other.

Jenny said, "I'm totally cool with it."

"It's a terrific idea," Annie said.

"It's settled then."

Stephen jumped up and headed for the stairs. "I've gotta pack."

It wasn't as simple as Cork had hoped. Nothing was simple anymore. There were no seats left on the flight he was taking. He got off the phone ready to put his fist through the kitchen wall.

Rose, who'd been sitting at the table with her rosary, said, "What about Mr. Parmer?"

"What about him?"

"He offered to help, didn't he? And you told me, didn't you, that he's got his own plane?"

It was a slim hope, but Cork was desperate. He pulled his wallet from his back pocket and plucked out the business card Hugh Parmer had given him. He noted the cell phone number, then turned the card lengthwise so that it again resembled a door. He made the call.

"Fly you and the boy to Wyoming? No problem at all, Cork," Parmer said without a moment's hesitation. "Glad I can be of help. I've got a couple of details to tie up here. If we flew out first thing in the morning, would that do? I could have you in Wyoming in time for breakfast."

Cork would have preferred flying out that evening but knew that if they did they'd arrive in the dead of night and couldn't do anything anyway.

"That would be fine, Hugh," he said. "Thanks."

"I'll drop by around five A.M. to pick you up. That ought to get us to the Duluth airport for takeoff about sunrise."

Cork put the phone down. If he'd just sold his soul to Parmer, he was surprised how little he cared. The truth was that, in the midst of so much need, what he felt most was an abundance of gratitude.

When darkness brought the search to an end in Wyoming that evening, Dewey Quinn called Cork to tell him that nothing had been found. Cork didn't tell the deputy he was coming. He figured Quinn would do his best to argue him out of it and the conversation would end up awkward for them both.

He called Sarah LeDuc, told her his plan, and promised to keep her informed. He also called Marsha Dross, who said she'd been expecting as much and wished him good luck. Finally he called Stephen's teacher and cleared his absence from school for a few more days. He drove to

Sam's Place and spent some time at the Quonset hut finishing a few details related to his PI business. He locked up and stood outside under a night sky that was slowly filling with stars. He walked to the end of the old dock. The water around the pilings was still and black. Far across the lake, the glimmer of lights from isolated cabins marked the distant shoreline. He remembered a night, years before, when he'd stood in this same spot with Jo. They'd been through hell. Their marriage had been chipped and broken and ready to fall apart. Yet under the sky that night, with the stars of heaven as their only witnesses, they'd made a vow to each other that had been sacred and true and binding. That night, far more powerfully than on the day they were wed, they pledged their lives to each other, their fortunes, their hearts, and their destinies.

Now, as he stood alone under that same sky, he made another vow.

"Wherever you are, I'll find you, Jo. And I swear to God, I'll bring you home."

NINE

Day Four, Missing 65 Hours

At night the emptiness of his bed drove Cork to the sofa, where he slept with the television tuned to CNN. He drifted between sleep and fevered dreams that were often driven by the reports from the news channel. Each time he woke, he remembered almost nothing except that the landscapes were bleak.

A little after 3:00 A.M., he was awakened by the sense that he was not alone, and he opened his eyes to find Rose sitting in the rocker. She had a throw around her shoulders, one she'd knitted as a birthday present for Jo. The only light came from the television, and in the constant shift of that hard glow Rose rocked gently back and forth.

Cork sat up.

"A woman and her daughter tried to escape," Rose said.

"What woman?" Cork struggled to bring himself fully awake.

"From the compound in Kansas. They shot them as they ran."

"The police?"

"Someone from the compound." She wiped her eye, dealing quietly with a tear. "The girl was only ten years old. What kind of religious community kills its mothers and its children?"

Cork had no answer for that.

"Here I am praying for Jo and for all of us. I should be praying for them, too, I suppose. Sometimes it just seems there can never be enough prayers." She took a deep breath and exhaled. "You were talking in your sleep."

"What did I say?"

"Nothing I could understand. It sounded angry."

That was probably right. He was afraid, and long ago he'd come to understand that translating fear into anger helped him deal with situations that threatened to paralyze him.

"Rose, I don't know if going out there will do any good."

"You have to go, though. You have to act, Cork. It's what you do best."

"What about you?"

"I pray. It's what I do best."

In what quiet comfort they could draw from each other's company, they sat until Stephen came downstairs with his suitcase. He looked at his watch.

"Mr. Parmer will be here in an hour, Dad. Have you even packed?"

"Last night."

"Should we, like, wait out front?"

"It's a little early for that."

"Maybe some breakfast first," Rose suggested, rising.

"That would be awesome, Aunt Rose."

Stephen dropped his bag by the front door, then stood at the window staring eagerly into a morning that still looked very much like night, as if he was trying hard to hurry the dawn. Cork showered, dressed, and brought his own suitcase downstairs. Mal was up now, too, drinking coffee in the kitchen and helping Rose. Stephen sat at the table, doing a lot of damage to a stack of pancakes. The girls came down a few minutes later. And shortly after that, Hugh Parmer arrived.

Cork introduced Parmer, and they all made a fuss of thanks, which Parmer accepted in a genuinely humble fashion. Stephen was eager to be off, so they were quickly and cleanly on their way to the Duluth airport in the dark of a very early November morning. Cork had cautioned Parmer to watch for deer, who were crepuscular creatures, apt to be lurking along the road as dawn approached. They made it to the airport without incident. Just as the sun began to rise over the vast inland sea of Lake Superior, Parmer's Learjet lifted off the ground, made a long curl to the west, and headed toward Wyoming.

After Stephen grew tired of looking out the window at the earth thirty thousand feet below, he turned to his host and asked, "Do you own this jet?"

"Yep." Parmer sat with a cup of coffee in his hand. "Lock, stock, and twin Honeywell engines."

"It must've cost like a million dollars."

"Several, Stephen. But in my work I need the freedom that having my own set of wings gives me."

"You build things, right? I mean like condominiums and stuff."

"Communities, Stephen. I develop communities."

"Dad says you're planning on trashing the shore along Iron Lake."

"Sorry, Hugh," Cork said.

Parmer laughed. "One man's vision may be another's nightmare, son. Your dad and I have a lot of talking to do. I think we've finished dealing through intermediaries. I believe we'll be working face-to-face on this from now on, man to man, which is the best way to do business, I think. But we're going to worry about that later. Right now you and your dad have more pressing concerns."

Stephen studied the interior of the Lear with continued admiration. "Maybe we could use your jet to look for Mom."

"I think you'll want something that maneuvers in and out of those mountains a little better. I'll bet we can arrange for that."

"We?" Cork said.

"Manner of speaking. But when I offered to help in any way I could, I wasn't just blowing smoke, Cork. If you want to arrange for your own aircraft in the search out there, you do that. Have 'em bill it to me."

"That's a lot more than I intended when I asked for your help, Hugh."

"And little enough for me to give."

Stephen said, "Were you always rich?"

"Nope. Grew up in West Texas working on the same spread where my father was a ranch hand. That's how I started out."

"How'd you get rich?"

"The truth is that I married the rancher's daughter. Didn't do it because she was rich. I loved that woman with all my heart."

"Still married?" Cork asked.

" 'Fraid not. Lost Julia almost twenty years ago to a drunk driver."

"I'm sorry."

"You'd think that after twenty years I'd get used to the idea." He looked out the window of the plane. "I hope you find your wife, Cork. I truly do."

The flight was smooth and uneventful, and shortly before ten o'clock the Lear touched down on a runway of the regional airport in Cody, Wyoming.

Cork had called ahead and arranged for a rental car, a Jeep Wrangler. After he confirmed that it was waiting, he and Stephen said goodbye to Hugh Parmer. They shook hands, and Parmer said, "I'm heading home, but if I hear that there was some way I could've helped and you didn't ask me, I'll be well and truly pissed."

"I'll be sure to let you know," Cork said. "Hugh, I appreciate everything you've done."

"We'll be talking," Parmer said. He ruffed Stephen's hair. "Your old man's lucky to have you along for backup. Keep him out of trouble, okay?"

"I will," Stephen said earnestly.

"And, son," Parmer added. "I sincerely hope you find your mother."

They drove southeast toward the Bighorn River, into a basin from which they could see the Absarokas to the west. The mountains were completely covered with snow, and at one point Stephen said solemnly, "They look like the teeth of a wolf." They drove between irrigated fields, where great rolls of hay lay wrapped in black plastic and wore a mantle of snow. They drove through rocky hills dotted with prickly pear cactus. They saw ranch houses in the distance, isolated, lonely-looking places, and spotted cattle grazing near gullies lined with cottonwoods. The farther south they drove the more rugged the land became, marked by the rise of long escarpments whose sharp cliffs were red as open wounds. Cork was surprised how little snow there was in the Bighorn Basin, in some places not much more than a dusting.

After an hour and a half, they came to Hot Springs, which proved to be a large town perched on the high ground at a bend in the Big-horn. On the far side of the river, steamy vapor drifted up from yel-low pools. Hot Springs had an old western feel to it, a community carved out of rock and bedded in sand. It was, in a way, colorful. Blue sky, blue river, blue-white mountains, red rock, yellow springs. The day was warm, the temperature in the high forties. In the hills above town lay pockets of snow, but in Hot Springs itself most of what had fallen had already melted away. They drove directly to the courthouse, an old building of tan brick, and they parked in the lot of the annex, a newer two-story addition that housed the Owl Creek County Sher-iff's Department and the county jail. Also parked in the lot were news vans from stations in Casper and Cheyenne with satellite dishes on top. Cork and Stephen went inside and found themselves in a small waiting area, empty at the moment, with two inner doors. One door was marked JAIL, the other AUTHORIZED PERSONNEL ONLY. There was a public contact window so dark Cork couldn't see what was on the other side. He walked to the window and spoke into the small grate embedded in the glass.

"My name is Cork O'Connor. This is my son, Stephen. We're here to see Deputy Dewey Quinn."

"Need to see some ID," came the voice from the other side.

Cork took out his driver's license and dropped it in the trough be-neath the glass, where a couple of fingers drew it in from the other side. A minute passed, then the license came back. "Have a seat," the tired, disembodied voice said.

They sat in a couple of uncomfortable black plastic chairs in the waiting area and didn't talk. Cork kept eyeing his watch and couldn't believe how slowly the minutes passed. All he could think of was how close they were to the search and how much precious time was being wasted.

Finally the Authorized Personnel Only door opened, and a man in a deputy's khaki uniform came out. He was of medium height, with dark brown hair in a crew cut. You could see in the deep tan of his face and the taut draw of the skin around his eyes and mouth that he spent a lot of time in the sun. Cork pegged Quinn at somewhere in his early thirties.

"Dewey?"

The deputy didn't appear happy to see him. "I wish you'd have let me know you were coming, Cork."

"Would it have made a difference?"

"I'd probably have tried to talk you out of it." He turned his attention to Cork's son. "Stephen?"

"Yeah. I mean, yes, sir."

He shook hands with them both.

"We're not here to cause you problems, Dewey," Cork said.

"I know. Doesn't mean you won't." He looked past them, out the front door, and said, "Oh, shit."

Cork glanced there, too, and saw a pretty blonde in jeans and an expensive-looking shearling coat sweeping toward the door from the parking lot.

"Quick," Quinn said, "follow me."

He hustled them to the door he'd come through, and they followed him inside.

Cork found himself in familiar territory. The Owl Creek County Sheriff's Department was not that different from the sheriff's department in Minnesota. There was a large common area and, along the perimeter, doors that led to other rooms and offices. To the right was the contact desk, currently staffed by a stout-looking deputy with a buzz cut and his sleeves rolled back. Beyond him was the dispatch desk and radio. The smell of fresh coffee filled the place.

"Who were you avoiding?" Cork asked.

"Felicia Gray. TV newswoman out of Casper. We're lucky because most of the media is up in Cody, where the Civil Air Patrol is coordinating the air search. Not as many reporters on this as there were at first. That standoff thing with the religious nut in Kansas seems to have grabbed everyone's attention."

Cork understood. A few missing Indians wouldn't be news for long.

"But we've got Ms. Gray," Quinn went on. "She's the one who broke the story about the pilot's drinking. She gets hold of you two, your nuts are deep-fried. She'll harass the hell out of you, believe you me. Probably can't avoid her forever, but you might as well delay it as long as possible. Bolger," he called to the deputy at the contact desk, and said by way of introduction, "the O'Connors. Miss Kiss-My-Pulitzer questions you about these two, you don't know anything, got that?"

"Ten-four, Dewey." He gave a two-fingered salute, then used the same gesture as a greeting to Cork and Stephen.

"Come with me." Quinn turned and walked briskly down a narrow hallway to a southwest-facing conference room where sunshine flooded through a long window. Beyond the glass, the streets of Hot Springs, lined with small houses and bared trees, ran toward the distant mountains. The conference table dead center was cluttered with maps and papers. A large topographic map hung on the wall opposite the window. It was studded with pins of various colors and lined with corridors crudely drawn with neon highlighters. There was a portable dispatch radio on a table against another wall. Several chairs were scattered about, all unoccupied at the moment.

"Like I said, the air search is being coordinated up in Cody by the Wyoming wing of the Civil Air Patrol," Quinn said. "Commander Nickleson of the Cody unit is in charge, and she's being assisted by units out of Big Horn and Jackson. We're in constant communication. This is where we've been handling things on our end." He swept his hand across the room. "When I say 'we,' I mean 'I.' We're a small department and we're stretched to the max. Cork, I swear to you, we're doing the best we can."

"Where's the sheriff?"

"Out on a domestic disturbance call. We still have our regular duties to see to. If he comes in, he probably won't say much. Just give you a look that'd scare a grizzly bear. Have a seat and I'll bring you up to date."

Cork took one of the chairs and Stephen another. Quinn walked to the map on the wall. He pointed to a black pin near the top of the map. The other pins and the highlighted corridors spread out south of it.

"This is where radar contact was lost." He moved his finger down a few inches. "This is where the snowmobilers reported hearing a plane fly low overhead. Now, normally a plane is going to follow certain flight lines, or vectors, dictated by the FAA. This is way off any vector. But if the plane was in trouble and if the snowmobilers were right, then the plane may have turned back and been trying to clear the mountains and find a flat place to land. Maybe the pilot hoped to make it to Casper. We just don't know."

Cork leaned his arms on the table and studied the map, which showed all of Owl Creek County and portions of the adjacent counties as well. "Have you sent planes over the area to the east, between the mountains and Casper?"

"Yes." Quinn studied the map and shook his head. "We've checked most of the logical locations, but it's a lot of country to cover and most of it's deep in snow."

Cork waved toward the window. "But there's not much snow here."

"Sometimes the mountain ranges—the Absarokas, the Bighorns, and the Wind River Range—divide the big storms and they end up sliding north or south of us. Creates a little microclimate here in the basin that's often quite moderate in the winter." He went back to the map. "We have nearly a dozen planes involved, CAP volunteers and a few pilots and aircraft on loan from the Air National Guard out of Cheyenne. And there's Rude's chopper. Several of the pilots are scanning the High Plains east of here, the rest are over the Absarokas. The mountains in the Washakie Wilderness area here"—he pointed toward one of the highlighted corridors—"are promising if you're thinking a plane might try an emergency landing. There are some very high, relatively barren plateaus where it might have a chance of coming down safely. We're looking particularly hard in that area. But there are two basic problems. One is the snow, of course. It's fallen so deep at the high elevations that it's covered everything." He kept his eyes on the map and hesitated.

"And the other problem?" Cork said.

He shot out a frustrated breath. "We're not at all certain that we're searching in the right places, Cork. Except for the report of the snowmobilers, we have nothing to go on after the plane dropped off radar. The pilot could have proceeded northwest along the same vector, hoping to poke through the storm. Commander Nickleson has planes searching that vector. He could have swung north toward the airport at Cody or southeast toward the one at Riverton. CAP planes are flying those areas, too. See, we just don't know."

Cork looked at the map and felt the weight on his shoulders grow heavier. "Even with a dozen planes it seems like a lot of area to cover."

"Believe me, it is," Quinn said.

"We saw a woman on CNN, the wife of one of the passengers, an Arapaho woman, I believe. She said her people were involved in the search."

"Ellyn Grant." Quinn didn't sound happy. "Yes, they're involved. They have one plane in the air. It's flying a search grid over this area. The Teton Wilderness." Quinn pointed southwest of the black pin where radar contact had been lost. "It's not a flight pattern that any pilot would logically follow, but she claims one of her people has had a vision of the plane coming down there. So that's where they're looking. She's not happy that we're concentrating on the Washakie and east." He sat down across from them at the table. "Okay, what did you have in mind?"

"I'm not sure," Cork said. He looked at Stephen. "We were kind of hoping we could go up in one of the planes."

"How about a helicopter instead?"

"Sure," Stephen jumped in.

"Our chopper pilot, Jon Rude, had a mechanical problem this morning. Delayed him a little. He's scheduled to take off in about an hour. I'll contact him, ask him to take you along. If he's willing. It'll be his call. Fair enough?"

"More than," Cork said.

"Where are you staying?"

"We haven't decided."

"The hotel that's on the grounds of the hot springs is excellent. A fine little place that's on the National Register of Historic Places. This time of year you should have no problem getting a room."

"Thanks, Dewey."

"Wait here. Let me give Jon a call."

He left the room.

"What do you think?" Cork said to Stephen.

"We're here and that's good. We're going up in a helicopter and that's good. And Deputy Quinn is really nice and that's really good."

The deputy had been gone only a few minutes when another officer entered the room. He was tall and bulky, and he fixed Cork and Stephen with the eye of a hunter.

"Who are you?" he said.

Cork stood up to introduce himself. "Cork O'Connor. And this is my son, Stephen."

The man made no move toward them to shake hands. "What are you doing here?"

"Waiting for Deputy Quinn."

"He brought you back?"

"That's right."

"Briefed you?"

"Yes."

"Do what he says, clear?"

"Crystal."

"All right then." He turned and left.

"Who was that?"

"Sheriff Kosmo would be my guess."

"Not very talkative."

"You got his message, didn't you?"

"Well, yeah."

" 'Nuff said."

A few more minutes, then Deputy Quinn returned. "Okay, we're all set. We'll meet Jon at the airfield in fifteen minutes. Did you see Sheriff Kosmo?"

"He stopped in to have a word," Cork said.

"One word, period," Stephen added.

Quinn laughed. "If Jim likes you, Stephen, you sometimes get two. All set?"

"Yes." Stephen leaped to his feet.

"Then let's go."

As they passed the contact desk, Quinn said to the deputy there, "Kiss-My-Pulitzer still around, Bolger?"

"Nope. I stonewalled her and she split."

"I'm ten-seven for the next hour, unless something new develops with the air search."

"I copy. Good luck, O'Connors," Bolger said.

"Thanks," Stephen threw back and gave him a wave.

Outside, the mountains to the west were blue-white under an azure sky. "The airfield's up there," Quinn said, pointing toward a massive ridge rising beyond the outskirts of Hot Springs in the direction of the mountains. "Just follow me."

He got into a departmental TrailBlazer. Cork and Stephen hurried to their Wrangler and followed the deputy out of the lot. They took a street called Carson that cut due west before winding its way up the ridge Quinn had indicated. They passed the town's water tower and what looked like a small, abandoned mining operation. At the crest of the ridge, the road divided. A sign pointed to the right and read, OWL CREEK GOLF COURSE—PUBLIC WELCOME. Quinn took the left fork, and Cork spotted the airfield immediately, a fenced area with several hangars and a couple of other small buildings beside a single runway. The gate was open, and they rolled through. Cork followed the TrailBlazer to the far side of one of the hangars, where they found the chopper and its pilot waiting.

Jon Rude's face was all about friendliness, from the laugh lines and the big smile to the wry glint of his eyes. He was Cork's height, just under six feet, and had a handshake that was firm without overdoing it.

"Thanks for letting us ride along," Cork said.

"No problem. Ever been in a chopper before?"

"A few occasions doing S and R back in Minnesota."

"That's right," Rude said. "Dewey told me you were in law enforcement for a while. What about you, Stephen?"

"I never have."

"You do okay on roller coasters?"

"Heck, yes."

"Then you'll be fine. We'd best be off. Got a lot of territory to cover." He addressed Quinn. "Any word from the others?"

"Nothing new."

"Okay, then. Stephen, you want to ride shotgun?"

"Sure."

"You'll need eagle eyes."

"I got 'em."

"Hop aboard and let's see what we can see."

TEN

Day Four, Missing 76 Hours

That's my place down there," Rude said. He banked the chopper in order for Cork and Stephen to have a better view.

They were flying low over a flat valley that was threaded down the middle by a stream lined with cottonwoods. The floor of the valley was covered with irrigated fields, mostly alfalfa. Rude's place consisted of a small ranch house, a barn, a corral, and a few outbuildings. From the air, it looked nice and neat. The nearest neighbor was a good half mile distant.

"I call her the Chopping R." Rude grinned.

"Do you ranch?" Cork spoke into the microphone attached to the flight helmet he wore. Rude had given flight helmets to both him and Stephen. Without them, the noise inside the cabin would have made verbal communication almost impossible.

"Yeah, but I can't make a living at it. Truth is, around here it's hard to make a decent living at much of anything, so I do just about everything. In winter, I fly skiers who like the extreme stuff up to remote slopes. In fall, I fly hunters. In summer, I do some crop dusting. Most of the rest of the time I contract out my services to BHPC."

"BHPC?"

"Big Horn Power Co-op. I fly their power lines doing inspection or giving a hand with repairs when they need me. My wife's taking classes down in Riverton to be a teacher. Soon as she's finished and gets herself a position at a school, things'll ease up a lot. I'll be able to spend more time with the ranch."

"Kids?" Cork asked.

"One. Gorgeous girl. Anna Marie. Six."

They left the valley, and the land rapidly turned harsh, almost desertlike. The grass was replaced by sand and rock and low-growing cactus and sage. The dusting of snow gave the place the alkaline look of an area where nothing could live. Wide, empty flats lay between ridges of barren stone, and as far as Cork could see in every direction there was no sign of human habitation.

"North section of the Owl Creek Reservation," Rude said. "Big place, not an acre of it worth shit. Maybe gas or oil underneath, nobody knows. We won't let anybody go looking."

"We? Are you Arapaho?"

"On my mother's side. German on my father's. Fifty-fifty."

The mountains loomed ahead, great, hoary giants whose crowns touched the sky. This close they were absolutely forbidding, and Cork felt his hopes take a bitter slide.

The chopper began to bounce and to be shoved right and left.

"Lot of downdrafts and crosscurrents as we head into the mountains," Rude said. "Can be tricky. You guys okay?"

"Yeah," Stephen said.

Over his shoulder Rude said something to Cork, but all Cork picked up on the headgear inside his flight helmet was static. He said, "I'm not reading you, Jon."

Rude made a sign for Cork to whack the side of his flight helmet. When Cork did, he could hear Rude again.

"Sorry," Rude said. "I've been meaning to get that looked at. In the meantime, if you can't hear, just give her a good smack." He pointed toward a massive formation in the distance, three peaks joined by a ridge that created a wall across the wilderness. "Up there, that's Heaven's Keep. Found a plane in that area yesterday. We thought at first maybe it was the one your wife was on. Turned out to be an old crash site."

Stephen said, "Why do they call it Heaven's Keep?"

"Know what a keep is?"

"No."

"The strongest part of a castle, the part that's hardest for an enemy to take. Looks pretty formidable, doesn't it?"

"Yeah. But what about the heaven part?"

"I always figured it's because it's so high that it feels connected to heaven. That's my explanation anyway. Now the Arapaho take a whole different approach. They call it Honoocooniinit. Basically means they consider it the devil."

Below them the land was covered with evergreens and seemed to have become a turbulent sea full of deep plunges and sudden rises that crested in knife-edged ridges of rock. They flew over meadows too small for a plane to land safely where the snow lay drifted deep enough to bury a house. They followed canyons whose rugged walls would smash a plane into small pieces. Over it all loomed Heaven's Keep, casting a long, dark shadow across the ice-white landscape.

"I'm heading toward the high plateaus just east of Heaven's Keep," Rude explained. "There are a few flat crowns up there above the tree line. It's the most likely place for a plane with engine trouble to attempt a landing. It's been gone over before, but I'm thinking that something buried in snow might be easy to miss. I'm taking my chopper in for a closer look."

"What about the black box?" Stephen said.

"The flight recorder? Small charter planes aren't required to carry them. Or a cockpit voice recorder either. And even if they had one, it wouldn't be much help in the search, Stephen. What we've been trying to get is a signal from the ELT. That's an emergency locator transmitter. In the event of a plane crash, the ELT is designed to send a signal that satellites can pick up and can be used to triangulate a position."

"Have you got a signal?" Stephen asked eagerly.

"No. And there are two main possibilities, one good, one not so good."

"Good news, bad news?" Cork said. "How about the bad news first."

"That would be that the ELT was destroyed by impact forces."

"The good news?"

"The plane landed softly enough that the ELT was never activated. That would mean there's an excellent chance of survivors. That's what we're counting on, right?" He gave Stephen a thumbs-up and got one in return.

They climbed rapidly, and Cork's stomach rolled at the chopper's pitch. Then Rude leveled out and they were flying over a treeless snowfield.

"If the pilot had any knowledge of the area, he might've tried an emergency landing here," Rude said. "It's not ideal, but it's better than most of the other options."

They flew a hundred feet above the snow, crisscrossing the field, which was several hundred yards wide and nearly a mile long. There were mounds here and there that stood out above the level of the rest of the snow.

"Boulders," Rude said. "But they're easier to avoid than a forest full of trees."

After half an hour, they'd found no sign of the plane and Rude banked north and east, heading toward the next plateau. He spoke over his shoulder again, and again Cork didn't pick up a clear transmission. He thumped the side of his helmet without effect, then took the helmet off to bang it harder. The cockpit noise was deafening. He gave the helmet another whack, put it back on, and heard Rude clearly this time.

"Ham sandwiches in the basket back there, if you're hungry," Rude said. "My wife made them. Plenty to go around. Lemonade, too."

Cork and Stephen hadn't eaten since breakfast. Cork found the basket and distributed the sandwiches. There was only the one thermos cup for the lemonade, but Rude said hell, he didn't mind drinking from the same trough.

They spent the afternoon flying over half a dozen sites, all above the tree line, all possibilities for an emergency landing though none was ideal, and all without a sign of the plane. When he realized fully the enormous difficulty of the situation, the lift of spirit Cork had felt at being involved in the search was replaced by disappointment. He saw the same dismal look gradually filling Stephen's face.

The sun was being eaten by the western Absarokas when Rude said it was time to turn back. It would be dark soon. As the chopper curled toward Hot Springs, he said, "What I don't understand is why the pilot, if he was having mechanical difficulty, didn't turn north toward Cody or south toward Riverton. Both have airfields where he could easily have landed. Why try for Casper? I mean, assuming what those snowmobilers heard was your wife's plane."

"Maybe they were wrong," Cork said. "Maybe the pilot did try for one of those airfields."

Rude shrugged. "We've gone over both those corridors. Nothing. Hell, if he'd only been able to make radio contact, at least we'd have some idea where to concentrate our search. As it is, we're kind of shotgunning it. Scattered, you know." He glanced at Stephen and added heartily, "But we're going to keep looking until we've covered every reasonable acre."

The mountains became deep blue in the twilight, and the canyons between were like dark, poisoned veins. Though the sun had dropped below the rest of the range, it hadn't yet set on Heaven's Keep, which towered above everything else. Its walls burned with the angry red of sunset, and it looked more like the gate to hell than anything to do with heaven.

As they flew back over the reservation, the land was black and empty as far as the eye could see. Rude, who seemed to read Cork's thoughts, said, "The rez covers thirty-four hundred square miles, an area the size of Rhode Island and Delaware combined. The number of people who live here could just about squeeze into a double-decker bus. It's empty, uninviting country. But to the Arapaho it's home and it's sacred."

A short while later, Rude set the chopper down on the landing strip at the Hot Springs airfield.

"You two have dinner plans?" he asked. "My wife's Italian. She makes pasta like you wouldn't believe."

"Thanks," Cork said, "but we've got to get ourselves into a hotel."

"Got one in mind?"

"Dewey Quinn recommended the hotel on the grounds of the hot springs."

"A good choice. When you're ready to eat, try the casino. Good food, good prices. Just a mile or so south on Highway 27. Can't miss it." He shoved his hands into the back pockets of his jeans and looked west, where darkness had swallowed the mountains. "Look, there's a lot of territory still to be covered. We'll give it another go tomorrow and every day after that until we find them."

"Can we go with you again?" Stephen asked. Cork was amazed at the hope still evident in his son's voice.

"Absolutely. I'll make sure Dewey knows that. Let's rendezvous here at oh-seven hundred hours."

"Seven o'clock," Stephen said.

"Right you are. I'll take a look at that helmet, Cork, but I won't promise anything."

"Thanks, Jon." Cork shook the man's hand gratefully.

Rude set about securing his chopper. Cork and Stephen got into their Wrangler and headed toward town.

ELEVEN

Day Four, Missing 82 Hours

The Excelsior Hotel was a sturdy little two-story structure of brick with a lovely courtyard whose centerpiece was a small octagonal pool fed by the hot springs. The night was turning cold, and a thin cloud of vapor that smelled faintly of sulfur drifted up from the pool, giving the courtyard a mystical appearance.

The woman at the front desk had passed along to Cork a message from Dewey Quinn, which was to call him at the sheriff's department. After they'd carried up their luggage, Cork used the room phone.

"How're you doing?" Quinn asked.

"Okay. We'd be a lot better if we'd located my wife."

"I wish I had something good to report from the other search planes." He didn't say anything for a moment. "Jon told me you're going out with him again tomorrow. You okay with that? I can ask one of the other pilots, if you'd like."

"We're fine with Jon as long as he'll have us. You work long hours," Cork said.

"I'm just about to call it, get myself something to eat."

"Dewey, thanks for everything."

"Just wish I could do more. Good night, Cork."

Next he called home and gave Rose a rundown of the first day in Wyoming. Stephen was in the room, and Cork wasn't as candid as he might otherwise have been. "There are lots of good people working hard out here to find the plane," he told Rose. "Also, there's a thing called an ELT that sends a signal if the plane has crashed. Nobody's picked up that signal. There's still plenty of reason to believe we'll find Jo."

He didn't mention that the snowdrifts were deep enough to bury a school, that the canyon walls could rip off wings and pulverize a fuselage, or that they had no idea if they were even looking in the right places.

"I'll keep praying," Rose said.

"And I'll keep you posted," Cork promised.

"Are they okay?" Stephen asked after his father put the cell phone away.

"They're fine. Worried, but fine."

"Worried?" Stephen said. "I remember when *worried* meant I was afraid you'd burn the meat loaf."

It wasn't really funny, but Stephen laughed, and Cork laughed, too, and he realized not only how taut their nerves had been drawn but how well, all things considered, Stephen was handling this. He threw his arm around his son's shoulders. "Let's go get a steak," he said. "I'm famished."

Half a mile outside of town, they passed a sign that told them they'd just entered the Owl Creek Reservation, home of the Owl Creek Band of Arapaho.

The Blue Sky Casino was, as Rude had said, on the highway, just about a mile south of Hot Springs. Compared to the Chippewa Grand Casino back in Minnesota, it was a modest-size establishment set in a kind of strip mall with an Old West façade—wooden sidewalk, wood overhang supported by wood uprights, hitching post railing. The BP gas station at the edge of the highway looked modern and jarringly anachronistic, but there was probably no way to disguise a gas pump. The Antelope Grill was attached to the casino but had its own entrance off the wooden sidewalk. The parking lot was only a quarter full.

The place smelled of meat on a grill, and the décor would have pleased Buffalo Bill. It was all about hunting, with trophy heads of deer and elk and antelope mounted above the booths, and a buffalo hide as big as the back end of a semi tacked to a wall near the entrance. The music of the casino slots funneled into the restaurant through the door that connected the two establishments. Cork and Stephen were seated near the bar and handed large menus. Cork asked if they had Leinenkugel's, and when he was told they didn't he requested a Fat Tire. Stephen asked for a Coke. They sat at the table, quiet and exhausted. Their drinks came and they ordered. Cork got the prime rib, Stephen a cheeseburger and fries.

"Feels like forever ago that we left Aurora," Stephen said.

"To me, too."

"I hope . . . ," Stephen began.

"What?"

Stephen seemed to be searching for the right words. "I hope we find Mom. I thought that once we got here it was going to be easy. But today . . ." He looked away and didn't finish.

"Still a lot of ground to cover, buddy. She's out there somewhere. We're going to keep looking till we find her."

"Promise?"

Now it was Cork's turn to look away. His eyes settled on the huge buffalo hide splayed on the wall. It seemed to him that what was left of the animal was trying to climb out of that place.

"Promise?" Stephen pressed.

Cork gazed into his son's dark, expectant eyes. "Promise," he said.

Stephen sat back, satisfied. "Look!" He pointed toward the bar, and Cork followed his gesture. "It's Deputy Quinn."

Sure enough, Dewey Quinn had just walked into the Antelope Grill. He was accompanied by a young blond woman, a real looker, dressed to kill. He'd changed into civilian clothes and was wearing creased blue jeans and a white sweater with a thick turtleneck. They walked to the bar. The woman sat on a stool, leaned toward the bartender, and said something that made him laugh. Quinn laughed, too.

"Should we ask him to eat with us?" Stephen said.

"He's got a date, Stephen."

"Please."

"I suppose it wouldn't hurt to ask. You want to deliver the invitation?"

"Sure," he said with surprising eagerness.

Cork watched his son cross the restaurant with a long, awkward gait and approach Quinn. The deputy turned to him and smiled. He introduced Stephen to the woman, who shook his hand delicately. Stephen spoke. Quinn looked toward Cork and carried on a brief discussion with the woman. She nodded, picked up the glass of white wine the bartender had given her, slid from her stool, and followed Stephen and Quinn to the table. Cork stood up.

"Stephen made us an offer we couldn't refuse," Quinn said. "Cork, this is my wife, Angie. Angie, Cork O'Connor."

She was younger than her husband. She had on a red dress that slid easily along the intriguing contours of her body. She wore gold earrings and a gold necklace. She smelled of a good, subtle perfume. Her hand, when she gave it to Cork in greeting, was soft and felt uncomfortably intimate in his.

To Cork's great surprise, his son pulled the chair out for her to sit. Like so much else about Stephen, whenever Cork saw him put into practice what had been drilled into him at home, he was still a bit amazed. Angie purred him a thank-you.

The waitress was there almost immediately. "Need a menu, Dewey?"

"We've already ordered," Cork told Quinn.

"Just give me the rib eye, rare, Estelle. And a baked potato, the works."

"Will do, honey. And you, Angie?"

"I'll have the chicken Caesar."

"And put that on our check," Cork said.

"No," Quinn objected.

"Please," Cork said. "A small way to say thank you, and, besides, I have an ulterior motive. I'm going to pump you for information."

"All right," Quinn said. "Thanks."

"It's nothing. We appreciate your kindness, right from the beginning."

"Kindness?" Quinn lifted the beer he'd brought from the bar and sipped. "You were sheriff of Tamarack County for quite a while. You dealt with your share of persons missing in those great North Woods, I'll bet."

"Sure."

"And weren't you always as considerate as you could be to the families involved? That's just being professional."

"It's different on this side of the situation, Dewey. It feels like a great kindness."

"Well, you're welcome." He lifted his bottle to Cork and Stephen in a kind of salute.

Angie drank from her wine and glanced around the place, as if restless or bored. Cork was sorry she had to be dragged down by what weighed on him and Stephen and, to a degree, her husband.

"Married long?" he asked her.

"Two years," she replied, smiling brightly. Flecks of her lipstick spotted her teeth, and Cork thought of a vampire or an animal feeding. "Dewey swept me off my feet." It sounded like a line she'd delivered often.

"We met in Kansas City, when I was there for a law enforcement conference," Quinn said. "Whirlwind romance."

"Big city," Cork said. "What do you think of Hot Springs?"

"It's a stop on the way," she said.

"Oh? To where?"

She put her hand on her husband's arm. "Dewey is a man with a future."

"FBI," Quinn said. "I'm thinking of putting in an application. I'm in charge of major crime investigations in Owl Creek County, and so I've got a lot of experience. But unless I decide to run for sheriff someday, I've pretty much hit the ceiling here."

"Lots of opportunity with the Bureau, I imagine. Good luck to you." Cork turned his beer slowly and studied the Fat Tire label. "Third day of the search. What now?"

"CAP keeps flying the grids southeast of where the plane dropped off radar. If they don't find anything, they start looking northwest, just in case the pilot decided to try to punch through the storm. Commander Nickleson believes that's a long shot. It's all air search now, but our ground S and R crews are ready to go as soon as we have an idea where to send them."

"It's . . . a big place," Cork said cautiously.

Stephen leaped in. "But we're finally able to look for Mom, and that's a really good thing."

"You bet it is," Quinn said.

Estelle brought their food and another round of drinks. As they ate, Quinn talked about Wyoming, or that part of Wyoming that lay within the far-flung boundaries of Owl Creek County. A diverse landscape, he said, with a diverse population. There were stark, beautiful badlands to the east, lovely pastoral country along the Bighorn, and a wide strip that was nearly desert that led up to the foothills of the Rockies. Finally there were the mountains themselves, all rugged wilderness.

"The Arapaho, the Crow, the Shoshone, they all fought over this area for a long time," he said, cutting into the last of his steak. "In the end, they pretty much lost everything to the white man. All that's left to the Arapaho is the Owl Creek Reservation, which is huge, but much of it not really suitable for human beings."

Cork said, "Jon Rude indicated there might be gas or oil out there."

"A lot of speculation about that, but so far the Arapaho have resisted pressure to let anyone look for it. They're afraid the land will be ruined. Hell, if you look at what's happened to a lot of the beautiful areas in this state that have mineral reserves, it's easy to see why they're concerned."

"I understand," Cork said.

"You're part Indian, right?" he asked.

"One-quarter Ojibwe."

Stephen's attention had turned from the talk at the table. "Hey, that's the woman we saw on CNN," he said, pointing toward the door that led to the casino.

Cork recognized the woman, too. The last time he'd seen her she was standing in front of the community center on the reservation, decrying the work of the Owl Creek County Sheriff's Department in the search for the missing plane.

"Ellyn Grant," Quinn said, clearly not thrilled.

"Her husband was a passenger on the plane," Cork said.

"He's the tribal chairman, and she heads up OCRE."

"Ocher? Like the color?"

"It's an acronym. Stands for Owl Creek Reservation Enterprises. The business arm of the rez. Oh crap, here she comes."

Ellyn Grant had stopped at the bar, where the bartender nodded toward Dewey Quinn. Now Grant wove her way among the tables and approached the deputy. In stature, there was nothing remarkable about her. She stood a few inches over five feet. She had dark brown hair done in a long braid, and a narrow face that didn't seem to have a lot of the physical look of an American Indian. She wore a calf-length jean skirt with a fringe, a brown leather vest over a blue cotton shirt, and elegant-looking cowboy boots. Her wrists were banded in silver set with turquoise, and large silver hoops dangled from the lobes of her ears. In person, she appeared less imposing than she had on CNN.

"Hello, Dewey," she said when she reached the table.

"Ellyn."

"I don't want to interrupt your evening, just wondering how your search is going."

"Not bad. And yours?"

"With only one plane, it's hard to cover much ground."

"If you were conducting the search in a logical area, maybe you'd have more help."

The woman eyed Cork and Stephen, but her face gave away nothing. Finally she looked at Mrs. Quinn. "Angie."

"Ellyn."

Dewey Quinn said, "This is Cork O'Connor and his son, Stephen. Cork's wife is one of the passengers on the plane with your husband."

"I'm sorry," she said to Cork, rather formally.

"Likewise."

She thought a moment. "She was the attorney, right?"

"Is the attorney," Cork said.

"Of course."

Stephen said, "We saw you on CNN the day before yesterday. You said they were searching in the wrong place for the plane."

She crossed her arms and shot the deputy a cold glance. "That's right, Stephen. I've been trying to convince Quinn and his boss to have some of the planes give us a hand looking in the right place."

"You said something about a vision," Stephen went on.

"Will Pope's vision."

Quinn broke in. "Says he saw an eagle come out of the sky and fly into an oblong box that was covered with a white blanket. One place that might fit the description is Baby's Cradle. It's a formation in the Teton Wilderness way to the southwest of where the plane dropped off radar." He raised his eyes to Grant. "Until we've exhausted the better possibilities, you're on your own out there, Ellyn."

"Better? Because some people—white people—drinking and driving their snowmobiles claim to have heard a plane?"

"It's a little more reliable lead than the vision of Will Pope."

"I had a vision," Stephen said.

Everyone looked at Stephen.

"What kind of vision?" Grant asked.

"I saw a white door in a yellow room. My mother went through the door and it closed behind her and I couldn't open it."

"Well, there you are," Grant said.

"There you are where?" Quinn said.

"Giant's Gate. The doorway to Baby's Cradle and Sleeping Baby Lake."

"Really?" Stephen appeared to have shed all his weariness, and his body fairly vibrated.

Grant turned her dark, cold eyes on Quinn. "Two visions to your what, Dewey? Blind logic? You go right ahead and do whatever you people need to do. We'll keep flying over Baby's Cradle. Nice to meet you, Stephen. Cork." She turned and walked away.

Stephen watched her go. "Could she be right?"

Cork looked to Quinn. "What do you think, Dewey?"

"Baby's Cradle isn't anywhere near any of the flight paths the plane might have followed. I suppose if there was instrument failure, Baby's Cradle might be a remote possibility. But I can't justify pulling planes off the search of the other vectors based on . . ." He paused.

"Visions," Stephen finished for him.

Quinn looked at him. "Yes."

Stephen sat back, sullen, and said nothing more.

"Stephen, Will Pope is not the most reliable man you'll ever meet. He has a fondness for alcohol."

"So? That doesn't mean he can't receive visions."

"No, but it certainly makes me cautious about what he says."

"You mean you don't believe him. Have you talked to him?"

"No."

"Well there you are."

Quinn's wife looked bored out of her mind. Cork said, "We're pretty tired. We've got another long day ahead of us tomorrow. Stephen and I are going to call it a night."

For a moment, Quinn looked as if he was about to say something more to Stephen, but he didn't. His wife looked as if she'd just been released from prison. She quickly folded her napkin, slid her chair back, and stood up. "Well, thanks for dinner. Dewey, it's still early. Let's gamble a little."

Quinn joined her, and she took his arm. "Cork, you're heading out with Rude again tomorrow, so I'll be in touch." He shook Cork's hand. "Good night, Stephen."

Stephen stared at his empty plate. "Yeah, 'night."

The couple walked away. As they headed toward the casino, Quinn slipped his arm around his wife's inviting waist.

After they were gone, Cork said, "If I were Dewey, I'd be making the same call, Stephen."

"You didn't see what I saw."

"No. But what you saw is open to interpretation, and how can you be sure this Giant's Gate is it?"

"Because from what Ms. Grant said it matches my vision."

"Stephen, there are probably lots of scenarios that would match your vision."

"Yeah? What about this Will Pope guy? What about his vision?"

"I don't know him so I can't answer that."

"Maybe we ought to get to know him. Maybe he's like Henry Meloux."

They talked more as they drove back to the hotel. Stephen was absolutely convinced now that looking east of the mountains was wrong. At the hotel, they carefully studied the map they'd bought at the airport in Cody, and Cork pointed out how far away from any reasonable flight pattern the lake lay. But the more they discussed the issue, the more adamant Stephen became.

"There's a door somewhere," Stephen said, "and Mom's behind it. All we have to do is find the door."

Finally Cork suggested a compromise. They would fly with Rude the next day and get his take on Baby's Cradle. Because he was part Arapaho, he might also have a reliable opinion about Will Pope. After they returned, they would find Pope for themselves and see what he had to say.

They got ready for bed and watched a little television, and in no time at all Stephen was sleeping. Cork lay staring at the ceiling. His mind was too crowded. He finally got up, put on his robe and slippers, dropped the room key card into his pocket, and went outside. He walked down the stairs to the courtyard, which was misty from the vapors of the pool. The night was cold and he knew he couldn't stay out long, but the air felt refreshing and what he could see of the sky was full of stars. He thought about Jo somewhere, staring up at that same sky—cold, lost, scared, maybe injured. He tried to shake off that image.

Against the black of the sky rose the nearer black of the Owl Creek Mountains. Beyond them, beyond the wide, desolate stretch of the reservation, lay more mountains, higher mountains. This was different country from home. This was a harsh, difficult place, and he hated it. Hated the way all the land rose up like walls. Hated how all that emptiness could so easily swallow a plane and its passengers. Hated that it seemed to be a land with no heart.

Henry Meloux would argue with him, he knew. Meloux would say that there was no part of Grandmother Earth that was without heart, without spirit. The fault lay not with the land but with Cork's expectations, with his own wounded spirit. Listen to the land, Meloux would probably advise. The land will reveal its heart. The land will tell you its truth.

But not that night. That night Cork heard only the chill wind that came off the high country in a long, empty sigh.

TWELVE
Day Five, Missing 94 Hours

Today we fly to Casper," Jon Rude said as they climbed into the chopper. "A couple hundred feet above ground the whole way. Bird's-eye view of every gulch and draw and butte from Meeteetse to the North Platte. How does that sound?" He winked at Stephen.

Stephen said, "Could we fly over Baby's Cradle?"

"Baby's Cradle?" Rude slipped his flight helmet on and began flipping switches. "You've been listening to Will Pope."

"Ellyn Grant," Cork said. "We ran into her at the Antelope Grill last night."

"Ellyn." Rude nodded. "Piece of work there." The rotors began their sweep. "Buckle in, gentlemen."

"What about Baby's Cradle?" Stephen said.

Rude scanned the area around the chopper, then glanced at Stephen. "See, the thing about old Will Pope's visions is that sometimes they're less the result of some spiritual visitation than they are of alcohol."

"Ms. Grant seems to think this one is real."

"Hell, maybe it is," Rude allowed.

"So what about Baby's Cradle?"

"You want my advice?"

"Yes," Stephen said.

"I think we ought to stick with the flight plan for today. I want to fly low and slow. If there's anything sticking out of some snowdrift on those high plains, I want to find it."

"What about the search of the mountains?" Cork asked.

"There are ten aircraft working the mountains. I talked with Dewey Quinn this morning, and he spoke with Commander Nickleson in Cody. We agreed that a low-level flight over the area between the Absarokas and Casper is worth a shot. If that plane tried to limp back to the airport and had to come down, it could be lying in a deep wash somewhere, buried in snow. That's what we call the Red Wall country. It's rough and it's empty. I'd rest easier knowing we took a good look at it. Wouldn't you, Stephen?"

"Yeah, I guess."

"And if we come up empty-handed, I'll take you to Will Pope myself and make the introductions."

"You know him?"

"I'm part Arapaho. I know everyone on the rez."

"All right."

"Okay, buckos. As Superman used to say, 'Up, up, and away.' "

They flew toward Meeteetse, a tiny western town where, Rude told them, Butch Cassidy had once resided. From there they turned southeast along the corridor that the plane, if it had indeed flown over the snowmobilers, would have followed back to Casper. They spoke little, and their eyes were glued to the ground below. Once they'd flown beyond the relatively gentle basin of the Bighorn, the land took on the feel of Armageddon, of upheaval and warring elements, a place where gods had battled and it was the earth that had suffered most. Long ridges had been chopped in half, leaving ragged cliffs the color of blood. In other places, the earth had been cut into deep arroyos or scraped to clean, hard flats. It appeared to be an area where nothing, human or otherwise, could possibly survive.

"Hole-in-the-wall country," Rude said. "This whole stretch is part of what used to be called the Outlaw Trail. Butch Cassidy and the Sundance Kid, Jesse James, just about every other desperado of that period was reputed to have hid out here at one time or another."

They reached the outskirts of Casper without spotting anything hopeful, and Rude turned back. He altered course so that on the return trip they'd fly over different country. The land below them was the same, however, just as empty of hope.

"Got stuck out here in a blizzard once," Rude said. "Not much more than a kid then. Tried to race a storm to Casper. Thought I was immortal. Wind came up, snow began blowing like a son of a bitch, next thing I know I'm way off the road, up to my windshield in a big drift. Got out to check the situation and suddenly I'm in a whiteout. Up, down, left, right, didn't mean anything. Confused as hell. Finally stumbled against my car and crawled inside to wait it out. Took a day and a half for the whole thing to blow over. By then, the snow was so deep, it completely covered my old Crown Victoria. Had me a couple of Snickers bars that I nibbled on and about a gallon of Mountain Dew. When the sun came back, I dug my way out, and a few hours later a plow came along. Was pretty hairy there for a while."

"Why'd you do it?" Stephen asked. He never stopped scouring the landscape below them, even when he was part of the conversation.

"Best reason in the world for a man to do stupid things, Stephen. A girl. She lived in Casper and I was desperately in love with her. Still am, for that matter. She's my wife."

They reached the airstrip at Hot Springs a little after 3:00 P.M. Rude radioed in and checked the status of the rest of the search effort. Through their own headphones, Cork and Stephen heard the reply: No one had spotted anything.

"You want, we can go back up and fly a grid. Or we can go talk to Will Pope. Your call."

"Will Pope," Stephen leaped in.

Rude looked at Cork.

"Pope," Cork agreed.

Rude radioed Dewey Quinn and explained what the plan was. Cork and Stephen had removed their flight helmets, so they couldn't hear the deputy's response. But Rude laughed and said into his mic, "Give 'em a break, Dewey. When they meet Will, they'll understand."

Rude shut down the chopper and explained that because it would be best to keep their visit to the reservation low profile, it would be more prudent to drive. They squeezed into his pickup and headed west.

* * *

Red Hawk lay beyond the Owl Creek Mountains, fifty miles from Hot Springs, at the convergence of two narrow streams. It was a small town in the middle of nowhere on a back highway that would be used only if you wanted to go to Red Hawk, which, from the poor condition of the road, Cork suspected not many people did. The village was a scattering of run-down BIA-constructed housing. At its heart was a school, a nursing home, a two-pump Chevron gas station with a mini-mart, a tiny stucco church named St. Alban, and the Reservation Business Center, which held the tribal offices. The business center looked new. Everything else looked as if it hadn't been worked on since the Korean War. Rude drove in from the alkali flats to the east. The day had been sunny and the temperature almost balmy. The snow was melting, and the grid of streets—half a dozen running north-south and again as many running east-west, most unpaved— had turned to mud. Will Pope lived at the end of a street that ran past the little church and was called St. Alban Lane. His trailer sat on cinder blocks. A gray station wagon, rust-eaten and mud-spattered, stood parked next to a big propane tank. Behind the trailer, a satellite dish was positioned to catch a signal from the east, and beyond the dish lay a hundred yards of snow-laden sagebrush that ended in a line of cottonwoods growing along a stream bank. There was nothing beyond the cottonwoods except the distant, inevitable collision of white earth and blue sky.

Rude parked beside the station wagon, and they all got out and walked to the trailer. Rude mounted the three steps to the door. As he lifted his hand to knock, a furious barking began inside and an old voice called out, "Who's there?"

"It's Jon Rude, Will. I'd like to talk to you. I brought some visitors. And I brought some beer."

The door opened just wide enough to reveal an old man wearing a ratty blue hooded sweatshirt, jeans faded nearly white, and a pair of thick black socks on his feet. Beside him stood a young German shepherd with its tongue lolling out.

"Beer?" the old man said. He gazed at them with an unspecific focus, and Cork quickly understood that the old man was blind or nearly so.

"Coors, Will. Know how you like it."

"You got someone with you?"

"Friends. Been showing them the country from my chopper. Mind if we come in?" He reached out and took the old man's hand and guided it to the six-pack he held.

The old man grasped the beer, turned around, and indicated his visitors should follow.

Compared with the glare off the snow outside, the trailer seemed especially dark. The curtains over the windows were drawn closed and there were no lights on. It took a moment for Cork's eyes to adjust. What he saw then was a place sparely furnished. A short couch, a stuffed easy chair, a standing lamp, a coffee table. In the kitchen area, there was a dinette with a Formica top and two metal chairs. On a stand in one corner of the room sat a big, new television. The television was on, tuned to a football game. The trailer smelled musty, as if long in need of a good cleaning.

"Listenin' to the Broncos beat the crap outta Oakland," the old man said, settling into the stuffed chair. He put the six-pack on the floor, where he could reach it easily with his right hand. Cork and Stephen sat on the couch. Rude stood near the old man. Will Pope held out a bottle of beer, waiting for it to be taken. Rude eased it from his grip and handed it to Cork. The old man offered a second, which Rude kept, and then he offered a third.

"You got us covered, Will," Rude said. "One of us is too young to drink."

"Yeah?" The old man twisted the top off his beer and took a long draw. "Which one?"

"Me," Stephen said.

The old man turned his head in Stephen's direction. "How old, boy?"

"Thirteen," Stephen said.

"Hell, I was drinkin' when I was thirteen."

"He might be, too, if I let him, grandfather," Cork said. "My name's Cork O'Connor. This is my son, Stephen."

The old man picked up the remote from the arm of his chair and turned the television off. He drank some more of his beer. The dog, who'd been sitting on his haunches next to Pope's chair, eased himself down and laid his head on his paws.

Rude said, "We wanted to talk to you about that vision of yours, Will. Baby's Cradle."

"Never said it was Baby's Cradle."

"From the description you gave, it seems pretty clear."

"In a vision, nuthin' is necessarily what it seems. What's your interest?"

"Cork's wife was on the plane that's missing."

"Ah." The old man nodded.

"When did you have the vision?" Cork asked.

"Come to me the night the plane went missin'."

"How'd it come to you, grandfather?" Stephen asked.

"Same as always. In a dream."

"You've had visions before?" Cork asked.

The old man looked peeved. "I'm a spirit walker."

"I had a vision, too," Stephen said.

The old man's eyebrows lifted. "That so?"

"I saw my mother disappear behind a door in a wall, grandfather."

"You sound like a *nahita* but you speak with respect."

"*Nahita?*"

"A white," Rude said.

"I'm white and I'm Anishinaabe, grandfather."

"Anishinaabe?"

"Ojibwe, grandfather."

"Mixed blood." The old man shrugged as if it wasn't important. He finished his beer and reached for a second. "Ojibwe. That what the whites call you?"

"Or Chippewa," Stephen said.

"They call us Arapaho. Hell, that's the name the Crow give us. We are Inunaina. Means 'Our People.' "

"Inunaina." Stephen tried the word.

"That's good, boy. What did you say your name was?"

"Stephen O'Connor."

"O'Connor. My great-grandfather was Cracks the Sky. The first agent this reservation had couldn't pronounce our Arapaho names so he give us names he could. Changed my grandfather's name to Pope. Not like the one in Italy. Some damned poet. Some folks got luckier. Ellyn Grant's people got named after a president."

"Would you tell us your vision, grandfather?" Cork said.

The old man took a long draw on his beer. "I seen an eagle come out of a cloud. Not like any eagle I ever seen before. Wings spread, all stiff, like it was frozen. It circled and glided into something looked like a bed only with sides to it."

"Like a cradle?" Rude said.

"Don't put words in my mouth, boy."

"I'm sorry, Will," Rude said.

"Go on, grandfather," Cork said.

"It landed and a white blanket floated down and covered it. That's pretty much it. Except that as it faded away, I heard a scream."

"From the eagle?" Stephen asked.

"No." He turned his face in the direction from which Stephen's voice had come. "Truth is, Stephen, it sounded to me like a woman."

"Grandfather," Stephen said cautiously, "do you have a feeling about my mother?"

The old man looked toward him with those eyes that no longer saw the light. He was quiet a long time. "Some people think of death like a hungry wolf, Stephen, and they're afraid of it. Me, I think death is just walkin' through a door and we go on livin' on the other side, livin' better, livin' in the true way, just waitin' for those we love to join us there. I got no feelin' about your mother, but I think you shouldn't be afraid. We all walk through that door someday. You understand what I'm sayin'?"

Stephen looked disappointed, but he said, "Yes."

The old man drank his beer and stared ahead at nothing.

"Anything else?" Rude said to Cork.

"No. That does it, I think. Thank you for your time, grandfather. *Migwech.*"

"*Migwech?*"

"In the language of the Anishinaabe people, it means 'thank you.' "

The old man held up his beer. "*Hohou.* Same thing in Arapaho."

THIRTEEN
Day Five, Missing 103 Hours

Outside Will Pope's trailer, Cork paused and looked around. There was no sign of life in Red Hawk. He could hear a distant motor that might have been a generator of some kind, but the streets were deserted. Late Sunday afternoon. Maybe everyone was watching the Broncos beat the crap out of Oakland.

"I'm not sure what that accomplished," he said.

"He's not like Henry Meloux," Stephen said, "but I like him."

Rude pulled his gloves on. "He was sober. That's real unusual for Will. Folks here on the rez treat him with respect because he's an elder, but most don't give any weight to his visions. I thought maybe if you saw him in his usual state you might understand why Dewey Quinn is skeptical."

"I still want to fly over Baby's Cradle," Stephen said.

Rude shrugged. "Okay by me. Cork?"

"Why not?"

"All right then. I'll get it cleared with Dewey for tomorrow." A tan Blazer passed the church, turned onto St. Alban Lane, and came toward them. There were emergency lights across the top, and the lettering on the door indicated that it belonged to the Bureau of Indian Affairs police. The Blazer parked in front of Pope's place, and an officer got out. He wore a leather jacket over his blue uniform. He was a stocky man with a broad face, dark eyes, close-cropped black hair, and teeth white as baking soda. He squinted in the sunlight, eyeing Rude, then Cork, then Stephen.

"Jon," he said, "you haven't been bothering my uncle, have you?"

"We just wanted to talk to him about that vision of his, Andy."

"Too many people been bothering him about that vision. Wearin' him out." He leveled his dark-eyed gaze on Cork. "Your name O'Connor?"

"Yes."

"I'm Andrew No Voice, chief of the Owl Creek Reservation police. I've been asked to escort you to the tribal offices."

"Who asked?"

"Ellyn Grant. You driving 'em, Jon?"

"Yep."

"Then come along."

No Voice returned to his vehicle and waited while Cork and the others got into Rude's pickup. As soon as Rude kicked the engine over, No Voice headed off and Rude followed.

"Ellyn Grant," Rude said. "Her eyes and ears are everywhere on the rez."

"She's got clout?"

"Big mojo. Smart woman, ambitious, educated, probably knows more about the Northern Arapaho and their history than anybody alive. Went to Stanford on a full scholarship, graduated magna cum laude. Any idea what an achievement that is for an Arapaho? Hell, she could've done just about anything she wanted, gone anywhere. What did she do? Returned home, married Edgar Little Bear, and launched herself on a one-woman crusade to get this reservation into the twenty-first century."

Cork eyed the sad-looking town around him. "Slow going," he noted.

"Things haven't gone as well for the Blue Sky Casino as everyone hoped. Hot Springs is too far off the beaten path. Still, the rez has a new business center. That road we came in on is slated to be completely redone this spring. Every enrolled member of the Owl Creek Arapaho gets a regular allotment check from the casino profits. It's not much at this point, but it's something. And, believe me, everybody here can always use a little something."

"And the Blue Sky Casino was Ellyn Grant's doing?" Cork asked.

Rude nodded. "Her idea beginning to end."

They parked in the lot of the Reservation Business Center, next to No Voice's Blazer, and followed him inside. Artwork filled the center's lobby: oils and watercolors, wood carvings, moccasins and purses and bags with beautiful and intricate beadwork, hand drums, and pottery. On a tripod sat a large sign that read "Absaroka Gallery. Fine Work by Arapaho Artists. One mile east on Highway 57."

"Nice work," Cork said.

"Lots of talent on the rez," No Voice replied with pride.

They passed a bulletin board crowded with notices and flyers: an announcement for a banquet to honor the high school football team, the Eagles; a lot of want ads; a big poster giving the warning signs for a meth lab. They approached a door with a small white plaque mounted on the wall beside it, identifying the office of Owl Creek Reservation Enterprises. No Voice swung the door open and stood aside for the others to enter.

"Here they are, Ellyn."

It was a large room with filing cabinets, a computer workstation, and a long table with half a dozen empty chairs around it. Grant sat at a desk of polished wood that was positioned in front of a window with a view of the empty powwow grounds not far away. Open before her lay a folder of documents with pages full of numbers. She was wearing glasses and held a yellow pencil. She smiled and said, "Thank you, Andy."

No Voice pulled the door shut and remained outside. Grant closed the folder, put the pencil down, stood up, and went to the long table. "Please," she said, "have a seat."

Occupying the center of the table was an architect's model, a miniature construct of a complex of connected buildings surrounded by miniature mountains with ski runs. The model was labeled: "The Gateway Grand Casino, a joint project of the Owl Creek Arapaho and Realm-McCrae Development."

"We didn't really have a chance to talk last night," she said. "And the Antelope Grill isn't the kind of place to have the kind of discussion I'd like to have."

"And what kind of discussion is that?" Cork said.

"People we love are missing. My husband. Your wife." She offered Stephen a look of deep sympathy. "Your mother. I've barely slept since I got word. And I've been all over Dewey Quinn trying to get him to expand the area of the search they're making."

"To include Baby's Cradle?" Cork asked.

"Exactly. With all due respect to Sheriff Kosmo, he's a nice guy but he'd need help finding his way out of a closet."

"It's my understanding that Commander Nickleson in Cody is in charge of the search."

"Dewey Quinn has lots of influence with Nickleson, and Quinn takes his orders from Jim Kosmo. If Kosmo says forget about Baby's Cradle, Quinn won't push it." She sat back, and for a moment her eyes drifted out the window toward the winter landscape of Red Hawk. When she looked at Cork again, she appeared deeply troubled. "You talked with Will Pope. What do you think?"

"I don't know Will Pope."

"I liked him," Stephen jumped in.

"I'm glad," Grant said. "I like old Will, too. A lot of people are eager to write him off because of his drinking, but this vision of his, well, it seems to me to have a lot of merit."

"Put yourself in the place of Sheriff Kosmo or Dewey Quinn," Cork said. "They're working with limited resources and in a desperate time frame. They're having to make decisions that seem to them the most judicious at the moment."

"Spoken like a member of the cop fraternity," Grant said. "But I understand you're part Ojibwe. Listen to that part of yourself."

"Wouldn't matter. I'm not in charge of the search and rescue operation."

"If Kosmo gets enough pressure from those of us with a sincere stake in the outcome, maybe he'll swing some of the search planes our way."

"Our way?"

"I need your help. Have you seen the most recent weather forecast?"

"No."

"Another storm system is heading this way. In a couple of days, it'll hit the Rockies and we'll get more snow in the high country. Anything not buried now will most surely be buried then."

All along, Cork had known they were working against impossibilities—the cold, the harsh terrain, the size of the search area, its emptiness. Yet he'd struggled to hold to a hope, however remote, that Jo and the others had survived the fall from the sky and that it was only a matter of finding them. Now even this fragile hope was about to be shattered. He tried not to show his devastation, tried not to let Stephen see.

"We have two days, Cork," Grant said.

"We're going to Baby's Cradle tomorrow," Stephen said. He still sounded buoyed by hope.

"That's good," Grant said. "But wouldn't it be better if other planes joined you? A few eyes are fine, but many eyes are best."

"Dad, we could talk to Deputy Quinn?"

"Talk to Kosmo," Grant said.

"All right," Cork agreed.

"And, Jon, why don't you give Lame Nightwind a call. He's been flying the Baby's Cradle area. He can tell you what he has and hasn't covered. Maybe you two can coordinate." She stood up, and the others did, too.

"What is this?" Cork asked, nodding toward the architect's model on the table.

"Our next venture," Grant said. "The Gateway Grand Casino. We're building it near the entrance to Yellowstone. When it's completed, it will be the largest casino complex between Atlantic City and Las Vegas."

"Looks like it'll offer a lot more than just gambling."

"World-class ski slopes, hundreds of miles of snowmobile and hiking trails, and everything else the Rockies and Yellowstone have to offer."

"The Blue Sky Casino must be doing better than it appears."

"It's doing well enough," she said and headed for the door. No Voice was still waiting in the hall. "We're finished here, Andy. Thanks for the help." She shook Cork's hand and then turned to his son. "It was a pleasure talking with you, Stephen."

"I didn't say much."

"We Arapaho have a saying: When there is true hospitality, not many words are needed."

He smiled. "Thanks."

Outside the sun was dropping behind the mountains. The light was fading fast. The dark blue shadow of the Absarokas had already swallowed the foothills, and Red Hawk was next. No Voice got into his Blazer and drove away. The town felt more deserted than ever. Stephen and Rude headed directly to the truck, but Cork hesitated for a minute in the parking lot.

The light of the setting sun fell against the little church of St. Alban on the opposite side of the street. The brass cross mounted above the entrance blazed for a minute as if on fire. As Cork stood watching, a small figure stepped from the shadow of the recessed doorway and looked in his direction. Cork saw clearly that it was a kid, probably no older than Stephen. He was Indian, Arapaho no doubt. He wore a jean jacket with some kind of insignia patch sewn on the shoulder. The kid stared, as if trying to burrow into Cork. Then he stepped back into the shadow of the doorway. It was only a few seconds, but there was something about the solitary figure under the blazing cross that struck Cork in a profound and unnerving way.

"Dad!" Stephen called. "Come on!"

Cork walked to Rude's pickup, performing without thought a procedure he'd trained himself to follow during his years as a cop: In his brain, he filed away the physical details of the kid where they would remain until he needed to retrieve them. If he ever did.

FOURTEEN

Day Five, Missing 105 Hours

It was hard dark when they reached the airstrip outside Hot Springs.

Rude said, "Why don't you come home with me and have a home-cooked meal? Diane makes a mean lasagna. And she loves company. You can meet my little girl, Anna. Apple of my eye."

"Thanks," Cork said. "But I want to track down Jim Kosmo."

"That won't be hard. He's fond of blackjack."

"So we'll find him at the casino?"

"Most likely."

"Thanks, Jon."

"I'll see you guys here tomorrow morning. Let's say seven."

"It's a deal."

They shook hands. Cork and Stephen climbed into their rented Wrangler and headed toward town. They went directly to the Blue Sky Casino, and, just as Rude had predicted, they found Sheriff Kosmo at a twenty-dollar-limit blackjack table with three small stacks of chips in front of him and no other players besides himself and the dealer. Kosmo was intent on his cards. He signaled for a hit, received the seven of hearts, and stood. The dealer showed a seven of clubs. He flipped his hole card, an eight of diamonds, and dealt himself a four. The six and five that the sheriff had in the hole gave him only eighteen. The dealer swept up the two blue chips Kosmo had placed as a bet.

"Sheriff," Cork said before the next hand was dealt.

Kosmo looked at him. "It's O'Connor, right?"

"That's right. I'd like to talk to you."

"Now?"

"Now."

Kosmo said to the dealer, "Roy, hold my place. I'll be right back."

"Sure thing, Jim."

They stepped away from the table and stood at the end of a line of slots. The casino wasn't busy, but you couldn't tell that from the noise the machines kept up.

"Okay, you've got me," Kosmo said. "Talk."

"Baby's Cradle," Cork said.

Kosmo's face was a broad stretch of flesh as unwelcoming as the Wyoming desert. "Dewey told me you were heading out to see Will Pope."

"Is there any way you can divert some of the search effort to that area?"

"Dewey's in charge of the operation. He makes the decisions."

"You're the sheriff."

"You were a county sheriff back in Minnesota, right? You know how it works. You put your best person in charge and then you stay out of their way. Have you talked to Dewey?"

"Not yet."

"He's working with the FAA, CAP, and our own S and R. He knows better than anyone what's reasonable. Talk to him. He says it's okay, it'll happen. Is that all?" He eyed the blackjack table, where the dealer stood looking bored.

"Any idea where I can find Dewey this time of night?"

"Last I spoke with him, he was still at the department."

"Come on, Stephen. The sheriff has more important things to do." Cork put his arm around his son, and they turned to leave.

"Look, O'Connor, if there's something you think we're not doing, I'd sure as hell like to know what that is."

"Forget it." Cork kept walking.

In the Wrangler on the way back to town, Stephen said, "Ms. Grant told us he was in charge. He says it's Deputy Quinn. What's going on, Dad?"

"I don't know, Stephen. Let's find Dewey and ask him. You hungry?"

"Yeah."

"After we talk to Dewey, we'll grab a burger somewhere, okay?"

Quinn was no longer at the sheriff's department. The deputy on the contact desk told them he'd left half an hour earlier. He didn't know where he'd gone. And no, he couldn't give them his phone number.

They grabbed cheeseburgers and shakes at a place called the Dairy Barn, then drove back to their hotel to eat. As they passed through the lobby, the woman at the front desk smiled at them, wished them a good evening, and picked up the phone. Two minutes after they'd stepped into their room, someone knocked at their door. Cork opened up to find the television reporter they'd seen the day before outside the sheriff's office.

"Mr. O'Connor, my name is Felicia Gray. I'm a reporter from Casper. Could I talk to you for a moment?"

"It's been a long day, Ms. Gray. We're tired and we're just about to eat."

"I understand you spoke with Will Pope today. What do you think?"

"I think the sheriff's people are doing everything they can to find that missing plane."

"Do you think there's anything to Mr. Pope's vision, or to Ellyn Grant's assertion that the vision indicates the plane went down in the Baby's Cradle area?"

"Pope didn't say that he thought his vision necessarily meant Baby's Cradle."

"If not Baby's Cradle, then where?"

"I don't know."

"Look, I talked with Will Pope myself. I was the one who broke the story. And I've got to tell you, it seems pretty clear to me that he's talking about Baby's Cradle. And that blanket over the eagle? That's got to be a blanket of snow, don't you think?"

"Even credible visions shouldn't be taken at face value, Ms. Gray."

"Meaning what?"

"They often require interpretation. Or that's my understanding."

"You're Native American, is that correct?"

"I have some Ojibwe blood in me."

"Then you'd know about visions and their interpretation."

"You want an interpretation, talk to Will Pope. Good night." He started to close the door, but she put out a hand to hold it open.

"Mr. O'Connor, I'm truly sorry for your situation. And I'm sorry if I seem aggressive. I'm just trying to put the story together. If you'd like to talk to me, I'm staying here. Room 217. I'm available anytime. Call my room or call me on my cell."

She handed him her business card, and after she'd stepped back, he closed the door.

While they ate, they watched television, CNN's continuing coverage of what had become known as the Hargrove standoff. The compound was surrounded, and Hargrove was threatening to blow everything sky-high if anyone tried to rush the place. The authorities weren't certain how many people were inside, but they did know a significant number of them were children. They were attempting to negotiate.

Halfway through their meal, another knock disturbed them.

"Damn it," Cork said and stomped to the door. "What?" he snapped as he opened up. Dewey Quinn stood there, looking startled. "Sorry," Cork said. "I thought you were that reporter."

"Felicia Gray? She was here?"

"Just a few minutes ago."

"What did she want?" He waved it off. "Doesn't matter. I got a call from the office. You dropped by looking for me?"

"Yeah. Come on in. Gray might still be out there."

When Dewey was inside, Stephen said, "Hello, Deputy Quinn."

"It's okay if you call me Dewey, Stephen. I understand you've been looking for me, Cork. Sorry to make this short, but my wife's waiting in the car."

"We talked to Will Pope this afternoon," Cork told him.

"And he has you believing in Baby's Cradle?"

"I think it's worth sending some search planes that way."

"Cork, when the question of Baby's Cradle first came up, I talked to Commander Nickleson. She was absolutely convinced that there was no merit in searching that area. Apparently it's a tough airspace to fly, and none of her pilots were particularly eager to try. Honestly, I agree with her assessment. There's no value in diverting planes to Baby's Cradle. But I'll tell you what. If Jon Rude is willing, I'll give him my blessing to join Nightwind."

"There's a new weather forecast, Dewey. Have you heard?"

He nodded. "Snow in a couple of days. Cork, we don't have any real idea where to look. I understand that if you don't check out this lead, you'll be left wondering. I don't want that. Go with Rude tomorrow and the next, if need be. In the meantime, we'll try to cover everything else."

Cork noticed for the first time that Quinn was wearing a sport coat and tie. "Going out?"

"My wife likes to dance. There's a place in Riverton." Quinn looked uncomfortable. "I have a life beyond the office."

"I know, Dewey. Have a good time."

"You guys get some sleep, okay?" He smiled wearily at them both and left.

Although it was late, Cork called his family in Aurora and filled them in. He tried to sound hopeful about Baby's Cradle. By the time he'd finished, Stephen had nodded off with his clothes on. Cork looked at his son, who was really not much more than a boy. This was hard business, something no boy should have to endure, yet Stephen continued to be strong and Cork was proud of him.

He put the room key card in his pocket and slipped outside. He went down to the courtyard, as he had the night before, and stood amid the vapors rising from the hot spring water that filled the small pool. He eyed the black sky and the stars and thought about the mountains to the west, which had begun to seem to him like malevolent, living things, angry giants against whom he felt puny and weak. And beyond those mountains was something worse. The fury of another storm. It seemed that all the great forces of the earth were mounted against him. And against Jo.

He closed his eyes and began to pray, but in the middle of the prayer, his mind took an odd turn. He saw, unexpected and startlingly vivid, the image of the blazing cross above the small church in Red Hawk and the boy who'd stood under it. He had an over-whelming sense that if he opened his eyes he'd find the boy before him now.

But when he looked, there was only the darkness of the night, the ghosts of the vapors, and the lost words of his prayer that had been cut short.

FIFTEEN

Day Six, Missing 118 Hours

When Cork and Stephen arrived at the airfield the next morning, Rude was already there with another man, bent over a map spread on the hood of Rude's pickup.

"Morning, guys," Rude said. "This is Lame Deer Nightwind."

Nightwind looked up from the map. "*Boozhoo*," he said. In response to the surprise on Cork's face, he brought out a relaxed smile. "I go to a lot of powwows. I can say hello in a dozen indigenous languages. That and 'I'll have a beer.'" He was no taller than Cork, a decade younger, lean and hard as rebar. He had eyes like shiny beetle shells, high, proud cheekbones, and that easy smile.

The sky was clear, the morning cold, the air dry. The southern Absarokas on the horizon were like a big wave rolling out of a calm sea. The men and Stephen stood around the hood of Rude's pickup, peering at the topographic map.

Nightwind drew a circle with his index finger. "This is where we're headed. You can see from the contours why it's called Baby's Cradle. These ridges form a box roughly ten miles long and five miles wide. At the bottom is Sleeping Baby Lake. It's a good-size glacial lake. It drains through a break in the ridge to the north—here." He nailed the spot with the tip of his finger. "The break's called Giant's Gate. That's where we fly in, and that's where things can get tricky. I've been telling Jon that when the wind comes out of the north, it funnels through Giant's Gate and whirls around inside Baby's Cradle like a hurricane. Kicks up snow so bad it's a blizzard in there. Can be plenty rough. Either of you prone to airsickness?"

"No," Stephen said without hesitation.

Cork said, "Don't think so, but it might depend on how bad it turns out to be."

"Wind's out of the west today, so not so bad," Nightwind said. "Jon's willing to give it a try."

Cork studied the map. "If Baby's Cradle is so difficult to get into, why would the pilot have flown in there?"

"Mostly it would have been by accident," Nightwind replied. "The ridge to the north is the lowest side of Baby's Cradle. Up here is where the last radio transmission from the pilot was made"—Nightwind tapped the spot on the map—"indicating he was descending from eighteen thousand feet. If he turned back and then decided he couldn't make it to Casper and headed instead for the Riverton airport"—he traced the line with his finger—"depending on the altitude he was able to maintain and the radius of his turn, he could have flown straight into Baby's Cradle."

"How about flying out of Baby's Cradle?" Cork said.

"Depends on the conditions, visibility, the trouble the pilot was experiencing with his plane. If he got in there and didn't begin a climb pretty quick, the ridge at the south end would've been hard to clear."

"Still game?" Rude said.

Cork nodded. "Let's do it."

Rude lifted off first and headed northwest. After Nightwind became airborne, he took the lead and Rude followed. They flew over the little valley where Rude had his spread, and then across the desolate landscape of the northern Owl Creek Reservation. Where the sun had heated the outcroppings, the snow had melted completely, leaving a patchwork of yellow or red rock surrounded by white earth in a way that reminded Cork of the mottled hide of a mangy dog.

After twenty minutes, Nightwind climbed steeply and banked to the north. Rude followed. Below them, the peaks of the southern Absarokas seemed to reach toward the belly of Rude's chopper as if to snatch it from the sky. In the distance, Cork recognized the immense, icy wall of Heaven's Keep, more imposing than anything else in that part of the range. The air currents grew powerful, knocking the helicopter around like a cat with a ball of yarn. Nightwind curled sharply to the west, and Rude stayed on his tail. Cork felt his stomach object to the maneuver, and he glanced at Stephen, who seemed not bothered in the least.

"We're lucky," Rude said. "Lame knows these mountains better than anyone I can think of. Hell, he's a better pilot than anyone I can think of."

"What's his story?" Cork asked.

"Don't know it all. Born on the rez, but no father ever came forward. His mother was caught up in booze and drugs. They found her dead in her trailer when Lame was just a kid. Story is he was sitting beside her like he was waiting for her to wake up. She'd been dead awhile, I guess. When they tried to remove her body, Lame went berserk, stabbed one of the guys with a knife. Andy No Voice swears it's true. Fierce little five-year-old protecting his dead mother." He shook his head, and Cork couldn't tell if it was out of admiration or bemusement. "An old uncle took him in. Kept to himself in a place he'd built way out to hell and gone in the foothills. Raised Lame like a little mountain man, hunting, fishing, trapping in the Absarokas. Somewhere along the way, his uncle died, don't know how. Lame got sent to live with his mother's cousin, woman who'd married a guy in Lander. That was Ellyn Grant's family. Gave them trouble, I guess. At seventeen, he took off to God knows where. Gone for a lot of years. Nobody heard boo from him. Then he shows up on the rez maybe half a dozen years ago. He's got himself a nice plane, some capital. Builds a place on the land where he'd lived with his uncle, snug up against the Absarokas. He still flies out periodically, gone for a few days or weeks. Nobody knows where, but everybody's got a speculation."

"Like what?" Stephen asked.

Rude shrugged. "He flies a Piper Super Cub, kind of classic among bush pilots. So could be he runs drugs or guns or smuggles anything from cigarettes to human cargo. He's kind of a swashbuckling figure around here."

Rude broke off suddenly and held up his hand to silence the talk

in the cockpit, and he resettled the radio headphones so that they covered his ears.

"We read you, Lame," he replied into his mic.

"There it is," came Nightwind's voice over the headset in Cork's
flight helmet. "Giant's Gate."

Rude pointed through the chopper's windshield. "Dead ahead," he
said.

Stephen leaned forward. Cork saw it, too, a high, rugged ridge
with a mile-wide break in the middle where a thread of white water
coursed through. Timber covered three-quarters of the ridge; above
that was bare rock buried deep in snow.

Static in Cork's headphones broke up the next transmission from
Nightwind, but he heard Rude's reply, "I read you, Lame." Rude turned
toward his passengers. "When we go in, Lame will maintain his altitude
and continue to scan the higher slopes. We're going to get as close to the
lake as possible. That's been a problem for him. Hold tight."

They swept into Baby's Cradle a hundred yards behind Nightwind's yellow Super Cub. Once inside, Cork saw swirls of snow kicking off the high faces of the ridges on both sides. The chopper slid
sideways, and Rude gripped the control stick and fought the powerful
shove of air currents as he guided the helicopter toward the lake far
below. From the snow line on the evergreens that covered the slopes,
Cork could see that the snowpack was already several feet deep. The
flat surface of Sleeping Baby Lake was covered with a solid blanket of
white, wrinkled where the wind had pushed the snow into long, rip-
pled drifts.

They spent a couple of hours flying a grid that took them across the
floor of Baby's Cradle first in a north–south pattern, then east–west.
There were several meadows, none more than a hundred yards wide,
not nearly large enough for a plane to land. They found no sign of
wreckage. Rude finally brought the chopper to a hover above the lake.

"I've been thinking about that vision of old Will Pope," he said.
"He told us the eagle went under a white blanket, so maybe the plane
went into the lake and is under the ice."

Cork nodded. "I've been thinking the same thing."

"To a pilot looking at an emergency landing, Sleeping Baby Lake might have presented an enticing possibility. But if that was the case . . ." Rude didn't finish with the obvious.

But Stephen did. He said, "They're all dead."

Cork looked at his son. Stephen's face gave away nothing, though the weight of his realization had to have been awful.

"Can we land?" Cork asked.

Rude shook his head. "I wouldn't risk it. No idea how thick the ice is. In one of the meadows maybe. But what good would it do?"

Cork said, "If there's a possibility they're here, Jon, we'd like to know one way or the other."

"I understand," Rude said. "I just don't know how to do that."

"Divers?" Cork suggested.

"Getting them up here would be hard enough. Then we'd have to clear snow and break a hole. And once they're in, it's a big lake to try to cover in the little time we have before the next storm hits."

"Please, Mr. Rude," Stephen said.

Rude was quiet awhile, considering. The wind lifted a sheet of snow off the lake and threw it at the chopper.

"I suppose we could use a magnetometer," Rude said.

Stephen looked puzzled. "What's that?"

"It's a device a lot of geologists and oil companies around here use. It measures variations in magnetic fields. A concentration of metal like the plane would probably register on a magnetometer. If we were going to try it here, we'd need a good handheld model."

"Where do we get one?"

"I suppose once we're out of Baby's Cradle, we could radio Dewey and have him start calling."

"What are we waiting for?" Cork said.

Rude told Nightwind, who'd been circling above, to rendezvous outside Baby's Cradle. Once there, he contacted Deputy Quinn and explained their thinking. Quinn said he'd see what he could do.

They flew back in somber quiet. Stephen kept his face turned away. Sometimes he stared at the pure blue sky, and sometimes at the mottled earth below. Cork had nothing hopeful to offer his son. At the moment, the prospect on the horizon was heartbreaking, and there was nothing he could do to shield Stephen from it.

Nightwind landed at the Hot Springs airfield ahead of them and was waiting when they touched down.

"Wish we'd come up with something more hopeful," he said, standing with his hands shoved in the back pockets of his jeans. "But tell you what. You get hold of one of those contraptions Jon's talking about, I'll be glad to go back up there and help out."

"Appreciate that." Cork shook his hand gratefully, and Stephen did the same.

Nightwind nodded to Rude in parting. "You know how to reach me, Jon."

After Nightwind left, Rude said, "Look, that offer of dinner last night is still good. Diane told me she's fixing a big pot of beef stew this evening. Don't know about you, but I'm so hungry I could eat a horse. What do you say? Good home-cooked meal with decent company?"

Cork put his hand on his son's shoulder. "What do you think?"

Stephen looked down the empty runway that pointed like a gray finger toward the mountains. "Stew's okay," he said quietly.

"It's a deal, Jon," Cork said.

"How about giving me a hand getting this chopper secured, Stephen? Then I'm guessing you guys might want to go back to your hotel, freshen up. We'll expect you in an hour or so. Think you can find it? Straight out County Seventeen west of town, five miles till you come to Banning Creek Road. Follow that north a couple miles. You'll see my place on the left."

"Thanks, we'll be there."

While Rude and Stephen worked on the helicopter, Cork looked toward the mountains. Even at this distance the top of Heaven's Keep was visible, a white crown on the Absarokas. From so far away, it seemed a regal, majestic formation. He knew on some level that this was beautiful country, but everything he saw here was coated in the possibility of utter loss and the promise of pain.

He hated Wyoming.

"Ready," Rude called.

Stephen trudged to the Wrangler, and Cork joined him.

SIXTEEN

Day Six, Missing 128 Hours

The ranch house was a green rambler with three towering cottonwoods in the front yard. A drainage ditch and a white rail fence separated the yard from the road. In back of the house stood a large barn with a connected corral and a couple of other outbuildings. Half a dozen horses browsed in a nearby pasture. A hundred yards to the west was an aluminum hangar and a landing strip. Hills rose above the southern side of the valley, chalk white with snow and barren as desert dunes. The sky above them was the faded blue of thrift-store jeans. Cork pulled up beside Rude's pickup, which was parked in the yard in front of the barn. When he got out, the smell of hay and fresh manure filled his nostrils.

The door of the barn swung open, and Rude strode out. He was wearing an old jean jacket, a cowboy hat, scarred boots, and pigskin work gloves with the palms worn to a shine. He tugged off his gloves as he came and greeted Cork and Stephen with "Howdy!"

"Jon, your place is even prettier from the ground than it was from five hundred feet up," Cork said.

"Come on in. Diane's got dinner under way."

They entered through the mudroom in back, where Rude removed his boots, which were caked with the residue from the barn floor. They went from there into the kitchen and the aroma of Italian spices. The room was large and bright, and at its center was an island, where a fine-looking woman stood with a long, sharp knife in her hand.

"Sweetheart, this is Cork O'Connor and his son, Stephen," Rude said.

She put the knife down and smiled. Her hair was light brown and hung to her shoulders. She had a long, lovely face. She wore a pale blue sweater and jeans. She wiped her hands on a dish towel draped over one shoulder and greeted them with a cordial clasp. "I'm Diane," she said. "Glad you finally let Jon talk you into dinner."

The sound of small feet across floorboards preceded the entrance of a child. She ran to her mother, grasped Diane's waist, and peered at the guests with shy interest.

"Anna, these are our friends. This is Cork and this is Stephen."

"Hi," Anna said. "I can dance."

"Tell you what, sweetheart," Rude said. "Let's all go into the living room and you can show our guests a little ballet, but only a little, all right?"

"All right," she agreed easily, turned, and danced her way out of the kitchen.

They ate a fine dinner, washed down with a good Chianti. Diane talked about her classes at the college in Lander and about her desire to teach. Cork told them a little about Aurora. The search for the missing plane was carefully skirted. Anna took a shine to Stephen and sat beside him and told him all about her stuffties. Stuffties, she explained, were her stuffed animal friends. After dinner she brought Stephen her favorites—a giraffe named Horace, a floppy-eared dog named Bop, and a unicorn named Uni. Rude asked Cork if he'd join him outside for a smoke, and the two men went through the mudroom, shrugged on their coats, and strolled out into the yard.

The moon was up, nearly full and flooding the valley with silver light that made everything look covered in frost. Yard lights from other spreads flickered up the valley. Rude walked to the fence that bounded the pasture. He brought out a pack of Marlboros and offered Cork a cigarette.

"Gave them up a few years back," Cork said.

"Wish I could." Rude lit up and shot out a cloud of silver smoke.

The horses in the pasture began to drift toward them.

"Fine place you've got here, Jon. Fine family," Cork said.

"I'm a blessed man and I know it, Cork." Rude studied the tip of his cigarette a moment. "Almost lost it all, though."

"Yeah? How's that?"

"Gambling. Never had a clue I'd be addicted. Then the Blue Sky Casino came along, and for a while I was spending all my time there. All my money, too. And finally money I didn't have. The casino"—he shook his head—"it's been okay for the Arapaho, I guess, but it's done a lot of individual damage around here."

"Still gamble?"

"Naw. Diane gave me an ultimatum. Told me to get help or she was leaving me and taking Anna with her."

"Worked, huh?"

"I belong to Gamblers Anonymous. I haven't set foot in that casino in over a year. Funny the things that can do a man in that he never saw coming." He laughed and held up his Marlboro. "I know all the heartache these things promise, and I'll stop one of these days. At the moment, I'm just real happy I was able to quit the gambling."

One of the horses whinnied and was answered somewhere in the distance, far beyond Rude's pasture. The sound made Cork sad, though he couldn't say exactly why. The truth was there wasn't much in the last few days that didn't affect him in this way.

"I wish I knew what to hope for you, Cork. We get our hands on a magnetometer and find the plane tomorrow in Sleeping Baby Lake, well, you understand what that'll mean."

"I know." Cork turned and looked back at the house, where the lights from inside shined warmly into the night. "I'll take one of those cigarettes."

Rude held out the Marlboros, and Cork pulled one from the pack. Rude snapped open his lighter and thumbed a flame. Cork bent and lit his cigarette. He drew the smoke into his lungs and closed his eyes. Whenever he smoked with Henry Meloux, it had nothing to do with the pleasure of the act itself. This was different. This was like running into a long-lost and very wicked friend.

"Feel like I've seduced you back to the dark side," Rude said.

"Not your fault. It's the circumstances."

For a while they smoked and didn't talk, then Diane called from the house. Inside, Anna had brought out a whole family of stuffties and was introducing Stephen to them all.

"This one is Jasper," she said, holding up a donkey. "He's kind of a joker. He makes the other stuffties laugh. If you want to keep him for a while, you can. Maybe he can make you laugh because you're probably pretty sad."

"Do I look sad?" Stephen asked.

"Yes. You're sad in your eyes. Here, take Jasper. He'll help. And you can give him back to me whenever you want to."

"Thanks." Stephen took the stuffed toy from Anna, though it appeared to trouble him.

They sat at the table again, and Diane served them cheesecake. As they were finishing, the telephone rang. Rude got up and went to the kitchen to answer. When he came back, he said, "That was Dewey Quinn. He's found a magnetometer."

In their room at the hotel, Stephen got ready for bed while Cork called home and gave an update. When Stephen had finished brushing his teeth, he turned on the television and tuned in CNN. The stuffed donkey Anna Rude had given him he put at the end of his bed, and then he crawled under the covers. He stared at the ceiling, but when the news turned to coverage of the standoff in Kansas his eyes were glued to the screen. The situation had continued to worsen. Hargrove seemed to be raving like a madman, threatening to detonate the explosives and kill everyone in the rural compound even though the authorities had so far refrained from any aggressive action.

"Do you think he'd really do that, Dad?" Stephen asked.

"People who see themselves in desperate situations sometimes do desperate, incomprehensible things," Cork said.

"Is everyone with him like that?"

"I don't know. It's hard to imagine that if you have children you'd be thinking that way."

"Maybe he'll let the children leave," Stephen said.

"Maybe." Though, in truth, Cork thought not. He wondered at

Stephen's deep concern over these people—these children—he didn't know. Maybe Stephen saw them as being a little like himself, caught up in something unthinkably horrific and over which they had no control. Maybe he thought that if the impossible situation on the plains of Kansas could somehow be resolved it would mean there was hope for the impossible in those rugged Wyoming mountains.

Cork went into the bathroom. By the time he came out, Stephen had fallen asleep.

It was just as well. He missed the breaking news from Prestman, Kansas. Gunther Hargrove had blown himself and his followers to kingdom come.

SEVENTEEN

Day Seven, Missing 144 Hours

The man from Luger Oil and Gas was named Harmon Bolt. He had enormous ears, a three-day shadow, the look of a hangover, and the smell of cigar smoke in his clothing. He was brusque and coarse, but he'd brought the magnetometer, so Cork forgave him everything. Bolt took the seat next to Rude. Cork and Stephen sat in back. Nightwind flew ahead, once again leading the way over the Absarokas. The flight out was quiet, except for Bolt, who kept hacking up junk that he spit into a dirty handkerchief. The magnetometer was stored behind Cork and Stephen. It was a yellow tube constructed of PVC, approximately four feet long and maybe two feet in circumference. Its rounded head and sleek body gave it the look of a torpedo. Bolt had explained that though he'd used it only on land, it was also designed for use underwater. "Treasure hunting and that kind of bullshit," he said.

They were all conscious of the weather. The storm front out of the northwest was barreling through Idaho. By late afternoon it would slam into the Absarokas, and heavy snowfall was predicted.

Though neither he nor Stephen had spoken of it, Cork understood that they were no longer thinking of finding Jo alive. Over the six days since her disappearance, with all the planes in the air and the search yielding nothing, they'd gradually left that hope behind. There was no moment, no event he could look back at and say, "Here. Here, I lost hope." There were even times when he wondered if he'd ever really had any hope. Now, staring at the back of Bolt's head, at the greasy hair badly in need of a cut, at the ridiculously large ears, Cork realized that what he'd been reduced to was a concern that, in a way, was almost pointless: Would they find her body?

They neared Heaven's Keep, and Cork saw that the towering wall of rock and snow and ice cast a long black shadow west across the Absarokas. It reminded him of the dark of an open grave.

Twenty minutes later, they swept through Giant's Gate. As soon as they entered Baby's Cradle, the chopper plummeted, caught in a sudden, powerful down current. Bolt hollered, "Oh shit!" and grabbed the passenger assist handle on the cockpit frame. Cork felt like he'd left his stomach a hundred feet above.

Rude seemed unruffled. "Going to be a little rough today," he said.

Below them, Baby's Cradle was a white fury. Rude gradually brought the chopper to a difficult hover a couple of feet above the surface of the snow near the northern end of the lake. Near whiteout conditions surrounded them, the result both of the wind and of the tempest caused by the chopper blades. Bolt had put a pair of snowshoes in the space between Cork and Stephen. Now Stephen passed them to him. Cork pulled the magnetometer from the storage area behind his seat and held it while Bolt zipped himself into his down parka.

"This is how it's going to go," Bolt said. He wasn't wearing a flight helmet, and he shouted to be heard over the noise of the chopper. "I'm going to open the door and situate myself so that I can get these snowshoes on. Then I'm going to drop down onto the snow cover. O'Connor, you'll hand me the magnetometer. I'm going to make two passes the length of the lake. That instrument'll pick up any variation in the magnetic field for a thousand feet around it. If the plane's under the ice, we'll know. Rude, you stay above me, far enough you don't add to this goddamn mess of blowing snow. Lose me in this shit, you son of a bitch, and I'll kick your ass from here to Arkansas. Got that?"

"Loud and clear," Rude said.

Bolt opened the door, and wind and snow screamed into the cockpit. He leaned down and spent a couple of minutes getting into his snowshoes, swearing a blue streak the whole time. Finally he hollered over his shoulder, "Ready with that instrument, O'Connor?"

"Ready!" Cork yelled.

Bolt tugged his mittens on and disappeared from the doorway. Cork opened his own door, and the wind struck him like a fist. He squeezed his eyes shut against the needles of ice and held out the magnetometer, which was snatched from his hands.

"Shut the door!" Rude called. "I'm taking 'er up."

The chopper rose a couple hundred feet above the lake. Below, they could make out Bolt, a figure in a dark green parka plodding south.

"You know him well?" Cork asked.

"Not really," Rude said. "He used to prospect for himself. He's been working for Luger for quite a while, but like most Wyoming men, he'd rather be independent. If it came down to it, he wouldn't think twice about telling the Luger people to go fuck themselves. Hard as a branding iron and nobody you'd want to spend time with. But it's a hell of a thing he's doing down there."

They followed Bolt the length of the lake, more than a mile, which took a little over an hour. At the southern end, Bolt cut to the west a couple of hundred yards and started back north, heading into the wind. Above them, Nightwind flew a broad circle inside Baby's Cradle. As Bolt began his long trek back through the deep snow that covered the frozen lake, Nightwind radioed a weather update. Static again prevented Cork from hearing Nightwind's transmission. Over his shoulder, Rude said, "That storm's moving faster than they predicted. Lame figures we've got at best another hour, before getting home safely becomes a serious question."

Cork watched the small figure below, which was obscured at times by sudden blasts of white. Bent into the wind, he moved more slowly now. Fatigue and the bitter high-mountain cold were probably working on him as well. Cork knew it would take much longer for the second leg of the sweep than it had for the first.

He leaned toward Rude. "If the plane had come in from the north through Giant's Gate and the pilot tried to land, he'd have ended up more toward the southern end of the lake, don't you think?"

"A reasonable assumption," Rude agreed.

"So even if Bolt doesn't make it all the way back to the north end, he'll still have covered the most likely area by the time we have to bring him in."

"I'd say that's right."

"Then that's the way we'll have to play it." Cork turned to his son, who looked troubled by the decision. "It's that or put us all in danger, Stephen."

"But won't there still be a question?"

"Hardly any," Cork said. "It's the best we can do under the circumstances. Okay?"

Stephen stared down where Bolt struggled against the elements, and finally he gave a silent nod.

The rate of Bolt's progress continued to deteriorate. Rude scanned the sky above Baby's Cradle, where dirty-looking clouds were piling up against the tops of the ridges. Bolt had made it just over halfway when snow began to fall, and Rude said, "We've got to pull the plug." He maneuvered the chopper to a spot a dozen yards in front of Bolt. The man came alongside and cracked the door open. He handed the magnetometer to Cork, then heaved himself in after. He turned on his seat and undid his snowshoes, which he handed to Stephen. He slammed the door, threw back the hood of his parka, spraying snow over the others, and howled, "Mother of God, it's cold out there!"

"Did you find anything?" Cork said.

"Nada," Bolt said. He pulled off his mittens and blew into his hands. "Christ, I can't feel my toes."

"There's a thermos of coffee in back, Harmon. Help yourself." Into his radio mic, Rude said, "We've got our cargo aboard and we're heading home. Do you read me, Lame?" The chopper began to ascend, and Rude brought it to a heading that would take them out through Giant's Gate. He shook his head in response to something that came through his headphones. "Negative. Harmon got nothing." He listened again and said, "That's a roger." He turned to the others. "We'll stay with Nightwind until we're clear of the mountains. Make sure the Absarokas don't swallow another aircraft."

They continued to be pummeled as they approached the gap in the north ridge, which had grown faint behind a gauze of blowing snow. In the battle between the little chopper and the wind, it was clear to Cork which of them was Goliath, and he began to be afraid they'd waited too long to get out. He feared for his own safety, but more he feared for Stephen, whose face was drawn taut and whose dark eyes were riveted on the icy ridge dead ahead, where thick coils of snow rose up into the air like snakes on the head of Medusa.

"God fucking damn it!" Bolt yelled. "You want me to get out and lift, Rude?"

"Easy, Harmon. We're going to make it."

Rude swung the chopper back the way they'd come, turning in an impossibly tight radius, so that Cork's stomach rolled. The helicopter climbed rapidly, and Rude swung it again toward Giant's Gate. The snow was falling more heavily now, and, along with what blew off the ridge, it appeared as if a white door had slammed shut before them.

Bolt's hand wrapped around his passenger assist handle in a death grip. "Jesus, you got any idea where we are?"

"I know exactly where we are," Rude replied in a tight voice, and added a few moments later, "We're through Giant's Gate."

They broke out of the blind of white, and Cork saw the mountains to the north, wrapped in dense clouds almost level with the chopper. Half a mile directly ahead, Nightwind's Super Cub circled in a holding pattern.

"We're clear, Lame," Rude said into his mic. Then to his passengers he said, "We're heading back."

The flight seemed to take forever, and the silence among the men in the little chopper was profound. At one point, Rude spoke with Dewey Quinn on the radio. Quinn reported that, like every other day, the search planes had found nothing. Above them, the clouds were rushing forward, and behind them the mountains were already nearly lost. The turbulence had increased, and there were moments when the chopper bounced like a rubber ball on a storm-tossed sea. Stephen stared out the window. Cork thought about the flight through Giant's Gate, about how afraid he'd been that they wouldn't make it, and he thought about Jo and what it must have been like for her as the plane dropped from the sky. And he wondered, wondered deeply, wondered sadly where she'd come to rest. And he wondered if he would ever know.

They set down at the Hot Springs airfield, where Cork and Stephen helped Bolt transfer his equipment to his old pickup while Rude secured the chopper.

Bolt paused before he climbed into his cab to leave. He looked into Stephen's eyes. "Son, I don't know if I ought to be wishing I found something up there. But seems to me since I didn't, maybe you still got something to hope for."

"Thank you for trying," Stephen said, and he shook the man's hand.

As Bolt drove off, Lame Deer Nightwind came from where he'd momentarily parked his Super Cub. "I need to get back to my own place before the storm hits. Anything I can do, Cork, let me know."

"You've already been a big help, Lame. Thanks for everything."

Nightwind put his hand on Stephen's shoulder. "I don't say this to many men, but I admire everything about you, son. I wish things had turned out different." He headed back to his plane and a few minutes later was airborne.

Rude stood in the gathering gloom of the afternoon. The first flakes began to fall, and he looked up at the sky. "Dewey'll call off the search, at least until this passes."

"He'll call it off for good," Cork said. "It's what I'd do. Where haven't we looked?"

Rude nodded. "I'm sorry."

"Not your fault. You did everything you could. We all did."

"You want to come over for dinner, you're welcome to."

"Thanks, but I think we'd like to be alone tonight."

"Sure." Rude reached out his hand one last time. "Take care, guys." He got into his pickup and headed away.

Cork and Stephen stood alone at the edge of the airstrip. The snow drifted down around them like ash from a fire. It was quiet and the air was strangely still, but that would soon change. Cork could feel it.

Even in the basin of the Bighorn River, where sometimes the storms didn't blow, something big was about to hit.

"She's gone," Stephen said. He stared toward the mountains. "She's really gone."

He'd held his back straight through the whole ordeal, but now Stephen bent and began, quietly, to cry.

Cork put his arms around his son and looked toward the mountains. Up there the snow was already falling heavily, burying everything more deeply. Beneath it, the grass and flowers of the meadows would lie dormant until spring, when they would rise again. Beneath it, animals lay curled in holes and in mountain caves where they would sleep through the dark, cold months ahead, and wake in the spring. And beneath it somewhere, God alone knew where, lay Jo, who would neither wake nor rise.

"Come on, Stephen," Cork said gently. "It's time to go home."

PART II
FOUND

EIGHTEEN

In the weeks and months after, as the details of Jo's final hour became known to him, Cork cobbled together a scene, played out again and again in his mind when he lay alone in bed at night, or while waiting for the pancake batter to bubble on the griddle, or in a thousand unexpected moments when the image would fall on him suddenly like a thief intent on stealing his heart. Small details differed: what blew in the wind across the hotel parking lot; Jo's private thoughts; the words exchanged between her and LeDuc, exchanges that Cork knew would have taken place but the subject of which—mending the rift in her marriage—came mostly from his own deep yearning. Some of the elements were, of course, true. What the shuttle driver had reported of the conversations in the van. The recording Jo left on voice mail. The final radio transmission from the pilot as he lost altitude. Cork never allowed himself to imagine beyond the start of that precipitous descent. He held himself back from going with Jo to her final moment. That was a place he knew his heart couldn't bear to be.

And so time passed, and although there were many periods when Cork yearned deeply for Jo, his life went on. And nearly six months later, the time finally came when he realized that for a full day he'd forgotten to imagine his wife's last hour. And he wept as if he'd betrayed her, though he knew it was not so.

"Stephen," Cork called up the stairs. "If you don't get a move on, we'll be late."

"I'm *coming!*" Stephen yelled back.

"That's what you said fifteen minutes ago. What's taking so long?"

Trixie came bounding down the stairs, and behind her came Stephen, tall and in a suit and tie.

"My God," Cork said. "You look downright handsome."

"I don't care about handsome. I just want to look nice."

"You look stunning, buddy."

"You don't look half bad yourself," Stephen said and gave his father a playful punch. "What time is Hugh picking us up?"

Cork glanced at his watch. "Should be here any minute."

"I've never ridden in a limo," Stephen said.

"Just a big car. I'm guessing that when you look back at all the firsts in your life, a limo ride won't even make the top twenty."

Stephen went to the window and checked the street. "How long do you think this'll take?"

"Couple of hours, maybe. Why? Got a hot date?"

"I'm going fishing with Gordy Hudacek. We're taking his dad's new boat over to Grace Cove to do some fishing."

"That's the cigarette boat with the twin Merc engines, right? Give me a break. That boat's all about speed. You're going to run it over to Grace Cove just to see how fast it'll get there."

"Well, sure, that's part of it. But we're going to fish, too."

"Middle of the day? Grace Cove?" Cork shook his head. "You won't even get a nibble. You want to catch something, you should be dropping a line off Finger Point."

"Dad, I've been fishing Iron Lake all my life. I know what I'm doing."

"Make you a deal, then. You catch anything in Grace Cove, I'll fry it up tonight, along with my special potatoes O'Connor, and I'll throw together some coleslaw. You come back empty-handed, you're responsible for dinner."

"Deal," Stephen said with confidence. "Is Hugh eating with us?"

"Haven't invited him. Should I?"

"Yeah. And tell him you'll be serving walleye."

In the long winter months following his mother's disappearance,

Stephen had done his grieving. He'd arrived finally at a place of acceptance and, in truth, had reached that place before his father. Cork believed that partly this was because, having gone to Wyoming, Stephen felt he'd done all he could for his mother. And partly it was because Henry Meloux had worked with Stephen to help him come to this understanding and others about death. And partly it was because Stephen still had his whole life ahead of him and so much of Cork's life felt gone. And partly—the worst part—it was because when Jo left she'd left in anger and Cork had never had a chance to make that right. He'd held a memorial service for her, and all the family had gathered. On one of the two plots in the cemetery that he and Jo had chosen together, he'd placed a simple granite stone that said "Beloved Wife and Mother."

Cork glanced out the window. "Limo's here," he said.

They headed down the porch steps and into the fine sunshine of a warm May morning. Hugh Parmer slid out of the limo and stood grinning at them. He was dressed in a brown western-cut suit, white shirt, and bolo tie. He held a tan Stetson in his hands. Or a cowboy hat of some kind, anyway. To Cork, all cowboy hats were Stetsons.

"Damn, Stephen, but don't you look good."

"Thanks."

"You know, I've got a granddaughter about your age."

"Don't go there, Hugh," Cork said.

"Hell, you ought to see the guys she dates, Cork. Jeans hanging halfway down their asses, holes in their T-shirts."

"Your generation's showing, Hugh."

"Guess you're right. Still, if I'd come courting Julia that way, her father would've horsewhipped me."

"Laws against that now. Probably then, too," Cork said. "Are we going to stand around bemoaning the younger generation all day, or is Stephen going to get his first limo ride?"

"Hop in," Parmer said and waved Stephen ahead.

It was a short ride to Sam's Place. When they turned onto the access off Oak Street, both sides of the road over the Burlington Northern tracks were lined with parked cars, and there was a stream of people walking in from town. The parking lot was filled, but a place had been saved for the limo. They parked and got out and were greeted by lots of locals, Cork's friends and neighbors. A platform had been erected under the pine tree next to the lake where usually Cork had a couple of picnic tables sitting. The North Star Pickers were playing bluegrass to an appreciative audience gathered there. A couple good long lines had formed at the serving windows of Sam's Place.

Cork said, "Let me check with my staff, then I'll join you guys."

He split off from Stephen and Parmer and entered the old Quonset hut through the side door. The smell was a familiar slice of heaven: grilled burgers and French fries hot from the oil. He headed up front to the serving area, where Judy Madsen, who managed Sam's Place when Cork wasn't there, was working fast and furious with three teenage girls, trying to keep up with the flood of orders. She was a retired school administrator, a no-nonsense but good-natured woman with time on her hands, who worked well with the high school kids who were Cork's usual hires.

"How's it going, Judy?"

"Been hit by a landslide," she replied from the grill, where she had half a dozen burgers and just as many hot dogs cooking. "If you wanted to shuck that sport coat and tie, you could roll up your sleeves and give a hand."

"Got ceremonial duties to see to first." To the teenage kids in aprons, he said, "You guys are doing great. Keep it up!"

They gave him quick smiles in reply and returned to their work.

"I'll come back and lend a hand as soon as all the business out there is finished, Judy."

She gave a grilling patty an expert flip. "If you don't make it, we'll be fine. But if this keeps up, a couple of extra hands wouldn't hurt."

"I'll be back," he promised.

Several boats had tied up to the dock. There were blankets spread along the shoreline of Iron Lake, and folks sat there eating food they'd purchased at Sam's Place or from baskets and coolers they'd brought themselves. At a long table, members of the Aurora Chamber of Commerce were filling balloons with helium and handing them to anyone who wanted one. Escaped balloons drifted over Iron Lake like birds lost from migrating flocks.

Cork found Stephen and Parmer shaking hands with Gary Niebuhr, mayor of Aurora, and Ted Hertel, who was a county commissioner.

"Just telling Hugh here how excited we are with the project," Niebuhr said to Cork.

"And how much we appreciate his willingness to work with us to make the development something we're all proud to have as part of our community," Hertel finished.

"Did you guys take that directly from the speeches you're about to make?" Cork asked.

Niebuhr laughed and looked at his watch. "You about ready?"

"As I'll ever be," Cork said.

"Then let's interrupt the music and get on with business."

They cleared the band off the platform, and Niebuhr spoke first. He welcomed everyone and told a lame joke about a man and a talking fish, and then he spoke for too long about the Northern Lights development and what a great thing it was for Aurora and for Tamarack County. Then he introduced Hugh Parmer.

Parmer didn't say a lot, but what he did say got an enthusiastic response. "This is a proud day for me, and this should be a proud day for all of you as well. Those of you who know the history of the Northern Lights development know that the vision has changed significantly in the last six months. Originally what we planned was to alter the shoreline of your beautiful lake by constructing condominiums rising almost at the water's edge. Which would have been pretty nice for the folks who bought condos, but not good at all for anyone else here. That's not what's going to happen now. Now, all the structures will be set back from the lake and the land between will be left pretty much as God created it, full of natural grass and wildflowers. Northern Lights is meant to add to the community and to take nothing from the beauty that has always been a part of this incredible North Country of yours.

"You have one man to thank for this change of heart—Cork O'Connor. I've worked closely with him for six months now, and let me tell you, when this man digs in his heels, ain't nuthin' gonna budge him. He refused to give in to any blueprint that would damage the lakeshore. He got his way, folks. And not only that, he got to keep Sam's Place, which we all know serves the best burgers anywhere in the great North Woods." This was met with a nice round of applause. Then Parmer went on. "The work of building the Northern Lights development will be done by men and women hired locally. It will contribute in every way to the growth of your economy, to the welfare of your citizens, and to the attractiveness of your community. That, ladies and gentlemen, is a solid-gold promise from Hugh Parmer."

Cork spoke next, said as little as he possibly could and still do the occasion justice.

A few others spoke, and then the band returned and the celebration went on. Cork shook a lot of hands, and finally he and Stephen and Parmer headed back to Sam's Place.

At the limo, Cork said to Parmer, "You have plans for dinner?"

"Nothing I can't change. Why?"

"Stephen insists he's going to catch enough walleye to feed us tonight. If he does, I promised him I'd fry 'em up. If he doesn't, he's responsible for the backup plan. What do you say?"

"Hell, I win either way. What can I bring?"

"Yourself. But leave the damn limo behind."

"It's a deal. You sticking around?"

"Yeah," Cork said. "I'm giving my staff a hand. We're doing a land office business today."

"What about you, Stephen?" Parmer said.

"I could use a ride back."

"Done." Parmer looked at the crowd and nodded his approval. "A fine day for us all, Cork."

"Amen," Cork said.

He started toward Sam's Place but stopped halfway when he heard his name called. From the milling of people, two women separated themselves and walked toward him. Cork didn't recognize either one. It was almost noon, and he stood in the warm sunlight, waiting, smiling at them both, with no idea of how dramatically they were about to change his life.

NINETEEN

The woman who spoke first had an intense, intelligent face, dark eyes that reminded Cork of ink drops on tissue, long black hair, and a figure that got his notice.

"Mr. O'Connor, my name is Liz Burns. This is Rebecca Bodine." She pronounced the last name "Bo-dyne."

Cork shook hands. "A pleasure to meet you both."

"We have something important to discuss with you," Burns said. "I wonder if there's somewhere we can talk, in private."

"Now?"

"If it's convenient."

Cork glanced at the long lines in front of the two serving windows. "Will this take long?"

Burns said, "I know you're busy, but when you hear what we have to say, you'll understand why it can't wait."

"All right. This way." Cork led them to the door of the Quonset hut and stood aside so they could enter. He came after them and closed the door. "Have a seat." He indicated the two chairs at the table. He went into the serving area, grabbed an empty stool, told Judy he would be in to help as soon as he could, and returned to the rear of Sam's Place. He set the stool at the table. "Can I offer you something to drink? Coffee, soda?"

"Thank you, no," Burns said.

"Well, then." Cork sat on the stool and looked from one woman to the other. The noise from the band and from the crowd came in through the open windows, the distracting sound of revelry. "Just a minute." He went around the room, sliding the windows closed. "That's better." He sat on the stool again. "So."

Burns said, "When I introduced you to Becca, did her name mean anything to you, Mr. O'Connor?"

"Call me Cork. And no, it doesn't ring any bells. Should it?"

"Becca?" Burns nodded her encouragement for the woman to speak.

"Mr. O'Connor—Cork . . ." The Bodine woman faltered. It reminded Cork of when his children were young and confessed to something worthy of punishment. She gathered herself and went on. "My husband's name was Clinton. Everyone called him Sandy."

Cork had been leaning toward her, smiling his encouragement, trying to let her know he wasn't someone she had to fear. But when he heard the name, he sat back and everything in him went stony.

Burns said, "That name means something. The pilot of the plane your wife was on."

"What do you want?" Cork said.

"To talk to you and to show you something."

"What could we possibly have to talk about?"

"I'm a lawyer, Cork," Burns said. "And I'm Becca's friend."

"You're representing her?"

He was speaking of the wrongful death suit that had been brought against her husband's estate because of his drinking the night before the plane went missing.

"Not technically."

"What is it you want?"

"Everyone who lost someone on that plane is a party to the lawsuit, everyone except you, Cork."

"Believe me, it's not because I don't hold Sandy Bodine responsible for the death of my wife."

"Why then?"

"I don't owe you, or you," he said, looking pointedly at the Bodine woman, "an explanation. I think we're at the end of our conversation." He stood up.

"Please," Becca Bodine said. "Please, just listen."

He'd struggled to get past his grief, to let go of his yearning for Jo, to begin to move on. He'd thought he'd done it. Now here it was again, threatening him in the form of a woman with a fearful look on her face and tears in her eyes.

"Goddamn it," he said. "You want to know why I'm not part of that lawsuit? I'll tell you why. I sold all that land out there for a million dollars. I don't need the money from a lawsuit. And I don't need the pain of dredging up the past and having it dropped in my lap again. And—" He broke off and turned away and stormed across the room. He stared out the window at the people and the colorful balloons.

"And what?" Burns said.

"I hate lawsuits. Nobody wins in the end except the lawyers. And, hell, the last thing we need is Indians suing Indians."

"You can help that not happen," Burns said quietly.

"Yeah? How?"

"Tell him, Becca."

"Mr. O'Connor—"

"It's Cork, goddamn it."

The Bodine woman sat back as if he'd hit her. Then she gathered herself and threw her next words like punches. "My husband wasn't a drunk. My husband wasn't irresponsible. My husband was a good, loving, hardworking man. And he didn't kill your wife or anyone else."

"Go sell it to Disneyland, Ms. Bodine, because that's the only place your fantasy might come true."

"You . . . you . . . you son of a bitch!" She stood and flew across the room. Her open hands rammed into Cork's chest and she shoved him powerfully backward.

"Becca!" Burns leaped to her feet.

"Why did you even think he might listen?" the Bodine woman said. "Let's go. He won't be any help at all."

Burns stepped between her friend and Cork. "Will you both settle down for a moment, please? Cork, give us a chance to explain. Becca, understand that what we're asking isn't easy."

"He won't listen to what we're asking," the Bodine woman snapped viciously.

"What is it you're asking?" Cork shot back with equal venom.

The door to the serving area opened, and Judy poked her head in. "Everything okay?"

"We're fine, Judy." Cork felt the heat of his anger passing. "We're fine. Go on back." He looked toward Burns. "So what is it you want?"

"We just want you to look at a videotape," Burns said. "That's all. Just look at a videotape."

"Of what?"

"Of the man accused of flying drunk."

"What's the point?"

"When you see the tape, you'll understand the point."

The Bodine woman stared at him and looked perfectly willing to have another go at him. "Well?"

"You have the tape?" he asked.

"Here." Burns went back to the table, reached into her large purse, and drew out the cassette, which she offered to Cork.

He took it and walked to the television on the stand in the corner. It was a combination TV-VCR-DVD that he sometimes used in his PI work. He hit the Power button, slid the tape into the player, and moved back to the stool where he'd been sitting. The screen was dark for a few moments, then a grainy, black-and-white image appeared. It was a long bar with ten stools. A bartender moved in the jerky way of people caught on security cameras. There were several people at the bar. The time-date in the corner told Cork the tape was shot in November, the night before Jo's plane went down. The bartender turned to reach for a bottle on the shelves back of the bar, and a man walked up to an empty stool and sat down. He wore a ball cap with a large brim. Though Cork couldn't see his face clearly, he recognized the man: Sandy Bodine.

"I've seen this tape before," Cork said.

"All of it?" Burns asked.

"Enough."

"Please, fifteen minutes is all we're asking."

Cork shut up and watched. The man drank, smoked, talked to the bartender, talked to the other customers, did all the things a man getting drunk at a bar would do. At the end of fifteen minutes, Cork said, "Okay, so what?"

"What did you see?" Burns asked.

"Exactly what I expected to see. Sandy Bodine doing what a pilot should never do the night before he flies."

"Getting drunk."

"Yeah. In a quarter hour, he downed two doubles of Jack Daniel's."

"My husband stopped drinking fifteen years ago," the Bodine woman said. "He's been a member of AA since. And even when he drank, he didn't drink Jack Daniel's."

"Fifteen years sober?" Cork asked.

"That's right."

"Was he often gone overnight on his charter flights?"

"It was pretty common, yes."

"Some men behave differently when they're away from their families."

"Not Sandy," Becca Bodine replied fiercely.

"Maybe," Cork said. "But there's a lot to suggest that there was more to your husband than you were aware of."

"Sandy was left-handed, Cork. Which hand does the man on the tape drink with?" Burns asked.

Cork thought a moment. "Usually his left, but occasionally his right."

"And he smokes with his left hand, too. But sometimes, he uses his right."

"So? He was a southpaw who sometimes was a switch-hitter."

"My husband was left-handed period," the Bodine woman insisted.

Burns said quietly, "It's easy to see that you're right-handed, Cork. Do you drink with your left hand?"

"I don't know. Maybe sometimes."

"Do you smoke?"

"Not anymore."

"When you smoked, did you ever smoke with your left hand?"

"I don't really remember."

"And did you smoke more when you drank?"

"What difference does that make?"

"He smokes one cigarette the whole time he's at the bar. One in two hours."

Cork shifted his gaze to the Bodine woman. "Did your husband smoke a lot?"

"A pack a day. He gave up drinking, but he couldn't kick cigarettes. He was happy enough to have the booze monkey off his back. Another thing. The bartender said this man bragged about his flying ability. He told everyone who'd listen that he could fly through the crack in the Statue of Liberty's ass. My husband was a modest man. He was no braggart. He was quiet, considerate, even a little shy."

"And did you notice that he never looks toward the camera?" Burns said. "He goes to the bathroom several times during the course of the whole tape and always keeps his head down so that the brim of the hat covers his features. The camera never has a clear shot of his face."

"All of which leads you to the conclusion that the man at the bar isn't Sandy Bodine?"

"He's Sandy's height and the same general build, but that's not Sandy."

Cork shook his head. "You're grasping at straws."

"This complete tape is nearly two hours long," the Bodine woman said. "I've watched it a dozen times. Let me ask you a question, Cork. If you watched a two-hour tape of your wife, even if you never saw her face, would you know just from the way she moves, from her body language itself, that it was her?"

"Maybe."

"Maybe?" She eyed him with disappointment. "Then you didn't know your wife. I knew my husband, and that's not him on the tape."

"The bartender and everyone in that bar IDed him from photographs," Cork pointed out.

"What they saw was an Indian drinking. And when they were shown a picture of my husband, they saw the same Indian. Indians all look the same to *chimooks*," she said, using the Ojibwe slang term for white people. "Maybe especially to Wyoming *chimooks*." She glanced away, through a window, and her dark eyes reflected the bright May sunlight outside. "Look, I stand to lose everything Sandy and I have worked for. But I don't care about that. The truth is I lost almost everything when I lost Sandy. What I have left that means anything to me is my son. I don't want him growing up with people telling him his father was a drunk and a murderer. I want him to know the truth."

"And what is that?"

"That's why we're here," Burns said. "We'd like your help in finding the truth."

"Why me?"

"You're not involved in the lawsuit. You're a private investigator. And you have a personal stake in the truth."

"You could hire any number of licensed PIs to do this."

"We did. A man named Steve Stilwell."

"Well?"

"He's vanished. We haven't heard anything from him in almost a week."

"Do you know what he'd been doing?"

"He went to Wyoming for a couple of days, interviewed some people out there, the bartender and some others who gave statements. Then he came back to Rice Lake. That's in Wisconsin. It's where Sandy and Becca live. Sandy operated his charter out of the regional airport there. He spent some time at Sandy's office and was scheduled to meet with us the next day. He never showed. We haven't heard from him since."

"Does he work for a firm?"

"No," Burns replied. "Like you, on his own. I've used him before. He's good. But now he's absent and that worries me."

Cork got up and walked a little, thinking. From outside, muffled by the closed windows, came the music of a fiddler on a hot riff and then the crowd exploded in applause. "Why would someone impersonate your husband?" he asked Becca Bodine.

"I've thought about it until my head hurts and I don't know. I just know someone did."

Cork looked at the television screen, where the jerky black-and-white security tape still played. If it was Jo on that tape, even if he couldn't see her face, he'd know it was her. He'd know it absolutely.

"Let me think about it," he said. "Can I keep the tape?"

"Of course."

"Are you staying in town?"

"My office is in Duluth," Burns said. "And my home is there. Becca is staying with me for the weekend." On the back of a business card, she wrote a telephone number. "This is my private cell phone. Call me there anytime."

The two women stood, and Cork walked them to the door.

The Bodine woman extended her hand. "I'm sorry I got so emotional."

"Not very Ojibwe of you," Cork said and smiled.

She shrugged. "Modern Shinnob."

"I'll call you tomorrow with my answer," Cork said.

"We appreciate your consideration," Burns said. "But we'd appreciate your help more."

After they were gone, Cork stood a few minutes looking at the tape on the screen, at the man his two visitors had insisted was not who he seemed. He didn't know what to think, but he felt slightly disoriented, as if the world around him had suddenly tilted.

"Cheese!" Judy Madsen called through the door of the serving area. "Cork, we're running low on cheese. And we could sure use your help up here."

"Be right there," Cork said and tried to turn his thinking to the matters of the moment.

TWENTY

The bluegrass sessions ended around four, and soon after, the crowd dispersed. At four thirty, Judy Madsen told Cork to go home, told him bluntly but gently that he'd been distracted all afternoon and had been about as useful as a wet kitchen match. Cork didn't argue. He took the videotape the two women had brought him and left the Quonset hut. Outside he stood in the sunshine watching the band platform being dismantled. The folks at the balloon table were packing things up. Some of those who'd come for the festivities lingered along the shoreline, eating burgers or drinking soft drinks from Sam's Place. At the small dock, a boat cast off and backed away while another waited its turn to tie up.

The day held still. Iron Lake was a calm blue reflection of the beautiful blue face of the sky. Cork looked across the big field that separated the lake from the town. Young wild grass grew calf high, and violets and pussytoes stood ready to bloom. A quiet, almost weightless sadness lay in his heart, because he knew that, despite the honest assurances of Hugh Parmer and the man's best intentions, everything he was looking at was about to change. Change was the destiny of all things, living or not. The best anyone could hope for was to have a strong hand in shaping what came next. Cork believed that was what he'd done. And believing made it easier to put recrimination behind him and make peace with what was inevitable.

His house, when he arrived, was empty. Not even Trixie was there to disturb the tranquillity. Stephen must have taken her with him, something he often did when he headed out. These days they were nearly inseparable. Cork took a cold bottle of Leinenkugel's from the refrigerator and went to the living room. He popped the tape into the VCR, sat down with his beer, and watched a good portion of what the security camera had caught.

If he hadn't been looking for something suspicious, he probably wouldn't have noticed the small details the women had pointed out: the man who was supposed to be Sandy Bodine, a southpaw, occasionally using his right hand and doing so with comfortable ease; the fact that the brim of his ball cap was pulled low, so that whenever he turned in the camera's direction much of his face was obscured; the effusive way he engaged the other patrons, buying rounds, making himself a presence, which, according to Becca Bodine, was not at all how her husband behaved. Individually, they were not big things, but taken together they were significant enough to make Cork uncomfortable. Another thing he pondered was why would a pilot do so publicly a thing that was so clearly at odds with flight regulations? As Cork watched, he wondered about other details. What brand of cigarette was the man at the bar smoking and was it the same brand Bodine smoked? How tall was the man and how tall was Bodine? The man in the video wore cowboy boots. Did Bodine?

The phone rang, and Cork jumped, startled out of his intensity. It was Stephen, calling from his cell phone. He was zipping back across the lake with Gordy Hudacek but without the promised catch. Cork told him to stop at Gratz's Meat Market on the way home, pick up three rib eyes and a loaf of garlic bread, and tell Gratz he'd drop by on Monday to make payment.

Cork hung up just as Parmer arrived. When Cork opened the front door, Parmer studied his face and said, "You look like a man who knows a mule kick's coming. What's the story?"

Cork pulled two beers from the refrigerator and played the tape for Parmer, pointing out the details that, if you were of a mind to question things, might make you wonder.

Parmer shook his head. "I understand what you're saying here, but I gotta tell you, Cork, I don't see anything you can take to the bank. In my experience, if you go looking for conspiracies, you're always going to see a figure lurking in the shadows, whether someone's there or not. It's human nature."

Cork nodded. "Yeah. Probably."

"What would be the point of it anyway? Why would someone go through all that trouble?"

"Let's talk outside," Cork said. "Stephen's on his way with some steaks. I need to get the coals going in the grill."

They went onto the patio in the backyard where Cork kept his Weber. He poured out charcoal and used a chimney to get the fire going. Then he stood in the early evening, beer in hand, staring across his empty lawn. There was a maple in the yard that his daughters and Stephen had spent a lot of hours in their childhood climbing like monkeys. Cork had built a small platform in the lower branches, where the kids often clustered in the gathering dark to tell ghost stories. The platform was still there, though his children had long ago outgrown the simple pleasures of ghost stories and climbing trees.

"Why would some guy spend the night in the bar pretending to be Bodine?" Parmer asked. "To discredit him?"

"It's possible," Cork said. "But why go to such extremes to discredit the man if nothing was going to come of it? Bodine flies out the next day, gets his customers to Seattle, everybody's happy. And if he's confronted about drinking, he'd probably be able to mount a good defense, witnesses who put him somewhere else at the time he's alleged to have been at the bar, so what's the point? But if Bodine isn't around any longer to challenge the impersonator, the charade gets carried off successfully. Unless you have a wife like Becca."

Parmer sat down at the picnic table on the patio. He put his beer on the tabletop and slowly turned the bottle as he considered things. "Okay, so what you're saying is that Bodine was already out of the picture when that guy walked into the bar?"

"I'm not saying it. Just following a line of speculation."

"For the sake of argument then, Bodine's already out of the picture. When?"

"Probably from the get-go. Changing pilots in Casper might raise some suspicion. If nobody on that flight actually knew what Bodine looked like, then it was probably never Bodine at the controls."

"But why?"

"I don't know, Hugh. Maybe they simply wanted to get rid of Bodine and to do it without a lot of suspicion involved. A man disappears off the street, that's one thing. A man disappears on a plane that's never found, that's another thing altogether."

"This all sounds pretty crazy, Cork, you know that, right?"

Cork checked the coals and rearranged them with a pair of tongs he kept for just that purpose. "If what the attorney told me is true, the investigator looking into all this has disappeared. You've got to ask yourself, what's up with that?" He heard Trixie barking in the front yard and said quickly to Parmer, "Not a word to Stephen, okay?"

"You got it," Parmer promised.

Stephen traipsed onto the patio, Trixie dancing at his heels. "You were right, Dad. They weren't biting in Grace Cove."

"But you made it there in record time, right?" Cork said. "How's that new boat?"

"Like a rocket."

"Stephen, that lake isn't there just for getting across quickly."

"I know, Dad. But a boat that does is a thing of beauty."

"Ah, to be fourteen again," Parmer said.

Cork threw the steaks that Stephen had brought onto the grill. He directed his son to grab the salad bag from the refrigerator and toss the contents in a bowl. He wrapped the garlic bread in foil and set it on the back of the grill to heat. In fifteen minutes, they were sitting at the picnic table, sliding their knives into meat done medium rare.

When the light was gone from the sky, they took their dishes into the kitchen, and Parmer said good night. Cork walked him out to his rented Navigator, which was parked at the curb.

"So what are you going to do about the Bodine woman's story?" Parmer asked.

"I don't know. Think about it some more."

"Let me know what you come up with. I'm in town for a couple more days."

"We'll see, Hugh."

"Thanks for dinner and the company. That son of yours is a great kid."

"Don't I know it. 'Night, Hugh."

He watched the Navigator pull away just as the streetlights came on. Behind him the screen door opened and banged closed, and Stephen leaped from the front porch and landed on the sidewalk. He loped to his father.

"Gordy just called. He's trying to put together a game of Risk. I'm headed over to his house."

Cork looked at his watch. "Home by ten."

"Eleven."

"Ten thirty."

"Deal."

Stephen raced away into the gathering dark. Cork watched until his son rounded the corner and was gone, then he went back inside and began cleaning up the dinner mess. All the while, in his head, he was picking up and examining the possibilities that Becca Bodine and Liz Burns had presented to him. The tape didn't nail anything. And as for the missing investigator, Cork had known more than a few guys in the business who succumbed to weakness—booze, women, gambling—that took them off everyone's radar for a while.

When he finished in the kitchen, he went to the room Jo had used as her office. Although he used it now for his own PI business, he'd left it pretty much the same: the shelves full of her reference books; the family photos she'd framed and hung; her plants, which he'd taken good care of. He never spoke of it to anyone, but whenever he was there, it was as if Jo was still with him. Her spirit haunted the room. Not in a ghostly way, but in the smell, the energy, the memories it held for Cork of walking in to find her bent over a case file, her hair fallen over her face like a veil of yellow-white silk, her blue eyes rising, the frown of her concentration vanishing, replaced with a smile that let him know she was happy to see him. And that she loved him.

He leaned against the threshold and let himself be swept into remembering, always a dangerous thing. When he finally pulled himself back, he wiped his eyes and turned away.

In the living room, he sat down to watch again the videotape from the Casper bar. Stephen hadn't taken Trixie with him, and the dog circled a few times, then settled on the carpet at Cork's feet, her head on her paws. Cork rewound to the beginning and studied the tape for almost an hour. He didn't believe he'd see anything more, but at the end of that hour he realized something about the man at the bar, something that made him stop the tape, rewind, and watch again carefully several of those moments when the man drank.

The guy in the video usually turned away from the bartender and the other patrons when he lifted his glass. He tipped his head down as he brought the drink up. What Cork realized was that the glass never touched his lips. It was a move done well and, in the moment, would have been hard to catch. Unless you scrutinized the tape, as Cork was doing now, you might easily miss the fact that the man at the bar wasn't drinking at all. The booze was going somewhere, but not down his throat.

"Liz, it's Cork O'Connor. I'd like to drop by tomorrow and talk to you and Ms. Bodine, if it's convenient."

"Of course. What time?"

"Mass here is over at ten thirty. I'll take off right away. I should hit Duluth around noon."

"That'll be fine." She hesitated, then ventured, "You sound anxious."

"We'll talk tomorrow," Cork said.

He made a call to Judy Madsen, explained that he needed her to cover Sam's Place tomorrow. No problem, she told him.

After he hung up, he went outside. He sat on the front porch swing, staring at the pool of light from the nearest streetlamp. He was thinking that, if it wasn't Sandy Bodine flying that plane, what else about the incident wasn't true? Though he wasn't cold at all, his body shook uncontrollably. Inside he was battling an ambush of fear and rage, fighting against a desperate desire not to be drawn again into a hopeless spiral of despair. For six months, he'd struggled with his grief and pain and tried to help his children deal with theirs. For six months, he'd worked to reconstruct his life around the raw, empty hole at its center. For six months, he'd fought to accept the reality that Jo was dead. Now, staring at that tiny island of light the streetlamp cast in front of his house, he thought with a shiver of hope, *What if she isn't?*

TWENTY-ONE

When Cork pulled off I-35 in Duluth and drove through the Canal Park district the next day, the sun was directly above him, glaring down from between sheets of starch-white cloud. He headed past Grandma's Saloon, across the Lift Bridge, and onto Park Point. Half a mile farther, he pulled into the driveway of the home that belonged to Liz Burns. It was a nice piece of property, a two-story of modern design with an unobstructed view of the vast, frigid blue that was Lake Superior. He parked his old Bronco behind a red Taurus with Wisconsin plates and stepped out into a stiff, cold wind that swept off the lake. He reached back inside for his jacket.

Burns greeted him at the door. She was wearing a maroon sweater, tight white slacks, and a tentative smile. "Thank you for coming, Cork."

Inside, the house was expensively furnished, mostly in shades of white set off with blue curtains that were the color of Lake Superior on a good day. Becca Bodine sat in a white, overstuffed chair. She held a glass full of a dark liquid cubed with ice. She eyed Cork warily as he entered the room, which Cork thought was good. In the business on which they were about to embark, caution would be an absolute necessity.

"Can I get you something to drink?" Burns asked from behind him.

"No, thanks."

Burns sat on the sofa. Cork took a wing chair to her left. Becca Bodine set her glass on a coaster on the coffee table. The tabletop was glass. On a shelf visible beneath was a large book with a lovely cover photo of the Aerial Lift Bridge and Park Point. The book was titled

Duluth: Gem of the Freshwater Sea. Cork laid the videotape from the Casper bar on the tabletop next to Becca Bodine's drink.

"I stand by what I said yesterday," he began. "Everything suspicious you saw on this tape could be the result of wanting to see something suspicious. I can't imagine it would be convincing to anyone else."

"So why are you here?" the Bodine woman said.

"Because I made some phone calls to colleagues in my line who know your investigator, Steve Stilwell. They told me he's not the kind of guy to go on a bender and leave a client high and dry. According to them, he's not the kind of guy to go on a bender, period."

"I tried to tell you that yesterday," Burns said.

"How good an investigator would I be if I just took your word? But there's another reason I'm here. I saw something on the videotape that you didn't, something that can't be explained away."

"And what's that?" Burns asked.

"The man at the bar doesn't drink."

"What are you talking about? We've seen the tape. He drinks like a fish."

"He does a good job of making it seem that way. But if you look closely, you can see that he pours the drink inside his shirt. You have a VCR handy?"

"In the den."

"Let's go have a look."

He followed Burns and Becca Bodine into another beautifully done room. A flat-screen television took up much of one wall. Beneath it, housed in a mahogany cabinet, was a VCR-DVD player. Burns turned on the screen, popped the tape into the player, and joined the others standing a dozen feet from the enormous screen. She pressed buttons on the remote, and the by now familiar jerky black-and-white image appeared, much enlarged. They stood in the quiet of the den, watching the silent movements of the man purported to be Sandy Bodine.

"May I have the remote?" Cork asked.

"Sure." Burns handed it over.

Cork fast-forwarded. "It takes a while before he gets careless and the camera catches what he's up to. Here." The bartender had just brought him another round and turned away. As the man at the bar bent to drink, Cork used the remote to slow the action. "Watch carefully," he said.

The man brought the glass gradually to his lips, then tilted it a split second before it connected. The glass emptied, but clearly not into his mouth.

"Oh, God," Burns said, and a huge smile broke across her face. "Oh, sweet God."

"Where is it going?" Becca Bodine asked.

"Could be something as simple as a hot water bottle that he's taped to his chest," Cork replied. "Though it's probably a little more sophisticated than that. He leaves to go to the men's room several times during the video. It could be that he uses the opportunity to empty what he's collected."

"Why?" asked Bodine.

"Because he wants to appear drunk without being drunk."

"But the taxi driver had to pull over so this guy could puke," Burns said.

Cork shrugged. "Finger down his throat."

"He wants to appear drunk without being drunk," Becca said. She frowned, thinking. "So he'd be in good shape to fly the plane the next day?"

"While having given the impression that he was in no shape to be piloting," Cork finished for her.

"Which brings us back to Becca's question," Burns said. "Why?"

"Mind if we go back into the other room?" Cork said. "This could take a while to sort out."

Burns ejected the tape and they returned to the living room. Outside, the wind had picked up, and through the long dining room windows, Cork saw the waves of Lake Superior breaking blue-white and furious along the yellow beach.

"I could use a beer," Burns said. "Anyone else?"

"I'll have one," Cork said.

"I keep a nice variety on hand."

"Leinie's?"

"Coming up. More Pepsi, Becca?"

"No, thanks."

Burns vanished into the kitchen, and Cork heard a refrigerator door open and close. He turned his attention to Becca Bodine, who was staring toward the long windows and the whitecaps of the lake beyond.

"You never doubted him?" Cork said.

Her face was Ojibwe—skin the color of wet sand, high cheeks, a broad nose, eyes like dark almonds. Those eyes drifted toward him, and she looked troubled for a moment, then confessed, "All the time. But I knew that was my weakness. I knew that if it was the other way around, Sandy would have believed in me no matter what the evidence."

Burns returned with two opened bottles, and they sat down again. For a moment, they drank quietly and Cork could hear the wind pressing against the house. One of the starch-white clouds blew across the sun, and the light through the windows turned gray and all the white in the house looked sullied.

"Why?" Burns said.

Cork cradled his beer in both hands. The bottle was like ice. "I've been thinking about that all night. The possibilities are just about endless, so we need to narrow things down. Did Stilwell give you any report on the progress of his investigation?"

"No, which isn't unusual. He usually touches base only when he has a question or when he has something significant to give me."

"Okay. So maybe we can assume that, before he disappeared, he hadn't found anything he felt ready to share with you. You say he disappeared after he visited Sandy's office at the Rice Lake airport?"

"Yes."

"So maybe he found something there."

"He called me," Becca said. "From Sandy's hangar. He told me he wanted to check Sandy's home office and he asked if I had a VCR at my place."

"Did he say why he wanted the VCR?"

"No."

"Did he go to your house?"

"I don't know. I wasn't there." She saw Cork's questioning look. "These days I spend a lot of my time at my sister's home near Hayward. It's hard being alone, raising a son. I try to be around family whenever I can."

"I understand," Cork said. "So he called your cell?"

"Yes."

"Did you hear from him again?"

"No."

"What time did he call?"

"I don't know. Maybe nine o'clock."

"P.M.?"

"Yes."

"So you have no idea if he went to your house?"

She shook her head. "But I told him where I keep a key hidden so he could let himself in."

"A VCR," Cork said. He scratched his neck and thought a moment. "He had a copy of this surveillance tape, right?"

"Yes. He said he'd watched it several times, but he never mentioned anything about seeing what you saw."

Cork rolled all this around for a moment and still didn't know what it meant. He looked at Becca. "Was there any reason someone might have wanted your husband dead?"

She seemed taken aback. "Sandy? No."

"Take a minute to think about it. Did he have enemies? Did he have associates that you didn't particularly care for, guys who maybe scared you a little? Were there clients in his charter business that he seemed circumspect about?"

"What do you mean?"

Cork shrugged. "A pilot flies his own plane, he can carry any cargo, human or otherwise, that will bring him a profit."

"You mean like drugs," she said coldly.

"Anything that needs to be carried under the radar."

"Sandy wouldn't do that."

"It may be that someone killed him, Becca. If that's true, there has to be a reason."

"Not his business," she said.

"All right. What about his personal life? He was a recovering alcoholic. Anything there we need to think about?"

"I told you, he stopped drinking years ago."

"No skeletons in the closet?"

"No."

"You don't need to answer so fast."

"You don't need to accuse him."

"Easy, Becca," Burns said. "He's just asking questions."

"I don't like his questions."

"Or is it that you don't like the answers?" Cork said.

"You're a real son of a bitch, you know that?" Becca said.

"What is it you're not telling me?"

"Fuck you."

"That doesn't get us anywhere."

She glared at him. He sipped his beer and waited.

She sat back and looked away. "Most of his business was flying Indians to powwows and other gatherings around the country. But a while back he flew a job for some Canadians, across the border. Afterward he was—I don't know . . . quiet. Maybe scared. He didn't talk about it, but I wondered."

"How long ago?"

"A couple of years. The business wasn't doing well."

"Any dealings with them since?"

"Not that I know of."

"Any speculation about the nature of what it was that he was paid to transport?"

"No."

"Any names?"

"No."

"Where did your husband keep his records?"

"Two places. His office in our home and his office at his hangar at the Rice Lake Regional Airport."

"You continue to keep his office at the airport?"

"Yes. Sandy had a yearly lease, and because of the FAA investigation and the lawsuit, it's just been easier for me to leave everything as it was."

"Has anyone handled the records since the plane disappeared?"

"The FAA investigators made copies of a lot of things."

Burns said, "And the attorneys for all the plaintiffs in the lawsuit. The originals should all still be there."

"Okay," Cork said. He sipped his beer. "There are other possibilities to consider. Most don't have to do with Sandy."

"What are they?" Burns said.

"There were six passengers on that plane. Maybe it was about one of them."

"Which one?"

"Got me." He reached for one of the coasters on the coffee table, put it in front of him, and set his beer down. "I've been thinking, what do we know about the people on that plane? With the exception of my wife, they were all Indian. So maybe it's something about being Indian. They were all tribal leaders. Anybody who knows tribal politics understands how contentious it can be. So maybe it was that. They were on their way to a conference in Seattle where a number of difficult topics related to mutual rez problems were going to be discussed and some resolutions hashed out. Maybe that was it. Or maybe someone just had a grudge against one of them and acted on it. I could go on."

"How do we figure out which it is?"

"Mostly we ask questions and try to eliminate possibilities." Cork reached out and picked up his beer, but he didn't drink. "One of the things that's clear is this: Whoever is behind it knew about the charter flight, about Sandy, and put together a pretty damn good plan to impersonate him. So that's a place to start. Becca, do you know who arranged the flight?"

"No."

"Would it be in his records?"

"I'm sure it would be. He was meticulous."

"I'd like to check his home office. And can you give me access to his office at the regional airport down there?"

"Of course."

"Okay. Tomorrow I'll drive to Rice Lake and have a look." Cork drank from the beer that had begun to warm in his hand. "Now, there's something else we need to discuss, and this is a little scary."

Burns said, "Steve Stilwell."

"That's right. I think we need to assume the worst. Someone took him out of the picture."

"They killed him?" Becca said.

"That would be my guess."

"Isn't it possible they just bought his silence?"

"Then he'd have stuck around and lied to you, told you he didn't find anything. And buying his silence is risky. He might decide to talk a blue streak to authorities later. I think he found something or he was getting close to finding something and they killed him. Which means they know you're looking into things."

"And that you're helping?"

"Maybe."

"Who's they? And should we be worried for our safety, too?"

"At the moment we don't know who these people are. I can't imagine that they're going to kill us outright. Too suspicious. If they decide to act, they'll figure a way, like they did with the plane, to get rid of us and make it look like it wasn't murder."

"Like what?" Burns said.

"How do you heat this house? Natural gas?"

"Yes."

"Then a gas explosion. Or a drained brake line on your car. Or carbon monoxide poisoning while you sleep. For guys who know what they're doing—and it sure as hell looks as if they do—the list is probably endless."

The women shot a glance at each other and the eyes of one mirrored the concern in those of the other.

"What do we do?" Burns asked.

"Whoever we're dealing with probably won't take any action until they believe we've found something that'll make the right people listen. In the meantime, I'm guessing that I'll be the guy they dog."

"Cork, we didn't mean to get you involved this way," Burns said.

"No? What way did you have in mind?" He smiled briefly, then he said, "I lost someone I loved, too. And if there's a human hand responsible, I've got to know. Stilwell operated out of Duluth, right, Liz?"

She nodded. "He's got an office in Canal Park."

"You know where he lived?"

"I can find out. Just a minute." She got up and vanished down the white tunnel of the hallway toward the den.

Becca stared into the Pepsi in her glass. The ice cubes had melted. She spoke without looking at Cork. "My husband was murdered, wasn't he?"

"I think he was probably dead before that plane lifted off from the airport in Rice Lake."

"I figured he was somewhere in those mountains in Wyoming. But his body is probably closer to home, don't you think?" Still she couldn't look at him.

"Yes, that's what I think."

"Do you think ..." She bowed her head, as if immeasurably weary. "Do you think you can find him?"

"I don't know. I'll try."

Finally she looked at him, and he saw in her dark eyes a sad determination. "I want to know what happened. No matter how terrible, I want to know."

"I understand," he said.

She got up, walked to one of the long windows, and stared at the angry lake.

Liz Burns returned with a slip of paper on which she'd written Stilwell's office and home addresses. She also brought a small handgun, a North American Arms .25 Guardian.

"I had a stalker once, a client who developed an unhealthy attachment to me. I bought this for protection."

"Know how to use it?" Cork asked.

"I fired at the range a few times after I got it. But that was a while ago."

"I'd visit the range again," Cork said. He looked toward Becca

Bodine, who was still at the window, staring at the lake. "Becca, do you have anything to protect yourself, should it come to that?"

She spoke with her back to him. "Sandy was a hunter. We have a cabinet full of rifles."

"And you know how to shoot?"

"Yes." She turned toward him, and her eyes were as turbulent as the lake behind her. "And I'd love the chance to prove it."

TWENTY-TWO

Canal Park was a thriving commercial district that had once been mostly warehouses and junkyards. Its name came from the cut of the shipping canal through which the great ore boats and other freighters traveled to reach the deep harbor. The old maritime buildings had been refurbished and remodeled and had become home to restaurants and boutiques and offices and lofts. Stilwell's office was in a building whose first floor housed a number of small shops and a funky little diner. The sign on the diner door said the soup that day was mulligatawny, and when Cork walked past, the tantalizing aroma of curry powder and ginger tried to seduce him. He passed a small bookstore and a souvenir shop, both nearly empty, and took the elevator to the third floor, which was totally deserted. The door to Stilwell's office was locked. Cork tried to peer through a long pane of translucent glass, but all he could see on the other side was bright sunlight and the dark suggestions of furnishings. The door had two locks: a dead bolt and a knob lock, each of simple pin-and-cylinder design. He pulled a pair of tight leather gloves from the outside pockets of his jacket and tugged them on. From the inside pocket of the jacket, he pulled a small leather case that contained a set of lock picks. He tried raking the dead bolt first but got nowhere. Then he used a pick and tension wrench and after a couple of minutes managed to slide the dead bolt. He quickly sprang the knob lock and slipped inside the office.

Cork stood for a moment, taking in the place. It was a one-man operation: a large desk with a computer monitor, phone, and desk calendar; two tan, five-drawer file cabinets; on the wall, a framed aerial photograph of Duluth; a healthy-looking rubber tree near the window; behind the desk, a deluxe computer chair in black micro-suede, and in front of the desk, a matching chair for clients. Cork walked to the desk and checked the calendar, which turned out to be of the *Far Side* variety. The page that was showing—a cartoon with a couple of lions and an idiot hunter—was outdated by nearly a week. Cork flipped back through the dates and saw quickly that Stilwell didn't use the calendar to track appointments. He checked the desk drawers, then went to the file cabinets, which were locked. He used his pick set again. Carefully he went through each drawer and found nothing of interest. He pulled a couple of client files, just to get a feel for how well Stilwell documented his work, and was impressed. It was clear that the man kept good records during an investigation. In the top drawer of the second cabinet, he found a folder marked "Bodine, C.," and he lifted it out. Inside were copies of expenses related to the investigation: an airline ticket to Casper, a hotel bill, a car rental receipt, restaurant tabs, records of phone calls, times, charges. Stilwell kept meticulous track of everything he'd spent on his client's nickel. But there were no other papers, no notes, nothing related to the substance of the investigation itself. Cork looked through the other drawers and found nothing else that seemed relevant.

He closed and locked the cabinets, then went to the desk, booted the computer, and found, as he suspected he would, that he needed a password to access the files. He turned the computer off.

He sat awhile in Stilwell's chair, staring out the window at the charcoal-colored brick of the building across the street.

In his own investigations, he was prone to keep copious records. He logged in his interviews—names, dates, times, salient observations that fell outside the interview material—and filed this information with the notes he made of the interview itself. He jotted down related thoughts, useful telephone numbers, potential sources. He kept maps, floor plans, photographs, sketches, anything that would help him in his visual recall or his conjecture. If he went solely on the basis of what was in the file for the Bodine investigation, he'd be inclined to believe that the only information of importance to Stilwell was the

cost of doing business. From what he'd learned in his calls to colleagues who knew Stilwell and from what he'd seen in the files for
Stilwell's other clients, that didn't ring true.

Downstairs Cork went into the diner and sat at the counter.
The place was hopping, and it took a moment for a waitress to come
his way.

"Coffee," he said. "Black."

When she poured it, he asked, "You work here most days?"

"Most," she said. She was maybe thirty, a lot of lipstick, eyeliner.
Blond, probably from a bottle. She started to walk away.

"Know Steve Stilwell?" he asked. "PI with an office upstairs?"

She turned back. "Who's asking?"

"A friend. Haven't seen him in a while. He's got a heart condition,
and I'm a little worried."

"Doesn't surprise me," she said. "He comes in almost every
morning. Always eats a heart attack breakfast. I haven't seen him
lately."

"Anybody else here might have seen him?"

"I'm here as much as anyone."

"Anybody been asking about him?"

"No. At least nobody's asked me."

"Thanks."

He drank his coffee and took the opportunity to scan the building
parking lot, where his Bronco sat. He figured that if Stilwell's investigation had, indeed, alarmed interested parties and they'd been shad-
owing Burns and Bodine, they were likely to be onto him, too. All he
spotted in the parking lot were empty cars and tourist types and nobody looking his way. He dropped three bucks for his coffee and a tip
and took off.

Stilwell's home address was a small bungalow in a nice residential
neighborhood on a steep hill. The street ran between stately trees
leafed with new green. It sloped sharply toward Lake Superior, which
sparkled at the end of the corridor like a wall built of sapphires. Stil-

well took nice care of his place. The yard grass was cut, and on either side of the walk leading up to the front porch, strips of earth had been turned and prepared for planting, though it was too early in the North Country to put in most varieties of flowers, still plenty of time for a killing frost.

Cork mounted the steps, entered the shadow of the overhang, and tried the door. The curtains inside were drawn across the windows. He left the porch and followed a flagstone walk around to the backyard. A huge red maple shaded three-quarters of the area. In the sunny northwest corner, Stilwell had put in a raised garden created out of railroad ties. The soil of the garden was clear of weeds, and a layer of compost had already been spread. The man was conscientious and clearly into his yard.

The back door stood at the top of a short flight of steps. The storm door wasn't secured, but the inner door was locked. Once again, Cork made use of his lock picks and was quickly inside. Which was good, because the moment he closed the door behind him, he saw, through the window, a woman leave the house next door and head toward her garage, carrying a plastic garbage bag.

He found himself in a narrow entryway. One side was lined with hooks, from which hung coats of varying degree of warmth. Below them were a pair of boots caked with dried mud, a pair of Adidas, and a pair of rubber galoshes. Beyond the entryway lay the kitchen, where everything was clean, not even a single dirty dish or utensil in the sink. Cork checked the refrigerator. Nicely stocked. He went into the dining room and then to the living room beyond. The woodwork of the bungalow had been wonderfully preserved and the wood floors finished with caramel-color stain under a coat of strong urethane. The furniture and the area rugs had been chosen to accent the rich color of all that beautiful woodwork. *Meticulous*, Cork thought again.

Then he spotted the birdcage near the front window. He walked to it and stared at the canary lying dead on the bottom. The seed feeder looked full, but on closer examination, Cork realized it held only feathery, empty husks. The water cup was completely dry. It appeared as if the bird had succumbed to either hunger or thirst or both.

Cork found an office off the living room. Bookshelves lined one of the walls. If the books there were any indication, Stilwell was a man of broad taste. The volumes were organized alphabetically by author, Heidegger between Hammett and Hemingway, Plato next to Proust, Steinbeck followed by Stendhal. There was a standing four-drawer file cabinet, but Cork found only personal files inside—tax documents, insurance information, papers related to Stilwell's home and his mortgage. He booted the computer on the desk and was confronted with the same situation he'd encountered at the man's business office: He needed a password.

He went upstairs. Two bedrooms and a full bath. One bedroom was clearly a guest room. In the other, the closet and dresser were full of clothing and there was a book on the nightstand—*Staggerford*—with a cloth bookmark slipped in midway. Cork checked the usual places, but found nothing related to the case he was interested in.

The final place he checked was the basement, which was unfinished and in which Stilwell stored nothing.

In the end, Cork stood for a long time in the living room of a clean, orderly house with a dead bird in a cage and an owner missing for a week. He was almost certain the man was dead and anything he'd left behind that would have helped point toward the reason and toward his killers had been removed. He had a clear sense that there was an enormous and brutal force at work, something ruthlessly efficient and certainly to be feared. And he had to assume they knew about him.

He left the way he'd entered, through the back door. He went around in front and walked to the house next door, where he'd seen the woman with the garbage bag. He rang the bell and waited. Thirty seconds later, she opened up.

"Good afternoon," he said with the most pleasant smile he could offer. "My name's Cork O'Connor. I'm a private investigator, a friend of Steve Stilwell's. I'm wondering if I could ask you a couple of questions."

"About Steve? Something's happened, hasn't it?"

She was a plump woman in her early fifties, with wispy red hair and green eyes that held a sudden worried look. She wore a red sweater with an embroidered moose in the center that seemed to be sliding down the ample slope of her breasts.

"Why do you say that?" Cork asked.

"He hasn't been home for days and I've been worried about Binky."

"Binky?"

"His canary. A sweet little thing. Usually when Steve's gone, he gives me a key and asks me to feed Binky. Not this time. So I've been worried, about him and about Binky."

"When was the last time you saw Steve?"

"He came back about a week ago from some work he was doing in Wyoming. He stopped by to get his key from me, and he brought me a spoon from Yellowstone to thank me. I collect spoons, you see. He was around that night, but I haven't seen him since."

"Have you seen anyone else at his house?"

"No. Well . . ." One side of her face squeezed up as she considered her next words.

"What?"

"I probably should have called the police or somebody," she said with obvious regret. "Three, or maybe it was four, nights ago I let Iago out. My cat," she explained. "It was like eleven o'clock. I wasn't wearing much, and I turned out all the lights first so nobody would see me in my undies, and then I opened the back door for Iago. He likes to prowl at night. Well, I could have sworn that when I did that, I saw someone slipping inside Steve's back door. It was dark, so I couldn't be sure. And I figured it was probably Steve anyway. But I haven't seen him since he got back from Wyoming so, yesterday I knocked on his door and tried to peek in his windows. I've actually been thinking about calling the police or something to make sure he's okay over there. But he's a private investigator and all, so I was afraid maybe that would be too nosy, you know?"

"I understand."

"You're a friend, right? And a PI?"

"Yes."

"Maybe you could call the police, then?"

"Sure."

"Will you let me know when you find out what's going on?"

"I'll do that. Thank you for your time."

"He's such a nice man."

"Indeed," Cork said and walked away.

TWENTY-THREE

He'd called Liz Burns on his cell phone, and when he arrived she and Becca Bodine had their jackets on. They went out the back way to a path that wound through a wall of sand to the beach beyond. The sun was out, but they zipped their jackets against the cold wind screaming off the lake. The waves rose like white-maned lions and roared as they came ashore. Burns looked back to where her home was visible above the top of the dunes.

"Far enough?" she asked.

"Let's keep walking," Cork said.

"You haven't explained what this is about."

"It's about the noise of the waves and the sound of the wind and how that might keep us from being overheard."

"By whom?"

"They," Cork said. "Whoever they are."

"The ones who killed Sandy?" Becca asked.

"Yes, them. They've been very thorough so far. It's hard to believe they'd be sloppy now. It's quite possible that they've tapped Liz's phone, maybe bugged her house. Yours, too, for that matter, Becca. Maybe mine by now."

The sun was at their backs, well into its descent, and it gave no warmth. Beside them, the broad, frigid body of Superior fumed and spit. Ahead, the sandy finger of Park Point stretched beyond the limit of their seeing. They were alone on the beach.

"You said you had a son, Becca. Where is he?" Cork asked.

"With my sister in Hayward."

"It might be a good idea if he stayed there for a while, and you stayed with Liz."

"Why?"

"It might keep him from ending up as collateral damage."

"Do you really think these people would go that far?" Burns asked.

"As nearly as I can tell, they've killed seven, maybe eight people already. Why would they stop now?"

"But what are they after?"

"I don't know yet."

Cork watched a gull negotiate the bitter wind and alight on the beach a dozen yards away. It snatched something from the sand and took off again. The wind kicked it, but the gull reeled, recovered, and soared away.

"Stilwell went down to Rice Lake to have a look at Sandy's offices and his records. He called after he'd been to the airport to ask about the VCR at Becca's place. And after that you didn't hear from him again. Is that right?"

"Yes," Burns said.

"Did Stilwell stay in Rice Lake during his investigation?"

Burns nodded. "He told me he'd checked in to a hotel and would probably be there overnight."

"When you didn't hear from him, did you call the hotel?"

Becca leaped in. "I called Rolfe Amundsen. He's the chief of police in Rice Lake. Sandy knew him pretty well. I asked him to look into it. He did and told us that Mr. Stilwell had checked in to the Best Western and checked out the next day."

"That's it?"

"Yes."

"Can you think of anything else that might help?"

Both women looked at each other, then at Cork, and it was clear they'd told him everything.

"You're still going to Rice Lake tomorrow?" Burns said.

"Yes."

"Shouldn't we bring in the authorities or something?" Becca said.

"And tell them what? Our suspicions? I was a cop for a long time,

Becca. Even if they're sympathetic, there's nothing at the moment they can do. Truth is, if I were on the other side listening to the story we'd tell, I'd file it away as a good one to share with the rest of the guys at the bar after shift's over." Cork stopped and looked at the long thread of empty beach. "Until we have something of substance, we're on our own."

Burns turned and looked behind them. "My house might be bugged. I feel like I've been violated."

"Don't talk about any of this in the house," Cork cautioned. "Don't talk on your home phone or your cell about this."

"How do we communicate with you?" Burns asked.

"I'll call when I get to Rice Lake to let you know I'm all right. If something's wrong, I'll use a code word. *Ikode.*"

"*Ikode?*"

Becca smiled. "It's Ojibwe. It means 'fire.' "

Cork said, "Do you have a key to Sandy's airport office, Becca?"

"No, but there's a set in the top drawer of the desk in his home office. It's on a key ring marked 'Hangar.' "

"How do I get into your house?"

"There's a key on a hook under the back steps."

"Aren't you concerned about your safety, Cork?" Burns asked.

"Sure. But I have an advantage over Steve Stilwell. I know there's a bogeyman in the shadows."

They headed back to Burns's house, and while she prepared hot coffee for them, Cork took a quick look for listening devices that might have been planted. Considering the care that had been taken in this affair so far, he didn't really believe he'd find anything. It would take, he figured, an electronic sweep to locate whatever bug they'd planted, if indeed they'd hidden one there. At this point, there was nothing he could be certain of.

They drank the coffee, and they talked awkwardly of small, inconsequential things. When Cork left, the two women walked with him to his Bronco and bid him good-bye and Godspeed. In his rearview mirror as he headed away, he saw Liz Burns put her arm around Becca Bodine, and they turned and walked together toward her house. A moment later they were gone from his sight.

TWENTY-FOUR

It was late afternoon when he returned to Aurora. He stopped at Sam's Place and checked in with Judy Madsen. She told him it had been a good day. Things had slowed a bit and they were doing fine. If he needed her to, she could handle closing. Cork kissed her cheek and told her she was the best, and she told him back that a kiss was fine but making her a partner was better. He said they'd talk. Soon.

In the back of Sam's Place, he unlocked the door to the cellar and went down. From an upright locker near the boiler, he took a handheld RF detector—a bug sweeper—and a phone tap detector. This was equipment he'd purchased nearly a year ago during an investigation he'd done for the Chippewa Grand Casino.

He swept that part of Sam's Place he used for his office and found no evidence of a bug. He checked the phone line. Nothing there. He told Judy he was heading off, and when he thanked her again, she said, "How soon is soon?"

At home, Cork found a note on the kitchen counter from Stephen saying that he was having dinner at Gordy Hudacek's house, okay? He'd be home by nine. Cork called Stephen's cell and told his son that he was back from Duluth, and, yes, he'd expect to see him at nine. He used the next hour to sweep his house for bugs and to check his own phone line. As nearly as he could tell, everything was clean. There were four possibilities: The people behind all this didn't particularly care about bugging him; they hadn't had time to bug him; the bugs they'd used were too sophisticated for his sweep equipment to detect; or he was mistaken in all his assumptions about what was going on.

Finally he called Hugh Parmer and arranged to meet him at the bar in the Four Seasons.

Parmer was waiting when Cork arrived, and the two men took a table near one of the windows that overlooked Iron Lake. Cork ordered a Leinenkugel's Dark. Parmer ordered a Cutty Sark and water.

"I need a favor from you, Hugh," Cork said. "A pretty big one."

"Name it."

"I'd like you to fly Stephen to Evanston, Illinois, in the morning."

"I can do that. Care to tell me why?"

"His aunt and uncle live there. I want him to stay with them for a while. I want him out of harm's way."

"Things are that bad?"

"They might be. I don't want to take a chance."

"Mind if I ask what's going on?"

Cork explained what he'd seen on the tape the night before, after Parmer had left. He told him about his day in Duluth and his growing concern that there was something solid in the conspiracy theory the two women had proposed to him. He said, "These people probably won't hesitate to kill again to cover whatever it is they've been up to."

"Which is what?"

Their drinks came, and Cork waited until the waitress was gone to go on. "I don't know yet, Hugh. But I'm going to do a lot of digging, see if I can uncover a nest of scorpions. If that happens, I don't want Stephen anywhere near me."

"I understand. I think it wouldn't be a bad idea to have some backup with you, though."

"You're probably right, but I work alone."

"After I drop Stephen off, it might be a good idea for me to fly to that regional airport in Rice Lake and meet you there."

"This isn't your business, Hugh."

"It is if I make it my business."

"This is a different kind of business from land development."

"I hunt deer and elk in the White Mountains of Arizona. I've hunted caribou in Alaska and gazelle in Africa. I know my way around firearms, Cork. And I wasn't always a land developer. I started as a ranch hand, an honest-to-God cowboy. You got any idea what kind of mettle that takes?"

"I'm not questioning your mettle, Hugh."

"And don't give me a lot of crap about feeling responsible if I'm hurt. A man chooses, and the consequences are on his own shoulders and no one else's. And just think about what kind of backup I'd provide, Cork. Hell, there's nothing in this world I can't afford to buy if we need it."

"Then why not buy me backup trained in this kind of thing?"

Parmer turned his head and looked away, an odd move for a man who'd have no trouble spitting in the devil's eye. He nodded, as if he was having a discussion with himself. Finally he looked at Cork and said, "Sometimes when a man gets too good at something, like buying land and putting things on it and making a lot of money in the process, what he does begins to lose its value to him. It's too easy. That's one of the reasons I took such an interest in the development here in Aurora. You were an obstacle. You stood in my way. That happens very seldom, and the old excitement kicked in. What you and I planned here for Iron Lake is something I'm proud of, really proud, because it could have been easy and ruinous, but your damn stubbornness, your love for this place, shaped the vision into something that will add to the beauty, not destroy it. At least, that's how I think of the project. My life is too simple these days, Cork, too easy. And for a long time, it's been all about me. I'd like to help because it feels important and because I care about the outcome. And also because it makes me feel alive. If you want me to hire backup instead, I will. I have excellent security people. But I feel up to the job and I'd like to do it."

The man was lean and hard and earnest. He'd come from common stock and risen out of the West Texas dust. He was clear-eyed about the contradictions of human nature and probably understood that inside the best of people there was always a war going on between the light and the dark, and that in anyone the tide of battle could shift at any moment, which meant trust was a dangerous thing. Parmer, Cork figured, would know when to trust. It didn't hurt at all that he could buy half of Minnesota if it came to that.

"All right," Cork said. "But you do as I say. Will that be a problem?"

Parmer grinned. "Not at all."

Back at home, Cork called Rose. She answered in a voice pinched with concern.

"Is everything all right?" he asked.

"Actually, no. Mal is in the hospital."

"Is it serious?"

"He's had a mild heart attack."

"Oh my God."

"He's all right," she said emphatically. "In church this morning, he complained of being short of breath and then of discomfort in his chest. He didn't want to make a fuss, but I insisted we go to the emergency room. They diagnosed him there. He's fine, really. They're keeping him overnight for observation, but he should be all right to come home tomorrow."

"Are you doing okay, Rose?"

"The worst was over before we really even knew what was going on. So, yes, I'm okay. We'll need to take a look at all the contributing circumstances and make some changes in our lives, I think. Mal has been driving himself lately. So the first order of business will be for him to slow down. I'm going to sit on him if I have to."

"Is there anything I can do?"

"No, Cork. And please don't think about coming down here to help. Mal wouldn't hear of it, and you've got plenty to keep you busy up there."

"You'll keep us posted?"

"Of course. I would have called, but I had my hands full." She paused. "But you called me. Was there something you wanted to talk about?"

"No, Rose. Just . . . keeping in touch."

They talked a minute or two more. Rose indicated she would call Jenny and Annie to let them know.

He hung up, aware that the option of sending Stephen to safety in Evanston was no longer available. He walked to the kitchen, stared out the window over the sink, and thought hard. The possibility that came to him was one he couldn't arrange over the phone. It would require some travel, and he had less than two hours of daylight left. He wrote a note to Stephen, then hurried to his Bronco and drove north out of town.

A light shone through the window of Meloux's cabin. Against the thin blue of the twilight sky, a thread of smoke rose up from the stovepipe that jutted from the cabin roof. The evening was still, and, except for the sound of Cork's footfalls on the well-worn path through the meadow, Crow Point was quiet. As he approached the cabin, Cork heard Walleye begin to bark inside. A moment later, the door opened and Meloux stepped out. Along with him came the succulent smell of hot stew.

"*Anin*, Corcoran O'Connor." The old man greeted him without any hint of surprise.

"*Anin*, Henry."

"I have made stew. Will you eat with me?"

The old Mide seemed to have anticipated his visitor and his need, something Cork had experienced so often with Meloux that he didn't question the old man's prescient ability.

"Thank you, Henry. I'm starved."

Meloux nodded and eyed him closely. "You have the look of a man hungry in many ways."

Cork offered his host a pouch of tobacco, which the Mide accepted without a word, and they went inside.

It was squirrel stew. The old man had shot the animal himself. Even though Meloux was well over ninety, his hand was still steadier than those of many men half his age. The stew was full of wild mushrooms, wild rice, carrots, and potatoes, and was spiced simply with salt, pepper, and sage. Meloux had also made drop biscuits. They ate without speaking. In the corner of the cabin where Meloux had set a bowl for Walleye, the old mutt slurped with gleeful abandon.

When they were finished, the old man said, "Now we will smoke, and then we will speak of the reason you have come."

From a deer-hide pouch hanging on the wall, the Mide took a stone pipe with a wood stem. He put two kitchen matches into the right pocket of his worn jeans and wrapped his gnarled hand around the pouch of tobacco Cork had brought him. He led the way to the fire ring beside the lake, where he opened the tobacco pouch. He pinched some of the contents and sprinkled it to the north. In the same way, he offered tobacco to the east, south, west, and finally let some of it fall into the center. Then he sat on one of the stumps that circled the ring, put a bit of tobacco into the pipe, and struck a match. As the mantle of night closed slowly around them, they smoked and then they talked.

Cork told Meloux of the things he'd discovered and what he suspected they might mean.

"Do you believe that your wife is still alive, Corcoran O'Connor?"

Cork shook his head. "For a little while, I entertained that hope. But I don't understand how it could possibly be. No, Henry, she's dead, but there's more to her death than any of us know. I want to find the truth."

"What will you tell Stephen?"

"I don't know yet."

"If you lie to him, he will know. If not now, eventually. I would think about what that means."

"If I tell him the truth, he'll want to help and I can't let him. He'll hate me for that as much as he would if I lied."

"The truth, a man can deal with."

"Stephen's not a man yet, Henry."

"He is not a boy either. If you treat him as a man, perhaps he will behave as a man."

"If I were Stephen and I knew what I know, nothing in all God's creation would stop me from going after the truth. Not even my father."

They sat in silence. A half-moon had risen in the east and cast a silver thread across the black water of Iron Lake. Near Meloux, Walleye sighed deeply, the only sound.

"Bring him to me," Meloux said. "Perhaps it is time to make a man of him."

"*Giigiwishimowin?*" Cork asked. He was speaking of the old way in which an Anishinaabe boy became a man. It involved a vision quest that required a boy to go alone into the woods and to fast until he'd been given a dream, a vision that would guide him as a man for the rest of his life.

"Yes," the old Mide replied. "The vision itself, if it is given to him, may help him to understand. And while he is seeking the vision, it would be a good time for you to do these things you must do."

"If I don't tell him the truth behind this, Henry, he may still see it as a lie."

"And what is the truth behind this, Corcoran O'Connor? You want him to grow into his manhood, do you not?"

"Of course."

"And you believe in the old way?"

"Yes."

"Then the truth of this is that you want your son to become a man and you want this done properly, is that not so?"

"Yes, Henry, I suppose that is the truth."

"Bring him to me tomorrow and I will prepare him. He will stay with me until it is finished."

"*Migwech*, Henry," Cork said, thanking his old friend.

They walked back to the cabin, with Walleye padding along behind in a tired way. Cork felt tired, too, weighted by the oppressive prospect of all that lay ahead. At the cabin door, he bid the old Mide good night.

Meloux slipped inside with his dog and closed the door.

By the light of the moon, Cork walked the trail back to his Bronco. In the woods on either side, the darkness was intense. But he knew those woods and knew what there was in them to fear, and passing through empty-handed was no concern. The darkness ahead, however, all that lurked within it and that was unknown to him, this was something else. And he was afraid.

TWENTY-FIVE

Cork had been concerned that for Stephen a few days away from school might seem like a holiday or an early summer vacation. But when he explained to his son the purpose of his visit with Meloux, Stephen had become solemn and accepted seriously the idea of a vision quest under the old man's guidance. Now they walked toward Meloux's cabin together, with Trixie trotting in front, taking in the scent of everything along the path. In the east, the rising sun was a red fire burning in the treetops. A heavy dew caught the color, and the meadow grass seemed hung with garnets. Walleye bounded from the open cabin door to meet them, and Trixie ran ahead. The two mutts, good acquaintances, danced together in a flurry of woofs and wagging tails.

Meloux stood in the doorway. Like the dew on the meadow grass, his dark eyes sparkled. "*Anin*, Stephen."

"*Anin*, Henry," Cork's son replied. There was a gravity in his voice that pleased his father. He shrugged off the pack he wore, which held his sleeping bag and clothing.

The old Mide looked at Cork. "There is no need for you to linger. Your part in this is finished."

"How long will this take, Henry?"

The old man shrugged. "I will send word."

Cork nodded. "*Migwech*." He turned to his son and offered his own version of an Ojibwe prayer. "May you learn the lesson in each leaf and rock. May you gain the strength and wisdom, not to be superior to your brothers, but to be able to fight your greatest enemy, yourself. And may you be ready to come before Kitchimanidoo with clean hands and a straight eye."

With the morning sun over his shoulder, the sky like mottled marble above his head, and a warm spring wind pushing at his back, Cork abandoned his son to the man he trusted most in the world and turned his feet to the trail through the forest. Beyond that lay a path that he suspected would be as dark as any he'd ever traveled in the great North Woods.

Hugh Parmer was waiting for him in the lot of the Four Seasons. Cork parked, grabbed a gym bag from the backseat of his Bronco, and tossed it into Parmer's Navigator. The two men got in, and they headed southeast on Highway 1 toward Duluth. They drove through the morning shadow of evergreens. In those places where the sun broke through the forest wall, it hit the windshield brilliant as molten gold. Cork was quiet, thinking of what lay ahead. Parmer, as he drove, drank from a cardboard cup of Four Seasons coffee.

"What's in the gym bag?" he asked after they'd passed beyond the limits of Aurora.

"Equipment I might need."

"Got a firearm in there?"

"No."

"The word I got in Aurora is that you have something against firearms." Parmer waited a moment, and when no reply came he said, "It seems to me that if a man wades into a pack of wild dogs he ought to expect to be bit. And he ought to be prepared."

"I don't want to have to explain myself at every turn, Hugh. You agreed to let me do this my way."

Parmer shook his head. "They've established the rules, and they're clearly not playing your way, Cork."

"You don't have to come with me."

"Relax. Just being the devil's advocate here."

"I'm going to explain this once and then we're not going to talk about it again," Cork said. "Two years ago a kid slaughtered a lot of his classmates and a teacher and a security guard at the high school in Aurora."

"I know. National news."

"What you may not know is that I was well acquainted with the kid. A lot of folks in town knew him and knew he was troubled. We weren't there for him when he needed us, pretty much ever. When he opened up in the high school, I'm sure this kid in his own warped thinking was wholly justified. I've killed men, too, and justified it in my own ways. But who's to say my reasons were any better than that kid's? You have a gun, Hugh, you risk the gun becoming the easy answer to a threat, especially if it's been the answer for you before. I'm no saint, and I'm not a gun control freak either. I just don't want the temptation that might come with carrying a firearm. I can't help thinking that, if I'm smart enough, the gun shouldn't be necessary."

"I don't know that smart is always the answer, Cork. I've known men who were born killers. Smart wouldn't have made any difference with them. What did you do with your firearms? Sell them?"

Cork shook his head. "I didn't want someone else using them. No, I put them in the hands of a friend for safekeeping."

"Indefinitely?"

"Permanently."

Parmer nodded, studied the road ahead, and began to whistle.

They drove to Duluth, crossed the Blatnik Bridge over the harbor, and entered Superior, Wisconsin, where they caught U.S. 53 toward Rice Lake. As they passed Solon Springs, a few miles south of Superior, Cork told Parmer to pull off for gas.

"Tank's still three-quarters full," Parmer said.

"Do it anyway."

Parmer did as he was instructed and pulled into a BP station. While he filled the tank, Cork cleaned the windshield of the mayflies that had plastered themselves across the glass.

"What are you hoping to find in Rice Lake?" Parmer said.

"What we know about Stilwell's investigation is that he'd talked to people in Wyoming. I'd love to find his notes on that, but there was nothing in his office files in Duluth. Then he came down to Rice Lake and spent some time at Bodine's airport office and maybe at his home. Then he disappeared. I'm thinking that whatever it was that got him killed—"

"You're sure he's dead?"

"For our own safety, I think we ought to assume that. So whatever it was that got him killed, there's a chance it had to do with what he found in Rice Lake."

"Records?"

Cork shrugged. "Could be anything, I suppose. I don't want to limit our thinking."

They took turns visiting the men's room and got back on the road. A few minutes later, Parmer said, "You've been spending a lot of time watching the mirror. Did that unnecessary fuel stop we just made have anything to do with it? Are we being followed?"

"If we are, they're a hell of a lot better at it than I am at spotting them," Cork said. "I haven't seen anything, but it never hurts to be cautious."

A little before 11:00 A.M., they pulled into the driveway of the Bodine home, a nice little rambler in a newer development on the western edge of Rice Lake. Cork found the key hanging from a hook under the back steps, exactly where Becca Bodine had told him it would be. They entered through the kitchen, which was clean and smelled of overripe bananas. In the living room, a comfortable scattering of toys lay about. Cars, Tonka trucks, Lego blocks, and on the sofa a plastic contraption that fired Nerf rockets. They found the room that Sandy Bodine had used as his home office. Becca had told him she'd left it exactly as it was when her husband used it. At first it was because of the investigation, then it was simply that she didn't have the resolve yet to clean things out, something Cork understood well. He returned to the kitchen, slid the gym bag from his shoulder, and took out the electronic sweep equipment he'd brought. He spent an hour going through the house and checking the phone line, but he found no bugs.

They hadn't spoken since before they entered. Now Cork shook his head and said quietly, "It could be that there's nothing. Or it could be that what they're using is too sophisticated for my stuff to detect." He put his equipment away and returned to Bodine's office. In the desk, he found the key marked "Hangar" that Becca had told him about. He also found the key to a file cabinet in the corner. He opened the cabinet and went through the files, drawer by drawer.

"What're you looking for?" Parmer asked.

"Anything that'll give me an idea about why someone would want Bodine dead. I don't know what that might be, but I'm hoping I'll know it when I see it."

He found the file on the flight that Bodine had made for the Canadians two years before. He pulled it out and handed it to Parmer. "See if you spot anything suspicious in there."

"Suspicious?"

"Whatever."

Cork went back to rifling through the files in the cabinet. When he'd finished he said, "Anything?"

Parmer shook his head. "Nothing extraordinary so far as I can see. He flew two men to a town in northern Ontario to fly-fish. All the paperwork seems to be here." He handed the file back to Cork. "Did you find anything?"

"It's what I didn't find that concerns me." Cork scanned the file Parmer had given him, then put it back where it belonged. "It appears to me that Bodine kept good records of every charter flight he made, and for every charter there's a signed contract. But the file for that final charter, the one to Seattle, doesn't contain a contract or a record of a deposit made to secure the flight."

Parmer nodded. "A strange omission for a man so organized."

"Omission? I don't think so. It's possible, I suppose, that the FAA investigators or the attorneys somehow ended up with the original."

"But you don't think so?"

"No. Stolen would be my guess. Before the investigators ever saw the files."

"What is it they don't want us to see?"

"It would tell us, among other things, who arranged for the flight. Whoever it was that wanted Bodine dead had time to plan things carefully. If we knew who made the flight arrangements, we might be able to get a handle on who could have been involved in planning his disappearance. It would be a lead to follow, anyway."

"Okay," Parmer said. "What now?"

"Let's have a look at the entertainment center in the living room."

"This isn't exciting enough for you?"

"Before he disappeared, Stilwell called Becca Bodine and asked if she had a VCR here."

"Why?"

"I'm not sure. Maybe the VCR will give us a clue."

But it didn't. The machine was empty. There were two shelves of videotapes and DVDs, mostly kids' things. Cork stood looking at the clutter of the living room.

"Okay, Sherlock, I'm waiting," Parmer said.

"We need to visit Bodine's office at the airport. But before we do that, there's another stop I want to make."

The Rice Lake Police Department shared a building with the Fire Department. It was one-story, a couple of blocks off Main Street, situated under the town's water tower. Inside, Cork slid his business card through the slot beneath the glass of the contact window and said to the woman on the other side, "I'd like to speak with the chief."

She was nonuniform, dressed casually. She came to the window and took his card. "Just a moment." She returned to her desk, punched in a number on her phone, and spoke quietly. She hung up and said to Cork, "He'll be right with you."

The chief came out almost immediately. He was a stocky, solid man, mid-thirties, with a Scandinavian look to him—blue eyes, blond hair, a ruddy cast to his face. He wore gold wire rims.

"I'm Chief Amundsen," he said.

"Cork O'Connor. And this is my associate Hugh Parmer."

The chief shook their hands. "Let's go somewhere we can talk."

He led them to a small meeting room, and they all sat around a table.

"What can I do for you, Mr. O'Connor?"

"We're looking into the disappearance of a colleague, a man named Steve Stilwell. He might have dropped by a few days ago to pay a courtesy call himself."

"As a matter of fact, he did," the chief said. He folded his hands. His fingers were like thick bratwurst. "He told me he was working for

Becca Bodine. A couple of days later I got a call from Becca. She hadn't heard from him and was worried. Asked me to check into it."

"Did you?"

"I did as much as I was able. Becca told me that he'd registered at the Best Western here in town. I checked the hotel and found that he stayed for a single night and left the next day."

"Checked out?"

"He never actually stopped by the desk. Express checkout, you know how that works. According to the hotel people, he didn't leave anything behind. That's pretty much the extent of my investigation. Seemed like there was nothing here to warrant anything more. He still hasn't popped up?"

"Not yet."

"Well, nothing personal, O'Connor, but in my experience private dicks aren't necessarily the most reliable of businesspeople. Could be he's on a bender somewhere."

"Could be," Cork allowed.

"He was looking into that business with the missing plane last fall. Is that part of why you're here, too?"

"That's part of it. Becca told me you knew her husband."

"Small town. Pretty much everybody knows everybody here. I went to high school with Sandy."

"Was he a drinker?"

"Oh, yeah. Back in the day he could drink the rest of us under the table."

"But he stopped drinking, right?"

Amundsen shrugged. "Around here. But Sandy was gone a lot. Hard telling how a man behaves away from home."

"Ever arrest him in relation to his drinking?"

"No. He didn't have an arrest record of any kind here." He smiled. "Stilwell asked me the same thing."

"Did he ask anything else?"

"Yeah, what I thought of Sandy. And he also asked if there was any bad blood between Sandy and anyone around here."

"What did you tell him?"

"That I liked Sandy. He was good people. And that, as far as I know, nobody here had it in for him. Of course, Sandy was Chippewa, and some folks, well, they've got ideas about Indians."

"Anybody like that that you'd be able to put a name to?"

The chief made a brief show of thinking. "Nope, can't say that I can."

"Thanks, Chief."

"Welcome. What do you fellas plan on doing while you're here?"

"As much as possible, we're going to try to do exactly what Stilwell did."

"I'd appreciate you keeping me apprised."

"We'll do that," Cork promised.

TWENTY-SIX

Becca Bodine had called ahead, and when Cork arrived at the Rice Lake Regional Airport, he was expected. He showed ID at the contact counter for the airport's fixed base operator, or FBO, the primary charter company, clearly a much larger enterprise than Bodine's one-man operation. He was given the key code to get the Navigator through the security gate and into the hangar area. From the outside, the hangar was unimposing, simply a moderate structure of corrugated steel painted a dull tan. Inside, perhaps because it was empty, it felt enormous and abandoned, like a high school gym long after the last game of a losing season. Overhead, exposed girders supported fluorescent lights. Through dusty windows, the midday sun cast dun-colored rhomboids onto the bare concrete floor. Metal cabinets lined the walls, and there were stacks of cardboard boxes labeled to indicate supplies. The air was cool and smelled unpleasantly of engines and the fuel and lubricants of engines.

In a far corner, Sandy Bodine had established his simple office. There was a large desk of gray metal with an overhead work light and a rolling chair. On the desk sat a big tin can wrapped in orange construction paper decorated with a child's drawings. The can held pencils, pens, and a ruler. The desk was shoved against a wall where two photographs hung. One was a framed family portrait: Bodine, Becca, and their son. The other was a large poster of a prop jet suspended in blue sky with the green earth far below. To the left of the desk stood a metal bookcase whose shelves were filled with aeronautical publications and rolled maps. To the right was a file cabinet that was a twin to the one in Bodine's home office.

Cork handed Parmer the key ring. "I'm guessing that little key is for the file cabinet. See what you can find."

"And I'm looking for what?"

"Pull anything on the Canadian charter a couple of years ago. And of course anything on the Wyoming flight. Other than that, anything that strikes you as odd."

"Okay. What are you going to do?"

"I have an idea why Stilwell asked Becca Bodine about a VCR. I'm going to check it out."

Parmer headed to the file cabinet and Cork began a slow search of the hangar. He walked along the walls, inspecting the stacks of cardboard boxes, checking under shelves and behind cabinets. He was moving along the final wall when he found what he'd been hoping for—cable wire concealed behind one of the tall cabinets. The wire ran up the wall to an industrial clock and appeared, at first glance, to be the clock's power cord. Cork braced himself and shoved the cabinet away from the wall. The cord entered the cabinet through a dime-size hole drilled through the metal backing. The cabinet door was secured with a padlock.

"Hugh," he called across the empty hangar. "Toss me that key ring."

Parmer sent it sailing with a fine throw, and Cork snagged it midair. He quickly flipped through the keys until he found the one that fit the padlock. When he opened the cabinet door, he said, "Eureka."

"What is it?" Parmer called to him.

"Exactly what I suspected. A security camera, a time-lapse VCR, and tapes."

Parmer joined him. He had two file folders. "The Canadian charter. And the Wyoming flight," he said.

Cork checked the VCR for a tape. The machine was empty. He looked at the shelf above, which held a row of tape cassettes, each marked with the dates during which the recordings had been made.

Parmer scanned the hangar. "Where's the camera?"

"Disguised as the wall clock," Cork said. "The dates on these cassettes indicate that each tape was created over a considerable period.

It's a motion-sensitive security system. The clock camera only operates when it detects movement."

"There's no tape in the VCR," Parmer pointed out.

"Exactly," Cork said. "Bodine wouldn't have left without activating his security camera, so the question is what happened to the final security tape. My guess is that Stilwell is the answer. He took the tape and headed to the Bodines' house, where he knew he could find a VCR and a television to view what happened in the hangar the morning Bodine flew out."

"Why not do that here?"

"I don't know. Maybe he didn't feel safe here. With good reason apparently."

"Is that what got Stilwell killed?"

"Could be."

"Why? What was on the tape?"

"I'm not sure. But maybe it was an image of the man who killed Bodine. Maybe it even captured the killing."

"You think he was killed here?"

"The first stop on that Wyoming charter was at the Aurora Regional Airport. It makes sense that whoever flew the plane flew it from the beginning, from right here in Rice Lake. If they wanted to get Bodine out of the picture without being seen, this hangar would be a good place to do that. And if they were careless and that wall clock did a good job of disguising itself, they might have been captured on film doing whatever it is that they did here."

"A lot of speculation."

"Got a better thought?" When Parmer didn't offer him anything, Cork said, "Let me see those folders." He checked the information on the Wyoming flight. "No contract here either," he said.

"What about the Canadian charter?" Parmer asked.

Cork leafed through the documents in that folder but didn't find anything that raised a concern. "From what Bodine's wife told me, her husband was in a temporary financial bind. It's possible the Canadian charter had to do with something illegal, quick money. Smuggling would be a good guess. Cigarettes, maybe, which are a big black-market item because of the tax in Canada. But I'm seeing only this one flight, and that seems pretty small potatoes for the kind of murder we're talking about with the Wyoming charter. I think there's something bigger at stake." He handed Parmer the folders to put back, then he continued his search of the hangar, poking into cabinets that weren't locked, looking into tool chests, finding nothing that seemed of any help.

"What next?" Parmer asked.

"If Bodine was killed here, whoever killed him had to get onto the airfield. Let's have a talk with the people in the office."

Because it was a security issue, the FBO contact who'd given him the key code sent him to speak with Gage Williams, the airport manager.

Cork knocked on the manager's door, and a firm business voice on the other side instructed him to come in.

Gage, he discovered, was a woman. She sat at her desk and eyed him over her reading glasses. Before her on the desk lay blueprints. She wore a white blouse with its long sleeves rolled back to her elbows. "Yes?" she said.

Cork introduced himself and Parmer. Gage Williams took off her glasses and used them to point toward a couple of chairs.

"I heard you were coming. We seem to have a regular stream of PIs through here lately. Did Becca fire the other guy?"

"He's out of the picture."

She folded her hands on the blueprints. "What can I do for you?"

"You can help us figure out how a man who might have wanted Sandy Bodine dead could have gotten onto the airfield and into Bodine's hangar."

She didn't move for several seconds. "You're not kidding."

"Not at all." Cork explained to her everything that had brought him to his conclusion.

"That's a hell of a story," she said when he'd finished. "I've got to tell you, it's not easy to buy."

"Humor us for a moment. If a man wanted to kill Bodine and fly his plane out, how could he get onto the airfield? Could he simply sneak on?"

"That would be extremely difficult. Since 9/11 we've tightened things up pretty good. We have PIDS now."

"PIDS?" Parmer said.

"Perimeter intrusion detection system," Cork said.

"There are security cameras everywhere," Williams said. "They feed directly into the Barron County Sheriff's Department."

"How closely monitored are they?"

"That I can't answer. But really, it would be difficult to sneak onto the field without being spotted." She sat back and toyed with her glasses. "Unless."

"What?" Cork said.

"I'm not sure I should be encouraging you, because, like I said, your story sounds pretty crazy. But if I wanted to get onto the field without raising suspicion, I'd simply fly in."

"Explain that," Cork said.

"We're a small regional airport. We don't have a control tower. Planes can land here anytime, day or night. If they're small enough, we don't even log them in or charge a landing fee. Unless they want to tie down overnight, we don't even keep a record of them. Conceivably a small plane could land in the dead of night and take off without us noticing."

Cork liked the idea, but there was a problem. "No record would exist."

"Not technically. But if they taxied anywhere near the terminal here, one of our security cameras should have picked them up."

"Any way we could look at the security tapes from the night before Bodine's last flight?"

"Actually, we use disks now, but sure. Wait here."

She left the office, was gone a few minutes, and came back with a disk, which she inserted into her computer. "This should contain the time frame we're interested in."

She turned her monitor so that Cork and Parmer could see the image, too, and she began to scan quickly through what the security cameras had caught. It wasn't difficult finding what they wanted.

There was nothing to see except empty tarmac for almost the entire period. But at 3:45 A.M., a small plane touched down and taxied past the terminal toward the charter hangars. It disappeared for a few minutes, returned, taxied back to the runway, and took off.

Williams said, "Now let's see what happened when it disappeared from the terminal cameras." She worked the mouse and, with a couple of additional keystrokes, brought up a view of the charter hangars.

The video image confirmed all Cork's suspicions. The plane taxied to the hangar area and paused for a few moments. A solitary figure quickly exited from the passenger side and slipped into the shadow of Bodine's hangar. The plane turned back for its return to the tarmac.

"Son of a gun," Williams said. "You were right."

"Any way to ID that plane?" Cork asked.

"Sure." She backed up the image and froze it as the figure was disembarking. "There, see that number on the tail? That's the plane's registration. That's all we need." She accessed the Internet and went to the FAA's aircraft registry site. In a few more moments, she smiled broadly, tapped the monitor with her finger, and said, "Voilà."

TWENTY-SEVEN

They stood in the airport parking lot, eyeing the western horizon. A thick mass of poisonous-looking green cloud had completely swallowed the sun. A fierce wind had risen, and Cork could feel the energy of a storm about to descend.

"That sky looks pretty sick," he said. "Could be hail."

Parmer put his hand on the rented Navigator. "It would be a shame to have this beauty assaulted."

"Let's pull into Bodine's hangar and see what develops."

At the security gate, they keyed in the code again and headed for Bodine's hangar. After he'd unlocked them, Cork retracted the big doors and Parmer drove the Navigator inside. They stood at the entrance, looking out at the airstrip, which lay empty under the threatening sky. The wind howled at the hangar, and the roof rattled as if it were about to be peeled away. Dust and grit peppered the walls with a sound like a rain of BBs.

The plane that Gage Williams had identified was a Cessna 400, Wyoming registration, owned by a company named Geotech West, which listed an address in Casper.

"Geotech West," Cork said, as much to himself as to Parmer. "Who the hell is Geotech West?"

"Let's find out," Parmer said.

He went to the Navigator and took something from the briefcase in the backseat. When he returned, Cork saw that he was holding a BlackBerry.

"The world at my fingertips," Parmer said. "Let's see what the world has to say about Geotech West."

At that same moment, a deafening roar commenced around them. Outside, hail the diameter of nickels began to hit the pavement and bounce like spit on a griddle. The hammering on the hangar drowned out any hope of conversation. Lightning slashed across the sky above the airfield, and the whole scene became an ice-white tableau. In almost the same instant, an explosion of thunder made the concrete under Cork's feet quiver. Within a few minutes, hail completely covered the ground. Within five minutes, the hailstorm ended, as suddenly as it had begun. Rain followed, falling in sheets blown nearly horizontal by the wind.

Cork said, "Will that thing still work in this storm?"

"We'll see," Parmer said.

"While you do that, I'm going to have another look around."

As he had earlier, Cork prowled the interior perimeter of the hangar, looking more carefully this time in every chest and crate and cabinet and barrel. A lot of what he saw he couldn't identify, tools and technical plane parts mostly. Near Bodine's corner office, he lifted the lid on a metal barrel and found an enormous supply of cloth rags. He pulled out handfuls and dropped them on the floor, thinking there might be something hidden deep in the barrel, but he reached bottom without hitting the jackpot. He began picking up the rags and stuffing them back in, then he stopped. In his hand was a wad of rags that weren't at all clean.

"Hey, Cork," Parmer called. "You might want to take a look at this."

"And you might want to take a look at this," Cork called back.

They met in the middle of the hangar, Cork with the soiled rags in his hands and Parmer, in a way, with the world in his.

"Is that what I think it is?" Parmer asked, staring at the wadded rags.

"I'm pretty sure it's not strawberry jam."

"Christ, there's a lot of blood. Where'd you find those?"

"Stuffed in a barrel."

"What do you think?"

"It's possible, I suppose, that Bodine cut himself."

"Severed an artery is more like it."

"It could be that these were used to clean up after he was killed. Or after Stilwell was killed. Maybe to wipe the hangar floor." Cork nodded toward the BlackBerry cradled in Parmer's palm. "What did you find?"

Parmer held the tiny screen toward Cork so that he could see the Internet display. "Geotech West advertises itself as a mineral exploration outfit." Parmer used his stylus to access another screen. "Here it says it's a subsidiary of Longmont Venture Partners. If we bring up Longmont"—and he did—"you can see that it's a company with a number of holdings, all dealing with mining and mineral technology. Now"—and he manipulated the screen again—"Longmont is a division of Fortrell, Inc., which has diversified interests. It owns a number of other companies. Wireless Technologies, Prism Optical, Realm-McCrae Development, Sanderson Aggregate, Alloy and—"

"Wait," Cork said. "Go back. Did you say Realm-McCrae Development?"

"Yes."

"Realm-McCrae. I know that name." Cork thought a moment but couldn't get a solid hold on the slippery memory. "Damn, I'm sure I know that name."

"Let's look a little deeper," Parmer said, working the BlackBerry. "Current Realm-McCrae projects include a housing subdivision in . . . wait a minute. I'll bet this is it. Says here they're working with the Arapahos in Wyoming to build a big resort casino."

"That's it! There's our connection, Hugh."

"Why would these people want Sandy Bodine dead?"

"Maybe it wasn't Bodine who was the target."

"Who then?"

"I don't know."

Parmer's stomach let out a long, mean growl. "Look, Cork, I hate to get basic on you, but we haven't eaten all day. I could use some food. Could we discuss this over a good steak and some beer?"

"I don't see why not. I think we're finished here for the moment."

"What are you going to do with those bloody rags?"

"Hold on to them. I don't know that they prove anything in and of themselves, but I'm not going to leave them here."

"Is that tampering with evidence?"

"You want to risk them being gone when we come back?" Cork said. He found a paper bag and put the rags inside. He set the bag on the backseat of Parmer's Navigator. Parmer pulled out of the hangar and into the rain. Cork closed and locked the hangar door and dashed to the SUV.

They ended up at the restaurant of a local country club, a nice place called Turtleback. They were given a table next to a long row of windows that overlooked the golf course. Far beyond that, rising on the other side of Rice Lake, lay the Blue Hills.

"Why do they call them the Blue Hills?" Parmer asked their waitress, a friendly woman who was probably someone's grandmother.

"There's often a blue haze that hangs over them," the woman said.

"What causes the haze?"

"Got me." She smiled.

Cork ordered a Leinenkugel's Creamy Dark.

"Good beer?" Parmer asked.

"I'm partial to it. It's a local brew."

"I'll have one, too," Parmer said.

While they waited for their drinks to arrive, Cork stared out the window, which was streaked with rain. The golf course was empty, and the Blue Hills were a vague suggestion behind the blur of the downpour.

"So what are you thinking?" Parmer asked.

"I've been going over in my mind the passenger list for Bodine's charter."

"Who were they?"

"George LeDuc, tribal chair of the Iron Lake Ojibwe. Bob Tall Grass, chair of the RBC for the Northern Cheyenne—"

"RBC?"

"Reservation Business Committee. An organization responsible for bringing business to the rez and overseeing the operations. Many reservations have something like it. Scott No Day, who was also on the plane, was responsible for that for the Eastern Shoshone."

"Okay, who else?"

"Edgar Little Bear, tribal chairman for the Owl Creek Arapaho. Oliver Washington, who was a Northern Cheyenne and also an attorney. And, of course, Jo and the pilot."

"Where were they going?"

"Seattle. To the annual conference of the National Congress of American Indians."

"Was there a reason they were traveling together?"

"They were all part of a committee that was supposed to deliver a report, something about the feasibility of an intertribal agency that would regulate Indian gaming. They met in Casper to go over the presentation, which Jo had prepared for them. Gaming is a huge issue in the Indian community. For a lot of reservations, it's the promise of a cold drink of water at the end of a long economic drought. But it doesn't always pan out that way. And among Indians, as among whites, the issue of the morality of gambling is a hot one. There are strong voices on both sides."

"Economic relief versus spiritual corruption?"

"Not just spiritual. The real corruption that can come with a casino is well known and well documented. I think that was one of the concerns the committee was going to address."

"Any idea what the report said?"

"I got the feeling from Jo that it wasn't anything particularly controversial."

"Still, is it possible someone didn't want the report delivered?"

"I suppose. But, hell, it was just a report and probably some recommendations. The Indian community moves pretty slowly on everything. Seems unlikely the presentation was something you'd kill a whole plane full of people over."

Their waitress delivered their beers. There were two additional bottles of Leinenkugel's Dark on her tray.

"I appreciate that you think of me as a two-fisted drinker," Cork said, "but at the moment, one beer'll do me fine."

The waitress laughed. "These are for those gentlemen over there." She indicated two men at another table.

"I admire their taste," Cork said.

She bent down confidentially. "They asked me for a recommendation, something local. I got the idea from you." She winked at him and headed away to deliver the remaining two beers. When she returned, she took their order and hustled toward the kitchen.

Cork sat back in his chair and sipped from his bottle. "What do Geotech West, Longmont Venture Partners, Fortrell, Inc., and Realm-McCrae have to do with this?"

"Quite simply, development is a way to launder money."

"How?"

"You know those Russian dolls, the ones where one doll fits inside another, which fits inside another, and so on? It's a structure often used in this business to disguise the source of investment money. So Geotech is owned by Longmont, which along with Realm-McCrae is a subsidiary of Fortrell. I'm guessing that isn't the end of this little doll game, but if we were able to get to the end, we might find someone who'd rather not have it known he's investing in a casino. I know a lot of people who know people. Why don't I make some calls tonight, see what I can uncover?"

Cork took a long draw on his beer. He could smell barbecue from the kitchen, and it made his mouth water. He put his bottle down. "One of the things I'm still wondering is who set up the charter flight."

"Without Bodine's records, is there any way you could find out?"

"Maybe George LeDuc said something to his wife. It wouldn't hurt to ask."

Parmer looked toward the restaurant door. "Think we're in the clear?"

"What do you mean?"

"You were worried we'd been followed."

"I'm still worried," Cork said. "I'll be worried until I have all the answers and all the evidence and put it into the hands of a cop I trust."

"You could be worried for quite a while."

Cork shook his head. "It's always a question of finding a thread to tug, then things usually unravel quickly. And, Hugh, we've found our thread."

TWENTY-EIGHT

Rain still fell heavily as they pulled onto U.S. 53 and headed north through Wisconsin toward Duluth. The food had been good and the day had been long and Cork was tired. He figured Parmer had to be pretty beat himself, and he'd offered to drive. The tires rolled over wet pavement with a constant hiss, and the wipers swept across the glass with a hypnotic *slap, slap, slap*. To keep them both awake, Parmer talked about poker tournaments he'd played in. He was an entertaining raconteur, and despite the odds against, Cork stayed awake too.

They were nearing Superior when a car approached from behind and drew alongside to pass. The road had been mostly empty, and Cork glanced at the vehicle. Through the dark and the rain, it wasn't easy to see clearly. Even so, Cork thought he recognized the man in the passenger seat, one of the two men from Turtleback to whom the waitress had recommended and then delivered the Leinenkugel's Dark. The car slipped ahead of them, eased into their lane, and continued to pull away. Cork thought about mentioning it to Parmer, but his companion was deep into a story about a smoky backroom game in a Houston country club and Cork hated to interrupt. They approached a bridge over the Amnicon River. Parmer was saying, "This guy had a tell you could see from outer space."

Later, Cork would recall what occurred next in harsh detail, as if it had happened in an excruciating dream in which time flowed like chilled honey.

First came the report, sharp in the way of a gunshot, except that the source was Parmer's Navigator itself, from the undercarriage up front. Next, the Navigator veered right and the beam of the headlights blasted across the guardrail at the south end of the bridge. The vehicle struck and the guardrail exploded. The headlights tunneled into the vast black of empty air, then slowly, dreamily, arced downward and puddled against the raging brown of the rain-swollen river. The circle of light contracted as the Navigator plunged and then hit dead center, like an arrow trued on a bull's-eye. The impact triggered the air bags. The slug to Cork's face knocked him nearly unconscious. Vaguely, he felt the river slap the Navigator sideways and the current snatch it roughly and shove it downstream. He knew he was cold and he knew he was wet and even on the edge of unconsciousness he understood what that meant.

He fumbled with his seat restraint. When he'd freed himself, he turned to Parmer, who lay slumped to the side. The river continued to invade the compartment, and the water had reached their waists. Cork released Parmer's seat belt, wrapped his arms around the man, and pulled him to the driver's side. He locked Parmer in a cross-chest grip and reached for the door handle. At that same moment, the Navigator slammed into something and came to a sudden halt. Cork tried the door. It wouldn't budge. He realized the current had wedged the vehicle against a fallen pine, which blocked his exit.

Water foamed around his chest as he maneuvered Parmer and himself to the other side of the Navigator. He tried to open the passenger's door, but the press of the river was far too powerful. He positioned Parmer against the seat back, stretched his own legs across the man's body, and kicked at the door window. It was awkward and the effort was further complicated by the rising water, but at last the window broke outward. The river rushed in. Cork muscled past Parmer and through the window. He reached back, gripped his companion's shirt in both hands, and hauled Parmer from the vehicle. Immediately the river grabbed them.

Cork clutched a fistful of Parmer's shirt in one hand and used his other to grasp at the branches of the fallen pine. His hand found a hold, but the rage of water continued to pull on him. The branch served as a pivot, however, and the force of the current swung him around. He entered an eddy behind the breakwater formed by both the pine and the body of the Navigator, where the power of the river was significantly weakened. Cork's feet found bottom. He steadied himself and hoisted Parmer onto the trunk of the fallen pine. He climbed up beside his companion and looked back at the bridge. A vehicle stood parked at the shattered guardrail. The beam of a flashlight shot along the course of the river and found Cork and Parmer. It held on them a long moment.

"Hey, you all right down there?"

"Yeah."

"Hold tight, buddy. I got the state patrol on my cell. They're on their way."

Cork called Liz Burns from the emergency room of St. Mary's Hospital in Superior, Wisconsin, where the EMTs had brought him and Parmer.

"Hugh insisted he was fine," Cork said into the pay phone. "The EMTs and the officers were just as insistent that we both get checked out."

"You're okay?" Burns said. "Both of you?"

"Not even any broken bones. We were lucky. But we could use a lift."

"We'll be there in twenty minutes."

"Uh, Liz, we could also use some dry clothes. Do you have anything?"

"I'll find something."

She brought Becca Bodine with her, and she brought sweat suits. One set was turquoise, the other pink. Cork and Parmer did rock, paper, scissors. Cork won. Parmer wore pink. The sweat suits, though roomy for Burns, didn't fit either man well, and Cork was glad when they left the hospital and the odd stares behind.

They drove back to Burns's place on Park Point, and when they were all inside, Burns said, "Let me throw those wet clothes in the dryer."

Becca said, "And I could make coffee."

"Great, I'd take a cup," Parmer said.

"Then we need to talk," Burns said.

Cork ached all over. They'd given him Tylenol 3 at the ER, but that only dulled the pain. Parmer was moving gingerly, too.

"No business for old men, Hugh," Cork said and offered a thin smile.

A few minutes later, they sat in the living room, sipping coffee from mugs. The rain had subsided, but Cork could still hear the angry crash of waves beyond the dunes. It was a sound much more pleasant to his ears than the mad rush of water he'd encountered in the swollen Amnicon River.

Burns said, "It wasn't an accident, was it?"

"It was certainly supposed to look that way," Cork replied.

"What did you tell the police?"

"A tire blew and I lost control. When they haul the Navigator out of the river, we'll see if we can tell what really happened. My guess is an explosive charge detonated by a signal sent from the car that passed us."

"You told me and Becca yesterday that something like this might happen," Burns said.

"Do we want to talk about this here?" Becca asked. She swept her hand across the room, reminding them that the place could be bugged.

"Hell, I don't care if they're listening," Cork said. "My guess is that they already know what we found in Rice Lake. That's why they tried to take us out."

Burns bent forward. "What did you find at Rice Lake?"

Cork explained about the record of the Geotech West flight and the thread they'd followed to Longmont Venture Partners, Fortrell, Inc., Realm-McCrae, and the casino development in Wyoming.

Parmer said, "Before I lost my cell phone in the river, I managed to make some calls to people I know who are tracking down the principal players in Fortrell, Inc."

"I don't understand what any of this has to do with why they killed my husband," Becca said.

Cork put his mug on the coffee table and leaned toward her. "Becca, I'm almost certain it was about something else and Sandy was just one of the people who had to be eliminated for these bastards to get whatever it was they wanted."

"Christ," Burns said. "Collateral damage."

Becca cupped her hands around her mug as if she was cold. "What happened to the plane?"

"I suppose it could still have simply crashed in the storm," Burns said.

Cork shook his head. "I don't think so. They went to a lot of trouble to get their man at the controls. I think they never had any intention of that plane arriving in Seattle. I think they went somewhere else."

"Where?"

"I don't know."

The sound of the waves outside came through the windows with a *shush*, like a mother quieting a child.

"Does that mean," Becca said, so softly it was barely audible and so near to hope it was heartbreaking, "that they might not be dead?"

Cork glanced at Parmer, who looked tired beyond measure. "Becca," he began carefully, "we found something at the hangar today. It was a bunch of soiled rags stuffed in a barrel. I believe they'd been used to clean up a lot of blood. I'm telling you this so that you know everything we know. What exactly those rags mean, I can't say. But if I had to guess, it would be that Sandy was taken out of the picture in his hangar before his King Air ever left the ground. I think there was a videotape of the attack and Stilwell found it. That's why he was killed. This is all speculation, but it's what I think."

Becca's face was hard and her dark eyes sharp. "Once I knew it wasn't him on the tape, I knew in my heart he was dead."

Burns asked, "What about the others on the plane?"

"I don't know. But I can't imagine why the people we're dealing with would have kept them alive."

"We still come back to the question of what happened to them and to the plane," Parmer pointed out.

Cork said, "After the plane went missing, an old Arapaho named Will Pope claimed he'd had a vision. He said he saw an eagle glide to earth and land in a box, where it was covered by a white blanket. It's possible the vision was about the plane. We checked what seemed to be the most logical location based on the information he gave us, and we found nothing. I'm wondering if we interpreted his vision correctly."

"What do you mean?" Burns said.

"I'm not sure. But maybe if I talk to the right people, I might have a better idea."

"Where do you find these people?"

Cork picked up his mug and blew away the steam before he sipped. "Mostly in Wyoming."

Becca was staying in one of the guest rooms. Cork insisted that Hugh Parmer take the other. Burns brought out a set of sheets, a blanket, and a pillow, and made up a bed for Cork on the sofa. After the others had gone to their rooms, she spent some time in the bathroom, then came out to where Cork stood at one of the big windows that faced the lake. He'd turned out the lamp. The storm had long ago passed, and the moon had risen out of Superior, a gibbous moon bright enough to turn the sand dunes white as snow. The moonlight filled the living room with a luminous glow. Burns came and stood beside him. He could smell the good, clean fragrance of the soap she'd used to wash her face for the night. Her hair was long and brushed full and fell elegantly over her white robe. She reached into the pocket of her robe and brought out her final offering of the night.

Cork looked at the Guardian in her hand. It wasn't at all a large weapon, and it was attractive in a way, with a beautiful wood-grain grip and a barrel that reflected a ghostly silver light. He shook his head. "No thanks."

"If they've been listening, they might come for us all," she said.

"I don't think so."

"Why?"

"Because when I was at the ER, I called a bunch of people and told them my suspicions, and if anything were to happen here, there would be at least a dozen good folks keeping the fire of this investigation alive. Whoever's behind this, the one thing they don't want is to bring a lot of attention and heat down on themselves. They blew one opportunity tonight. I think the next one will be carefully thought out and far from here."

"And it will be you they target."

"Probably."

"Then shouldn't you be armed and ready?"

"Ready, yes."

She leaned her shoulder against the window glass and stared up into his face. "You were sheriff once. Didn't you carry a gun then?"

"I did."

"But something happened?"

"Yeah, something happened. I got tired of the weight."

She held out the Guardian. "It's so light you'll barely notice it."

"Not the kind of weight I was talking about."

She sighed and pocketed the firearm. "I know." She pushed gently away from the window. "I suppose I should go to bed."

Cork said, "If you want to stick around, it's fine by me. I'm too wired to sleep. And I wouldn't mind the company."

She stayed.

"You and Becca, friends long?" he asked.

"We go way back. We met when we were going to school in Madison. We remained in touch, remained friends. When the whole mess with Sandy came up, she asked for my help."

They were quiet for a while.

"Big house," Cork finally said.

"Big for just me, you mean."

"Nope. Big, period."

She laughed softly. "Sorry. It's a line I get sometimes. Men—or some men, I should say—seem to think there's something wrong with a woman liking to be alone."

"I figure it's something that depends a lot on what you're used to."

She thought about that. "Becca has a hard time being alone in her house in Rice Lake."

"Two places I get lonely," Cork said. "My wife had an office in our house. It's still hard to be in there sometimes."

"And the other?"

He shrugged. "The bed's too big. I still sleep on the half I've always slept on."

The talking died again. The only sound came from the waves breaking on the shore beyond the dunes.

"You loved her." It wasn't a question.

"That I did. And though it doesn't do me any good, I still do."

"You won't let yourself hope that she might still be alive?"

"It wouldn't make sense." He eyed the bone white dunes. "You should go to bed."

"You're right." She looked like she was going to say something more but just said, "Good night," then turned and walked away.

He stayed at the window. When he was sure he was alone, he said quietly, "And it would hurt too much."

TWENTY-NINE

After breakfast the next morning, Burns drove them into Duluth, and Parmer bought a BlackBerry to replace the one he'd lost to the river the night before. Then she took them to the airport, where Parmer rented another Navigator and they said their good-byes. Parmer took the wheel. They arrived in Aurora shortly before noon, and their first stop was the Tamarack County Sheriff's Office. Marsha Dross was one of the people Cork had called the night before from the emergency room.

"It's a fascinating story, Cork, but you understand that you have no proof of anything. Not a single shred of solid evidence."

"There's the videotape that shows the man in the bar in Casper wasn't really drinking."

"It's suspicious, of course, and it would probably be useful in the civil suits that have been filed against Bodine, but it proves nothing criminal. And why would anyone go to so much trouble? You still don't have a motive. Or bodies, for that matter."

"I believe I'll find the motive in Wyoming. Maybe the bodies will follow."

They sat in Dross's office, where the windows were open to the fresh breeze of the late spring day and to the coos of a couple of doves courting in the branches of the maple on the front lawn. Her desk was awash in budget documents, and Cork recognized the worn look on her face from dealing with an aspect of the job no sheriff enjoyed.

"What are you going to do when you get to Hot Springs?" she

went on. "You lay all this out, and there's not enough substance for the Owl Creek County authorities to do anything."

"That'll have to be their decision."

She laughed in a tired way and swept her hand over the documents on her desk. "I can tell you right now that if I were them and as strapped for money as we are here and as most sheriffs' departments tend to be, I wouldn't commit any resources based on your story."

"Doesn't matter. I'll do my own investigation without their help. I've done all right so far."

"Yeah, you almost got yourself killed." She sat back and folded her hands, and in the quiet all they could hear was the sound of the doves cooing. "What do you want from me, Cork?"

"Well, it relates in a way to your last comment. That we almost got ourselves killed."

"Okay." She looked at him, her face puzzled.

"If we don't come back, I'd be much obliged if you took up the flag, so to speak. Make sure the job gets finished."

She studied him. "And what about Stephen?"

"He'll want to help you. Let him do what he can."

"I mean, what *about* him? If you don't come back, he's an orphan."

"God and Henry Meloux willing, he'll also be a man. It will be something he'll have to deal with, and he will. He'll still have family."

She shook her head slowly. "You're really going to do this."

"I am."

She looked at Parmer. "You, too?"

"Call me crazy," Parmer said with a smile.

At Parmer's hotel, where Cork had parked his Bronco, the two men parted ways, with an understanding that they'd regroup no later than two o'clock. Cork went home to throw things into his suitcase, and then he drove to Henry Meloux's place.

He found the old Mide sitting near the fire ring beyond the rock outcropping at the end of Crow Point. Meloux had a small fire going, and into the flames he fed sprigs of sage and shavings of cedar. Walleye lay near, drowsing in the warm sun.

"*Anin*, Henry," Cork said, approaching.

"*Anin*, Corcoran O'Connor. Sit."

Cork sat on one of the cut sections of log placed around the fire ring.

"It is not yet finished," the Mide said.

"I didn't think it would be, Henry. He's doing okay, though, right?"

"How he is doing is in the hands of Kitchimanidoo. But his spirit is fine and strong and his desire is true. I would not worry, Corcoran O'Connor."

"Henry, there's something I need to ask you."

"Then ask."

"There is a man in Wyoming, an Arapaho. He's a spirit walker."

"I have heard of such men."

"He is also a man who drinks."

"Sometimes dreams are like knives. They wound. And for some dreamers alcohol helps the pain."

"He had a vision about the missing plane. We checked it, but it didn't pan out. I wrote it off as drunken nonsense. But now I'm wondering about that vision."

"Tell me."

Cork explained what Will Pope claimed to have seen.

The old Mide shook his head. "I cannot tell you about his vision. I do not know this man. You have met him, yes?"

"Yes."

"Then you should be able to answer your own question."

"I believed him, Henry. But when we didn't find Jo, I chalked it up to his drinking. Now I don't know. Maybe we simply misinterpreted the meaning."

"Another key without a lock."

Cork looked at him.

Meloux explained, "Stephen, too, had a vision that he has not yet understood."

"The white door," Cork said.

"You are being given much," the old man said. "The spirits are on your side. That is a good thing."

"Why don't the spirits just tell us things, Henry? How come they make it so hard?"

The old man laughed. "I think it is like this. The spirits shoot an arrow. It is past us before we can see it clearly. But if we follow, eventually we come to the place where it has lodged. And we realize the arrow is not important. What is important is the place it has guided us to."

"One more thing, Henry. Where I'm going, this place I might come to, it looks like it's going to be full of folks who'd prefer me dead."

"Ah," Meloux said and nodded. "You want me to return your firearms."

"No, that's not it. What I want is for you to help Stephen understand if I don't come back."

"What is there to understand? You have seen the road you must walk and you will walk it. Long ago, your own father walked a road out of your life. Did you understand?"

"Yes. But it hurt like hell."

"I did not say it would be easy for Stephen."

"*Migwech*, Henry."

"I have done nothing yet," the old Mide said. "Stay a bit and we will smoke and send to the spirits our wish that you return."

After he left Meloux, Cork drove a series of logging roads that took him eventually to Allouette, the main town on the Iron Lake Reservation. He pulled up in front of the Mocha Moose, the coffee shop owned by Sarah LeDuc, and went inside. The sound of Bill Miller's Indian flute came from the CD player on a shelf near the back. There weren't many customers, and Cork knew most of them. Normally he'd have received a good welcome, but there was a decidedly chilly current in the place that was blowing in his direction. Sarah stood behind the counter with her back to Cork.

"*Boozhoo*, Sarah," he said.

She turned with a smile of greeting on her face, but when she saw who it was, the smiled dropped like a shot bird.

"Could I talk to you for a minute?"

"I'm kind of busy right now," she said.

"It's important."

"Wouldn't have anything to do with you working for the woman whose husband killed George?"

Word had spread quickly. It didn't surprise him. On the rez telegraph, information seemed to move at the speed of light.

"Sarah, listen to me—"

"Look, not all of us are millionaires. The money from that lawsuit, it'll go a long way to helping us out since we don't have George."

"Sarah, will you just listen for a minute?"

"I don't understand you, Cork. Why would you help these people? Why would you want to hurt our case?"

"What if I could prove to you that Clinton Bodine wasn't drinking? What if I could prove to you that he wasn't even flying that plane when it disappeared?"

"I'd say you were a liar or a magician."

"Sarah, I'm almost certain he was killed before his plane took off to pick up George and Jo. He wasn't even on the plane. Or if he was, he was stuffed in the luggage compartment and in no condition to complain."

"You're serious?"

"Absolutely."

"So . . ." She squinted, trying to put together in a few seconds what had taken Cork a couple of days to understand. "So, what exactly is going on?"

"I don't know. I'm trying to find out, and maybe you can help."

"How?"

"Did George talk to you about the National Congress of American Indians in Seattle?"

"Of course. George talked to me about everything."

"He and Jo were working on a report that had to do with gaming regulations."

"Yeah, I read it."

"Was there anything remarkably controversial or threatening in the report?"

"Not at all. It came down to recommending an oversight group. George had pushed for it because he was concerned that if we didn't regulate ourselves the government would be more than willing to step in and do it for us. A couple of months ago some of the people organizing this year's congress contacted me and asked if George kept a copy of the report in his files. I found it and sent it along. It's supposed to be on the agenda this November."

"Jo told me that George asked her to fly with him to Seattle. Did he arrange for Bodine to fly them?"

She thought a moment. "I think it was one of the Wyoming people. But honestly, Cork, that was so long ago I couldn't say for sure."

"That's okay."

"But, you know," she said, "I believe it had some connection with powwows. I don't remember how exactly, just that George mentioned it."

Cork mulled it over. "Bodine's wife said he often flew groups to powwows around the country. It was a big part of his business."

"Does this help?"

"Everything we learn helps."

A thought came to her, and her face looked deeply troubled. "If Clinton Bodine wasn't flying that plane, who was?"

"That's one of the things I'm trying to find out. And I think I'm on the right track. Somebody tried to kill me yesterday."

"Cork, no!"

"Oh, yeah."

He told her what he'd been doing for the last forty-eight hours.

At the end, she looked stricken. "That poor woman. She lost her husband, too, and all these months I've been thinking such horrible things about him. I've been steeling myself for this lawsuit, trying not to see her as someone I should feel any pity for. But she's just like me, isn't she?"

"Pretty much. I think you'd like her if you got to know her."

She put both hands on the counter, and her dark eyes were aflame. "What can I do to help?"

Cork loved her for that, loved how quickly her ice had turned to fire. It was part of what George LeDuc had loved about her, too.

"If you think of anything, call me. Use my cell number." He gave her one of his cards. "I'm going to Wyoming today to ask some questions out there."

"You be careful."

"I will."

"And you'll let me know what you find out?"

"You can bank on it."

He turned to leave but was stopped by the fragile hope in Sarah's next words. "Cork, if what we believed isn't true, is it possible—"

He spun and cut her off. "No. They're dead, Sarah. That's the one thing in all this that is true. They're dead."

She nodded and looked down at the wood floor. Cork left her that way.

THIRTY

Cork stopped at the house and checked Jo's computer. He located the file that contained the report she'd prepared for the National Congress of American Indians. He scanned it quickly and could see nothing particularly threatening about it.

When he arrived at the Four Seasons, he found Parmer waiting. They took his rented Navigator and headed back to Duluth, where Parmer's private jet was being readied for their departure.

"I got a call while you were gone," Parmer said. "From the people I asked to look into Fortrell. We're heading into stormy weather here, Cork."

"We're already in it, Hugh. What about Fortrell?"

"The money for a lot of Fortrell's investments, and probably for the Realm-McCrae casino project, comes from loans secured from the Western Continental Bank of Denver. Western Continental is a legitimate investment bank, but it's also known to be a funnel for money from investors hiding behind the veil of foreign private banks. PBs they're called in financial circles. The chief value of PBs is the confidentiality of their services. They operate outside the constraints of banks in this country and are able to handle money for their clients with great secrecy. Because they're banks, they can move large amounts in ways that individuals can't. They're the perfect mechanism for laundering.

"As nearly as my people can tell, the money for the loan came from a PB in Aruba, the Antilles Investment Bank. There are a number of PBs that operate out of that island, and many are suspected of being favored by the mob. The Antilles Investment Bank is one of them."

"Okay, let me get this straight. You're telling me that, in the end, the money trail for building that casino leads back to organized crime?"

"I can't say for sure, but it certainly seems like a reasonable speculation."

"Doesn't anybody check on these things?"

Parmer shook his head. "There's so much development going on that unless something raises a red flag, nobody notices. Now a casino is probably a little different. It might get more scrutiny. But my guess is that all it would take to be certain nobody asks the wrong questions would be plenty of green delivered to the right hands. Happens all the time. And even if questions are raised, we go back to the beauty of the veil of the PB. Who's to say for certain where the money came from?"

"That might explain a lot," Cork said. "But it still doesn't explain why they wanted Bodine's plane to disappear."

"Maybe that report you told me about, the one Jo put together on Indians regulating gaming themselves?"

"I read it," Cork said. "Just a lot of recommendations. It didn't have any teeth. And Indians don't do things quickly, without a lot of consideration and talk. Even if there was general agreement that the recommendations were a good thing, it would take a very long time for anything to happen."

"Was there something really damning in the report, something that pointed fingers?"

Cork stared at the empty road ahead. "I don't think the report is what this is about. I don't think we've found the reason yet."

They landed in Casper at 4:00 P.M. Cork rented a Jeep Wrangler, and they drove to the address they had for Geotech West, which turned out to be in a strip mall at the edge of the city. The place was locked, and when he peered through the storefront window, Cork could see that the furnishings were Spartan at best. He went to the business next door, a print shop, and spoke to the middle-aged guy who came to the front counter and turned out to be the owner. He told them he never saw anybody in the Geotech West office. He figured it was some fool prospecting enterprise that had gone bust. There were a lot of those in Wyoming, he said.

Outside, Parmer said, "Like I told you, a doll inside another doll."

Next they drove to the hotel where Jo and the others had stayed the night before their plane vanished. At the front desk, Cork asked to speak with the manager, and when she appeared Cork handed her his business card.

"Of course I remember them," she said. "Because of what happened to them, they're hard to forget."

"They all stayed here?"

"Everyone on the plane, yes."

"Even the pilot?"

"Him, too, as I recall."

"Did you notice anything unusual while they were here?"

"No. Except one of them put up kind of a stink just before they left. He lost his glasses and claimed he was blind without them. He couldn't find them in his room. Had us looking in the trash and in laundry bags. Hell, everywhere."

"Did you find them?"

"No. Seems to me his wife promised she'd send him a pair when she got home."

"His wife?"

"Yes, she was here with him. She didn't go on the plane, though. Lucky for her."

"Do you remember which of the guests it was who lost his glasses?"

"I don't recall his name, but it was one of the older gentlemen."

"What do you recall about his wife?"

"Much younger."

"Does the name Edgar Little Bear ring a bell?"

"I really couldn't say. It's been such a long time. But it is funny that you're asking me these things. Felicia Gray from Channel Five asked me pretty much the same things."

"When was that?"

"A few weeks ago, shortly before she died."

"She's dead?"

"Oh, yeah. Big news in these parts. Her car went off the road in the badlands west of here."

"An accident?"

"I think she blew a front tire and lost control."

Cork checked in with the county sheriff's office and got the location of the accident. It was an hour west of Casper on the road to Hot Springs and easy to spot. The highway had been chiseled along a cliff face, and on the south side there was very little shoulder and a precipitous drop-off. A new section of guardrail had been put up to replace the portion damaged in the accident. Cork and Parmer stood on the edge looking down a steep slope that was punctuated with sharp rocks, prickly pear cactus, and squat clumps of sagebrush. At the bottom lay a dry wash that appeared to be full of dust as white as chalk. A huge boulder there was blackened along one side, evidence of fire.

"Wonder what she found that got her killed," Cork said.

"If we're lucky, we'll find it, too."

"And if we're luckier we won't end up down there afterward."

They checked in at the Excelsior Hotel in Hot Springs, then drove west. It was getting late. The sun had set behind the mountains ahead of them, but there was still plenty of light, and in the valley where Jon Rude had his ranch, the spring grass looked blue in the twilight. They turned onto the gravel drive and drove up to the house. Cork saw Rude's daughter, Anna, standing at the pasture fence, in deep communion with a horse on the other side. He and Parmer got out and walked to the girl.

"Hello, Anna. Remember me?"

She eyed him intently and nodded. "You're the man Daddy helped look for your wife."

"That's right."

"Did you find her?"

"No, I didn't."

She studied his face in the twilight. "Are you sad?" Her own face seemed prepared to be sad with him.

"Sometimes I am, Anna. But mostly I'm puzzled right now, and I need to talk to your father."

"He's in the back with my mom." She pointed toward the yard behind the house.

"Is this your horse?" Parmer asked the girl. The bay kept poking its nose between the slats of the fence to nuzzle Anna's hand.

"Yes. His name is Brownie."

"I have a horse, too," Parmer said. "Her name is Lullabye."

"Do you get to ride her?"

"Oh, yes. We ride a lot together."

"Me and Brownie do, too, but only when my mom or dad can come. I can't ride him alone."

"You will someday," Parmer said.

"When I'm bigger."

"When you're bigger," Parmer agreed with a serious nod.

They left Anna and Brownie at the fence and walked to the backyard. They found Jon and Diane Rude staking out the contours of a large garden. A power tiller stood silent but ready. Rude carried a hammer and a bundle of wooden stakes. Diane had a big ball of string. When Rude spotted Cork, he dropped his bundle of stakes and came striding across the lawn. "My God, Cork. What a surprise."

"Jon, this my friend Hugh Parmer. Hugh, Jon Rude. And the lovely vision with her hands full of string is his wife, Diane."

Parmer shook hands with the couple and offered pleasantries.

Rude hung the hammer through a loop on the utility belt he wore. "Why didn't you let us know you were coming?"

"Came up kind of quick, Jon," Cork said.

"Are you hungry?" Diane asked. "There's chicken and a good marinara sauce still warm in the kitchen."

"As a matter of fact, I could eat," Cork said. "Hugh, Diane's an extraordinary cook."

"Jon made dinner tonight," she said. "A man of many talents, my husband."

"Come on in," Rude said, waving them toward the house. "And while you eat, we can talk about what brings you back to our neck of the woods. Pleasure, I hope."

Cork said, "We'll talk."

Anna played in the living room with a bunch of her stuffed animals, carrying on her end of a lively conversation. In the dining room, over a plate of good food, Cork explained why he was there.

"Jesus," Rude said when he'd heard it all. He sat back. "Jesus." He looked from one man to the other. "You're serious?"

"Never more so," Cork said.

"You really believe that somebody posing as this Bodine flew the plane and landed it somewhere?"

"That's what I believe."

Diane poured Cork another cup of coffee. "Landed it where?" she asked.

"That's what I'm hoping your husband can tell me."

"Me?" Rude looked confused.

Cork spooned a little sugar into his coffee and stirred. "In Will Pope's vision, the eagle landed in a long box and was covered by a white blanket. We figured it to be Baby's Cradle. But what if it wasn't? What if we interpreted the vision wrong?"

"You really believed old Will?"

"I believed him."

"Truth is, so did I," Rude confessed.

"Okay, so you know this country from the air as well as any man, I'd guess. Where else could you land a plane?"

"There are a few private airstrips."

"Where would they be?"

"Let me get some maps."

"First say good night to your daughter," Diane told him. "I'm putting Anna to bed."

The girl came in and kissed her father. She said a cordial good night to Cork and Parmer, and then followed her mother to the back of the house.

For the next half hour, Rude guided the two men along the topography east of the Wyoming Rockies, where the land was a pastiche of rugged buttes, alkali flats, dry gulches, grassy hills, and broad river valleys full of agriculture. He marked the airstrips he knew of but acknowledged they were dealing with a huge area and he probably didn't know them all.

"How about this?" Cork suggested. "What if we drew a line created from two points? The first would be where the plane dropped off radar and the second where those snowmobilers reported hearing it fly overhead. We extend the line east and take a look at what the nearest strips along it would be."

"As good as anything," Rude agreed.

When they'd done this, they found the estimated line of flight would have taken the plane southeast of the Washakie Wilderness, well north of the Owl Creek Reservation and the town of Hot Springs, across the badlands south of the Bighorns, and, if it could have flown that far, well into the empty grasslands of Thunder Basin. There were three private airstrips that Rude had marked near enough to this line to make them of interest.

"Okay. Those are the airstrips we consider checking. Where else could that plane have landed?"

"For a safe landing with a turboprop like a King Air, you'd need a hard, flat surface at least twelve hundred feet long."

"Any salt flats around here that might work?"

"No, but we've got some alkali flats east of Shoshoni that might fill the bill." He put his finger on a spot well to the south of the line they'd drawn on the map.

Cork shook his head. "Doesn't feel right. Too far to fly. What's the land up here like?" He tapped the map east of the Washakie Wilderness.

"Some ranchland. Some gas and oil development. But if there's a flat enough stretch with few enough rocks to land a King Air safely, I don't know it."

"What if they turned north?"

"Meeteetse and Cody up that way. Comparatively speaking, lots of folks."

"South?"

"The Owl Creek Reservation. And almost no people to speak of."

"Any private landing strips?"

"Only one that I know of. Belongs to Lame Nightwind."

Cork saw the connection immediately and sat back. "Jesus."

In that same moment, Rude had the same realization. His eyes narrowed in dark understanding, and he said, "Your Indian pilot."

THIRTY-ONE

Let's not rush to judgment," Cork cautioned. In his years as a cop, he'd seen often enough the mess that could result from leaping to conclusions.

"But it fits," Rude said.

"Okay, what's his motive?"

"Whoa, hold on a moment," Parmer said. "Who's this Nightwind?"

"The pilot who guided us into the mountains when we were looking for Jo's plane," Cork said. "He's Arapaho."

"What's he like? Is he a man who could do this kind of thing?"

"He seemed decent enough when he helped us search Baby's Cradle," Cork said and looked to Rude.

Rude sat back and considered. "Lame's got secrets, no doubt about it, but then who doesn't? He was gone for a lot of years. People say that he's been all over the world. Rumors have him as CIA or Special Forces. Some folks believe he was involved with the drug cartels. Others say the mob. Or smuggling or a mercenary. Lame never talks about his past, so who knows? Depending on what you believe, he's either Robin Hood or the bogeyman."

"What's the bogeyman side?" Parmer asked.

"We had a pretty bad drug problem a few years ago," Rude said. "When Ellyn Grant came back, the problem was huge. Mexican dealers had established themselves on the rez by marrying Arapaho women, and they used the rez as a depot to distribute every illegal substance under the sun. We didn't have the resources to fight back. Hell, nobody had jobs, and a lot of Arapaho got sucked into dealing because the money was good. Those who weren't dealing were getting high on the merchandise. Not much Andy No Voice or the DEA could do about it because it was a family thing and nobody would talk. Ellyn took on the drug dealers and she won, but probably she couldn't have done it without Lame Nightwind. See, what happened was the Mexican dealers simply started disappearing. Here one day, gone the next, one by one, and those that left never came back. It's possible they returned to where they came from, but that's not what most people on the rez think. Popular speculation is that Nightwind was turning them into coyote food somewhere out in the vast emptiness of the rez where no one would ever find their bones. The authorities didn't go looking for them and the dealers who didn't just disappear got so spooked they cut and ran."

"So you think he's quite capable of killing?"

"He can be dangerous, I'm sure of that, but I don't think of him as a bad man. As far as killing goes, I'd guess he's plenty capable provided the reason is compelling enough."

"So what would his motive have been?" Cork asked.

Parmer said, "We've already figured this is about the Yellowstone casino, haven't we?"

"I can suggest a motive."

Cork turned and found Diane standing at his back. She'd come in silently from putting Anna to bed. How long she'd been standing there he couldn't say.

"What motive?" he said.

"Love." She walked to the table and stood beside her husband with her hand affectionately on his shoulder. "Lame Nightwind is in love with Ellyn Grant."

Cork's eyes jumped from Diane to her husband. "True?"

Rude shrugged. "Gossip."

"I volunteer two days a week at the Singing Water Shelter in Red Hawk," Diane said. "According to the women there, Lame has always been in love with Ellyn, all the way back to when they were kids."

"Is she in love with him?" Cork asked.

"I don't know. But her husband was a man nearly old enough

to be her grandfather, so if not love, maybe something more physical."

Rude said, "I suppose there could be something between her and Nightwind, though I've never seen it."

"This is a big, empty territory, Jon," Diane pointed out. "If you were careful, it wouldn't be hard to carry on an affair without being observed."

Rude glanced up at his wife. "You seem to have given this a lot of thought. Should I be worried?"

She laughed. "Be afraid. Be very afraid."

Rude shook his head. "Grant and Nightwind? I don't know."

"Men can be dense." Diane patted his head affectionately.

"Even if there's something between them," Rude went on, "I'd say he's second in her affection, well behind the Arapaho people. She really does see herself as a kind of savior here."

"How do you mean?" Cork asked.

"After she took care of the drug situation, she wanted to tackle the poverty of the rez. Edgar Little Bear argued for opening the land to the oil and gas companies. Hell, they've been eyeing the Arapaho holdings for years. Ellyn was opposed. Not just opposed, she was furious. She was sure the mineral exploration would destroy the land. When she couldn't get Little Bear to budge, she married him and moved him in ways that words couldn't. That's how she got him behind the Blue Sky Casino."

"Sacrificed herself for the sake of the Arapaho, is that what you're saying?"

"Little Bear wasn't exactly a prize catch. We all respected him enormously, but like Diane said, he was one pretty tough old piece of jerky."

"And his breath could have knocked over a buffalo," Diane added.

"Everyone on the rez understood what she was doing, probably even Edgar," Rude said. "He knew he was getting himself a hell of a bargain."

"So Nightwind loves Ellyn Grant, and maybe he'd do anything for her. And Ellyn Grant loves the Arapaho and would do anything for them. How does the disappearance of the charter help either of them?" Cork asked.

They lapsed into another thoughtful silence. Finally Rude said, "The Gateway Grand Casino up at Yellowstone."

"How?"

"Edgar Little Bear didn't like the idea of the casino at all. A few weeks before he disappeared, I went to a meeting of the tribal council where they discussed the Yellowstone plan. Little Bear asked me to be there and to talk to the council about my gambling problem. After I spoke, he told the council he knew a lot of other people with the same problem, white and Indian. He was afraid the casino was damaging the spirit of the Owl Creek Arapaho. He thought a bigger operation would only create a bigger problem. He pointed out that the Blue Sky Casino wasn't exactly bringing in the flood of revenue Ellyn had promised, and he was afraid that this project, if it failed, it would ruin the reservation."

"How did Ellyn respond?"

"With all kinds of charts and graphs and projections that promised we'd end up richer than God."

"Sounds persuasive."

"It was. But you didn't know Edgar Little Bear. He was a great presence. People looked up to him. The council listened. Their big concern was the money. And Little Bear offered a solution. He proposed once again that the Arapaho begin talking with the oil and gas interests."

"How did that go over?"

"The council was willing to consider it, but Ellyn hit the warpath. Which didn't seem to bother Little Bear, so I figured they'd already discussed this between them. She argued that the companies would rape the land, but Little Bear was sure that, with proper oversight, the Arapaho could make sure that didn't happen. He talked about available new technology and a new sensitivity to the environment. I don't know about the Ojibwe, Cork, but the Arapaho consider things long and carefully before making any decisions. The plane disappeared before the council took up discussion again. When they did and the conversation finally ended many weeks later, Ellyn Grant had persuaded the council to support the Gateway Grand Casino."

"Which might not have happened if Little Bear had been around?" Cork said.

"Exactly."

Parmer said, "Maybe it's not one or the other. Maybe it's both love and politics. With Little Bear out of the picture, the way is clear for Nightwind and Grant to proceed with their relationship and for the casino project to go forward."

"But why such a complicated plan to get rid of Little Bear?" Cork said.

"Because if Edgar had just disappeared, everyone would have looked immediately at Lame Nightwind and Ellyn Grant, and Ellyn would have lost all her credibility to lead," Rude said. "But if it's the weather that was responsible and a whole plane full of people disappeared along with him, then nobody suspects a thing."

"It works," Cork agreed. "In theory. But we still have no proof. If we could just tie Nightwind to the missing plane."

"I've been thinking about that," Rude said. "I've been thinking about Will Pope's vision. He saw the eagle descend from the sky and glide into a box, where it was covered with a white blanket, right? What if the box was an airplane hangar and the white blanket was the snow on the roof?"

"Does Nightwind have a hangar along with his private airstrip?" Cork asked.

Rude smiled. "He does indeed."

"Can you draw me a map that'll take me there?"

"I'll take you there myself."

"No, from this point on you stay clear of us. Things could get difficult, Jon."

"That doesn't worry me."

Cork said, "Maybe not, but I'll bet Diane doesn't like the idea."

Rude looked up at his wife, who said, "If Cork really needs you, I won't stand in your way. But I'd prefer to know you're safe. I'd like

Anna to grow up with a father." She didn't smile, and Cork understood that everything she said was true.

Rude spent a long moment weighing his response, then gave a nod. "All right."

When they returned to their hotel, the desk clerk signaled to them as they passed. She was a woman of Indian descent, India of the subcontinent. She wore a smart blue suit and had an ornamental spot in the middle of her forehead. She smiled and handed Cork a note.

"The sheriff was here earlier. He asked me to give this to you."

"Thank you." Cork opened the note. It said, "Call me. Kosmo." He'd written both his office phone and his cell phone number.

Upstairs in the room that, for safety's sake, he and Parmer had decided to share, Cork called the Owl Creek County sheriff. Because it was late, he tried the cell phone first.

"Kosmo."

From the background sound, the harsh music of casino slots, Cork knew where the man was.

"This is Cork O'Connor."

"Heard you were in town. I'd like to have a talk with you first thing in the morning, O'Connor."

"It'll have to be early, Sheriff. I've got a full day planned."

"Make it seven. My office."

"I'll be there."

When Cork ended the call, Parmer said, "Well?"

"We've been summoned."

"What do you think?"

"I don't know. Tomorrow will tell. Been a long day. Let's get some sleep."

"Hang on. Something I want you to see." Parmer hefted his suitcase onto his bed and opened it. He dug under some of the clothing and drew out a large handgun, a Ruger Blackhawk.

"Four seventy-five caliber?" Cork asked.

"Yep."

"That's a substantial piece, Hugh. Could bring down an elephant. Planning on hunting while you're here?"

"I figure it'll stop any critter, elephant or otherwise, intent on doing us harm."

"Got a permit?"

"Wouldn't be without one. I also have a permit for this." He reached back into his suitcase and drew out a slightly smaller firearm, an S & W Sigma 18. He held it out, offering.

Cork shook his head.

With a shrug, Parmer put the gun back. "It'll be here if you decide you want it."

Cork laughed. "I honestly don't believe they'll break down our door during the night. If they're going to jump us, they'll do it in the middle of nowhere."

"Lot of nowhere out here. And won't it be a good thing that I have a gun that'll bring down an elephant?"

Cork said, "I'm going out for some air. I'll be careful to watch for elephants."

He left the room and walked to the courtyard, where the little pool was filled with water from the hot springs. He stared up at the clear black sky and the stars, and thought about Stephen, who was alone in the deep Minnesota woods, staring up at the same sky. He drove out of his heart any worry about his son. Stephen had spent much of his life in the forest, and he understood its ways. He was in the keeping of the spirits of that land and under the watchful eye of Henry Meloux. Cork's only concern was whether Stephen would be granted the vision he sought. And over that, no man had control.

The night was cool but still much warmer than any had been when he'd stood there months earlier during his first search for the missing plane. Those cold nights he'd held desperately to hope. What he held to now was something very different, a resolve like a hard fist in his heart. After months of torturing himself, he'd finally stopped re-creating in his mind the morning of Jo's disappearance, which he'd accepted as the morning of her death. Then Liz Burns and Becca Bodine had brought him the videotape. And now he understood that much of what he'd imagined, particularly the ending, was untrue. There probably had been no problem with turbulence, no sudden tilting of the wings, no long, irrevocable slide toward earth. What had been the true end for Jo? The kiss of a gun barrel against the back of her head? Did she know what was coming? Oh Christ, did she know?

Alone in the courtyard under the black sky, Cork stared down at his empty right hand and closed it slowly until it was a rock of bone and flesh.

THIRTY-TWO

The next morning at seven sharp, Cork and Parmer stood at the public contact window of the Owl Creek County Sheriff's Office. Dewey Quinn was on the desk and buzzed them through the security door. He left his chair and greeted Cork with an enthusiastic handshake.

"The sheriff told me you were in town. Good to see you."

"Dewey, this is a friend of mine, Hugh Parmer. Hugh, Dewey Quinn."

"A pleasure," the deputy said. He looked at Cork questioningly. "Here for . . . ?"

"Just here, Dewey. It's been a while."

"And the snow's starting to melt in the high country," Quinn said. "I don't want to discourage you, Cork, but it'll be a while before enough of it's gone to expose the plane."

"Thanks, Dewey. I'll keep that in mind."

"The sheriff's expecting you. He told me to send you right in."

Sheriff Kosmo stood at a window, his back to the door, which was open. Cork stepped inside, Parmer behind him. Kosmo had his hands clasped against the small of his back. He seemed intent on what lay beyond the window glass.

"Sheriff?" Cork said.

Kosmo didn't turn. He said, "Have a seat, gentlemen."

Two chairs with shiny metal frames and orange plastic seats and backs had been set before the desk. Cork took one and Parmer the other.

"Tell me why you're here," Kosmo said.

"Because you asked me," Cork replied.

Kosmo turned to them. He looked like a man who hadn't slept in a month. Bags of flesh hung under his eyes. His face was waxen and his lids heavy. A tall man, he looked down at them. "No, tell me why you and Mr. Parmer are here in my county."

"I'm searching for answers to a few questions that have come up lately."

"What questions?"

"About the plane that went missing with my wife aboard."

"Until we locate it, we all have questions."

"When do you expect that will be?"

The sheriff gave a moment's thought. "When the snow in the high country has melted sufficiently."

"I don't think you'll find it," Cork said.

"Any particular reason?"

"I don't think it's in the high country."

That seemed to catch Kosmo by surprise. His brows lifted, and a little energy came into his eyes. "Oh? Where do you think it is?"

"That's one of the questions I'm here to answer."

The sheriff walked to his own chair and sat down. He folded his hands on his desk. "What makes you think it's not in the mountains?"

"A PI name of Stilwell came here a couple of weeks ago. Probably checked in with you. A courtesy call."

"What of it?"

"He's gone missing."

"Well, I can pretty much say for certain he left this county in one piece."

"What about Felicia Gray?"

"What about her?"

"She was asking questions about the plane crash, too. And she ended up dead in a gulch."

"That was an accident."

"Funny, as soon as I started asking questions about the missing plane, I had the same kind of accident. Only I was luckier than Ms. Gray."

Kosmo sat back and gave him a long, dark, weary look. "Tell me straight what's going on here."

Cork laid it out for him: the mob connection, the money laundering, the possibility that Ellyn Grant was complicit in it all, including
the missing charter. He didn't tell Kosmo everything. Not wanting to
show every card he held, he said nothing about his suspicion that
Nightwind was the pilot or about what he suspected was the relationship between Nightwind and Grant.

Kosmo listened without interrupting. At the end, he took a breath
that sounded like a bull's snort and said, "You believe this?"

"Give me another read," Cork countered.

Kosmo slid his rolling chair back, stood up, and returned to the
window. Through the glass panes, Cork could see the main street of
Hot Springs, its storefronts and businesses, mostly old buildings that
had started as one enterprise and now housed another. It was clearly a
town looking for a way to survive.

"Let me explain something, O'Connor. For a long time, Hot
Springs had a lot of life in it. Folks used to come for the waters, stay
awhile, spend money. It was a destination. Now? Hell, everybody in
the United States has got a hot tub in their backyard full of water that
doesn't stink. No reason to come to Hot Springs anymore. Last couple
of decades, things have been hard for folks around here. White *and*
Arapaho."

"My guess is that they've always been harder for the Arapaho."

"Maybe so. But that casino gets built up near Yellowstone, it's
going to bring a lot of traffic through Hot Springs wouldn't otherwise
come this way. People'll stop here for the waters and for the Blue Sky
Casino." He looked over his shoulder at Cork. "You got any idea the
revenue that could bring into this county?"

"Some. We've got a casino in my county back home."

"Tell me something. What if your casino shut down?"

"Who says we're here to shut down the Arapaho casino?"

"I'm looking at the larger picture, O'Connor, the total fallout."

"You make it sound like we intend to detonate a nuclear device."

"Economically, the effect could be the same."

"You're a lawman, Sheriff. Shouldn't you be concerned about the
law?"

"My concern is the well-being of Owl Creek County. Let me tell you something else. We had us a drug problem here a while back. Significant problem, centered out on the reservation. Bunch of Mexican drug dealers married Arapaho women, began using the reservation as a base for their operation. Us, state drug task force, DEA, none of us could break it up because none of the Arapaho would talk. Family business, you know. And, hell, lot of those folks out there are dirt poor, out of work. The drug money was pretty good. Know who took 'em on and beat 'em? Ellyn Grant. Did it by offering hope mostly, a different kind of hope than the drug money and all the evil goes along with that. Stood up at great personal risk. That woman can be a pain in the ass, sure, and we don't always see eye to eye, but there's much about her to admire.

"Now, I'm not saying I don't understand your motive in coming here. It's a crazy story you tell, but you obviously believe there may be some truth to it, so I get how you must feel. What I'd like is for you and me to reach an agreement. While you're in my county, I expect an open exchange of information. Whatever you need from me or my people, you've got it. In return, I want to know where you're going, where you've been, and what you've found. Fair enough?"

"All right."

"What's your itinerary for today?"

"Sightseeing in general."

"Sightseeing? You've got to do better than that, O'Connor."

"Best I can do right now. Is that all, Sheriff?"

Kosmo looked at him a long time, dark and disappointed. "I'll be watching you, O'Connor."

"I'm sure you will, Sheriff."

Cork stood, turned with Parmer, and they left. He stopped to talk with Quinn at the contact desk.

"You remember that TV journalist who died in a car wreck a few weeks ago, Dewey? Felicia Gray?"

"Of course. A real tragedy, that."

"She was out here just before the accident, is that right?"

"Yeah. But she was out here a lot. Did a number of stories about the Arapaho and the casino. Always digging. I heard she wanted a job in an important television market. Denver, place like that. Maybe she thought if she came up with something big, it would be her ticket out. Believe me, I understand."

"Who investigated the accident?"

"We did. It happened just inside our county line."

"You find anything unusual?"

"No. Pretty clear her front tire blew. Just bad luck it happened on a curve."

"Yeah. Bad luck. Thanks, Dewey."

"Sure. Going to stick around and wait for the snow to melt?"

"We're going to stick around," Cork said.

Outside, Parmer asked, "Do you really intend to keep your promise to the sheriff?"

"About as much as he intends to keep his promise to me."

They drove north out of Hot Springs on the highway toward Cody. Ten miles out of town, they turned west onto Horseshoe Creek Trail, a dirt road that followed a thread of water toward the distant Absarokas. The route that Rude had carefully laid out for them would take them through the north part of the Owl Creek Reservation, then southwest to their destination, a total distance of seventy miles over dirt tracks that could hardly be called roads and that, Rude had warned them, were often barely navigable.

Cork had been born and raised in Tamarack County. To him, the place he lived was alive with energy—the dance of sun off water, the song of trees in wind, the electricity of a forest just before a storm—and everywhere he looked there was only beauty. What he'd seen of the Owl Creek Reservation felt to him blasted and barren, and he wondered at the deep love the Arapaho held for the land they called home. There was a certain desolate splendor he could understand. The long ridges and buttes sculpted of red rock, the yellow sand, the pale green sage and spiked cactus, the bruised mountains looming against the iridescent sky. To be alone in such a place could, he understood, help you to an awareness that you were in the heart of a great spirit. It could also, if you were ill-prepared, scare you to death and probably kill you. It seemed a land impossible to love.

Two miles off the highway, they crossed an old wood bridge over the creek, and after that the road was rough and the going slow. Cork often kept the Wrangler to a crawl as he maneuvered up and down tiers of bare stone or around boulders strewn along the bed of a dry wash.

"You're from the West," he said to Parmer. "What's the difference between a gulch, a wash, and a draw?"

Parmer said, "A wash has water in it more often than a gulch or a draw. A draw can be a temporary situation and not so pronounced. A gulch has been around and will be around for a while. It's deeper than the other two. That help?"

"Is that true or just Texas bullshit?"

"Made it up on the spur of the moment, but damned if it doesn't feel right to me. Rattlesnake." Parmer pointed toward a coil on a flat sun-blasted rock to the right ahead.

"How do you know it's a rattler?"

"Check out the pattern of its skin. Diamondback."

As they approached, the snake uncoiled and vanished on the far side of the rock.

"Hard country," Cork said.

"My kind of country," Parmer said. "Reminds me of West Texas. The beauty of empty places."

They found the connection that Rude had marked on the map, another road as desolate as the one they'd just traveled, heading toward Red Hawk, which was thirty miles to the south. Rude had given them this circuitous route at Cork's request. Cork didn't want anyone following where they were headed that morning. The new road was a little easier and led across low, barren hills. Small trees sometimes greened the banks of creeks where the snowmelt from the Absarokas ran. After twenty miles, they turned west onto another dirt track, rumbled over a cattle guard, and shot through a gap in an endless line of barbed-wire fencing. A sign affixed to a fence post at the side of the road read: NIGHT FLYING RANCH. NO TRESPASSING. They were now on land owned by Lame Nightwind.

They drove another half hour toward the mountains, passing cattle grazing on the low, distant hills. They climbed a rise among the foothills of the Absarokas, which were spotted with lodgepole pines. At the top of the rise, they looked down on the house and outbuildings of Nightwind's ranch.

Cork killed the engine and reached to the backseat for a knapsack he'd packed that morning. He pulled out a pair of field glasses and got out of the Jeep. Parmer joined him. For the next couple of minutes, Cork scanned the ranch compound. There were four large structures: the ranch house; a long, low building near it that, from the wide doors, he took to be a garage; the barn with its corral; and another building so close to the barn that, without binoculars, Cork might have been fooled into thinking they were both part of a single construction. The area around the ranch house wasn't landscaped. It had been left in its natural state. The architecture of the house, which was built of wood and rock, made the structure seem formed from the ground on which it stood. The garage was of the same design. The barn and the other outbuilding were the same red as the desert cliffs. Hay, rolled into round bales big as hippos, lay stacked against the north wall of the barn. Enclosed by a rail fence was a large pasture where several horses grazed. The pasture grass was being irrigated by a large impact sprinkler that flung out powerful bursts of water.

Cork swung the binoculars to the east. Through a trough between two hills the gray tarmac of Nightwind's airstrip was visible. He handed the glasses to Parmer, who did his own scan of the scene.

"I don't see anybody," Parmer said.

"Inside maybe." Cork spotted something to his right. "Give me the glasses." Cork took a look at a thread of smoke rising from behind a long arm of exposed rock nestled against the side of the hill a quarter mile west of the ranch compound.

"What is it?" Parmer said.

"A small cabin. Smoke's coming from a chimney. I can't see much."

"Nightwind?"

"I don't know."

"What now?" Parmer asked.

"We announce our presence, or we have a look at the airstrip and hangar first."

"If we let Nightwind know we're here, we might never get a look at what's in that hangar."

"My sentiments exactly."

Cork turned the Jeep around and headed back down the rise. When they were well out of sight of the ranch compound, he struck east toward the hills that hid the airstrip. After ten minutes of careful maneuvering over rugged open ground, he parked in front of the hangar that had been built beside the strip. A steady breeze swept along the face of the foothills. The wind sock attached to the top of a pole planted at the tarmac's edge pointed south.

They left the Wrangler and walked to the hangar door. Their shadows slid up the siding like the rattlesnake that had slithered off the rock that morning. Cork tried the door. It was locked. There were windows, but they were covered with dust, and when he wiped the glass he couldn't see any better what was hidden inside. Parmer had separated from him and disappeared around the far end of the hangar.

"Over here," Cork heard him shout.

He found Parmer holding a windowpane that was tilted open.

"You find it like that?" Cork asked.

"No, but it was unlocked. Mind if I go first?"

Cork held the window while Parmer climbed inside, then Parmer did the same for Cork. The hangar sheltered two planes. One was the yellow Piper Super Cub that Nightwind had flown during the search for Jo. The other wasn't Sandy Bodine's missing Beechcraft King Air, but it was a single engine.

"If that's a Cessna Four Hundred, we're in business," Parmer said.

Cork felt every muscle draw taut as they skirted the Piper Cub and approached the other plane. Cork wasn't familiar with aircraft, and it wasn't until he saw the word *Beechcraft* on the tail that he realized it was a dead end.

"Damn," Parmer said. "I suppose it was too much to hope for."

They did a brief search of the hangar and found maintenance records and a flight log, which showed a lot of activity, but none of it to Wisconsin.

"What now?" Parmer asked.

"Now we go up to the house and announce ourselves to Night-wind."

"And what? Ask him what he did with the plane and the people on it?"

"Maybe. Maybe we bluff him a little and see if we can get a feel for the cards he's holding."

"One gambler to another, that's a risky strategy unless you know your opponent."

"Got a better suggestion?"

Parmer said, "Your game. You deal the cards."

They exited the way they'd entered. As they rounded the corner of the hangar to return to their Jeep, they were confronted by a lanky man with a rifle. He was Indian, Arapaho, Cork guessed. Maybe sixty. He wore scuffed cowboy boots, jeans, a denim work shirt, and a beat-up brown cowboy hat. His face was deep in the shadow of the hat brim, but his dark eyes were clearly visible and clearly hostile.

"You take another step, I'll have to shoot," he said. "Put those hands on top of your heads."

When they'd obeyed, he pulled a walkie-talkie from a holder on his belt and spoke into it.

"Nick, you there?"

"Yes."

"Bring the pickup down. I've bagged the coyotes. I think we ought to kill 'em and skin 'em."

Those hard eyes stared from beneath the brim of the hat, and Cork understood that the man wasn't kidding.

THIRTY-THREE

He told them to sit with their hands clasped on top of their heads. They sat on the ground in the sun and squinted up at him.

"Who are you?" Cork asked.

"I work for Lame Nightwind."

"Where's Nightwind?"

"Gone."

"We were looking for him."

"People who are looking for him don't sneak in the back way."

"We were lost," Cork said.

"And that's why you crawled through the window into his hangar, cuz you were lost?"

Cork gave it a moment, then said, "Any chance you'd believe me if I said yes?"

The hardness of the eyes seemed blunted for an instant, and Cork thought the man might actually laugh. Instead he said, "You just sit tight and we'll see what's what."

"Worked for Nightwind long?" Cork asked.

"Been breaking and entering long?" the man shot back.

"Technically we just entered," Cork said. "The window was unlocked."

"Technically I could probably shoot you. So why don't you just close your mouth and be quiet."

The rifle in the man's hands made the advice seem more than reasonable, and Cork followed it.

The only sound the isolation of that distant piece of the reservation offered was the soft sweep of wind. Under different circumstances, Cork thought maybe he could appreciate that aspect of the place.

In a few minutes, the thump and rattle of a truck over hard terrain reached them. A pickup came into view, heading down the dirt track from the ranch compound. It stopped near the Arapaho with the rifle. The sun reflected off the windshield in a way that made the driver invisible to Cork. The door opened. A boy got out, a kid no older than Cork's own son. Like the man, he was Indian.

"You call No Voice?" the man asked.

"He's on his way."

Cork realized he'd seen the young Arapaho before, on his first visit to Red Hawk. The kid had stood beneath the burning cross that hung over the front door of the mission in the reservation town. He seemed to recognize Cork, and he spoke in Arapaho to the man with the rifle. The man looked at Cork in a different way.

"You the one who lost his wife when that plane went down?" he said.

"Yes."

The kid spoke again in Arapaho. The man spoke back, angrily. He jerked his head toward the pickup. The boy walked to the truck, dropped the tailgate, and rummaged in back. He returned with a roll of duct tape.

The man with the rifle said to Cork, "My grandson's going to toss you the duct tape. I want you to tape your friend's hands behind his back. Then toss the duct tape to my grandson."

Cork did as he was instructed, binding Parmer's hands together at the small of his back, then he threw the tape to the kid.

"Turn around, hands behind your back. My grandson'll do the same to your hands. You try anything, I'll blow your head off."

The kid secured Cork's hands and stepped back.

"Climb into the truck bed," the man ordered.

Cork and Parmer did as instructed. The kid slammed the tailgate shut and got behind the wheel.

"You two sit tight. We're going up to the ranch house. Anything stupid and you're dead. Understand?"

The man got in the cab, and his grandson drove them to the compound. The truck drew up to the outbuilding next to the barn. There were three doors—two large doors for the entry of vehicles and one smaller door for human use. The Arapaho with the rifle got out and entered the building through the smaller door. A moment later one of the big doors swung up mechanically. The boy drove the truck in and parked next to a yellow Allis-Chalmers backhoe with a blade mounted on the front. A couple of ATVs were parked there as well. Shovels, picks, pry bars, and other digging implements hung from hooks on the walls. There was a long workbench and above it a Peg-Board full of hand tools. The building smelled of oil and grease but was clean. The older Arapaho dropped the tailgate.

"Get out," he said.

Cork and Parmer scooted off the truck bed. The kid joined his grandfather.

"Sit down," the grandfather said to the two men.

They sat in the shade of the outbuilding. The kid said something to his grandfather in Arapaho, and the older man shook his head. The boy looked disappointed. He headed toward the rear of the outbuilding and returned with two folding chairs, which he set facing Cork and Parmer, some distance away. He sat in one, his grandfather in the other, with the rifle across his legs.

"Is Nightwind gone a lot?" Cork asked.

"No talking," the Arapaho said.

"You live in that cabin we saw up there in the hills?"

"Another word, I stuff this rifle butt down your throat."

No more words were spoken. Half an hour later, Andrew No Voice, chief of the Owl Creek Arapaho Police, arrived. He climbed from his Blazer and stood with his arms crossed, looking down at Cork and Parmer.

"Understand you gentlemen've been involved in a little breaking and entering."

"No," the older Arapaho said.

No Voice glanced his way. "Message I got said that was the case."

"They were snooping, that's all."

"Snooping? You sure got 'em trussed up good for snooping."

"A misunderstanding," the Arapaho said.

No Voice looked at the kid. "That right, Nick? Just a little misunderstanding?"

"Yes," the kid said.

"I want them off Nightwind's land," the older Arapaho said. "I want them gone, and I don't want them to come back."

"Prefer charges," No Voice said, "and I can guarantee they won't be back."

"No. No charges."

"Where's Lame?" No Voice asked.

"Gone."

"All right." The policeman was clearly not thrilled with the Arapaho's position. "I'll take 'em into Red Hawk, deal with them there."

"We have a Jeep," Cork said. "It's down at the hangar."

"Let's get it and get you two out of here."

"Mind cutting us loose?"

"I'm not inclined to do that just yet."

He herded them into the back of his Blazer and drove to the hangar.

"Who's got the keys?" he asked.

"I do," Cork said.

No Voice opened Cork's door. "Get out."

After Cork complied, No Voice turned him roughly, took a pocket-knife from a pouch on his belt, opened the blade, and slit the tape that bound his wrists.

"You drive the Jeep," No Voice said. "Follow me to Red Hawk. I'll keep your partner in my vehicle. Just a little insurance in case you're inclined toward a different destination."

In the Jeep, Cork followed No Voice back up the dirt track to the compound. The Arapaho and his grandson still stood in the shade of the outbuilding. Cork waved as he passed to let them know he bore them no ill will. They didn't respond, just stood watching as the two vehicles kicked up dust on their way out.

THIRTY-FOUR

Red Hawk drowsed in the May afternoon sun. Several pickups stood parked at the Chevron gas station and mini-mart. On the porch of the senior home across the street, two white-haired women rocked and watched No Voice's Blazer and Cork's Jeep crawl past. In the playing field behind the school, a bunch of kids were kicking a soccer ball around. No Voice pulled into the parking lot of the Reservation Business Center. He got out, opened the door for Parmer, and was in the process of cutting the tape that still bound Parmer's wrists when Cork pulled alongside and parked.

"Inside, O'Connor," No Voice said. After they'd entered, he pointed to the right. "End of the hall. I'm right behind you."

As they approached, Cork realized they were headed to the office of Ellyn Grant.

"We're expected?" Cork said.

"Oh, yeah. Go right in."

Beyond the door, much of the large office was still occupied by the miniature rendering of the Gateway Grand Casino.

Ellyn Grant looked up from her desk. Her face was the color and hardness of desert sandstone. She'd been writing, but she put her pen down very deliberately.

"Thank you, Andy. You can wait outside."

No Voice retreated and closed the door.

"Mr. O'Connor, we meet again. And you must be Hugh Parmer," she said. "I'm Ellyn Grant."

Parmer nodded and said, "Ah."

"I understand you two gentlemen have concerns about our casino development."

"Actually, Ellyn, my concerns go way beyond your casino."

"I'd be interested in hearing them." She flipped her hand in invitation toward two empty chairs, and the men sat. "Well?"

"I'll tell you what," Cork said. "You ask me a question, something you'd like to know, and I'll give you an answer. In return, I'll ask you a question and you give me an answer. Keeps us on equal footing."

"I could simply have you thrown in jail."

"Not here. No Voice has no jurisdiction over whites accused of breaking the law on the rez. But I suppose you might have the right influence with Sheriff Kosmo. Problem is that it doesn't get either of us any of the answers we're looking for."

She weighed his proposition. "All right."

"What would you like to know?" he said.

"That's a question, Mr. O'Connor. I thought I got to go first." She gave him a cool, satisfied smile. "It's my understanding that you believe the plane that went missing with my husband and your wife aboard didn't crash in the mountains. What do you think did happen to it?"

"I think it was flown somewhere and landed."

"Flown where?"

Cork held up his hand to stop her. "My turn." He leaned forward. "Is Lame Nightwind in love with you?"

His question clearly caught her off guard. "I'm sure I don't know."

Cork sat back. "Hell, if you're not going to tell me the truth, I'll just throw a few lies your way, too. We'll get nowhere."

For several seconds, she stared at him without blinking, and he thought of the Sphinx of Egypt.

"Yes," she finally replied. "He's in love with me."

"He's loved you since you were kids, isn't that true?"

"My turn," she said. "Where do you believe the plane landed?"

"My best guess at the moment is Nightwind's airstrip. Forget about the question I just asked. I'm going to assume that he's loved you forever. So my question is this: Do you love him?"

"No," she said. "And yes."

"Care to explain?"

"That's another question." She picked up the pen she'd been using and toyed with it. "If you think the plane landed at Lame's airstrip, you must believe that he was involved. I'd be interested in knowing why you believe this."

"We know that it wasn't Clinton Bodine who flew the plane," Cork told her. "I believe he was dead before the charter ever left the ground in Wisconsin. But everyone agrees that the pilot who flew out of Casper was Indian. Nightwind told me last year when I met him that he flew to a lot of powwows. So did Clinton Bodine. It's not hard to imagine that at some point they bumped into each other. That was probably what gave Nightwind the idea for the pilot switch. We also know that your husband was opposed to the Gateway Grand Casino. He was a problem that needed taking care of."

"What do you mean?"

"He needed to be removed from the picture. Killed. Which you helped with."

"You think I would actually take part in something like that?"

"Depends."

"On what?"

"Who you love more, your husband or the Arapaho. The way I see it, you were in trouble. Or more specifically, the Owl Creek Reservation was in trouble. You'd promised wealth you couldn't deliver. You built your little casino thinking it would bring in good money to fund all your fine improvements. But it didn't work out that way because Hot Springs is too far off the beaten path. All those millions of people headed to Yellowstone stay to the south or to the north, and neither the Blue Sky Casino nor the healing spring waters are enough to entice them to make a detour.

"So there you are, trapped. You've invested whatever resources the rez has in an enterprise that's going south. Your husband's answer is to open the reservation to gas and oil exploration, which you see as rape. Then maybe something like this happens: Some people come to you, offer you a sweet deal. They'll carry your debt. Hell, maybe even provide cash for some of those improvements on the rez so that your credibility holds together. And in return you use the sovereign status of the Arapaho to help these people build a casino, the biggest between Atlantic City and Las Vegas, at the doorway to Yellowstone. It's a partnership that promises the kind of income you'd always dreamed of for the Owl Creek Arapaho. Only one problem. Your partners aren't nice people. They're the kind of people who make people disappear. And when your husband doesn't come around to your way of thinking, he needs to be one of the people who disappears."

"I had nothing to do with anyone disappearing."

"No? You were with your husband in Casper before the plane left that morning, is that correct?"

"Yes."

"And his glasses went missing?"

"I don't really remember."

"He would have been pretty blind without them?"

"I suppose so, yes."

"Which would be necessary, because if he could see when he got on that plane, he'd have recognized Nightwind. Maybe Nightwind alters his voice some and your husband is none the wiser."

"That's absurd."

"You want to hear something really absurd? You knew all along that the plane hadn't gone down in Baby's Cradle, but you and Nightwind kept pointing us there. Why? Because Will Pope's vision was true and you had to misdirect us so that we wouldn't be thinking about what his vision was really telling us. But we're going to figure that out, Ellyn, and when we do, your whole card castle is going to tumble."

"That's enough," she said. "We're finished."

"Let me tell you one more thing. If I were you, I'd be very careful and I wouldn't travel alone. Because the closer we get to the evidence we need to prove these things, the greater a liability you become to the people behind all this."

She laughed harshly. "I've dealt with tough people before, Mr. O'Connor. They don't scare me. And if what you say is true, it seems to me that you and your friend are the ones who ought to be careful.

It would be much easier for these people, if they exist, to simply make *you* disappear."

"True enough. On the other hand, the more folks we talk to, and believe me we've talked to a lot, the more will come asking the same questions if we vanish. Easier, it seems to me, to cut the threads that tie these bad people to the missing plane. And those threads would be you and Lame Nightwind."

The door opened, and Dewey Quinn walked in with No Voice behind him.

"Sorry to break in like this, Ms. Grant," Quinn said, "but I need to take these men back to Hot Springs. The sheriff would like to see them."

"That's all right, Dewey." She gave Cork one last look that seemed chipped from flint. "Our business is finished."

"Think about it, Ellyn," Cork said. "And if I were you, I'd talk to Nightwind, tell him to watch his back."

"Good day, gentlemen."

Quinn and No Voice escorted them out to the parking lot, where Quinn shook hands with his colleague.

"Love to see 'em charged with something," No Voice said.

"I'm sure Jim'll let you know what he decides, Andy. Thanks."

Before No Voice headed to his Blazer, he said to Cork and Parmer, "You men, I catch you on the rez again, I'll be happy to dispense a little of my own Arapaho justice. Understand?" He got into his vehicle and left.

Quinn said, "Mr. Parmer, you mind driving the Jeep? I'd like to have a word with Cork on the way back."

"No problem."

They headed out of Red Hawk along the potholed road toward Hot Springs. Behind them, the sun was just dropping into the grasp of the mountains. The late afternoon light turned the sage nearly gold and made the barren hills seem dipped in honey.

"Sheriff's pretty hot under the collar," Quinn said.

"I can imagine."

"Said you screwed him on a promise you made."

"I guess I did."

Quinn glanced his way. "Look, he doesn't let me in on things sometimes, so I feel like I'm trying to play in a ball game but I've got no bat to swing with. You mind telling me what's going on?"

Cork didn't see any reason not to. While the sun finished setting behind them and the desolate land the Arapaho called home turned blue-gray in the twilight, Cork filled Quinn in completely.

"Ah, Jesus." The deputy slapped the steering wheel. "It all makes sense now."

"What makes sense?"

"Little things. They don't seem like much separately, but when you put them all together they make a clear picture."

"What little things?"

Quinn shot out a hot breath and seemed angry with himself. "When I was helping coordinate the search for the plane last year, the sheriff insisted I keep all the aircraft involved out of airspace over the reservation. He told me he wanted to be certain the most probable routes were given the highest priority."

"Nightwind flew us over the rez on the way to Baby's Cradle."

"Sure. He'd know exactly where not to fly. The sheriff was almost fanatical about no one else going there."

"I was under the impression you and the Civil Air Patrol commander made the decisions about the search."

"Kosmo sometimes gave me certain directives, and that was one. And here's the kicker. A few days before the plane went missing, we received a report of unusual activity on the north part of the reservation. Somebody spotted heavy equipment moving along one of the back roads up there. Only you can't really call them roads. Anybody who doesn't know the area well would get lost trying to follow them."

"I tried following a few of those today," Cork said.

"The concern was that somebody was doing some unauthorized prospecting on the reservation, probably oil and gas exploration. Happens sometimes. Kosmo and No Voice said they'd handle it. Went out, came back, claimed it was a bullshit report. Nothing to it."

"What's this got to do with the missing plane?"

"I'm getting to that. We had us a pretty severe drug problem a few years back. Mostly the problems came from the reservation."

"We know about that."

"I worked with guys from DEA who said that drug dealers will sometimes take a vehicle or a plane that's been used to transport the product and bury it. Makes all the evidence disappear easily. Now, think about Will Pope's vision, Cork. What if the cradle was a hole in the ground? These people buried the plane, and the snow that was falling covered it completely. The white blanket Pope talked about."

Cork sat back, letting it all play out in his mind. "And that heavy equipment was used to dig the hole."

"And probably to scrape out a runway."

"You have any idea where this was?"

"I can check the files for the report to be sure, but I have a pretty good idea. There's a box canyon up that way with a nice flat run right up to it. If I were going to create a landing strip, that's where I'd do it."

"Can you show me on a map, Dewey?"

"I'll go you one better. I'll take you there myself. I've got lots of vacation saved. I'll take a day tomorrow. Ten miles north of town on the highway to Cody, there's a cutoff for a road called Horseshoe Creek Trail."

"I know the road. That's how we headed out this morning."

"Okay. A couple of miles in you come to a place where the road crosses an old wood bridge over the creek. Meet me there at sunup and we'll head out together. I'll bring some shovels and some other digging tools. I also got me a pretty good metal detector from the days when I was doing a little prospecting myself."

"Throwing in with us, you could be headed into a lot of trouble, Dewey," Cork said.

"I don't just work here, I live here. If there's something dirty in this county, I have to know." Quinn frowned and hesitated a moment. "I hate to say this about my own people, but I've got no idea who might be tainted. It's best if we don't say anything to anyone until after we've had a chance to check this out thoroughly. I'd say that includes Jon Rude. I know you trust him, but we have to be sure."

"I agree."

"And I wouldn't risk any calls. God only knows who might be listening."

"All right."

"Look, I hope you understand what I'm about to say. Christ, I hope I'm all wrong about this. He's a strange man sometimes and hard to figure, but I like Jim Kosmo. I'd hate to see him go down."

Cork said, "If he had anything to do with Jo's death, I'll take him down with my own hands."

THIRTY-FIVE

Nightwind." Kosmo squinted as if he was trying to picture something in his mind's eye. "And you figure he's the Indian pilot who took Bodine's place."

Cork and Parmer sat in the sheriff's office, in the same orange plastic chairs they'd occupied that morning. Kosmo seemed restrained. If he was angry, he was keeping it well in check.

"It fits," Cork said.

Kosmo sat at his desk. The big man's head was framed by a hint of blue lingering in the twilight sky visible through the window at his back. It struck Cork like a faded halo. The overhead light was off, and the room was lit by the lamp on his desk. It created a small, illuminated circle that enclosed the three men.

"What do you know about Nightwind?" Kosmo asked.

"He's in love with Ellyn Grant. So maybe he'd do anything she asked, including murder."

Kosmo sat back and studied the two men, companions in the light, then he said, "When I was a kid, there was a family lived down the street from us. The Halbersons. Had this German shepherd they called Pooch. Most days they kept him tied to a leash on the front porch. That dog was real unusual. I never once heard him bark. He'd just sit there all day long, watching everything and everybody. Mailman would slide mail into the box at the gate, dog just watched. Paperboy came by, tossed the evening paper in the yard, dog just watched. Us kids, we'd holler at him, make faces, sometimes throw things just to try to get a rise out of Pooch. No dice. Just looked at us like we were, I don't know, bushes or something. One kid, Harvey Groat, he swore the dog was blind or deaf or retarded. We all dared him to go into the yard and see if he could get Pooch to bark. So Groat, never the swiftest boat in the fleet, opens the gate, creeps into the yard, gets one foot on the front steps, and Pooch is up. Lunges so hard and fast he snaps the leash and he's all over Groat, chewing the hell out of him. Groat's screaming and we're screaming and finally the front door jerks open and Mr. Halberson comes flying out. Kicks the shit out of Pooch before the dog finally retreats and leaves Groat be. Groat, he ends up getting a few dozen stitches. Carries the scars to this day. Pooch, he got put down for the attack, which was a shame because he was only doing what he'd been trained to do, which was protect that family and its property. You know, during the whole incident with Groat, that dog never uttered a sound. I bet he went to his death without a whimper."

"And the point is?" Cork said.

"Nightwind, he's just like that dog, O'Connor. You never hear him. He never makes trouble. But you always have the feeling that, if he wanted to, he could give you a whole lot of hurt real fast. I was you, I'd stay clear of him.

"He called me before you got here. Said he didn't want any charges brought. Said it was all a kind of misunderstanding. Me, I'd just as soon toss you in a cell for a while. Probably couldn't make anything stick. And I've been checking on Mr. Parmer here and I know that he's richer than Rockefeller and would most likely haul in a whole cadre of lawyers to make my life miserable. So I'm just going to let you go. Mark my words, though. You make any trouble for me, for those folks on the reservation, hell, you spit on the sidewalk, I'll come down on you like old Pooch on Groat, don't think I won't."

All the light had faded from the sky, and what framed Kosmo now was black night. Cork was quiet for a moment, then asked, "It doesn't matter to you what I'm trying to accomplish here?"

Kosmo brought his hand up to his face and used his thumb to rub his eyebrow. "I have sympathy for your situation, O'Connor. I just don't buy your read of the circumstances."

"Why? Because it craps all over this dream you and everyone here have for Owl Creek County?"

"No. Because if you really listened to yourself, you'd realize how crazy it sounds. And because you haven't been able to offer one solid piece of evidence in support."

"Why do I get the feeling I could dump a garbage truck full of evidence on your desk and it wouldn't make any difference?"

"See, O'Connor? You're reading me all wrong. And because I know that, I know that your own reading of this whole situation is way off target."

"Fine, Sheriff. You just sit there. I'm going to gather myself a garbage truck full of evidence and I'm going to dump it in your lap. Then let's see what kind of lawman you are."

"You've got me all figured out, have you?"

"Right down to the lint in your boot socks."

Kosmo scooted back from his desk, taking himself out of the light. "I guess at the moment there's nothing else to discuss."

"I guess you're right. We're free to leave?"

"Oh, yeah. But if I were a betting man, and I just happen to be, I'd lay odds that we'll be talking again real soon."

Cork and Parmer left. As they passed Dewey Quinn in the common area, Quinn gave them a surreptitious thumbs-up.

In the parking lot outside, Parmer said, "That could have been worse. I thought he'd tear us both new assholes."

Cork looked back up at the window of the sheriff's office. He could see the light from the desk lamp inside. "I think Sheriff Kosmo would prefer to deal with us in a more private way. I had a long talk with Quinn on our way here. Very enlightening. Let's grab ourselves a couple of steaks and some beers and I'll tell you all about it."

They ate at the Bronco Saloon on Main Street, a place where the nostalgia for the Old West was clearly evident in the Remington prints and the photos of roundups and brandings and bronco bustings that hung on the walls. Cork had first arrived in Wyoming with certain preconceived ideas that came from Zane Grey and Louis L'Amour, and from John Wayne and Randolph Scott. Everyone wore Stetsons and spurs and walked a little bowlegged from a lifetime mounted on the heaving flanks of cow ponies. But judging from the people he'd seen on the streets of Hot Springs, folks in Wyoming bought their clothes from JCPenney and Lands' End, same as people in Minnesota. The kids were partial to baggy jeans and printed T-shirts and baseball caps worn askew, and they rode skateboards instead of steeds. The culture of the Old West, if it ever really did exist, had been tamed and replaced by the uniformity of the Walmart–strip mall–McDonald's homogenizing of America. It was happening in Minnesota, too. Hell, it was happening everywhere in the world.

Over a juicy rib eye and a couple of draws of Fat Tire beer, Cork related to Parmer the conversation he'd had with Quinn.

"You did a good job back there not tipping your hand to Kosmo," Parmer said. "Are you going to let Liz and Becca know?"

Cork took a final bite of steak, laid his fork down, slid his plate away, and shook his head. "I don't want to get their hopes up if it turns out to be nothing."

"It won't be nothing. There's something to this."

Cork shook his head. "Until we find it, I don't want to risk letting the other side know what we know. I'm not sure there's a safe way to talk to Liz and Becca."

Parmer laid his own fork down and folded his hands above his plate. "Cork," he began tentatively, "if it's there . . ." He hesitated, then tried again. "Have you thought about . . ." Once more, he seemed at a loss to know how to proceed.

"Yeah? Go on."

"What I'm trying to get at is this. If we find the plane, what's inside won't be pretty. Have you considered that?"

"Whatever's inside, Hugh, it can't be worse than not knowing. I don't care how bleak the truth is, it's better than living with the question. Do you understand?"

"I think so."

"Good. Then let's get out of here. We need a good night's sleep."

But a good night's sleep didn't come to him. Cork lay awake a long time considering Parmer's question. He assumed that if the plane had been buried, the bodies had been left inside. Six months. Six months in an airless tomb. What would remain of the woman he loved? He tried not to think of that. He tried to think of Jo as she'd been, smart and loving and dedicated and beautiful.

The plane had become a crypt, and what was inside wasn't Jo, he told himself. It would be like the dirt and rock that surrounded it. It would be what had once been earth becoming earth again. And Jo? Jo was somewhere else. Beyond pain. Beyond fear. Beyond anger. Beyond caring. These were the burdens of the living.

Long after he lay down, he finally fell asleep, oppressed by the weight of being alive.

THIRTY-SIX

At sunup next morning, they found Dewey Quinn waiting where he said he'd be, at the old wood bridge on Horseshoe Creek Trail. Quinn wore a straw cowboy hat, faded jeans, and work boots that looked pretty new. He drove a white pickup that had been recently washed, but the tailgate and rear panels now carried a patina of brown dust, courtesy of the dirt road. Quinn directed Cork to park the Wrangler among a gathering of cottonwoods fifty yards north of the bridge. Parmer grabbed the knapsack they'd brought. Everyone piled into Quinn's pickup and headed west for the Absarokas, forty miles distant, lying low on the horizon, the snowcapped peaks like sharp teeth gnawing on the blue bone of sky.

"Once it all fell into place," Quinn said, over the squawk and hammer of the suspension, "I could've kicked myself. This box canyon we're headed toward, it pretty much sits in the shadow of a mountain that has no official name, no name that appears on a map anyway. But the Arapaho have a name for it. I can't pronounce it to save my soul, but it means Eagle Cloud. In Will Pope's vision, the eagle dropped out of a cloud into a box. That'd be the canyon, I figure. It was right out there in front of me. I just didn't see it."

"Nightwind and Grant did a pretty good job of misdirection," Cork said.

"I still feel bad. I could've saved you a lot of grief."

"Nobody could've done that, Dewey. Let it go. What's done is done. And we're closing in on the answers now, thanks to you."

"Thank me when we've actually located the plane."

After forty minutes, they left the road and struck northwest, cross-country. The undercarriage of Quinn's pickup had an unusually high clearance, and the suspension was tough, both of which Cork commented on.

"Like I said, I used to prospect some before I was married. Wanted to be a rich man. I needed a vehicle that could get me into places only snakes and maybe mountain goats could go. Saw a lot of the backcountry that way. That's how I knew about Eagle Cloud and this canyon."

The ground rose in swells of red and yellow rock. Quinn kept to the troughs of the ridges, weaving the pickup among great blocks of shattered stone. This was an area of upheaval, of cataclysm, Cork thought. The nearer they came to the mountains, the more pronounced was Heaven's Keep. It thrust above the rest of the range in stark, foreboding grandeur, looking in every way like a fortress, an unassailable hold of secrets.

They came to a dry wash full of sand the color of bread crust. As Quinn started down, Cork said, "Wait a minute, Dewey. Hold up."

Cork got out, walked into the depression, and knelt in the sand. Quinn and Parmer joined him.

"What is it?" Parmer asked.

"Tire tracks," Cork said. "Somebody's been this way."

Dewey said, "That's unusual. This isn't exactly on a standard road map." He knelt, too. "On the other hand, no telling when these tracks were made. We haven't had a good rain here in a while."

"Why would anyone be out this way?" Parmer said.

Quinn shrugged. "Prospecting, maybe."

"Maybe," Cork said. He stood up and looked toward the mountains. "I think we ought to be prepared for a reception, though."

"Who could know?" Quinn asked.

Cork said, "It wouldn't surprise me if these people know everything."

They returned to the pickup. Quinn dropped the tailgate and hopped into the bed. He stepped around the shovels and pick and pry bar and the metal detector he'd loaded that morning, and he bent over a toolbox secured to the side. He unlocked the lid, lifted out a box of cartridges, and tossed them to Cork.

"Hang on to those," he said.

He locked the toolbox, nimbly leaped to the ground, and slammed the tailgate shut. From the rifle rack affixed to the back of the cab, he pulled down a flat-sided, lever-action Winchester that had been cradled there. He slid half a dozen cartridges into the magazine and looked at Cork.

"You a good shot?"

Cork considered the weight in his hands. "Used to be," he said, "but I haven't fired one of these for a while."

Quinn squinted at Parmer. "Can you shoot?"

"I was born to it. But I have my own weapon." Parmer grabbed the knapsack and pulled out his Ruger.

Quinn said, "Let's do it this way, then. Cork, you drive and I'll ride shotgun. It might be a little rough, but it'd be good if you rode in back, Hugh. Somebody tries to hit us, we can both respond. I need to stay in the cab and guide Cork."

"Works for me," Parmer said.

Cork took his place behind the wheel. Parmer settled himself in back. Quinn sat on the passenger side with the rifle cradled in his hands. They headed off once again, and half an hour later, without incident and without seeing any further evidence of another vehicle, they arrived at their destination.

It was clear from a distance how, in a vision, the formation might appear as a bed or a box. The sides were dark red, like rough-finished cherrywood, and the floor of the canyon was dirt of the same color. It was half a mile long and a couple of hundred yards wide. It sat on a flat plain maybe a mile square that lay at the very base of the foothills. Behind it rose a small mountain that Cork figured had to be Eagle Cloud. This was the only large, flat area he'd seen all morning, and he understood why Quinn thought an airstrip could have been scraped there.

As they approached the opening to the canyon, Cork stopped the pickup and got out. His eyes swept the scene before him, east to west. Quinn and Parmer came and stood beside him and saw the same thing: a long, narrow band of earth, clear of rock and sage and all debris, leading directly into the canyon.

"They landed here," Cork said. "The sons of bitches brought the plane down right here."

"Where do we begin?" Parmer finally said.

"In the canyon, at the end of the strip they cleared," Cork said. "If I was going to bury a plane, that's where I'd do it."

They drove into the shadow of the canyon a hundred and fifty yards to a place where the makeshift airstrip came to an end. There, very clearly, they saw a long rectangle where the earth had been disturbed. It was like a grave in a cemetery, old enough to have lost the mounding of dirt but still new enough not to blend in completely with the ground around it. Quinn dragged his metal detector from the bed of the pickup, clamped the headphones on, and ran the instrument over the area, all the time nodding to the others confirmation of their suspicions.

When Quinn finished, Cork asked, "Can you tell how deep it is?"

"No, but I'd say not deep. The readings are strong." He looked back at the cleared strip behind them. "They didn't bother to cover their tracks. Probably figured nobody would ever come out here. And if they did, the plane was out of sight. Unless you were really looking for something, like we were, hell, you probably wouldn't even notice."

"Well," Parmer said. He looked at the others. "Shouldn't we start digging?"

They spread out and began. At just over two feet, they struck metal. Parmer's shovel found the plane first. Cork and Quinn left their own excavations and joined him. Together they cleared a large rectangle of white fuselage that sloped right. They dug a pit following the downward slope of the plane. Two men worked in the ground while the idle man stayed above with the rifle, watching for any trouble that might arrive. Parmer and Quinn relieved each other, but Cork refused to take a break. By midmorning, they'd created an excavation deeper than they were tall that ran for nearly eight feet along the plane and extended half a dozen feet outward. They'd uncovered the upper part of the door and cleared the latch. Cork carefully wiped the dirt from the mechanism and tried the handle. He leaned the weight of his body and the will of his spirit into the attempt, and he let out a cry as if the effort hurt him. The handle didn't yield. He yanked and swore, grabbed his shovel and raised it to deliver a blow, but Parmer's hand restrained him.

"Easy, Cork. We can't open the door yet anyway, not till we've cleared the rest of the dirt. Let's worry about the handle then, okay?"

Cork stood frozen, the shovel poised. He was deep in the grip of a desperation that, as the door had revealed itself, had coiled tighter and tighter around his heart.

"We're almost there." Parmer waited, and when Cork didn't respond, he said, "If you damage the latch, we might not get inside at all."

Cork finally heard the wisdom in the words. He stepped back, took a few deep breaths, and nodded. They'd cut crude steps into the side of the pit as they dug, and now Parmer climbed out and disappeared. He returned with bottles of water they'd packed that morning. The men drank and wiped at the sweat and grit on their faces, and considered in the silence of their own thoughts the prospect of what lay before them. Finally they returned to their labor.

On a shimmering crest of heat, the sun continued to rise. The only sounds were the occasional buzz of a flying insect, the dull *chuk* of the blades biting dirt, and the grunts of the men as they broke the earth free and catapulted it from the hole.

An hour past noon it was finished. They'd cleared the door. Parmer examined the latch.

"A lot of grit jammed in there," he said. "Some water and a brush might clean it out." He looked up at Quinn, who stood above, at the edge of the pit, holding the rifle.

Quinn nodded and left the hole. He returned with a bottle of water. He also brought a sponge and a soft-bristle scrub brush, which he said he used to wash his truck. Parmer unscrewed the bottle cap and poured half the contents around the handle, then took the brush and with short, careful strokes began to clean the grit from the mechanism.

Cork stood watching, aware from the throb in his chest and thickness in his head that his heart rate, and probably his blood pressure, was spiking. Sweat ran down his face and soaked his clothing. All of this, he understood, was a physical manifestation of something that had nothing to do with the long hours of exertion. Parmer was methodical and thorough, maddeningly so, and as the minutes dragged on, Cork struggled to hold himself back from leaping at his friend, grabbing the water and the brush, and attacking the door.

At last, Parmer sat back. "You want to give her a try, Cork?"

He'd been waiting for this moment, but now that it was here, he felt suddenly weak, unequal to the task. He shook his head. "You go ahead."

Parmer braced himself and gave the handle a steady pull. Nothing happened. He relaxed, settled himself once more, and again pulled hard. This time the mechanism gave. He shoved the door open fully, leaving a gaping entry. Inside was utterly dark, and from it poured the foul stench of entombed putrefaction.

"We'll need a flashlight," Quinn said. He disappeared.

Parmer was studying Cork. "You okay?"

Cork didn't answer. He was thinking, *Not Jo. That's not Jo inside.* He felt himself reeling, falling backward. Suddenly he was staring at the pure blue rectangle of sky framed by the edges of the pit, and for a moment he was back on Iron Lake as a kid on a raft on a summer day staring up and thinking that in heaven the angels must be dressed in fabric made from the sky, it was so perfect.

Then Parmer's voice brought him back. "Just stay down, Cork."

Quinn clambered into the hole. "Whoa, what happened?"

"He fainted," Parmer said.

Quinn waved a hand briskly in front of his own face. "It's the smell. Enough to gag anyone."

"I'm fine." Cork sat up and leaned back against the side of the pit.

"Here, have some water," Parmer said.

He gave Cork the bottle he'd used to wash the handle mechanism clean. There were still a few swallows in it. Cork finished the water, and Parmer said to Quinn, "There's another bottle in my knapsack in the truck."

"Got it," Quinn said and took off.

Cork sat looking at the open door and feeling faint again. "I don't think I can go in there, Hugh."

"No reason you have to, Cork. Let Quinn and me handle that. You just stay here."

"I should go," Cork said.

"No, you've come as far as you need to. What's in there, you don't have to see."

"I should go," Cork said again. "But honest to God, Hugh, I can't."

"I understand."

Quinn came back. He handed the bottled water to Cork.

"Okay?" Parmer said.

Cork nodded.

"Dewey, you and me are going inside," Parmer said.

"All right." Quinn accepted the situation without comment.

The two men stood up. Quinn set his rifle against the fuselage, turned on the flashlight he'd retrieved from his truck, and led the way into the plane.

Cork tried to drink some water, but his throat was dry and he choked. He stared at the black beyond the door and forced himself not to imagine what was inside. He heard Quinn and Parmer talking in voices too low for him to catch the words. He felt the tension in him building, roiling up from the pit of his stomach.

And then Parmer stood in the doorway of the plane, eyeing Cork in an odd way.

Every muscle in Cork's body had drawn taut, and he felt ready to explode. "Well?"

"They're in there," Parmer replied. His face held a puzzled look. "They're all in there except for one, Cork. Your wife's not on this plane."

THIRTY-SEVEN

Cork staggered up. "What did you say?"

Parmer shook his head in bewilderment. "She's not in there, Cork. Jo's not in there."

Quinn came out looking grim and unsteady. "Christ, enough to give anybody nightmares."

Cork grasped Quinn by the shoulders. "Did you see her?"

"No," Quinn replied. "Five bodies. They'll be a bitch to ID, but all definitely male."

Cork grabbed the flashlight from Quinn and pushed between the two men into the foul-smelling plane.

What greeted him was an eerie scene. The cockpit was empty. He'd expected that. In the cabin, the passengers sat in their seats, still wearing the oxygen masks that had deployed from the compartments above. The skin of their faces had drawn back, and skeletal grins peeked out from the sides of the masks. Their eye sockets were empty, and they seemed to watch Cork with black stares. The liquefaction of internal organs had caused the bodies to collapse inward, giving them an exaggerated gauntness. They hadn't decomposed a great deal, the result, Cork supposed, of the airless crypt where they'd been entombed. He walked slowly between the seats until he came to one that was empty, next to a window, where he saw a briefcase lying on the floor.

"Cork, what happened here?"

He turned and found Parmer just inside the door, Quinn at his back.

"Shot," Cork said. "All of them in the head at close range. Small caliber. A twenty-two would be my guess. The bullet stays inside the skull, ricochets off the bone, and destroys the brain. Work of professionals."

Parmer stared at the dead men, sitting before him in a repose that seemed almost peaceful. "You're telling me that they just sat there like that and let someone execute them?"

"That's exactly what I'm telling you."

"That doesn't make any sense."

"Where's your wife?" Quinn asked.

"She was here." Cork leaned over the body next to the empty seat. From the long gray hair, he was pretty sure it had been George LeDuc. He lifted the briefcase from the floor. "This is hers." He pointed to the cushion of the empty seat. "I don't see any blood. Maybe she wasn't shot like the others."

"Then where is she?" Quinn persisted. He seemed perturbed that she wasn't there.

Cork didn't have an answer. He felt almost giddy. Jo's mysterious absence from that macabre scene was the first glimmer of hope he'd had since the plane went missing.

"This smell's making me sick," Quinn said. "Let's get out of here."

Cork took a long last look around, then followed the others. Outside, his two companions stood motionless at the top of the pit. As he climbed the crude steps to join them, he saw what had made them freeze. A couple of men stood facing them, holding handguns.

"That's right, O'Connor," one of the men said. "Come on up and join the party."

Cork stood next to Parmer, kicking himself for letting his guard down. He was thinking they must have been hiding among the rocks of the canyon wall, waiting for their chance, and when all three men had entered the plane, they'd wasted no time in seizing the advantage. He was thinking about the rifle still in the pit, propped against the fuselage. He was thinking that, given a moment of distraction, he could be in the pit with that rifle.

One of the men was tall and slender with brooding lips and sleepy eyelids that made him look tragically poetic. The other, the one who'd spoken, was like a washing machine—plain, square, and efficient. Cork recognized him. He'd seen him before, in the Turtleback restaurant in Rice Lake, ordering Leinenkugel's on the waitress's recommendation, and again that same night, framed in the rain-streaked window of a car that passed Parmer's Navigator only moments before the front tire blew.

"You're a hard one to get rid of, O'Connor," the man said. "I kind of admire that, don't you, Mike?"

"Makes me warm all over, Gully," Mike said.

"I was being sincere, Mike. Then you have to go and interject uncalled-for sarcasm. That's disrespect."

"Whatever," Mike said.

"We'd have made an appearance earlier," Gully said, speaking toward Cork and the others, "but I hate to interrupt good men while they're working. Also saved us the trouble of digging a hole for your bodies. Now we can just toss you in with the others, fill that hole back up, nobody's the wiser."

Quinn suddenly began walking toward the two men. "Jesus," he said. "You almost blew it. O'Connor spotted your tire tracks on the way here." He took a stance next to Mike.

Cork said, "Dewey?"

Quinn shrugged and smiled affably. "Services to the highest bidder."

Cork said, "Couldn't become a rich man by prospecting so you took an easier route?"

"Got a wife with expensive tastes. Money makes her happy. Makes me happy, too."

"People have died for your happiness, Dewey."

"People die for all kinds of stupid reasons, Cork. By the way," he said to his cohorts, "O'Connor's wife isn't in there."

Gully shot him an evil look. "The fuck you saying?"

"I'm saying she's not in there. She should be there, dead like the others, but she's not."

"Mike, check it out."

Mike took his lean, poetic-looking self into the pit. He was gone a minute, and when he returned he came with a string of words few poets would normally use in rhyme. He walked toward Gully with his hands open and empty and his face confounded. "Bitch isn't there, Gully. Just like Quinn says."

With his free hand, Gully slapped his partner's shoulder hard. "Goddamn it, I told you to cap her."

"I did. I just couldn't shoot her in the face. I told you, she looked too much like Rita. So I put one in her heart. Hell, if that didn't kill her, I figured she'd suffocate."

"Obviously she didn't. Fuck!"

"What do we do?" Quinn asked.

"Get rid of these two and cut our losses," Mike said. "We'll put 'em inside with the others and bury the plane again. Then see if we can figure how the woman did the Houdini thing."

The two thugs were less than a dozen feet away. If they were any good with their weapons, Cork didn't stand a chance of reaching the rifle in the pit before they nailed him. But he figured at this point, he had nothing to lose. He was just about to make his move when two shots rang out from the top of the canyon wall and two rounds burrowed into the dirt near the killers' feet. The men spun and crouched, swinging their weapons toward the line where the top of the canyon wall met the sky. Cork grabbed Parmer, and they both dove for the pit. They weren't alone. Dewey Quinn leaped in after them.

Cork took Quinn. He grabbed the man and heaved him against the pit wall. Quinn lashed out with a fast fist that caught Cork just below his left eye. Cork took the blow, then lunged forward, burying his shoulder in Quinn's gut, and he wrapped his arms around the deputy. Quinn tried to dig his knee into Cork's stomach and hammered at the back of his head, but Cork held on. He lifted Quinn off his feet and threw him to the ground. Quinn tried to come up. The toe of Cork's boot buried itself in the soft tissue below Quinn's jaw, and the man's head snapped back. It hit the fuselage with a hollow thud. Quinn lay on the ground, facedown. He moaned and struggled to rise, but Cork sat on his back, pinning him in the dirt.

He'd been vaguely aware of gunfire. And now he saw that Parmer had the rifle, had positioned himself on the steps, and was pulling off rounds over the edge of the pit. At the moment, there wasn't any return fire. Parmer held off squeezing the trigger. He glanced down at Cork.

"They both got away," he said. "Do we go after them?"

"What about the shooter on the wall?" Cork asked.

"Nothing since those first two rounds. How's Benedict Arnold there?"

"Just the way I want him. Alive and rattled." Cork got up and grabbed one of the shovels. He rolled Quinn over and put the digging edge of the blade to the man's throat. "I'm very much inclined to separate your head from the rest of you, Dewey. Then I'll just throw the two pieces in that plane and bury it again. Nobody'll ever know."

Quinn looked up at him. It wasn't fear in his eyes so much as resignation.

"Tell me what you know," Cork said.

Quinn began to talk.

THIRTY-EIGHT

They drove back the way they'd come. When they reached the junction with the road they'd traveled the day before, they took it southwest, following the line of the mountains toward Nightwind's ranch.

With the shovel blade at his throat, Dewey Quinn had told them everything. There'd been no report of mysterious activity on the rez involving heavy equipment. He'd concocted the story to draw them out to the canyon where they were to be dealt with. As far as he knew, Kosmo and No Voice weren't involved, but Nightwind was, and Ellyn Grant. He didn't know anyone higher up the food chain than Gully and Mike. Their last names? He didn't know that either. They never dealt in last names. He blamed his wife for his involvement.

"You got any idea how tough it is keeping a spoiled woman happy? Christ, I was in debt up to my eyeballs."

"And then Gully and Mike came along and offered you a way out."

"Nightwind sent them. That guy's like the devil. He knows how to get to you."

"What did they want you for?" Parmer asked.

It was Cork who answered. "They needed a man on the inside of the department, a guy who could keep them informed and if necessary remove the complications of the law. Who better for that than the officer responsible for the investigation of major crimes in Owl Creek County? When Felicia Gray's car took that plunge, I'm sure Dewey here was quick on the official determination of cause. A tragic accident. And all it took to buy his soul was money. Hell, Dewey, I thought you had your eyes on a job with the FBI."

"There's no cop job in the world pays like they were paying me." Despite his disgrace, he'd eyed Hugh Parmer and managed a look of disdain. "Not all of us have the luxury of being rich."

Quinn sat between them now. They'd tied his hands with twine from his toolbox, and they'd bound his ankles as well.

Cork used Parmer's cell phone to call Jim Kosmo and tell him about the plane buried in the canyon under Eagle Cloud. When the sheriff asked where he and Parmer were at that moment, Cork wouldn't say. Which didn't sit at all well with Kosmo. Big surprise.

The compound lay in the blue shadow of the foothills. Cork parked Quinn's truck, took the binoculars from the knapsack, and got out. Parmer joined him, and for several minutes they studied their objective.

The place seemed deserted. Cork spotted the pickup that the Arapaho kid had driven the day before, parked in front of the barn. Although he couldn't see anyone moving about, the barn door was clearly open.

"Well?" Parmer said.

"There may be someone in the barn."

"How do we handle this?"

"Approach on foot, do our best to surprise him."

"What about Quinn?"

"We leave him with the truck."

"What if he tries to get away?"

Cork hauled Quinn out of the cab. He hopped the deputy to the front of the truck and sat him on the bumper. "Toss me that roll of twine," he said to Parmer. He bound Quinn to the grille. When he stepped back, he said, "Dewey, we come back and I find you gone, I'll hunt you down and shoot you like a rabbit, don't think I won't."

Cork grabbed Quinn's Winchester from the rack in the cab. Parmer, who was holding his Ruger, gave a long look at the rifle, then another long look at Cork. But he said nothing.

They made their way down the slope, which was covered with short, coarse grass and punctuated by large rocks that protruded from the earth like the bows of sinking ships. Moving carefully rock to rock, they took several minutes to reach the barn. From inside came the sound of someone whistling. A Roy Orbison tune. "Running Scared." Cork peered around the edge of the open door. The older Arapaho who'd greeted them on their first visit to the ranch was standing at a worktable, a screwdriver in his hand, laboring over a piece of sheet metal. Cork saw no one else. He signaled to Parmer, and the two men slipped inside. They approached the Arapaho, who suddenly stopped his work and spun. When he saw them, he reached toward a rifle that lay on the bench next to the worktable.

"Hold it right there," Cork said.

The Arapaho froze, a foot of empty air between his hand and the weapon he'd gone for.

"Move away from the firearm," Cork ordered.

The Arapaho sidled a yard to his right.

"Where's Nightwind?"

The Arapaho didn't answer.

"You always work with a rifle close at hand?"

"In this country," the man replied, "you never know what kind of animal might be sneaking around. It's my job to protect this property and the livestock on it."

"Where's Nightwind?" Cork asked again.

"He's not here."

"That's not what I asked."

"I don't know where he is."

"Suppose I go up to the house and have a look-see?"

The Arapaho gave no sign that he cared one way or the other.

"Sit on the ground," Cork told him.

The man sat.

"Watch him, Hugh. I'm going to see if I can rustle up a little Nightwind."

"Careful, partner."

Cork stood at the barn door and studied the house a long moment. He slipped out and dashed to the outbuilding where the ATVs and heavy equipment were kept. From there, he ran to the garage and took a quick look inside. One of the spaces was empty. Which didn't necessarily mean anything. He sprinted to the house and approached the front door. Locked. He eased along the side of the house and checked the windows as he went. The curtains were open. There appeared to be no one inside. He came to a side door, which was also locked. He used the butt of Quinn's rifle to shatter one of the panes in the mullioned window, and he reached inside to free the lock. With his hip he nudged the door open and popped inside. Room by room he crept through the house, satisfying himself that it was empty. The place was simply furnished, decorated with artwork like the kind on display at the gallery in the Reservation Business Center. A framed photograph on the mantel in the living room caught his eye. It showed two young people holding hands, with foothills at their backs, and with Heaven's Keep looming above the whole scene like a guardian angel. The young woman was Ellyn Grant. The young man was Lame Nightwind. It must have been taken twenty years before and in a happier time. They were holding hands and smiling.

Cork returned to the barn.

"He's not there." He stood at the open door and eyed the thread of woodsmoke rising in the foothills half a mile away. "There's somewhere else he might be, though. Let's pay a visit to your place."

"No," the Arapaho said.

"Yes," Cork said. "And we're going to take your pickup. You drive."

The Arapaho stood his ground and would not move.

"All right," Cork said. "We'll tie you up, leave you down here, and we'll still take your truck."

"All right," the Arapaho said. "I'll drive you there."

They left the barn, and at the pickup Cork said, "Hugh, give me your gun. I'll ride up front with our host. You take the rifle and hunker down in back so nobody can see you." To the Arapaho, he said, "Any shooting starts, you take the first bullet."

"You'd really shoot me?"

"You want to find out?"

"Nightwind isn't at my cabin."

"I'd like to see that for myself."

"Only my wife is there. You'll frighten her. She won't give you any trouble, I promise. None of us will."

"Fine. Then this should be easy all the way around. Let's go."

The Arapaho slid behind the wheel, and Cork took the seat next to him. He held Parmer's Ruger in his lap with the muzzle toward the man driving. Parmer lay down in back with the rifle beside him. They took off and followed a dirt road that wound through foothills dotted with lodgepole pines. As they approached the cabin, Cork saw that it was built among a gathering of cottonwoods. Nestled into the fold of the hills, with smoke rising from the chimney, it looked like a good, peaceful place to live. Cork hoped he wouldn't find Nightwind there. He hated the thought of bringing violence to the Arapaho's home. But if it would help him find Jo, he'd raise hell in heaven itself.

The Arapaho braked to a stop fifty yards from the cabin. A sheepdog, black and white, left the porch and trotted out to meet them. The dog hesitated and must have caught the strange scent of Cork and Parmer, because it began to bark fiercely. Cork saw a curtain move in a front window.

"Go on," he said to the Arapaho. "Pull all the way up."

The man took his time. When they were parked near the porch, Cork said, "Slide this way. We're getting out the same side." He opened his door and used it to shield him from the cabin as the Arapaho maneuvered out. Parmer jumped from the pickup bed and stood beside Cork.

"Walk to the house and keep in front of us," he told the Arapaho.

"You're scaring my wife," the Arapaho said.

"If Nightwind's not here, she has nothing to fear."

The door opened before they reached the porch, and a woman appeared. She wore her hair in a long, graying braid. She had on a tan blouse and a long green skirt, embroidered along the hem. Around her waist an apron was tied, and she wiped her hands on it as she looked the men over. She spoke to her husband in Arapaho. He replied in the same language.

"What are you saying?" Cork asked.

"She wants to know who you are. I told her."

"Told her what?"

"Men looking for Lame."

"Lame's gone," she said.

"We'd like to take a look inside, ma'am, just for our own peace of mind."

The woman glanced at her husband, who spoke again in Arapaho. She stood aside, leaving the way clear for them to enter.

"After you," Cork said to the Arapaho.

Inside, the air was sharp and redolent with the aroma of cooking chili peppers. Parmer stayed with the couple while Cork checked the rooms. The place was cozy and simple: a small living room and kitchen, a bathroom, and two bedrooms. One of the bedrooms was decorated with posters of aircraft of all kind. A biplane, a World War II Sabre jet, a stealth bomber. Plastic airplane models hung from strings tacked to the ceiling boards. When Cork returned to the others, he said, "Your grandson, he wants to fly?"

The woman made no reply, but her husband gave a diffident shrug.

"Where is he?"

"Out," the Arapaho said. "Riding."

"Where's Nightwind?"

"I told you. We don't know. He comes. He goes. He doesn't have to tell me. He's my boss, I'm not his."

"Have you seen a woman with him? A white woman, blond?"

"No," the man said.

His wife spoke to him in Arapaho. He hushed her harshly.

"What did she say?"

"That she's afraid you're going to kill us."

"We're not going to hurt you," Cork said to her.

She eyed the Ruger in his hand, and he lowered it to his side, muzzle toward the floor.

"I just want to find my wife. If you know the truth and if you're hiding Lame Nightwind, it could be bad for you. You could be charged with a crime."

"What crime?" asked the Arapaho.

"Aiding and abetting a known criminal."

"You know that Lame's a criminal?"

"I do. At least five people are dead because of him."

"We don't know where he is, and that's God's truth. We don't know when he'll be back. And we don't know anything about a blond white woman."

Cork looked at the Arapaho's wife, who looked at the floor. "All right," he finally said. "Let's get out of here, Hugh."

They left the cabin and walked across the hills to where they'd parked the truck. Quinn was still bound to the grille.

"Didn't hear any gunshots," the deputy said. "Guess you didn't find Nightwind." He offered a cruel and satisfied smile.

"See if you can find something in his toolbox to cut that twine," Cork told Parmer. To Quinn he said, "I'm thinking, Dewey, that you're lucky to be with us at the moment. You're one of the threads that tie these people to the bodies in that plane. Makes you a liability. With us, you face jail time. With them, it would be a more permanent, and probably painful, resolution."

Parmer brought a pair of wire clippers from the toolbox and cut Quinn free from the truck.

Cork said, "Now let's make sure Nightwind can't fly out of here."

They drove to the hangar next to the airstrip, and Cork used a pry bar from Quinn's toolbox to force the door open. Parmer pulled Quinn from the truck, and they all went in together and stood between the Piper Cub and the Beechcraft that Nightwind kept parked there.

"He's flown bush with this plane," Parmer said.

"How do you know?"

"He's modified it. Larger tires for soft fields, a larger engine for short field and heavy loads."

"What would keep this plane from flying, Hugh?"

"I'd say the simplest thing would be to damage the prop."

"Sounds good," Cork said. "Seems to me I saw a small sledgehammer in Dewey's toolbox. That ought to do the trick." He went to the truck and came back with the sledge. He ran his hand along the Piper Cub's single propeller. "Wood," he said, a little surprised.

"Not really so odd. A wood prop is lighter, runs smoother, and if you get a tip strike, it shatters like a bunch of toothpicks, so there's less chance of damaging the entire assembly. Pretty simple to replace, too."

"How do you know so much?"

Parmer shrugged and offered an affable grin. "I know a good deal about a lot of things."

Cork took a firm stance in front of the Super Cub and swung twice before the prop blade snapped and splintered. Then he did the same to the prop on the Beechcraft. He stepped back, satisfied. "That should keep him grounded."

"What now?" Parmer said.

"Now we follow the only other thread we have left. Ellyn Grant."

THIRTY-NINE

They arrived in Red Hawk at sunset, under a sky that flamed. They went to the Reservation Business Center, but it was closed for the day. At the Chevron gas station and mini-mart, they asked the man behind the counter if he knew where Grant lived. The man, an Arapaho, fat and tired-looking, shook his head. Cork figured he was lying. On the reservation, on any rez, the rule of thumb when it came to outsiders was to feign ignorance.

In the absence of a better plan, they drove through town. When they came to the little mission of St. Alban, Cork saw activity in the yard beside the church. A number of women were decorating with flowers and streamers, talking and laughing as they worked. Among them strode the priest, tall and white-haired, wearing his clerics and collar, joining in the work and in the gaiety. Cork pulled onto the gravel shoulder of the street and parked. He and Parmer got out. As Cork entered the churchyard, he caught sight of the brass cross above the front door, which was burnished with the reflection of the fire in the sky. Again he recalled the evening months before when he'd spotted the Arapaho kid standing under that same cross as it burned in that same way.

When the two strangers appeared, the women fell silent. The priest, whose back was to the street, turned and watched Cork and Parmer approach.

"Yes?" he said. He wasn't hostile, but he also wasn't particularly welcoming.

"Father, I wonder if we might have a word with you?"

"Of course." The priest turned back to the gathering. "I'll be right back. It's looking so lovely, you know. A fine job." He glanced at the red evening sky. "Afraid we'll have to call it quits soon."

They walked some distance away. The women returned to their preparations, but they did not talk and their eyes followed the men.

"My name is Cork O'Connor. This is Hugh Parmer."

They shook the priest's hand, which was firm and callused.

"Frank Grisham," the priest said. "The Arapaho here call me Father Frank. Are you two gardeners?"

"I beg your pardon?" Cork replied.

"Your fingernails," the priest said. "They're packed with dirt. And your clothing looks like you've been crawling around in a compost heap."

"Sorry, Father. We didn't have a chance to wash up. We're trying to locate Ellyn Grant."

In the red light, the priest studied Cork's face. "You've asked that question of someone here already."

"Yes."

The priest nodded. "Everyone's a little suspicious of white people asking about Arapahos. The first assumption is that you're cops."

"Don't worry, we're not."

The priest said, "You're not from around here."

"Minnesota," Cork told him. "Hugh's from Texas."

"It's none of my affair, of course, but would you mind telling me why you're looking for Ellyn?"

"I think she may have information that will help me find my wife."

The priest waited, as if expecting more explanation from Cork. When he realized there was nothing more coming, he said, "And you think your wife is here?"

"It's complicated, Father. I really need to speak with Ms. Grant."

As he considered, the priest ran his gray eyes over every inch of the two strangers. Finally he came to a decision. "She lives there." He pointed beyond the churchyard toward a modest, one-story house at the end of the next street. A light was on inside. Behind it was an open field. "You say you're not police, but I come from a family of Boston cops, and, son, you've got cop written all over you."

"Retired," Cork said.

The priest laughed and shook his head. "That's like saying 'retired priest.' You never really step away."

"Thank you, Father. I appreciate your help."

They returned to the truck and to Quinn, who was still tied up inside.

"You think you'll get anything out of Ellyn Grant, you're barking up the wrong tree," Quinn said.

"We'll see."

Cork made a U-turn on the empty street and headed to the house the priest had indicated. The place was surrounded by a squat picket fence painted green. Parmer shoved his gun into his belt at the small of his back and pulled out his shirttail to cover it. He followed Cork through the gate and to the front door. Cork knocked. A shadow slid across the curtains, which were lit from inside. Cork waited, then knocked again.

The door opened, and Ellyn Grant stood before them with a rifle in one hand and a small glass filled with amber liquid and ice in the other. Cork smelled whiskey.

"Are you going to shoot us or offer us a drink?" he asked.

Grant looked at Quinn, who hunched between Cork and Parmer with his hands bound.

"I ought to shoot you," she said, though she spoke without rancor.

"We need to talk," Cork said. "We found the plane you buried." He glanced at the whiskey she held. "But I'm guessing you already knew that."

"The plane I buried? I don't know what you're talking about."

"That's not what Dewey says."

"No? What does Dewey say?"

She spoke slowly, and Cork figured the drink in her hand was not her first.

"You really want us to stand here and discuss this in such a public way?"

She thought it over and finally stepped aside. Once they were in, she closed the door and locked it. Cork found himself in a small, comfortable living room decorated with much of the same kind of

Arapaho art he'd seen in Nightwind's home. Grant led them down a short hallway to the kitchen, which was at the back of the house and was illuminated by the overhead light and by the last of the daylight. A bottle of Canadian Club, more than half empty, sat on the table. A chair was already pulled out, and Grant dropped into it and laid the rifle across the tabletop. Cork drew out a chair for Quinn and shoved him into it. He sat in one of the other chairs, and Parmer took the last.

"My wife wasn't on the plane with the others, Ellyn," Cork said. "What happened to her? Where is she?"

"I don't know anything about your wife."

"Quinn swears you're involved up to your eyeballs. He says you knew everything."

She looked at Quinn and shrugged. "Then it's my word against his, isn't it?"

"Who were you expecting, Ellyn?" Cork nodded at the rifle on the table. "Gully and Mike? They'll be looking to clip those threads that tie anyone to them."

Grant didn't respond.

"Even if we have trouble connecting some of the dots, the big picture is crystal clear, Ellyn. There's no way your Gateway Grand Casino will ever get off the ground."

"We'll find another way to bring revenue to the reservation," she replied, as if unconcerned.

"Maybe the Arapaho will, but you won't be helping them do it. You and Lame Nightwind are finished here."

"Lame had nothing to do with anything."

"We know he flew the charter plane."

Grant took a long drink of the whiskey.

"I'm willing to bet he did it for you," Cork said. "I'm willing to bet he did it all for you because he loves you. See, love is something I know about because I lost the woman I love. What did you do for Lame, Ellyn? Did you love him? Or did you just use him so that you could be the great savior of the Arapaho?"

Grant closed her eyes against his words, and a softness came into her face that might have been the effect of the alcohol. She was quiet for a long time. Beyond the kitchen windows daylight continued to fade.

"Love," she finally said and smiled. "Of all the Great Creator's great creations, it must be the most sacred and shapeless." She opened her eyes and looked dreamily at Cork. "I love Lame Nightwind, oh yes. And I love the Arapaho. And I love this country, the Owl Creek Reservation, even though to the eyes of a *nahita* it probably looks like a wasteland. I love the vision I had for my people. And I'm just drunk enough, Cork O'Connor, to say that in my way I love you because you've shown me something important. You're right. There won't be any Gateway Grand Casino, no easy way out for the Owl Creek Arapaho, but I've come to understand that maybe it's for the best. Maybe Edgar was right. Trading on the weakness of others makes us weak as well. The Arapaho have always been a strong people. I lost my faith in our strength. We have endured much. And we have much yet to endure. But endure we will." She lifted her glass in a toast and drank again.

"Ellyn, what happened to my wife?"

She considered him and shook her head with drunken sympathy. "You love her, don't you? Lucky man. Lucky woman." She stared out the kitchen window at the darkening sky. "That white door your son saw? She's behind it."

"What do you mean? What white door? Where?"

Grant took a long, deep breath, but before she answered, the window glass shattered and her head flew back as if she'd been kicked in the face and her chair tipped over and she tumbled to the floor. The next shot hit Dewey Quinn, caught him in the right shoulder and spun him out of his chair and onto the kitchen floor. Parmer lurched from his seat and hugged the floor. Cork grabbed the rifle from the table. It was a Marlin carbine, and he worked the lever to be sure there was a round in the chamber. He crawled to the wall next to the shattered window.

"Kill the light," he told Parmer.

Parmer scrambled across the floor, hit the wall switch, and the kitchen went dark. Cork and his companion cautiously peered through the window. Two figures were racing away across the field behind

Grant's home. Cork leaped to the back door, fumbled with the lock, finally flung the door open, and tore outside. He caught sight of the two men again just as they ran into a line of trees that followed a stream on the far side of the field. Headlights came on, and a black Jeep Cherokee sped away. Cork knelt, lifted the rifle to his shoulder, and pulled off four rounds. Near the bridge at the other end of the field, the Cherokee swung onto the paved road and rocketed away.

Cork ran back to the house and found Parmer on his knees next to Ellyn Grant. There was a hole the size of a nickel above her left eye and beneath her head a rapidly spreading pool of blood.

Quinn lay on his back, groaning, the clothing over his right shoulder a wet mess of red.

A furious pounding came from the front door. "Open up!"

Cork went quickly to the living room, unlocked the door, and swung it wide.

Andrew No Voice stood there, weapon drawn. At his back were a number of Arapaho, and among them stood the tall, white-haired priest. "Put your gun down! Do it now!" No Voice ordered.

Cork laid his firearm on the floor.

FORTY

Sheriff Kosmo arrived by helicopter, courtesy of Jon Rude. Through the window of No Voice's office, Cork watched the chopper land in the gravel parking area. The headquarters of the tribal police was a long, narrow one-story cinder-block construction at the southern edge of Red Hawk. It was separated from the school grounds by a field of irrigated alfalfa. As soon as the helicopter touched down, Kosmo leaped out and headed for the headquarters's door. No Voice didn't get up when Kosmo walked in. He just nodded toward Cork and Parmer and said, "All yours, Jim."

Kosmo stood with his beefy arms crossed, staring down at the two seated men. "You talk to 'em?"

"Yeah," No Voice said.

"Don't suppose you wrung a lock-solid confession out of 'em."

"They were cooperative. And they didn't do it."

"How do you know?"

"Earl Vixen, next house up the street from Ellyn's, he was out in the yard with Kong, that Chihuahua of his, waiting for his dog to take a crap. Corroborated O'Connor's account of the men firing from the field out back. It took a while for Earl to stroll over here. Told me he didn't say anything to anybody cuz he was concerned someone might come looking for him, too. He's still here. I got him in a back room working on an official statement. Bottom line is that at the moment a lot of folks in Red Hawk are under the impression these two killed Ellyn. I've had some pretty irate calls already. I didn't want to turn them loose until I was sure they had safe passage to Hot Springs."

"I'll have Rude fly them back," Kosmo said, then he addressed Cork. "You able to ID the guys?"

"I didn't see them, but I have a good idea who they were. One calls himself Gully. The other is Mike."

"Last names?"

Cork shook his head. "They were the two who tried to take us out at the plane."

"Them and Dewey, right?"

"That's right."

"Where's my deputy, Andy?"

"In a holding cell in back. He's got himself a pretty good flesh wound. I had Grace Lincoln from the clinic come over and clean him up and sew him closed. He'll probably have a nasty-looking scar, but he's in no danger. Want to talk to him?"

"In a bit."

Rude strolled in and stood just inside the door. "Good to see you two alive," he said. "Want me to stick around, Sheriff?"

"Yeah, I want you to give these two a lift back to Hot Springs. For a while we'll need to keep them out of harm's way." Kosmo turned back to Cork and Parmer. "We found the plane. DCI's on their way up from Cheyenne. They'll process the scene." He looked at No Voice. "I asked 'em to send someone over here to go over Ellyn's house, too." He eyed Cork. "Five bodies onboard, all male. So. Where's your wife, O'Connor?"

"That's what I wanted to talk to Ellyn Grant about."

"Did she tell you anything?"

"Yeah. She said Jo's behind a white door."

"What's that mean?"

"She didn't have a chance to explain."

"Got an idea?"

"None."

"You came straight to Red Hawk from the plane site?"

"No. We stopped at Nightwind's ranch on the way. He wasn't there."

"Find out where he is?"

"The Arapaho there—"

"Ben Iron."

"Right, and his wife, they claimed they didn't know."

"You thought Nightwind might have an idea where your wife is?"

"I figured it wouldn't hurt to ask him."

"These two guys, Mike and Gully, would they know?"

"I doubt it. They seemed genuinely surprised that she wasn't there with the others."

"Maybe she dug her way out?"

"Maybe. But we didn't see any sign of that," Cork said.

"She was definitely onboard?"

"I found her briefcase under the only seat not occupied."

"So how do you explain her absence?"

"I have no explanation."

"All right. I'm going to head down and have a word or two with my deputy."

"Mind if I come along?" No Voice said.

"Be my guest, Andy. You two gentlemen just relax. I might want to talk some more after I hear what Dewey has to say."

When the two law officers had gone, Cork said to Rude, "So, you're the sheriff's personal escort these days?"

Rude grinned. "I'm the fastest transport to a remote location. Around here we all lend a hand when we can. Truth is, when Kosmo called and told me what was going on, I wanted to see for myself. Any idea what's going on?"

"I'll tell you, Jon, I've been looking at it from every angle, and it's got me stumped."

"You think she's alive?"

Cork rubbed his eyes with the heels of his hands, overcome with weariness. It was the long day, the hard labor of the dig, the fact that he had no answer to Rude's question.

"I'm not going there yet, Jon," he said.

"Sure." Rude nodded. "I understand."

Kosmo came back. "You two are free to go. I'd like you both in my office early tomorrow. I'll need formal statements."

"Did Quinn tell you anything?" Parmer asked.

"He's reluctant at the moment, but I'll be talking to Dewey all night. By the time I see you in the morning, there won't be anything he knows that I don't." To Rude he said, "I'll have one of No Voice's men transport me and Dewey. Thanks for your help." He didn't leave immediately. Instead he turned to Cork. "O'Connor, I'm sorry I gave you such a hard time. I apologize. But this, hell, this is such a bizarre situation. Look, from here on in, I'll do everything I possibly can to help you find your wife. That's a promise."

"Thanks," Cork said.

Kosmo gave a parting nod and left.

"All right," Rude said. "Let's get this show on the road."

The moon was up. All the way back, Cork stared at the ground below, a vast emptiness punctuated at great distances with solitary yard lights. It made him think of the cold universe where an eternity separated the stars. Jo was somewhere in all that hollow space. God alone knew where. Alive? No, that was too much, too painful a hope to lose again. If she was alive, wouldn't she have let him know? And how could it possibly be? She'd been in the plane with the others. Mike shot her in the heart. There was no sign that she'd dug herself out. Hell, she couldn't even have opened the door, the dirt had been packed against it so firmly. Yet she was not there. It was Houdini. It was magic. Or, it was a miracle.

They landed at Rude's ranch. He gave them a ride from there to where they'd parked their Jeep on the Horseshoe Creek Trail that morning. By the time they were ready to separate, it was well after midnight. They stood among the cottonwoods beside the trickle of the creek. The moonlight was so bright it was like silver fire burning shadows into the ground.

"What do you have planned for tomorrow?" Rude asked.

Cork shook his head. "I'm fresh out of ideas. I've followed every lead I can. I expect Lame Nightwind knows we're on his trail, and I'm guessing he'll stay vanished. From what you told me, Jon, he knows those mountains well enough he could disappear there and never be found."

"True. But he'd be leaving everything behind."

"With Ellyn Grant dead, maybe there's nothing for him to come back to," Parmer said.

Rude crossed his arms and looked up at the moon. "You want my take on it, Lame won't be satisfied until he's dealt with whoever killed her. At the moment, he probably thinks that's you."

"We won't have to worry about Nightwind. Gully and Mike'll be gunning for him. Another thread they need to cut," Cork said.

"I'd love to be there when those guys face off," Parmer said. "Little Bighorn meets the St. Valentine's Day Massacre."

Rude extended his hand in parting. "You need anything from me, Cork, just holler."

"Thanks, Jon."

Rude took off, heading home, and Parmer got in the Jeep. Cork stood by himself, staring at his shadow, black against the ground. It seemed to him he was looking into a bottomless hole, and he felt empty. He'd been so close to finding Jo, and then he'd lost her. Again. And he had no idea anymore where to look.

"Cork?" Parmer called.

After a long moment, Cork said, "I'm coming."

FORTY-ONE

The next morning, the ring of the phone in his hotel room startled Cork awake. He fumbled with the receiver.

"Yeah?"

"Mr. O'Connor? This is Father Frank Grisham."

"Yeah, Father. Just a second." Cork sat up and tried to blink the sleep from his eyes. The room was bright with sunlight. He looked at the clock on the nightstand. Eight thirty. "Okay, Father. What can I do for you?"

"I need to speak with you. It's urgent."

"Can we talk over the phone?"

"No, this needs to be done here at St. Alban, face-to-face."

"All right, Father. I can be in Red Hawk in an hour."

The call had awakened Parmer. Cork told him what was up, and Parmer threw back his covers and got out of bed.

Cork was dressed and had just finished brushing his teeth when Sheriff Kosmo called.

"O'Connor, I thought you'd like to know this. The DCI team from Cheyenne started working the scene at the plane first thing this morning. They figured out why those passengers just sat there and allowed themselves to be shot. The masks that dropped and they put over their faces? The oxygen tanks that fed them had been switched for nitrogen. The DCI people tell me that would have knocked out anyone wearing a mask. Except for the pilot. His mask was fed from an oxygen tank. These people, O'Connor, they thought of everything."

"Has the DCI team found anything else?"

"Nothing we don't already know about, but it's early. I still want to see you and Parmer here at the department for a formal statement."

"We'll be there before lunch."

Parmer had already gone downstairs for the hotel's complimentary continental breakfast. Cork joined him and grabbed coffee and a roll to go. As they headed out to the mission in Red Hawk, he filled Parmer in on his conversation with Kosmo.

"So, Jo was probably unconscious like the others," Parmer said. "And if what Gully and Mike said is correct, she was also in the plane when they buried it. Did she wake up and get herself out somehow?"

"If she did, why didn't we see any evidence of her digging?" Cork replied. "And why didn't I hear from her?"

"Maybe she got out and got lost in the area. Out there, there's nothing for a million miles."

"And the pixies filled in the hole she dug?"

"I know. Nothing makes sense."

The morning sun was behind them. Cork was at the wheel. He looked west across the empty country toward the Absarokas, where a dark bank of clouds was pushing up from the back side of the range.

"You happen to hear a weather report?" he asked Parmer.

"Yeah, a front's moving in. Rain down here, maybe a lot. Snow at the higher elevations." He yawned and settled back against the headrest. "Wonder what the priest wants to talk to you about."

"I'm thinking it has to do with Ellyn Grant. Maybe he knows something about her and Nightwind that might be useful. We'll find out soon enough."

As they pulled into Red Hawk, they spotted Andy No Voice coming toward them in his Blazer. Both vehicles stopped as they came abreast, and No Voice leaned out his open window.

"What are you doing here, O'Connor?"

"Business with the priest at the mission. Any word on Lame Nightwind?"

"Nothing. Kosmo and me made a visit to his place at daybreak. He wasn't there, hadn't slept in his bed. Possible, I suppose, that those two men who took out Ellyn Grant did the same to him and left his body for the coyotes somewhere, but I'd be surprised if anybody could get the drop on Lame Nightwind. More likely he's lying low, trying to figure his next move.

"I've got most of my force out patrolling the back roads, what of 'em we can. We might get lucky. I'm headed to the hospital in Hot Springs. They got Deputy Quinn there for observation. The DCI folks are going to interview him this morning. I want to be there for that."

"I'll talk to Kosmo later," Cork said, "see if Quinn gave up anything new."

No Voice looked back at the quiet town. "This might not be the safest place for you two. There are still people in Red Hawk who think it was you killed Ellyn."

"We'll keep that in mind," Cork promised. "And we'll be careful."

"All right then." No Voice lifted his hand briefly in a parting gesture and headed away.

Cork parked in front of St. Alban, and he and Parmer got out. The mission door was open, and the priest stood just inside, out of the sun. When they approached, Father Grisham said, "Your friend needs to wait outside. This is for you alone, Mr. O'Connor."

"I'll be in the Jeep," Parmer said.

Cork followed the priest into the mission. It was a small sanctuary with a lot of statuary that looked locally made. The crucifix above the altar was hewn from wood and roughly carved. The windows were opaque gold, and the light coming through had a golden hue. There were flowers everywhere, as if in preparation for a wedding, and Cork thought about all the women who'd been there the night before, decorating. Two people sat in the last pew, a woman and a boy. When they heard the men coming, they stood and turned. Cork recognized them. The Arapaho woman and the kid from Nightwind's ranch.

After glancing into his face for a brief instant, the woman looked down.

"You know who these people are, Mr. O'Connor. They're good people, and they have something they need to tell you."

Cork waited. The mission was quiet, peaceful. It felt safe.

"Go ahead, Adelle," the priest urged gently. "Tell Mr. O'Connor exactly what you've told me."

The woman spoke toward the floor. "We didn't mean any harm. We didn't know what else to do."

"Just tell him, Adelle."

The woman glanced at her grandson, who also looked at the floor. "When Nick was not much more than a baby, his father killed a man in a fight and went to the prison in Rawlins. He's still there. His mother died two years later. We've raised Nick. My husband is a good man, and he tries to do right for our grandson. But a boy, he wants adventure. Lame Deer Nightwind is adventure. Nick, he follows Lame everywhere. One day late last fall, Lame loaded his big machine onto a trailer and got ready to leave."

"Big machine?" Cork asked.

"His backhoe," the kid said.

"When Nick asked him where he was going, Lame wouldn't say," Adelle went on. "He was very mysterious. As soon as he was gone, Nick saddled a horse and followed. He does this kind of thing."

"You knew where Nightwind was going?" Cork asked the boy.

Nick shook his head. "But out here there's nobody. It was real easy to follow the tracks his truck and trailer left."

"Did he go to the box canyon north of the ranch?"

"Yes," Nick said. He risked a glance upward into Cork's face. "I hid in the rocks on top of the canyon wall and watched him clear a long strip with the blade on his backhoe. I figured right away what it was, but then he did something I didn't understand. He dug a big hole at one end. When he was finished, he left the backhoe and the trailer and drove off. I rode home. The next day he put Dominion into a trailer and headed toward the canyon again."

"Dominion?" Cork asked.

"His favorite horse," Adelle said.

"Go on, Nick."

"He came back riding Dominion."

"What did he do with the truck?"

The kid shrugged. "I wondered that, too. The next morning he flew away. He was gone for a couple of days, then the clouds came and

I knew there was going to be a big storm and I worried about his truck. I saddled one of the horses and rode out to the canyon to make sure things were all right there." He hesitated.

"And were they?"

"I could tell there was a lot of snow coming down in the mountains already, but nothing was falling here yet. Just before I got to the canyon, I heard a plane flying low over the foothills. I saw it come out of the clouds and bank for a landing on the strip that Lame had cleared. It touched down and taxied into the canyon and then I couldn't see it anymore. I tied up my horse and climbed the canyon wall. I saw the plane in the big hole Lame had dug, and Lame was there with two other men. The two men went into the plane, but Lame didn't go in with them. Then I heard a bunch of shots inside and they came back out. Lame got on his backhoe and buried the plane. Then he loaded the backhoe on the trailer and hauled it away with his truck. The two men who were with him drove away, too."

He stopped and went back to looking at the floor.

"And you went down there?" Cork said.

The kid shook his head. "I should have. I had an idea what happened in that plane. But I was scared. Lame's horse trailer was still there and I figured he'd come back for it and I didn't want him to catch me, so I left and went home."

"Did you tell anyone what you saw?"

"No."

"My wife was on that plane. But she's not there now. Do you know why?"

The boy lifted his eyes to Cork's face. "I went back and got her."

"You?"

"Yeah. I couldn't stop thinking about that plane, and I had to know. The next day I went back. I took a shovel. It was still snowing and blowing, but it wasn't that cold and I knew the way. When I got there, I saw that Lame had already come back for his horse trailer. There was snow over everything, but I could still see where the plane was buried. It was kind of mounded like. I started digging. The ground was still pretty loose, and it wasn't hard. It took me a couple of hours, but I finally uncovered the door. When I opened it, it was bad inside.

All those guys sitting in their seats, shot in the head, blood all down their faces. I wanted to turn around and just run, but I heard a noise. It came from the back of the plane. I was scared, but I went back there anyway. That's when I saw her. She was shot different from the men. Shot here." He pointed toward the middle of his chest. "She wasn't dead. She looked at me and tried to say something. But all she could do was make a little sound. I didn't think I should move her, so I found a blanket and put it over her and I tried to make her understand that I'd be back. Then I rode home and told my granddad."

"Your husband knew?" Cork said to Adelle.

"The story isn't over," the woman said. "Before you judge him, please just listen."

Cork wanted to grab the kid and shake the story from him, the whole thing, in an instant. Struggling to sound patient, he said, "Go on."

"My granddad drove his truck. We went back inside the plane. The woman was right there where I left her. She was unconscious. My granddad carried her to the truck and put her inside. He said we couldn't leave the hole open, so we filled it back in, and spread snow over it real careful so it was hard to tell we'd been there. Then we brought her home."

Cork could contain himself no longer. He reached out and grasped the kid's shoulders. "What did you do with her?"

"Let him go," Adelle said. She pried Cork's hands from her grandson and gathered Nick under the protection of her arm. "If it weren't for him, you and your friend would be dead now. He saved you yesterday. In that canyon."

"You? You fired those shots?"

The boy nodded. "I was at the barn. I heard Lame outside talking on his phone. I heard him say the buried plane would be a good place to get rid of O'Connor. I knew that was you. I told my granddad. He said we should stay out of it, but it didn't seem right to me. So I rode out. I took my rifle. I don't know. It seemed like a good thing. I got there and you already had the hole dug. Then the men came out from where they'd been hiding and I knew they were going to kill you. So I tried to shoot them. But I missed. I guess I was kind of scared."

Cork gathered himself and shoved aside his impatience and his anger. "Thanks," he said more quietly, then asked, "What about my wife?"

Adelle continued the story. "We hid her and we nursed her. She was hurt bad, but we didn't know what to do."

"Why didn't you take her to a doctor?"

"Because we would have to tell the truth. And they would know what Lame did and they would put him in jail. Lame's been good to us. We didn't want trouble. And if Lame was sent away, we didn't know what would become of us."

"He didn't know about her?"

"Not at first. We were . . ." She looked down. "We were afraid of him. But she just got worse and worse. And finally my husband said we had to tell Lame. Lame had to figure what to do."

"How did Nightwind take the news?"

"He was mad, like we knew he would be. I thought he was going to hurt Nick."

"I knew he wouldn't hurt me," Nick said.

"We told him the woman needed help," Adelle went on. "She needed a doctor. He said that if the people who'd shot her knew that we knew, he couldn't protect us and they'd kill us all."

"What did he do?"

"He made us leave the ranch for a few days in case those men showed up looking for us. When we came back, she was gone."

"Did he say what he'd done with her?"

Nick said, "I asked him if he killed her. He said no and I believed him."

Cork looked at the Arapaho woman. "And you? Did you believe him?"

"I wanted to. But I don't know. She was gone and I tried to forget. And then you came back looking for her. And we"—she put her arm around her grandson and drew him to her—"we decided that you needed to know the truth, whatever it cost us."

"Does your husband know you're here?"

"Yes. He stayed at the ranch. He believed he should let Lame know what we're doing."

"Where is Lame?"

"I don't know. He left last night and still wasn't back this morning."

The priest said, "I'm sure that by now he knows about Ellyn Grant, Mr. O'Connor. Word on the reservation travels remarkably fast. And he's probably aware of what you know and the danger it presents to him. I can't imagine that he'll simply wait around to be arrested, though Lame isn't a man easy to predict."

"Yesterday we made sure that he couldn't fly away," Cork said. "And there aren't a lot of roads out here and No Voice says his guys are patrolling, so if he tries to drive there's a good chance he'll be spotted. But sometimes, Father, a cornered man just hunkers down and waits."

"And then what?"

"That's always the question."

A woman rushed into the mission and stood just inside the door, breathing hard. A ball cap was pulled over her long hair and shaded her eyes. She wore faded jeans and a T-shirt with an image of four Apache warriors holding rifles. The caption for the image read HOME-LAND SECURITY. FIGHTING TERRORISM SINCE 1492.

Cork recognized her, though he couldn't remember her name. He'd seen her the night before at the office of the tribal police. She was a dispatcher.

"What is it, Lee?"

"I just spoke with Chief No Voice on the radio. He's on his way back, but he said I should come over and tell this to Mr. O'Connor." She looked at the woman and the kid. "I suppose it's good you're here, too, Adelle. It's about Ben."

"What about him?" Adelle asked.

"We just got a 911 call from Lame Nightwind's ranch. Your husband's been shot, Adelle. It doesn't sound good, but it's not fatal."

"Who shot him?" Cork asked.

"I don't know."

Cork spoke again. "Who made the call?"

"Lame Nightwind," the dispatcher said.

FORTY-TWO

It was thirty miles to Nightwind's ranch. Cork drove like a madman. In the dust raised behind him, Father Frank and the Arapaho followed in the truck they'd driven to Red Hawk. Ten minutes after they left town, Cork's cell phone rang, and he handed it to Parmer.

Parmer answered, listened, then turned to Cork. "It's Sheriff Kosmo. He'd like you to stop immediately and wait. He'll have men out here as soon as he can and an ambulance."

"Tell him to go to hell."

Into the phone, Parmer said, "Sheriff, I'd have better luck trying to stop a bulldozer with a feather duster." He listened again, then held out the cell phone to Cork. "He wants to talk to you."

Cork took the phone, snapped it shut, and handed it back to Parmer. Then he bore down even harder on the accelerator.

Half a mile from Lame Nightwind's ranch compound, Cork stopped. "Check your Ruger."

Parmer opened the glove box where he'd placed the weapon. He pulled the firearm out, ejected and checked the magazine, then slapped it back into place. Cork swung himself out of the Jeep and opened the back door just as the Arapahos' truck drew up behind him. He lifted out Quinn's Winchester, which he'd kept.

Adelle, Nick, and Father Frank got out of the pickup and hurried to the Jeep.

The priest frowned at the rifle in Cork's hands. "Is this necessary, Mr. O'Connor?"

Cork checked the magazine to be sure it carried a full load of rounds.

"I've got no idea what we might be walking into, Father. It could be Lame Nightwind or it could be a couple of professional killers. I just want to be prepared."

"Mr. O'Connor, I understand your eagerness—" the priest began.

"Father, what you understand or don't isn't important to me. Nightwind may be the only man alive who knows where my wife is. I intend to get some answers from him."

"What if you kill him first?" the priest said.

"I'll make sure that doesn't happen."

Cork pushed the priest aside, got into the Jeep, and handed Parmer the rifle. Adelle Iron rushed to his door and stood looking at him very afraid.

"What about my husband?"

"I'll do what I can," Cork said. "But until we know the situation, you and Nick and the father stay back. Do you understand?"

He didn't wait for her to answer. He kicked the engine over, and as soon as she stepped away, he sped off.

A hundred yards from the ranch house he pulled to a stop and scanned the compound. Except for the horses grazing in the pasture behind the barn, nothing moved. Two hawks circled on thermals above the foothills, and beyond that the face of Heaven's Keep, distant and brooding, looked down. A line of dark clouds had begun to mount from behind the Absarokas.

Cork reached for his rifle. "Stay here and cover me," he said to Parmer. "I'm going to check the house."

He used the protection of the boulders that were a natural part of the landscape and made his way toward the ranch house.

Behind him, Adelle Iron parked the truck next to Parmer and the Wrangler.

Cork reached the porch and bounded up the steps to the front door. He waited, then tried the knob. The door was unlocked. He nudged it open but kept to the side, out of sight. When nothing happened, he kicked the door wide and slipped inside. He scanned the living room and the dining room beyond. He listened carefully but heard nothing. Then he sensed movement at his back. He spun and found Parmer in the doorway.

"Easy, Cork. Just me."

Cork turned back to the interior of the house. He motioned with his hand for Parmer to follow. Slowly, carefully, they went through the whole place. Nightwind wasn't there. They returned to the Jeep.

"My husband?" Adelle asked.

Cork shook his head.

"At the cabin," she said.

"Wait here until we're sure." Cork's attention became focused on the outbuildings. He sprinted to the garage and peered through a window. Nightwind's pickup was parked inside, along with a Jeep Cherokee. Cork turned to Parmer, who'd shadowed him.

"His vehicles are still here. He's around somewhere. We're going to check the outbuildings one at a time. I'll go first, you cover me."

Parmer was dripping sweat. His shirt was soaked dark. He put a hand on Cork's shoulder. "The sheriff's people will be here in an hour or so. Sure you don't want to wait?"

Cork wanted to scream so bad he could barely speak to Parmer. What he managed to say was this: "I have to know about my wife. If God himself were coming in an hour, I wouldn't wait."

For an instant, Parmer's grip tightened on Cork's shoulder, then released. "All right, I'm with you. Whatever it takes."

Cork ran in a crouch to the next outbuilding, where Nightwind kept his backhoe. He tried the door. It opened easily. Inside, except for the silent bulk of the great machine, the place was empty. He motioned Parmer to join him, and he nodded toward the barn.

Cork slipped along the front wall toward the barn door, which was pulled wide open. From inside came a steady hum that Cork couldn't identify. He motioned Parmer toward the rear of the building. Parmer climbed a rail fence and disappeared in back. Cork reached the door and edged his left shoulder and his head around the threshold. Slowly, the scene revealed itself to him. The barn was in disarray, tools and materials thrown about as if in the heat of an angry battle. A chair sat in the middle of the room. It was empty, but an uncoiled length of rope lay like a long, dead snake on the ground around it. The hum continued, coming from the corner of the barn that was still hidden from Cork's view. His finger nestled the rifle trigger, and he eased himself farther into the barn.

What he saw stopped him cold.

A body hung upside down, its ankles tied to a rope that ran through a pulley suspended from a rafter. It was male, nude, eviscerated. Entrails hung from the gaping wound and lay in the dirt directly below. The body was black with a skin that seemed to ripple. Flies. Thousands of them. The source of the hum Cork had heard.

Parmer entered through the back door and came to where Cork stood.

"Jesus," he said. "Is that Ben Iron?"

Because of the flies, Cork couldn't tell. He walked to the hung body and nudged it with his rifle barrel. The flies dispersed. The body slowly rotated. Cork looked at the face.

"It's Gully," he said.

Parmer glanced around. "Where's Mike?"

"Over there." Cork walked to a stall where a body lay thrown on a bed of hay. Most of the lower jaw had been blown away, but enough of the face still remained for Cork to see clearly who it had been.

"What's with the chair and the rope?" Parmer asked. "He tied Gully there first, then decided on this?" ·

Cork shook his head. "I can't make heads or tails of Nightwind."

"Where is he?"

"Only one place that I know of left to look."

At that moment, the Arapaho truck sped past the barn.

Cork ran to the door and watched the trail of dust rise as the truck raced toward the cabin. "Goddamn it! Come on, Hugh."

Under the threatening sky, they hightailed it to the Wrangler and followed the truck into the foothills.

When they reached the cabin, the truck was empty and the cabin door was ajar. Cork heard voices inside, talking loud and fast. He heard Adelle cry out. He grasped his rifle and jumped from the Jeep. Parmer leaped out the other side. The priest appeared in the doorway. He looked stricken and beckoned them forward. They came cautiously. Cork held his rifle ready.

"Nightwind's gone," the priest said.

Inside Cork found Ben Iron lying on the sofa. He was conscious but not in good shape. He'd been beaten severely, his face a mass of bruise and swelling. His midsection had been wrapped in gauze, and there was a large red stain over the left side. His wife sat beside him, fussing over his injuries. Nick stood behind them.

"Where's Nightwind?" Cork said.

Ben Iron stared at him and said weakly, "Where you'll never find him."

"What happened, Ben?" the priest asked.

Through lips swollen and crusted with dried blood, the man answered, "A visit from the devil, Father."

FORTY-THREE

Soon after Adelle and Nick had left that morning, the two men came. They did it quietly and caught Ben Iron in the barn. They shot him and then tied him to the chair. They were looking for Lame Nightwind. The Arapaho didn't know where Lame was. They called him a lying redskin and laid into him. While they were at it, Lame slipped into the barn. He shot them both. Mike, he killed instantly. Gully wasn't so lucky. Nightwind strung him up, tortured him until he confessed to killing Ellyn Grant, then went on torturing him until he was dead.

The Arapaho was only semiconscious through most of this. When Nightwind had finished working on Gully, he took Ben Iron to the cabin, laid him on the sofa, saw to his wound, and declared he would survive. Iron told him where his wife and Nick had gone. Then Nightwind went away, and after that everything went black.

He remembered next that Nightwind shook him awake and told him people were on their way to help him. And he put a note in Iron's pocket and told him good-bye.

The next thing Iron remembered was his wife and grandson and the priest coming through the cabin door.

Cork walked to the sofa, reached into the man's pocket, and drew out the note.

The ranch belongs to you now, Ben. The papers are in my desk. I have unfinished business. Any man who tries to follow me is a dead man.

Cork read the note again. "Follow him where? His truck's here and he can't fly his planes."

"I didn't see Dominion at the barn," Nick said.

Adelle looked out the open cabin door. "He probably went into the mountains."

"Where would he go up there?"

"Anywhere he wants to," Iron said. "He knows the Absarokas better than anyone."

"He has a cabin up there," the kid said.

"Nick," his grandfather said and cut him off with a look.

"Where?" Cork said.

Nick stared at the cabin floor and didn't answer.

Adelle said, "Ben, this man hasn't hurt us in any way, and all he wants is to find his wife."

"Lame's been good to us," Iron said.

"He's the cause of this man's sorrow, Ben," Adelle said. "At least give him the chance to find his wife."

"Lame'll probably kill him anyway," the kid said.

"Nick," his grandmother snapped at him.

Iron squeezed his eyes closed in pain and finally gave in. "It's supposed to be near Heaven's Keep, but nobody except Lame knows where," he said. "His uncle built it. Hunted and trapped out of it. Hid it somewhere nobody could stumble across it. There's a trailhead not far from here. Lame always takes it. But God alone knows where he goes."

Cork walked to the door and looked toward Heaven's Keep, which he could no longer see because it had become shrouded in clouds spilling in from the west.

"I'll need a horse," he said.

Nick and Parmer accompanied him to the barn. Inside the doorway, the kid stopped and stared, horrified, at the hanging man.

"I'd cut him down," Cork said, "but he needs to be left like that for the police."

After that the kid did his best to avoid looking. He chose a dapple gray named Aggie. Next to Dominion, this was the best horse on the ranch, Nick said. While the kid saddled him, Cork and Parmer went to the ranch house to collect supplies.

"Look, I understand where you're coming from, Cork. But you can't go alone."

"I'm not putting anyone else in jeopardy, Hugh."

"You know anything about horses, Cork?"

"No."

"I can't turn you loose in those mountains trusting your fate to an animal you don't understand."

"I don't figure I'll need my horse for long, one way or the other."

Into a canvas sack he'd brought from the barn, Cork had thrown a can of baked beans, a couple of cans of tuna fish, a can of peaches, a jar half full of peanut butter, most of a jar of strawberry jam, and a box of saltines. He opened a drawer and found a can opener, a spoon, and a sharp knife, all of which he threw into the sack.

Parmer grabbed him roughly. "Look at me. What the kid said is true. Nightwind'll probably kill you. If you're alone. Two of us stand a better chance."

"This is way more than what you signed on for."

"Hell, it's been way more from the beginning. I'm not going to let you cut me loose at this point no matter what. We do this together."

"I'm wasting time here, Hugh."

"Then just say yes, damn it."

Cork thought it over quickly, under the press of time, and gave in. "All right."

Parmer smiled. "Let's get cracking."

They left the kitchen and headed toward a room Cork had seen in his earlier reconnoitering. In Nightwind's study, he found what he was looking for, a gun case containing some fine-looking armaments. The case was locked. Cork smashed the glass, reached inside, and pulled out a Savage 110. He looked at Parmer and waited for the man to comment on the firearm in his hands.

Parmer simply nodded and said, "Nice piece." He reached into the case and chose a Weatherby. "Wonder where he keeps the cartridges."

"In the equipment shed," Nick said from the doorway. "He has scopes there, too."

"My horse is ready, Nick?"

"Yes."

"Mind getting us those cartridges and scopes?"

"Okay. Lame's got sleeping bags, too. I'll bring those." He saw the rifle in Parmer's hands. "I'll saddle Hornet for you. A good horse, trust me."

Cork went to the closet in the front entryway. He grabbed a fleece-lined jean jacket that was hanging there. Parmer took a leather jacket, also lined with fleece. Cork slid a Stetson from the closet shelf and tried it on. Too big for him, but it fit Parmer nicely. There was a gray stocking cap hanging on a peg, and Cork took that instead.

Nick brought them the cartridge boxes and the sleeping bags, and they returned to the barn for the horses. Parmer saddled his own mount, speaking quietly to the animal as he worked. The kid went into the tack room and brought out scabbards for the rifles. Cork was walking his horse out of the barn when Kosmo showed up.

The sheriff came with two deputies. No Voice followed in his Blazer, accompanied by two of his own officers. They arrived in a cloud of dust and drew up in front of the barn. The officers got out, weapons drawn. Cork walked out to meet them.

"Where's Nightwind?" Kosmo asked.

"Gone into the mountains."

Cork related the salient details of the story the Arapaho had told him, then he handed the lawman Nightwind's note.

Kosmo read it and looked into the barn behind Cork, where Nick and Parmer were readying the second mount. "You're going after him?"

"Hugh and me."

"What's the unfinished business he mentions?"

"I don't know," Cork said.

"You go up there and he'll kill you both."

"He's the only one who knows the truth about my wife, so it's a chance I'm willing to take. There's something you ought to see." Cork jerked his head for Kosmo to follow.

"Wait here," the sheriff said to his deputies. Inside, when he caught sight of the body strung from the rafter, Kosmo stopped as if he'd walked into a wall. "Jesus Christ. Who is it?"

"Gully. Mike's in the stall over there. They came looking for Nightwind."

No Voice joined them. When he saw Nightwind's handiwork, he whistled. "Like a goddamn slaughtered cow. Who is it?"

"One of the guys shot Ellyn Grant," Kosmo said.

"Where's the other one?" No Voice asked.

The sheriff nodded toward the body in the stall.

No Voice couldn't take his eyes off the bloody spectacle hung from the beam. "Lame did this out of pure meanness?"

"I got no idea what's in his head," Kosmo said. "Where's your granddad, Nick?"

"At our cabin," the kid replied. "Those men hurt him, but he'll be all right."

"EMTs are on their way from Hot Springs. Be here pretty soon." Kosmo turned to Cork. "You really intend to go after Nightwind? Just you and Parmer?"

"I don't have much choice, Sheriff. I hope you're not thinking of trying to stop me."

"Hold off for a while," Kosmo said. "In three hours I could have a dozen men mounted to go with you."

Cork shook his head. "You see those clouds. It'll be raining pretty soon down here. That means snow in the mountains. By the time you get it all together, his trail'll be covered. We head off now, we have a chance."

Kosmo threw a stern look at Parmer. "You understand what you're walking into? You could well end up just like that man there."

Parmer said, "I understand."

The sheriff shoved his big hands into the back pockets of his jeans and studied the mountains through the doorway of the barn. "Christ, I don't like this."

"I'm not exactly doing cartwheels, Sheriff," Cork said. "But if there's a chance of getting my wife back, I'll do whatever I have to."

Kosmo looked at the butchered man for half a minute, and in the quiet as he considered, the only sounds were the snorts of the horses and the ripples of their flanks as they shook off the flies.

"It's still a free country, O'Connor, and I don't suppose I've got any legal way to keep you from going. But let me give you a few things that'll help."

Outside, he took two ballistic vests from the trunk of his cruiser and gave one to each of them.

"Got these babies through a special Homeland Security grant. They provide Level Three protection. They'll stop anything up to a .308 caliber, full metal jacket round. Unless Nightwind has armor-piercing ammo, you're covered."

He also gave Cork a Falcon II handheld radio. The last thing he offered was a topographic map of the area.

"I'm going to maintain a command post here at Nightwind's place. Take care of that radio. It's set on our search and rescue frequency. Provided you're somewhere high enough that the topography doesn't block the signal, we'll hear you."

"We've both got cell phones," Parmer said.

"Yeah, well, good luck getting a signal in the Absarokas. However you do it, keep me apprised of your situation as best you can."

"All right," Cork said. He looked to Nick. "You willing to show us that trailhead your granddad talked about?"

"Yes. It's not an official trail or anything, it's just how Lame goes into the mountains. But it leads to a national forest trail that begins north of Dubois and cuts into the Washakie Wilderness. It's not a good trail, and it's hard going. Almost nobody but Lame ever follows it."

"Can you show us?" Cork said, and he unfolded the topographic map Kosmo had provided.

It took Nick a minute to orient himself, and then he said, "It kind of runs like this and will take you right to the base of Heaven's Keep."

Cork folded the map and slipped it among his gear. He and Parmer mounted, and Cork swung Nick up behind him. Under a threatening sky, they rode away.

FORTY-FOUR

They dropped the kid a couple of miles beyond the cabin where the trail—a thin, bare line in the coarse grass—led along a stream through a stand of lodgepole pines.

"Follow the stream," Nick said. "It'll take you maybe five miles into the mountains to a pond. On the other side of the pond it joins the Dubois trail. If you think you're lost, just look for Heaven's Keep and head toward it."

"Thanks, Nick," Cork said. "You've been a big help."

"Lame's not a bad man," the kid said.

"He's done bad things," Cork said.

"Father Frank says that sometimes even good men do bad things."

Parmer said, "Nick, you keep listening to Father Frank."

"We've got it from here," Cork said. "Go on back. I'm sure your grandparents need you."

Nick stood unmoving, reluctant to abandon them, and even after Cork and Parmer had urged their horses into the pines, he remained a long time, watching.

The trail wasn't difficult to follow. The ground was soggy from the spring melt, and Nightwind's horse had left clear tracks in the muck. They rode all afternoon and climbed in altitude, and the air grew colder and the clouds thicker and after a while a drizzle fell. They got out the ponchos they'd packed and put them on and kept riding. They began to see patches of snow in those places the sun didn't hit. Eventually the trail became covered with slush that was full of hoofprints marking Nightwind's passage. Late in the day it began to rain in earnest, but they rode on until they could no longer see because of the darkness.

They camped without a fire at a place where the trail broke from the heavy cover of pines and led across an alpine meadow. Just beyond the trees on the far side, the land climbed a steep slope with a rocky face that even in good daylight would have been dangerous to attempt. They positioned themselves along a stream where the horses could water. With the stub of a pencil he'd found in the pocket of his coat, Parmer had been tracking their progress on the map Kosmo had provided, and he calculated that they'd gone nearly fifteen miles. While Parmer hobbled their horses for the night, Cork tried the radio in order to report their final location, but he got only static. They settled in between two fallen trees that provided some protection and didn't light a fire for fear Nightwind might see.

"How much farther, you think?" Parmer asked as they sat eating tuna and crackers.

"To the cabin? Only Nightwind knows that."

"Think he knows we're following?"

"He'd be a fool to believe that somebody wasn't."

"How do you think he'll do it? If he decides to jump us, I mean?" Parmer didn't sound nervous, just interested.

"I've been trying to think like Nightwind," Cork said. "What is it he really wants out of this?"

"To get away?"

"Get away to what? The woman he loved is dead. He's given up his ranch. And I keep thinking about that note. Unfinished business. What business?"

"I hope to God we have a chance to ask him," Parmer said.

In the rain and without moonlight or even the ambient light of the stars, they were nearly blind. Parmer, just a few feet away, was almost invisible. Only from the occasional snort and the clap of a shoe on an exposed stone did Cork know where the horses were hobbled.

"Cork?"

"Yeah?"

"Do you really believe it's possible Jo's still alive?"

Cork didn't answer.

"I mean, where would he have kept her all this time?"

"I don't know what's possible anymore. I couldn't have imagined that anyone would survive what happened in Bodine's plane, but she did."

"Could she be his unfinished business?"

"I wish I knew, Hugh. I wish to Christ I knew. Let's get some sleep."

He pulled his blanket around him but didn't sleep immediately. He spent a long time staring into a dark that was full of things unknown.

In the night, the drizzle turned to snow, and in the morning, in a shroud of falling white, the two men rose, donned their body armor, mounted their horses, and continued after Nightwind.

They rode through the day without incident, the whole time in snowfall. Periodically they stopped to rest the horses, but only briefly. In the afternoon, the snow came down harder and a wind kicked up. The blowing mess cut their field of vision to less than a hundred yards. Nightwind's tracks became harder to follow. Cork knew that the snow and the clouds would bring an early dark, and he was worried he would lose his quarry. Every hour or so, he or Parmer tried to raise Kosmo on the radio, to no avail. They both understood that until the weather cleared they were cut off and alone.

Late in the afternoon, they came to a stream that issued from what appeared to be a deep canyon. The tracks of Nightwind's horse led beside the stream and into the canyon.

Parmer checked the map. "Dead-ends a couple miles farther."

Cork balked at following the tracks. In a canyon, if Nightwind knew he was being followed, it would be easy for him to establish a vantage above and pick them off. And the dead end was doubly disconcerting. Cork's natural inclination was to climb to higher ground and try to track from above. But if he did that, he might lose Nightwind for good and in doing so lose any hope of finding Jo.

"We split up here," he finally said. "You head up, follow the rim. I'll stay below with the stream."

Parmer looked ahead into the canyon. "If he's going to jump you, this is where he'll do it."

"It's where I'd do it," Cork agreed.

"If that happens, do your best to keep him busy," Parmer said. "I'll get behind him as fast as I can. If you hit the end of the canyon and nothing's gone down, backtrack and I'll meet you here and we can figure what to do next."

They shook hands. Parmer turned his horse up the slope and began to mount toward the canyon rim. Cork made sure the magazine on his Savage 110 was full, and he chambered a round. He cradled the rifle across his lap and urged his horse ahead at a walk.

In the protection of the canyon, the wind ceased to be a problem, but the snow still dropped a translucent curtain all around. Above him, the rock walls, dotted with juniper and scrub brush and jumbles of broken rock, rose up and disappeared in the snowfall. The ground snow was deeper here, sometimes reaching midway to the horse's knees, and the only sign of the trail was the mess left by the passage of Nightwind. Judging from the lack of drift in the prints, Cork figured the man wasn't far ahead.

Fifteen minutes into the canyon, the trail ended abruptly. The prints of Nightwind's horse simply stopped. The snow ahead was unmarred, as if the man Cork had been tracking had vanished into thin air. He realized that Nightwind had backtracked and was behind him.

He spun his horse just as the first shot came. Cork felt a club hit him in the middle of his chest, and he was knocked from the saddle. He hit the ground and his horse charged back the way it had come. Cork lay facedown in the snow, still as death. His chest hurt like hell, but the Kevlar vest Kosmo had provided him had stopped a round that would have pierced his heart. He waited, barely breathing. Finally he heard the crunch of Nightwind's boots in the snow. The man stopped a couple of feet away.

"Christ," Nightwind said. "Didn't I warn you?"

He stepped closer and knelt. He laid his rifle in the snow and slid his hands under Cork's body to turn him faceup. Cork made his move. As he rolled over, he reached up and grabbed Nightwind's coat. He caught the man off guard and flung him easily to the ground. Not two feet away from Cork lay the rifle. He snatched it up and swung the barrel toward Nightwind, who'd scrambled to a crouch and was about to launch himself.

"Move and you're the dead man," Cork said.

Nightwind froze. He studied Cork, his body tensed while he weighed his options. Finally he relaxed, abandoned his crouch, and stood to his full height. "Now what?"

Cork rose to his feet, keeping the rifle trained dead center on Nightwind's chest. "Now you tell me about my wife."

"And then what?"

"Then I take you back."

Nightwind shook his head. "I don't think so."

"You're not in a position to bargain."

"On the contrary, I've got what you want most and I don't intend to give it to you without getting what I want in return."

"Which is what?"

"You let me go."

"I can't do that."

"Then your wife is lost to you forever."

Cork said, "Not necessarily. Right now I'm thinking I might string you up and have a go at you the same way you did Gully."

Again Nightwind shook his head. "Uh-uh. That's not you, O'Connor."

"You have no idea what I'm capable of. Especially where my wife is concerned."

"I know you love her and I know how that feels. My whole life Ellyn's been everything to me. Whatever I've done and tried to do it was for her. That freedom I'm asking you for, it's about her and about love."

"How so?"

"Why do you think I headed into these mountains? Just to run?

Hell, I've got nothing to run to. Everything I care about is gone. Ellyn. My ranch. A future. I figured up here I could regroup and then go after the men who killed Ellyn because I'm damn sure they'll be coming after me. It would have been easier for me if you hadn't crippled my planes."

"You already took care of the men who killed Ellyn. Gully and Mike."

Nightwind laughed, a bitter sound. "I'm talking about the men behind all this, the ones really responsible for Ellyn dying. Mike and Gully were nothing. They were like tools in a shed, used to get the dirty work done. No, the guys I'm after, the guys pulling all the strings, with their money and their power, they're going to be almost impossible to get to. But I know who they are and I know how to get to them. And swear to God I'm going to make them pay. You think Gully suffered, that was nothing."

"Tell me who they are. The law will get them."

"The law is a turtle. This needs to be finished quickly."

"How do you know these men?"

"I've done jobs for them over the years."

"You brought them to Ellyn?"

"Yeah." He didn't seem happy about admitting it. "She was desperate. The little casino in Hot Springs, it was going nowhere, and building it put the rez deep in debt. These people, they were drooling to get their claws into an Indian casino, and they have the money to make a huge project happen. She thought it was the way to help the Arapaho. She was afraid Little Bear's plan would end up with the big oil companies fucking the land and the people on it because that's the way it's always ended. I told her these men were dangerous, but she was sure she could handle them. Fact is, she wasn't doing too bad until you came along."

"Whose idea was it to get rid of Little Bear on the charter flight? Yours?"

"We worked it out together. With some help from Gully and Mike."

"Ellyn couldn't persuade him any other way?"

"He couldn't be bought. And he was too old to be swayed anymore by her other obvious charms. Me, I was happy just to get him out of the picture."

"Yeah, and how'd it feel murdering all those people, murdering Sandy Bodine?"

"I've killed men before, O'Connor. From what I've been told, you have, too, so don't go all sanctimonious on me. We both had our reasons."

"What did you do with Bodine's body?"

"Burial at sea, so to speak. On my way to Aurora, I flew over Lake Superior and dumped him. You know what they say about that lake? Never gives up her dead."

"What about Stilwell?"

"That wasn't my doing. Mike and Gully said they sank the body in a bog somewhere in the Wisconsin woods. God only knows where." Nightwind eyed him levelly. "So how about it? You going to let me go?"

The wind sent snow between them and against them, and Cork felt the cold kiss of it on his face.

"How do I explain it to the wives of the men who died on that charter plane? How do I explain it to Becca Bodine?"

"Tell 'em you did it for love. They'll understand."

"And if I let you go, you'll tell me where my wife is?"

"That's the deal."

"How do I know I can trust you?"

"Same goes for me. As soon as you have what you want, what's to prevent you from shooting me? Mexican standoff, O'Connor."

Nightwind grinned, lifted his hand as if it were a gun, and pointed it at Cork.

The shot came from behind Cork and above him. Nightwind's body jerked with the impact of the round, and he looked startled, then his knees buckled and he dropped to the ground and lay bleeding into the snow. Cork went to him quickly. Nightwind stared up into his face and blinked several times as if stunned.

"Lame?"

Nightwind grunted. "Should've known you wouldn't come alone."

Cork heard the scrape of boot sole on rock, and a moment later

Hugh Parmer was at his side holding the Weatherby he'd taken from Nightwind's ranch.

"Why did you shoot?" Cork said angrily.

"I thought he was going to shoot you."

"He didn't have a weapon, Hugh."

"I thought . . ." Parmer looked at the wounded man's empty hand. "Christ, I couldn't see. The snow, Cork."

Nightwind coughed blood. "Looks like neither of us gets what we wanted, O'Connor."

Cork set his rifle down and gently lifted Nightwind and cradled his head. "Lame, I swear to God I'll deliver these men to justice. Just tell me who they are. Tell me where my wife is."

Nightwind breathed with great difficulty, and a sickening rattle came from deep in his throat. He said, "You love her, O'Connor, and love's brought you a far piece. This is hard country. It's full of hard men, but you bested them all. There's a good deal in you to admire. If love was everything, you'd have what you came for. But there's one thing love can't do. It can't give you back the dead. You won't see your wife again. Not in this life."

"I don't believe you."

"She's been dead since almost the beginning."

"If she's dead, where's her body?"

"A place you'll never find without my help."

"Tell me."

Nightwind struggled for breath, then said, "Give me your promise you'll go after these men. Even if the law can't get to them, you will."

"You have it."

"Something to write with? I don't want you to forget."

Parmer pulled out his wallet and plucked a piece of paper from among the folded currency. He dug inside his coat and drew out the pencil stub.

As Nightwind spoke, Parmer wrote down the information he provided, which was the name of the place Cork would find Jo, the names of the three men responsible, the name of a bank in Denver, and the number of a safe-deposit box there.

"In the box," Nightwind said. "All the evidence you need to get these guys. Been gathering it for years. Insurance policy, you know? Photos, tape recordings, records. Your wife. Others before her. It's all there. In the hands of a good prosecutor, it'll put these assholes in the gas chamber, I swear it." He grabbed hold of Cork's coat sleeve. "Get them, O'Connor. Promise me you'll get them."

"I promise."

Nightwind let go.

Parmer handed the paper over, and Cork read the name of the place where Nightwind had said he would find his wife. He was baffled.

"Bonita, Mexico?" he asked.

"In Sonora," Nightwind said, nearly breathless.

"I don't understand."

"You will."

Parmer said, "Maybe we can bind your wound, Lame."

Nightwind shook his head. "It's over. Just let me go."

Cork told Parmer to round up the horses. Parmer looked down at Nightwind. Then he looked at the rifle he'd used to fire the fatal bullet. Finally he turned and walked away into the snow to find the horses.

It wasn't exactly over. Nightwind lingered for another hour. He spoke no more and struggled simply to breathe. Cradled in Cork's arms, he stared up at the falling snow, and when the snow stopped and the wind blew the clouds away he stared up at an evening sky filling with stars. The canyon ran near the foot of Heaven's Keep, and the great formation stood white and imperious in the last light of day. At the very end, just before Nightwind took his final ragged breath, his eyes drifted to the cold face of rock, and it seemed to Cork that a sense of satisfaction settled over Lame Deer Nightwind, as if he'd just been given the answer to a great question. Afterward Cork followed the dead man's gaze to the top of Heaven's Keep, which appeared to be among the stars themselves, and he thought that maybe if he climbed there he could look into the face of God and understand all the tragedy that had brought him to that place.

But in his head he knew that he would never climb. And in his heart he doubted that he would ever understand.

FORTY-FIVE

It was an old Spanish mission, whitewashed stucco, set amid saguaro cacti and creosote bushes, with the Sierra Madres in the distance under a cloudless blue sky. Blooming bougainvillea climbed the courtyard walls, and the flowers of a large garden grew in the shade of desert willows. At the center was a fountain bubbling softly.

In the office where they sat waiting, Cork, Stephen, and Parmer could hear the fountain through the open window.

There was a knock at the door. A man and a woman entered. The man was dressed in an expensive gray suit and wore a blue silk tie. The woman wore tan slacks, a white blouse, and an embroidered blue vest. She was older than the man. Her hair was gray and her eyes were calm brown.

Cork and his son and Parmer stood, and they all shook hands and sat down together around the table.

The man in the suit had a small mustache, thin and black against his olive skin. He spoke with a Hispanic accent. Cork had met him earlier, briefly. His name was Ramirez. "I have brought Sister Amelia. She was responsible for your wife while she was with us."

Sister Amelia smiled graciously. "I'm sure there's much you want to know."

"She couldn't be saved?" Cork's most burning question.

The man in the suit answered. "When Mr. Nightwind delivered her to us, our doctors examined her thoroughly. By the time she arrived, there was no hope. The MRI showed the bullet lodged against her spine and surrounded by infection. There was also evidence of significant brain damage due, our doctors suspected, to oxygen deprivation."

"She was trapped in a buried airplane," Stephen said.

Ramirez lifted his hand gently to stop Stephen. "We're a hospice center, son. We're concerned primarily with helping those who come to us make a peaceful passage to the next life. Because many of our clients have backgrounds they would prefer remain a secret, we ask no questions and seek no explanations. Our location, far from prying eyes and prying officials, ensures that in their final days the privacy of our clients is respected. You understand."

"Was she in any pain?" Cork asked.

"Our doctors made sure that she was not," Ramirez said.

"Was she conscious at all?" Stephen asked. "Did she say anything?"

"No." Ramirez looked toward Parmer. "We have details to discuss of her transport back to the States—on your aircraft, yes?"

"That's right," Parmer said.

"Perhaps you and I could handle this for the moment. Sister Amelia, I believe, has something she would like to show Mr. O'Connor. Sister?"

She looked kindly at Cork and at Stephen. "Would you follow me?"

"Sure." Cork glanced at Parmer. "Thanks, Hugh."

"No trouble, partner."

They left the office and strolled through the courtyard, which was filled with the fragrance of the flowers and the gentle murmur of the fountain.

In the days behind, the groundwork for justice had been laid. The men Lame Deer Nightwind was after were Donald and Victor Arbuela, who were brothers, and a brother-in-law, Thomas Quintanna. Cork was sure they didn't know Jo and had nothing against her personally. To them her death was simply business. They all lived in Miami and claimed to be in real estate. In the photographs, they were balding men with skin tanned the color of a grocery store paper bag and faces as mundane as lettuce. Cork wasn't surprised that they didn't look particularly evil. He'd seen the face of evil enough to know that more often than not it was dreadfully ordinary. The safe-deposit box in the Denver bank had yielded damning evidence against the three, evidence of years of corruption, fraud, theft, and murder by men who thought they were untouchable. The U.S. attorney in Denver, a woman named Sheila Cannon, who carefully evaluated the evidence, assured Cork they were not. He told her of Nightwind's belief that justice moved with the speed of a turtle. Cannon said maybe so, but in the end the turtle always won the race. Cork understood Lame Nightwind's doubt about the ultimate ability of the law to prevail, and he chose not to share with Cannon his intention, if the law failed, to keep his promise to Nightwind.

He had retrieved his son, who'd returned from his solitary time in the woods having received the vision he sought. Stephen hadn't told Cork what that vision was; perhaps he never would. But the change in him was obvious, and the quiet strength in his young, dark Anishinaabe eyes was compelling. Cork believed that Stephen was fully prepared for the final responsibility that lay before them.

Halfway across the courtyard, Cork paused and turned to Sister Amelia. "How did Lame Nightwind know about this place?"

"Several years ago he was hired to deliver a dying man to us. This man's name, if I divulged it, would be well known to you. His deeds were dark and infamous. Here, he was a different man. I have often seen this. Confronted with the prospect of soon standing before God, unable to hide behind lies and artifice and pretense, people see their lives differently. I'm thankful I don't have to be responsible for judging their time on earth. My duty, my calling, is simply to help prepare them for their audience with the Lord."

"And my wife? How was she at the end?"

Sister Amelia began to stroll again. "I was with her constantly. She never spoke. She never regained consciousness. But, Mr. O'Connor, I felt a strength in her that surprised me. Do you know the poem that says, 'Do not go gentle into that good night'?"

"Not really," Cork said.

"It's about death. At first, your wife did not want to go gently. She did not want to die. Or rather, there was something she wanted very much before she died."

"What?"

"I didn't know. She had no way of telling me. But I believed absolutely there was unfinished business so important to her that she couldn't let go of life until somehow she'd seen to it. In my experience, the only force powerful enough to make death stand back that way is love. So I believed it had to do with love. I prayed with her. I told her that whatever was holding her to this world, God would take care of it. She heard me, Mr. O'Connor, and she believed. And she finally let go."

"You were with her?" Stephen asked.

"I was holding her hand." She walked a few steps and stopped and looked with great compassion into Cork's eyes and Stephen's. "I believe I understand now what was keeping her here. We knew nothing about your wife, Mr. O'Connor. Your mother, Stephen. That's sometimes the way it is when people come to us. We had no idea that she had a family who didn't know where she was or what had become of her. I believe that's what held her. I believe she wanted you to know. And now God has taken care of it."

They continued on and passed through the wall of the old mission and came out into the bright sunlight of the desert, where a cemetery had been created. White stone stood against yellow sand. There were green cacti and sage-colored desert plants among the grave markers and the monuments, and all these elements fit together in a starkly beautiful way.

"Many of those who come to us don't wish to go back for burial," Sister Amelia said. "They have their reasons for wanting their final rest to be here. With your wife, we had no choice, of course. And Mr. Nightwind was quite generous in his request for her disposition. Your wife is there."

She pointed toward a large mausoleum at the center of the cemetery. The structure was built of stunning white marble, with a door as white as ice. Cork stopped as if he'd hit a wall, and he stared. He felt that he'd been blind all along but under the blaze of the desert sun the scales had finally fallen from his eyes. He glanced at his son, who had seen it, too.

Sister Amelia touched his arm. "Are you all right?"

"Yes," he said. "It's just that we know this place. Stephen saw it a long time ago in a vision. A big yellow room with white rocks and a white door and behind it his mother. We didn't know what it meant."

Sister Amelia put her hand gently on Stephen's shoulder. "Perhaps that she would be waiting for you here. That she was always meant to be waiting for you here. Would you like to go inside?"

"Yes," Stephen said. He walked forward on his own.

But Sister Amelia took Cork's hand, guiding him, because his eyes had become blind again, this time with tears.

EPILOGUE

Nancy Jo O'Connor was laid to rest in the cemetery in Aurora on a lovely May afternoon when the sun was saffron yellow and the sky was cornflower blue. It was a simple graveside ceremony in the place where before there'd been only a memorial headstone. Cork was there. Jo's children and her friends were there. Rose and Mal were there and Hugh Parmer and Becca Bodine and her son, who finally knew the truth of their husband and father. And Liz Burns was there. Although she'd never known Jo, the part she'd played in Cork's search had brought her into the lives of the O'Connors in a powerful way.

Cork looked around him at those who'd loved his wife, especially his children. Jenny and Anne were practically grown women, beautiful and strong. There was still a good deal about Stephen that was changing, but much of the fine man Cork believed he would become was already obvious. Jo would have been proud of him. She would have been proud of them all.

They prayed and they wept, and at the end they turned together and headed back to their lives. All of them except Cork, who lingered at the grave. When he was alone, he spoke quietly.

"There's something I need to say to you, Jo. It's been in my heart a long time, ever since we argued and you left. I hope you can hear me, sweetheart." He laid his hand on the polished coffin, where sunlight ran along the grain and gave the wood the look of sweet honey. "I just want to say I'm sorry. And I want to say I love you." He closed his eyes and took a deep breath. "And I have to say good-bye."

He took his hand away, turned where the others had gone, and followed them into the beauty of that day.